Planet of the Orange-red Sun

Series Volume 11

Magi, Witches, Swords, and Superstitions

Planet of the Orange-red Sun Series

Volume 11
Magi, Witches, Swords, and Superstitions

by Vic Broquard

Copyright 2010, 2011, 2012, 2014 by Vic Broquard

Second Edition; ISBN: 978-1-941415-28-3

http://www.Broquard-ebooks.com
Broquard eBooks
103 Timberlane
East Peoria, IL 61611
author@Broquard-eBooks.com

Artwork by Crooked Willow Studios.

For Morgan and L. Ron Hubbard

Table of Contents

Chapter 1 It's My Life

This is my story, and I'll damn well tell it my way! I'm Nia Elain Compton. I'm eighteen years old, when the real tale begins. I know. My first and last names don't jive. I've known that since I was a little girl. I was adopted. Ah, that explains it all, you say. Ha, you don't know the half of it! Okay, I'll admit it. I don't know it all either; neither do my parents, mom and dad, Captain Henry and Mary Compton. Right, those aren't their real names either. They're originally from Descartes-3, where women wear fashionable lip plate ornaments. Mom once told me their original names, but I could never figure out her native click language, let alone pronounce it. She told me no one else could either, and that's why they changed their names. Doesn't explain my name. To date, no one can or has. But I digress. Who cares about names, really? They're just labels, but I keep looking for answers. Answers yield knowledge. It's a universal truism that knowledge is power. I'm proof enough of that, as you'll soon see.

Dad is forty-three and captain of the deep space exploration ship, the Eagle's Seed, out of Descartes-3. Damned if I know why it's called that, except perhaps because eagles soar independently above worlds. Mom is a year younger and their navigator; she's brilliant at complex math. Sometimes, I wish I were, but only sometimes. The Eagle's Seed has, or had rather, twenty of us onboard, including me. I've always been onboard. No, I wasn't born in deep space — that much I know. Why? Because mom told me that when she was twenty-one, she was exposed to some deadly radiation that made her sterile. So I know I wasn't born on this ship. You can do the arithmetic on that one. And yes, that's why they adopted me. Mom and dad wanted to have children, and this was the only method available to them. They claim that they got me when I was a baby, only a few months old. I don't know if that's true or not.

The earliest thing I can remember is mom tucking me

into bed one night. I must have been three perhaps, maybe four. I remember her telling me stories of high adventure among the stars, but I just loved the dull throb of the engines, propelling the ship along at sub-light speed. It puts me right to sleep — that was my pacifier, like a blanket that others might use. Now, I really am digressing.

It all began just after I turned eighteen. We'd been gliding among the stars for months, when Roger, our astronomer, located a potentially habitable planet. That's the purpose of the Eagle's Seed — to search out new planets and civilizations for the mighty Imperium. They are a greedy lot, if you ask me, but then I'm rather biased, particularly after all that's happened to me. Now, I am getting ahead of myself. This is harder than it looks, all right? I'll admit it, but I'm going to tell this tale my way. After all, it's mine to tell, damn it.

Roger identified this new world as Metcalf-4. The star is a yellow dwarf, known in the Imperium catalogues as #149325, but commonly called Metcalf in this sector of space. The four represents the fourth planet out from the sun. Damned if I know what is on the other three that are closer. Never been there — don't care to, either. Okay, technically, it's not a dwarf star; it's a smaller main sequence star. True dwarfs are lots smaller in luminosity and lie far below the main-sequence, though rather parallel to it.

Metcalf-4 has three moons orbiting it, quite strange, since they are all about the same size. Of course, many gas giants have quite a large number of satellites, some barely rocks, hardly classifiable as moons. Yet, these three are rather large and have different orbital periods. Roger explained all this to me and mom did the math, but I wasn't paying too much attention to all that. They were pretty and looked cool; that's what mattered to me.

What matters to me? Mom and dad. I loved them, and they really did love me. Not a day goes by when I'm not reminded of the tender loving care they gave me while I was growing up. Honestly, in hindsight, I can truthfully say I really did need a whole lot of love when I was little. I was supposed to be dad's little boy, but that didn't quite work out right. I was born different, very different, as I now know. Back then, I didn't realize that detail. My folks didn't either; obviously, they wanted a little boy and thought that's what they were adopting. Back then, even I sometimes thought of myself as a boy. Well, that's in the past now. Periods will do that to you, you know.

Dad did one thing very right. I'm alive today because of it. I remember him saying, "You have to be totally independent, Nia. The only person in the universe that you can ever count upon is yourself. I've been incredibly lucky to have found your mother, but I never expected to find someone like her." In spite of everything else, both mom and dad continued to push me towards being wholly independent. Sometimes, it hurt, though — physically, that is.

Looking back on it, dad was right. Every time we docked on civilized worlds, he made me continue my martial arts training, whether I wanted it or not. Isn't hindsight just perfect? I now know that is what has saved my life countless times. But that's getting ahead of the story. I began taking lessons when I was six, and my last one was before we left Descartes-3 on this last exploration trip. I was seventeen then. Okay, I admit it; I am deadly with my feet. I have had to be.

Want to be, you ask? What did I want to grow up to be? Does a teen really ever truly know the answer to that one? Perhaps, it is more like fate intervening, leading you to your calling. I'm not a philosopher, but that doesn't mean I'm ignorant and uneducated. Far from that! What do you think I did all those years flying around the galaxy in the Eagle's Seed? Shoot, until Metcalf-4, all together, perhaps one of my eighteen years was planet-side, and the rest of the time we were in space, searching out new worlds. So, no, I've never attended an Academy or formal school. Don't care to either.

But that doesn't mean I didn't get educated. That duty fell to mom, mostly. When she wasn't on navigation duty, she was my teacher. Although math was her strong suit, it wasn't mine. I did learn all the basics, but I excelled in physics or so everyone on the ship told me. If I'm going to be wholly honest with you, I needed to be good at physics. I had to find alternate means to do many things, back then. Levers, fulcrums, forces, angular momentum, these and more I made extensive use of, not only in my martial arts training, but in ordinary living. I had to, if I was to be independent. Actually, I really didn't have any choice about learning to be independent. Dad and mom saw to that.

"No, I'm not going to help you clean up your room, Nia Elain," mom declared. I remember that day well. My room was a shambles. I hadn't put things back when I was finished playing with them. Mom had to step over all sorts of things just to get to my bed. All my whining about it being impossible for me to do that fell on deaf ears. Now, I know better. Mom was probably crying inside, all the while displaying a stern, unrelenting face. Dad probably did too. Damn, I wish I could see and talk to them again! There's so much I would dearly love to tell them, but then doesn't everyone who has lost someone they've loved? Sorry, waxing sentimental on you.

Back to the beginning. I find it best to start at that point. We landed on Metcalf-4 near a small, primitive village, if you can call it that, high in the right-hand side of the foothills of a rugged mountain range. Yes, we had completed an initial flyover of the planet. Our geologist, Tom, detected vast mineral deposits around here, along with some particularly potent germanium-alloy crystals. Hence, dad chose this location to set down and explore. The flyover told us this planet had a small native population of some kind, but there were no signs of a real civilization, not like on Descartes-3, for example. Mom suggested that perhaps the world was culturally in its stone age, but she could not be sure until we landed and took a look at the natives. Perhaps, it might help you, if I jumped ahead and told you that the world was in a transitional period. A late hunter-gatherer culture was being overrun by an agricultural based, bronze weapons culture.

Natives mean a people who certainly don't speak your language. This is always a first-contact problem, which we explorers continually have to face. You land and are greeted by people, who not only look strange to you and have unusual customs, but speak in an unknown language. What did you think? That they'd speak your language? Ha! Well, if I am good at things, one that I excel in is languages. Probably, that's because with so little to do while on these nearly year-long voyages drifting along through space, I listened to nearly every language disk on the ship. Mom used to tease me that I could speak a hundred different languages, excepting her own, the click language of Descartes-3. Damn, I just remembered I promised her that I would one day learn hers, and I haven't kept that promise, not yet anyway, but I eventually have, but I'm getting ahead again.

Like I said, I am good with languages, especially picking them up rapidly. Since I was fourteen, dad allowed me a key role during our first contacts with the native populations we encountered. Of course, others were there with me. One group turned out to be cannibal head hunters. They had a severe protein shortage. That encounter was a bit dicey, but I'm digressing again.

Once we landed, I was part of the three-person team that established contact with this small village. As I stepped out of the ship and onto the rocky ground, I was wearing my light blue tank top, heavy jeans, and my usual slip on shoes. I use my toes a lot still. My top was getting too small for me again. I am very well developed. No, actually, extremely well endowed. Okay, mammothly well endowed. Already, my breast size is H, whoppers, three times the size of mom's. Okay, I admit I was quite pleased when, at ten, they began developing. I was becoming an adult, like mom, or so I thought back then. At that time, if I knew how big they were going to get, I wouldn't have been so elated that I was maturing, but that's another story entirely. Let's just say I cut a quite striking appearance and leave it at that.

The site was extremely hilly and densely forested in places, with bare rock outcrops dotting the landscape. The trees were a mixture of pine and oak, I think. Mind you, I am not an expert on trees. As we walked the mile to the village, dodging underbrush, I began to smell pine smoke from their cooking fires. I love that distinct odor, rarely found on civilized worlds, except as an artificially-made scent — I hate those things. Before long, we entered a relatively open patch. The small village lay before us.

If I am honest, it was small, but quite similar in many

ways to others that I'd seen during our many years of exploration. The quaint, small homes were made of wood and mud. Waddle and daub construction, it's technically called. I know; it's crude, but homey, as I was about to discover. I counted twelve such dwellings. Estimating four people per home, that gave me a crude guess that we might be encountering perhaps fifty here. A dozen children were playing in the open, dirt-covered spaces around the homes. A stone-walled, circular well lay centrally located. Off to the right side of the village, I spotted a number of hides strung out on wooden drying frames. The children went barefoot, but wore leather loincloths — shorts might be a better description. The adults wore more substantial clothing, leather constructs, for the most part. One middle aged woman was drawing water from the well, as we made our appearance at the very edge of the village. She cried out an alarm, naturally. The children ceased their play, running quickly to their homes. The woman also let her bucket fall and dashed away. Aliens can have that affect, you see.

Strangers have that impression on locals, I've noted that many times. After all, what would you think if a very strangely dressed group came walking into your hometown? This was to be expected, just as what followed was. Within seconds, several men came out, carrying weapons. I say weapons, but I ought to be quite clear here.

Within civilized worlds, weapons are usually d-guns. They shoot disintegration beams and are designed to drill two-inch holes in the target. You might suppose, as I once did, that if you fire a d-gun in a certain direction, then the beam will drill that hole into everything in its path out to its maximum range. And you'd be as wrong as I was. If that was the case, and if you shot one off in a spaceship, then that would result in a hull breach and likely the destruction of said ship. No, these d-guns have limiters, a feedback sensor that automatically ends the shot, as soon as it hits something that it disintegrates. Nice safety precaution. While there are other weapons on civilized worlds, mostly those are ancient projectile guns, which are only used for sporting events and historical re-enactments.

6

These men carried crude bows and arrows, short swords, and long knives. The swords were strapped around their waists with a leather sheath and belt. The knives were in a leather holster strapped to their legs, usually their left leg. I presumed this was because they were right-handed.

"Hello." I began saying, repeating it in many different languages, smiling and looking as friendly-like as I could. Look, if a stranger appears at your house and starts speaking a host of different foreign languages, all the while smiling, eventually you are bound to start talking yourself.

They did. Several began chatting among themselves, before one tried to address us. Okay, I admit it. I'm hot with languages. Hearing them talk briefly and having a good idea what they were most likely to be saying, I decided their language was quite similar to a Slavic language I knew. I quickly began speaking in that one. Instant recognition. Amazing how people's expressions change when you are suddenly being at least somewhat understood by others.

"Hello. We are sky people. We are just visiting your world. I am called Nia Elain Compton. What is your village called? What's your name?" I said. Okay, I am also a chatterer. I probably ought to have limited myself to just one question at a time.

Of course, having a mammothly well-endowed, young woman making first contact with men also plays a role, especially when she is wearing a thin tank top, revealing quite a cleavage. The men began to smile and talk to me, all the while eyeing my bosom. By now, I'm quite used to stares. I'd been stared at all my life. So what's new? At least, I quickly discovered their language was quite similar to the Slavic that I knew, though not the same, and that we could understand each other fairly well. On the other hand, Peter, who was with me, had a pocket recorder, and was recording everything that was being said. Later, the others would be studying it to learn their language well enough to get by rather primitively.

Did ya catch that one? Sky people? One thing I've learned about landing on more primitive worlds is the term "sky people" is easily grasped, especially if some of them saw the ship landing. While their language wasn't Slavic, it was close enough. The men understood me, and the ice was broken. Of course, we had to endure many repeats of, "Sky people. Sky people. Ya. Sky people."

As is often the case, such an exchange is then followed by the whole village coming out to see the sky people for themselves. We're a curiosity, naturally. What I always find interesting is just what they subsequently offer us to drink or eat. I will admit I'm into exotic foods and beverages. I think you rather have to be, if you are in this line of work, though I've never liked eating bugs. Fortunately, this time they didn't offer us any creepy, crawling creatures.

A young teen close to my own age came out, carrying a copper cup. "Hi. Berry juice. I Jelena Kish. Drink," she said, purposely speaking slowly and in a rather baby-talk manner."

"Thanks, I'm able to understand your language somewhat. I'm Nia Elain Compton."

"Oh, you have a very bad accent. The berry juice is very good. We welcome great guests with it. Please, the other wives are giving your men some too," she explained. "Did you get all that?"

I sat down and used my feet to lift the cup up to my lips. "Mostly. Thanks. Say, this is really good, Jelena," I replied and continued drinking it. The other two followed my lead. "They don't speak your language yet. I have to translate. What's the name of your village?"

"Jovan. Have you really fallen down from the sky above? Did the fall hurt you?" she asked, innocently, but with a note of disbelief in her voice.

"Sure. No, we're fine. Want to come and see our sky ship?" I asked, knowing full well that everyone in the village wanted just that — to come and see for themselves. After all, if your world did not have spaceships, wouldn't you be quite curious to see a real spaceship that has just landed nearby?

They did and we did. After that, the ice was completely broken. Dad asked me to hang around the village, building up a solid language database, while they did their mineral prospecting. I have to tell you up front that I have no interest in minerals or prospecting. So I leapt at the chance to visit with others my own age, even if their culture is vastly different from mine.

Naturally, for the first couple of days, the villagers plied me with questions. Some, I could answer; others, I could not. After all, how do you explain hyper-drive to a primitive person? Or the Imperium, for that matter? You can't. So you make do. After the newness of us wore off, I began to enjoy myself and my new friend, Jelena.

I found out that she was a year older than I was. She was slightly taller than I was, six feet, I'd guess. Jelena wore a supple leather dress with colorful beads sewn into various geometric designs across her bodice. She had curly, blonde hair that quite possibly had not been cut, falling to her waist, though she usually kept it tied back in a ponytail. Her face was round with a prominent nose, rounded cheeks, and sparkling, blue eyes. I thought she was rather attractive. She too carried a long knife in a sheath strapped to her left leg on the outer side. Thus, I figured she was right-handed and was correct again.

She saw an eighteen year old who stood about five-nine. My hair is wavy and richly black, but quite thick and with a sheen to it. I've kept the split ends trimmed, and it drapes over my shoulders, falling to my waist as well. She and I share tastes in our hair. That is one of the first things we chatted about. However, I use the fall of mine to hide my shoulders, giving the appearance that I've no arms, which is the way that I prefer it. My eyebrows are rather bushy as well; my lips are quite full. My eyes are black too. I think my face appears rather stern to others, somewhat elliptical, but that's only my own opinion. Incidentally, I don't think of myself as being particularly attractive.

We chatted endlessly, while she gave me a tour of her village. Of course, she soon brought up the topic that I knew was coming. It always had — whenever I met new people. "What's wrong with your arms? They look so weird," she finally asked what had been bothering her since we first met a few days ago.

This is a really hard question to answer. "I didn't used to have any," I answered. Immediately, I found myself recalling a talk with my mother. I was four years old, I think. "Why I don't have arm-things like you and dad?" I asked her, innocently. I'd begun to see the world and others in relation to my own self. It's rather hard not to see such a significant difference in bodies. I remember back then, I was learning how to use my feet to feed myself at the dinner table, and noticed mom and dad had these seemingly extra appendages, which they used for all manner of useful things. "How come I don't have them? When will I grow mine?"

"Honey, your body is different. You don't have any. You see, normal babies are born with them, but somehow you weren't given any. Possibly, it is what we call a birth defect — something went wrong," mom tried to explain this to a four year old. I can tell you now she failed utterly. I recall her adding, "Someday, dad will get you some arms. I promise."

I was satisfied. Heck, my attention span was awfully short back then. I was more interested in the cookies and ice cream mom was dishing out. After that simple explanation, I was satisfied for many years. Honestly, what you don't have, you don't miss. As mom and dad kept telling me, "You do it your way." I did just that, though I will admit that, until I was around ten years old, I spent a lot of time trying to figure out how to do things for myself. One thing, which really helped me, is my incredible flexibility and keen sense of balance. My own theory is that bodies compensate.

That reminds me. One time when I was twelve, I had to show off to mom and dad. While standing on one foot, I raised my other leg straight up, while my torso and head went perfectly horizontal. Mom was quite pleased and called it the vertical splits. Funny how you remember things when you least expect them.

Sorry, digressing again. As I said, I didn't think any more about that until I was twelve and had my first period. Talk about embarrassment! You don't know the half of it! That's when I received my first discussion about the birds and the bees, but from both mom and dad! That's because my body is that of a hermaphrodite. I've got both sexes in one body, though I appear as a female, and I consider myself a female. I don't think I was ever more embarrassed than that night when they explained all this to me. Until then, I figured I was just like mom, when in fact I was like both of them.

That's also when I realized once more that I was physically very different from my parents. Still, dad did promise me that soon he would pay the doctors on Descartes-3 to regrow my arms. I remember clearly how much that cheered me up. Back then, I thought if I had arms like mom and dad and everyone else did, then I wouldn't be different. I was rather naive, I know, but I was only twelve and dealing with my first period.

For several years, we didn't get back to Descartes-3 long enough for that to be done. When I was seventeen, we finally did, just before we departed on this trip to Metcalf-4. In hindsight, I wish dad hadn't spent all that money trying to get my arms regrown. Something didn't work out right with them, but that's getting way ahead here.

When I landed on Metcalf-4, my newly growing arms were quite tiny and very weak. I couldn't hold the cup that Jelena offered me the first time we met. I could brush the hair out of my face, but little more. The doctors did say that it would take time for them to regrow fully, perhaps years. Still, having really tiny arms attached to my shoulders looked positively weird. Even mom thought so. I overheard her and dad talking about them. She thought something had gone very wrong. Dad agreed with her and promised to take me back to the doctors when we returned to Descartes-3.

I came out of dreamland and attempted to answer Jelena's question. "Sorry, Jelena. I got distracted. I was born without arms, but a few months ago, my dad took me to the doctors to get some grown. I don't think it's working quite right. About all I can do with them is brush my hair out of my face."

"I'm sorry, Nia. It must be awful for you," Jelena replied, very sympathetic.

Ordinarily, I get rather testy when others heap sympathy on me. I don't want your pity or sympathy. I don't need it either. However, something about her sincerity kept my slight rise in hostility at bay. "Not really, Jelena. You can't miss something you've never had. I just have other ways of doing things. I use my feet a lot. I'm quite flexible."

"Do all the sky women not have arms like you?" she

11

asked, again quite innocently.

"All of the women I've met have two arms, just like you and everyone here does. I'm the freak." I regretted saying that. I don't consider myself a freak, but then perhaps I ought to. I certainly am quite different. I was not about to undo my jeans and show her what else I had.

This is when I was taken by surprise. Jelena replied, "Okay. I think I understand, Nia. I am a witch. Well, a witch in training, actually. My mom's our village witch, and she's teaching me all that she knows. I've never come across any cure that regrows lost arms or legs or anything like that, but I'll ask her tonight."

"A witch? What do you do? Cast spells on people?" I asked. This time, my own ignorance showed. She'd turned the tables on me. I was totally in the dark over the significance of her revelation.

Jelena laughed. "Hardly. We are healers. We know what herbs and potions can cure all sorts of things. We help deliver babies too. Only last week, I helped Nikita heal a nasty cut that she got. Witches are healers, you see. We also make all sorts of potions, even love potions." She giggled after mentioning that last one.

I didn't see, but accepted the fact. Little did I know just how important Jelena would later become to me. Since we both felt as if we'd just revealed some deep secrets about ourselves to each other, she and I continued to chat, but we knew from that moment we were destined to become best friends.

While the days passed, I spent the daytime hours with Jelena. Honestly, while dad and the others were here, I had nothing else to do. Besides, if you spend months cooped up on a small spaceship, you relish the opportunity to spend time out of doors, especially on a world free of all forms of pollution. Descartes-3 really stinks, in my humble opinion.

I learned something about the local dangerous creatures. There were deadly vipers, but not here in the foothills. Instead, bears and wild boars were sometimes encountered. One also had to be alert for raiding parties. Bad men sometimes raided villages, carrying off slaves. That explained the bows and short swords, I concluded. Overall, those few weeks living among the villagers and sharing their meals and chat was truly enjoyable.

One day, Jelena was asked to forage for more herbs for her mother. "Can I tag along?"

"I'd be offended if you didn't," Jelena teased me. "I've made you a sack you can slip over your head and help carry the things we find. I love to wander the hills. You never know what really interesting things you can find. You don't have to worry about the bears or wild boars. I've got us covered." She waved one of her small pouches she had tied to her waist belt. That's when I noticed that today she carried numerous small leather pouches around her waist. "My remedies. Never go out into the wild unprepared."

Shortly, she slipped a leather strap over my shoulders and head. A very large, leather collection bag hung from it. "Cool," I replied. "Can you teach me about the herbs and such?"

As we began walking through the woods, she answered, "I can try, but not everyone can learn. Mom says we witches are rather rare — that we alone are attuned to Nature. I can feel the plants. They tell me what they can do to help me. Do your people ever talk to plants?"

I stifled a giggle. Talk to plants? Hardly. Well, I've heard some looneys who claim that they talk to their houseplants, but no one takes them seriously. I answered honestly, "No. I didn't think plants can talk."

Jelena giggled. "Oh they certainly do, only you have to listen to them. They are very soft spoken, you know." I didn't know, but kept quiet and followed her lead. Little did I know then!

Within a short time, I was completely lost. The trees looked all the same to me. The rock formations blended together, totally disorienting me. We were not following any kind of path that I could see, but then I chalked that up to my own inexperience with such things. Some protruding rock formations thrust up like jagged fingers, pushing their way through the unyielding ground, which seemed loathed to allow the rock to be visible. Then again, perhaps the trees and the brush wanted to refuse the rocks fingers. Or perhaps, foothills are just harbingers of the actual mountains, which I knew were just to the west of where our ship landed.

I was amazed with Jelena for she wasn't lost at all. This was her homeland. I guessed she could probably find her way around here in the dark. Before long, she began collecting bits of plants or used her knife to dig up some roots. She patiently explained to me what each was for, but homeopathic remedies were far beyond anything I had ever been exposed to. I'm afraid most of what she was explaining to me floated right through my mind, like the air that we passed through on our walk.

If one of us space people got sick or injured, we simply headed to our shipboard medical machine to be patched up in short order. Even I, knowing almost nothing about medicine, could operate the menu-driven machine, naturally making the selections with my toes. Hence, I don't think I was a very good student for Jelena. Still, my ignorance didn't bother her in the slightest. I sensed she was enjoying my company and the opportunity to show me a bit of her life.

We rounded a bend. The way was blocked by a stand of trees, but that wasn't the reason the Jelena suddenly froze. I halted abruptly, nearly bumping into her. Then, I gasped audibly. A giant bear was just ahead of us! Okay, it looked giant to me. I've never seen a bear before and certainly not in the wild. "Stay still a moment while I convince him to leave us alone," Jelena whispered.

While she was fumbling with a small pouch, I eyed her long knife, wondering if it could be used somehow to stop the bear. To my eyes, the blade looked terribly small and the bear, terribly big. Jelena made no attempt to draw her knife, however. Shortly, she had a pinch of some kind of powder in her fingers. She tossed it up into the air. I saw tiny particles outlined in the sun's rays, filtering through the green canopy above us. They twinkled and showered down before us.

As I watched in complete disbelief, the bear began sniffing. It rose up for a moment. I thought for sure it was about to attack us, but then it let out a yeowl, turned, and moved quickly away from us. Jelena pivoted and said, "You can't outrun a bear nor can you out-climb one. They are fast, but they hate certain odors. I sprinkled some dried, decomposed flesh plant. Once he smelled it, he took off fast. It's safe now."

"Amazing, Jelena. Amazing. I can see that you really know your stuff," I praised her, greatly relieved. "I was worried there for a minute. It was really big!"

Jelena giggled. "I hate to bust your bubbles, Nia Elain, but that was a young one, not even fully grown. Probably a yearling, two at the most. Come on; we've got lots more to find for mom. You have to see this place in the late fall. The reds, yellows, oranges, browns — just breathtaking." I tried to imagine how it must appear, but could only recall some photographs I'd once seen. Perhaps, I thought, we might be here long enough for me to see the fall foliage in its splendor.

We hiked on for hours, before stopping for lunch beside a trickling stream. I got down on my knees, leaned over, and took a long, welcome drink. I don't think I've ever tasted water as clean and pure as that stream! I rather wished I could bottle a year's supply and take it back with me. For a moment, I toyed with that very idea. Shipboard, we have recycled water, pure H_2O as they say. Bland. Besides, I always imagine I was drinking what I got rid of in the toilet the previous day — everything is recycled on the ship.

While I went on about how great tasting the water was, Jelena merely giggled and set about making a small fire. She took out some dried meat and a small pot. After putting the meat into it, along with a number of vegetables from other pouches, she scooped some water into the mix and put it onto the fire. "I like to let it soak some and simmer before we eat. Let's sit back and relax for a while. Tell me about flying among the stars. Is it fun?"

While the food cooked, I talked about some of my trips. I tried to tell her about my favorite locations, flying close to the gaseous nebulae with all their glowing, wispy filaments of gases. I doubt she could picture it from my descriptions, but she seemed to enjoy hearing about it. Sometime later, she pronounced the meal ready and produced two spoons, handing one hesitantly to me. Quickly, I slipped off my shoe and took it between my toes. Giggling, we began sharing the stew. That's what I called it anyway. It tasted very good indeed. It hit the spot, as far as I was concerned. Yes, cooking is another thing I'm no good at. Mom says I am the only person she knows who can blacken a pot while boiling water for tea. Sometimes, I've wondered if that will impact my chances of marriage, but always other considerations dwarf this one, as you can well imagine.

That done, she washed the pot and spoons in the creek, but I insisted on drying them. Again, she watched me carefully to see how I could manage that. Mom taught me well. I always do my part. Jelena relaxed some, seeing I was actually doing it acceptably. "You just have different ways to do things. I see that now, though I have to admit, Nia Elain, I didn't believe you at first."

"No one does. Mom and dad taught me to be very independent and to always do my share of the work," I explained. After that, we continued our searching for roots and herbs.

About an hour later, Jelena suddenly stopped, startling me. "What's up?" I looked but didn't see another bear or anything, just more forest, rocks, and bushes. She held her hand up, indicating silence. I obeyed. I heard her sniffing, rather like a bear. I emulated her.

"The wind has changed. Worse, I smell something. I need to see better. I'm going to climb that tree so I can check this out," she explained, suddenly very serious.

"What's up? Danger?" I whispered, though I didn't see any immediate threat.

"Not sure. Have to check it out. It's early this year, if it's the wind. Can you climb a tree?"

No one had ever suggested that I'd ever need to climb a tree. I looked at it and sighed. "Nope. Now that's something I can't do. I don't think so, anyway." I watched as she scampered up, limb over limb, as though she'd done this everyday of her life. Later, I learned that she had. She'd been a tomboy and loved to climb nearly anything. A few minutes later, she returned to the ground, standing before me. From her very serious mien, I knew something was wrong, but what?

16

"It's called the Slave Wind. Usually, it comes in the late fall, but it's coming early this year. The wind blows down the far distant Slava Mountain. It picks up some really dangerous pollen and dust. We have to find shelter right now before it hits us hard." Her voice bordered on panic.

"Can't we run back to the village?" I asked.

"Too far. It will catch us out in the open. We'd be doomed. Come on. I think I know where we might be safe enough from the Slave Wind. There's a cave not far from here. This way. Hurry. Can you run?"

"Sure. Lead on, Jelena. I'm right behind you." At first she merely jogged, thinking perhaps I couldn't run or keep up. Soon, she saw I could and picked up her pace considerably. I stayed far enough behind her to avoid getting the backlash from some of the tree branches and bushes that she'd pushed out of her way. Me, I just ducked them. I have a very streamlined figure and am quite agile on my feet.

I could definitely now feel the wind. It was sharply cold on my exposed skin. I wished I'd worn something less provocative than my thin tank top. In my defense, I can put it on and take it off easily. That is one reason I often wore them. There was also a distinctive odor in the air as well.

Panting heavily, we found the cave she mentioned. I was a bit amazed that she just ran on into it, without first making sure there wasn't a bear inside it or something equally dangerous!

In fact, as we stopped deep inside the jagged, brownish cavern, there was a large bear already in here! I panicked and was about to turn tail and run, when between gasps Jelena said, "It's all right. It knows the Slave Wind has come. It's terrified of it too, and it knows we are seeking shelter from it here as well. It won't bother us, as long as we don't bother it. In times like this, all of Nature forms sort of a truce in hostilities. Come on. Let's sit down. This is going to be a bad one."

I chose to sit closer to the entrance than Jelena. Silly me. I had her between me and the bear. Not my finest hour, I agree, but I was scared. What the devil was going on here? "So what is with this wind? Why the danger? What's that smell?"

"You smell it too. God, I hope we'll be protected enough in this cave," Jelena replied. She was twisting her hands, and I sensed she was very frightened of this wind, but why?

Jelena finally caught her breath and nervously explained. "The Slave Wind is really, really bad, Nia. Like I said, it usually comes once in the late fall, but it's early this year for some reason. Everyone around these parts knows about it, including the animals. It causes all manner of delusions. Whatever you think you are seeing, feeling, or believe is happening, trust me, it probably isn't real. If caught out in the open, people and animals go absolutely crazy. It's deadly. Mom once told me that her father got caught in one, and he killed himself afterwards. She said he thought he was being eaten alive by giant centipedes, and thinking that, he was jumping into the river, but instead, he jumped off a cliff. People and animals die from this Slave Wind."

She continued, "That's the best thing that happens — to die right away. Others go mad afterwards. I had a girlfriend, Kolina, who got caught in the Slave Wind. She went insane afterwards; it turned her into a babbling idiot. Our village elder finally had to put her down. That was three years ago. It does other strange things to people's minds, too."

"This sounds really bad, Jelena. What strange things?"

She lowered her voice to a whisper, "Some say that the Slave Wind is what gives the Magi their powers. They are great sorcerers. Mom says if someone starts doing strange things, you know, like starting fires, then they've been infected with the Magi Madness, and the only cure is to get the person to a trained Magus right away. Either that or put them down before they go crazy and burn the forest down."

"What is a magi anyway?" I asked. "What's a sorcerer? We don't have such people where I come from, I don't think," I inquired, somewhat nervously. This was sounding worse and worse.

"Great and powerful wizards, sorcerers. They cast really powerful spells," she replied, equally nervously. I surmised that for some reason this topic scared her.

I racked my memories for anything related to spells. "You mean like turning someone into a toad?" I know. It was just a silly fairytale that mom once told me, but until you've actually witnessed a magus and his or her spells, you really haven't any notion of what they can do.

A nervous giggle answered me. "No, silly. At least I don't think they do that. I've heard they can create great balls of fire that can easily kill you. They can be here one minute, and the next, they are some other place, far away. They can change their shape into almost anything, even into that bear behind us. They have terrible powers, and some are really bad, but mom always tells me some are good too. I don't really know, though. I've never met one, and I hope I don't meet one. They can enslave you worse than this Slave Wind or even the evil slaver men. That's what I've heard anyway. So whatever happens, don't believe any of it. Not until the wind is gone."

"Sounds scary. How long will the wind last?"

"Don't know. Maybe a day, if we are lucky. It's not supposed to come this early. Mom is going to be very worried about us. I hope someone tells your Sky People about the Slave Wind."

Now, I did have a tense stomach! If the Slave Wind were this bad, what would happen to my parents and the others who were out surveying the planet for minerals? I had no way to contact them. This was supposed to be just another fine, late summer's stroll in the woods, back by suppertime. Now, it was turning into a nightmare.

We sat there in silence for a while. Then, I think it began, at least I began seeing things. Bugs. A host of bugs appeared on the opposite cavern wall, crawling, swarming over the rocky surfaces, hundreds of them. I hate bugs. I think I said, "You stay over there on your side of the cave," but who knows if I really said such a thing. They certainly didn't stay there. As soon as I spoke, they began swarming over onto me. I remember saying to myself, "Not real. Not real! Not real!"

The bugs vanished, replaced by glowing lights. Next, the cavern walls began to morph into a chocolate cake! Suddenly, I was hungry, starving. I seemed to be trying to eat the cake, rather frantically, I might add. "It can't be real!" I think I said.

The cake vanished, but a giant monster with great wings, huge claws, and fangs appeared in its place. Saliva drool down it's hideous chin. It eyed me hungrily. I think I was screaming now. No, I distinctly seemed to be thrashing at it with giant arms, arms I know that I have never had. As I realized that detail, the monster vanished.

Sheets of colored lights appeared, pretty and serene, oh so beautiful! Now, this was an hallucination I enjoyed seeing. Aesthetic? Absolutely. It reminded of the shimmering gas clouds I so loved to watch from the ship's view ports. I watched the lights for some time, admiring them. So beautiful. No, so ugly, because just then, men wearing gas masks of some kind came walking into the cavern, at least, I think they were men.

I tried to make the men go away. They were interfering with the pretty lights, but they didn't, so I ignored them. Now, the lights turned into a grey void. I was and felt lost, alone, so alone. I felt like crying and did so, I think. Lost. Helpless. Not real. Is real. Alone. I tried to walk, then run. Running. Running as fast as a gazelle. I have to get out of this void. I have to find my way home. Run, Nia Elain, run. Why am I not out of breath? Don't know, but run anyway.

After a time, I saw I was getting nowhere at all. The grey void was all around me. Now, I couldn't move or so it seemed. I tried to walk, to run, but couldn't. Sleep. Yes, I am tired. Sleep to rest. That's the answer. Sleep. I closed my eyes, at least I think I closed what I thought were my eyes. Can you think while you are sleeping? That question perplexed me, though I continued to think about it, but my breathing became harder and harder. Am I suffocating while I sleep? Open your eyes. Can't. Why? Best sleep. It's all a nightmare anyway, not real.

Am I awake now? I seemed still to be in a grey void, but now I could see others. Two men. I feel something over my face. Being carried. That's good. Mom always carried me when I was very little. I had an image of mom holding me in her arms. It felt so peaceful, so comfortable. No, not mom. Men. I tried to wiggle out of his grasp, but my feet seemed fused together somehow, as if I only had one very wide leg. How strange. I feel like my body is slumped over the man's shoulder. Turning my head, I see another man. He has a gas mask over his face too, but he's got Jelena over his shoulder. Her legs are tied up together. So are her hands.

Now, I see a shimmering, giant circle of light, a glowing torus, taller than the men. We are moving towards it. At least, there *is* something in this grey void. Maybe we are leaving the void. That would be good. I'm lost in here, but maybe not alone. Jelena is over there; I think she is. Not real, maybe it's not real. Where's the bear? I look around but don't see it. That's good. Bears are big.

The men are carrying us through the glowing torus. That's good. I want to get out of this endless void. Maybe I will wake up. Maybe the dream is ending. I see a large campsite. Many men. Men with swords. Rough looking men. They need a bath. I wonder when they last had one. Maybe never. What's happening to us?

The man sat me down beside Jelena. To my left, I saw three other women. He pulled a mask off my face. Hey, gently, I think I said. He walks away to a campfire. Maybe we are camping out somewhere.

"Nia, Nia, are you awake?" It was Jelena; she was whispering. I turned and saw that her legs were tied up, strangely so. Someone had wrapped a rope around her legs above her knees about ten times and then another ten times just below her knees. The rope then went in between her legs and the two bands, pulling them quite taught. Another band of ten loops was around her ankles, but again, another one was wrapped between her two ankles and over the thick loops, drawing them quite taught. I looked at my own legs. They were tied identically. I looked to my left. The other three had their legs tied in the same manner. Our hands were similarly tied together at our wrists, but they were out in front of us, not behind our backs. Still, the world was filled with the greyness of the void. But perhaps, it was clearing up some. I hoped so anyway. I was more than ready for this nightmare to end.

"Nia! We've been captured by slavers! They have a magus with them! That was a transporting torus they took us through! I don't know where we are. Are you awake? Are you all right? Nia?"

"Here, I think. Slavers? What do they want?"

A man walked up to me. "Look at this one, boss. Magus Sileny is going to love this one. Look at those knockers. Here," he bent over, a long knife in his hand. Is he going to slit my throat? No, he cut my nice tank top. Hell, he cut it in half! I tried to flinch, to move away, and to cover my partial nakedness. I know they are monsters, but I don't want others to see them. All the men came over to me and stared. One even played with them a bit, "They're real all right, fellows!" I think I spat on him, but I'm not sure if that was real or not. He gave them a slight slap; that did seem to sting, but I ignored the men, as best I could. What is going on?

Jelena cried out, "Leave her alone!" Someone slapped her across her face. These are not nice men, I thought. I know, my mind wasn't working properly at all. That's the best thought I could think of at the time.

A voice called out, "Leave her alone. The magus will take it out on you, if she's harmed." The man seemed suddenly quite scared and said something indicating he hadn't hurt me. "Come on; grab some chow." Chow? I was hungry or was that also an hallucination? I couldn't tell. I just wanted my tank top back, but it lay cut to pieces on the ground. I liked that tank top. Gradually, I slipped back into the greyness that seemed to surround the world around me. Perhaps, I had not yet woken up. Not real.

Motion caught my attention. Several motions, actually. I roused. This was all so surreal, so strange. Hallucinations simply aren't fun, I decided, praying the nightmare would soon end. It didn't. It had only just begun.

Chapter 2 Rescue

From the corner of my eye, I saw movement — seemed to be another woman, slipping silently around the perimeter of the campsite. A man to my left took a hold of the ropes binding her hands. He gave her a giant pull, bringing her up to her feet. She cried out from the pain and wobbled a bit. Like all of us, she couldn't move her feet at all. The man continued to pull on her arms. "Hop, bitch. Hop. Over to the wagon." As I watched, the poor woman tried to hop, as he continually pulled on her tied arms. I saw a crude wagon not too distant.

After he sat her in the wagon, he did the same to the next one, and then the next one, right beside me. I sensed her pain, when he jerked hard on her arms, pulling her up. I could feel her fright, as she was forced to hop over to the wagon, joining the other two. At least he lifted her up and sat her in the wagon. He walked back to me, but I also saw there were six of these gruff looking men here. Then, it happened. It forever changed my life.

There are times in one's life when you do something that affects your entire destiny. I remember mom telling me about hers. It was that day when she first met dad. Wait! I'm digressing again. Sorry, even trying to recall what was happening during this traumatic event is really difficult.

The unshaven, filthy man, the one who had sliced my favorite tank top, came before me. He grabbed my very tiny arms by the ropes that bound my little hands together. He gave a giant upwards pull on them, thinking he'd be pulling me onto my feet just as he had the three women before me. Pain! Excruciating pain shot through my shoulders! The grubby man fell over backwards, hitting his butt hard on the ground, crying out in shock and pain. His hands still held the ropes and my arms. He'd pulled the tiny, baby-like arms right out of my shoulders! He recoiled in shock.

Me? Pain shot through my shoulders, and I reacted! All I could think of was something that Jelena had said to me. Fire. Pain equals fire. I wanted to lash out at the man who had hurt me. Fire. An intense flame engulfed the grubby, prone man. His screams were hideous. Serves him right, I thought.

At the same time, I saw that woman who was sneaking around the outer edge of the campsite, just beyond the campfire's illumination. She carried a sword, and she thrust it into the back of another one of the distracted men who had captured us. Good, I thought. Clanking sounds. I turned my head and saw another man had stepped into the light of the fires. He was fighting with another of our captors. Good, I thought. No, bad. Four others were making for the backstabbing woman and the other man. Pain. My shoulders throbbed. I felt something warm flowing down my sides. Pain. Pain equals fire. A ball of intense flames suddenly appeared, engulfing the four men, who added their startled screeches to the din. The woman with the short sword stepped back. She was wary or perhaps even afraid. Pain. Pain equals fire. Now, the campfires seemed to explode into roaring infernos, two of them. I passed out, at least I think I did, but I continued to hear voices.

Was that Jelena's voice? "Quick! Cut me loose. I am a witch. I can heal her, she's bleeding to death!"

Another female voice countered, "Where's the magus?"

"Don't know. She and I got caught in the Slave Wind. Two of these men captured us in the cavern where we took refuge. Please, cut me loose before she bleeds to death!" That was Jelena again; I'm sure of it. Later, Jelena told me all about what had happened to us.

"Okay, I don't see anyone else here." She cut Jelena free. "You fix her up. I'll cut the others free. Name's Kisha, by the way."

"Jelena. Get them to make me some boiling water. I'll need a bunch of rags and their hands too, if I'm to save her. Please hurry." Jelena quickly began rummaging through her many bags, setting certain ones out before her. Shortly, two women came running over to help her. One carried some rags. "Good. I'll place them where I need them, and you press them up tightly to her shoulders. We have to stop the bleeding, before it's too late."

She spotted the third woman working on preparing

some hot water and relaxed a bit, focusing on my bleeding shoulders. "How strange, the arteries are so tiny. That's going to help."

Across the way, Kisha stood over the smoldering remains of one of the men. Using her sword, she poked about his body, dragging a necklace out of the mess. "This is mine. I told you that you should not take my necklace. You should have listened to me, you beast!" Kisha spat on the remains, pocketing her necklace. She walked over to the other man, "Well, Vlad, I see you got your man."

"Yah, but where's the magus? Them four burst into flames. Where's the magus?"

"Damned if I know, Vlad. This is the strangest fight yet. Got my necklace back. Thanks for your help. Looks like we rescued some women from the slavers. Bet we don't get any reward for it though."

He laughed, "Hardly. We came after your damned necklace. I hope it was worth it. Whatever. Is that other one going to make it? How come she had such tiny arms? Ah well, doesn't matter, does it? She's as good as dead anyway. Probably ought to let her die. It's merciful, you know." He sounded awfully apathetic.

Kisha shrugged, wiping off her sword before sheathing it. "Probably, Vlad. You don't see me helping them, do you? Best that she dies. She'd be helpless if she lives. Pity. Those are some knockers she's got. Never seen any that big before."

"You suppose I should help them?" Vlad asked. "Doubt it will do any real good though."

"Nah, help me search these fellows. Who knows what valuables we might get. Besides, we can sell their weapons and horses. Get a pretty bit of silver for them, I reckon," Kisha suggested.

"Money, that's all you thieves think about, isn't it?"

"Hey, money makes the world go round, Prince of No Where," Kisha retorted. "You don't want to get your hands dirty, I can see that. Why don't you search all the other things, and I'll deal with the corpses," Kisha suggested, knowing that she'd probably find what was really valuable. He nodded, and the two set about a thorough search.

Later, when she finished, Kisha examined the cooking pot. "Hey Vlad, there's still some grub in the pot. How about something to eat? Find any good stuff?"

"Yah, a fighter has to eat after a big battle. Nothing much, just some blankets and stuff," Vlad replied. "But then I didn't expect to find much. They are just pathetic scum." He sat down on a log before the fire and helped himself to a copper plate of the stew. "We split fifty-fifty?" he finally asked, seeing the small pile of coins and gems she'd collected from the corpses.

"I'm an honest thief, Vlad. Of course, we split fifty-fifty, as we agreed on. Kisha never backs out of her agreements. That's all I found, excepting what we can take back and sell. Take your half. I suppose I ought to go check on the five women and see if the poor one with the mammoth boobs has died."

"Be best if she did, don't ya think? I do," Vlad replied with his mouth full of stew.

Kisha walked over to the five women. As she approached, Jelena looked up and sat back. "There, I believe I've got her stabilized now. Fortunately, her arteries were quite small. We've got the bleeding stopped. I've given her something to make her sleep. Thanks for rescuing us. Which one is the magus? That was a magus spell, wasn't it? Where are we anyway?"

"Damn! Poor thing. You know, witch, she shouldn't have been healed. How the devil is she going to live now?" Kisha didn't answer any of her questions. "You've doomed her to a pathetic existence or don't you realize that?"

Jelena came to my defense. "Hey, she's my friend! She didn't used to have arms anyway. She didn't use those small arms for anything, except brushing her hair out of her face. She uses her feet. Really well, I might add. She's not helpless, if that's what you are thinking."

"All right, all right! Don't get so riled up, witch. Yes, those definitely were magus spells, fire elemental for sure. I've no idea where the magus was at. He certainly hasn't revealed himself. Perhaps, he doesn't want to be seen. Damn, the Slaver Magus is going to be really pissed with us, but then he

26

shouldn't have had his henchmen steal my necklace here. I told the bastard I would be coming after him to get it back. Stupid man. Didn't listen. Paid the price. Sticker here got him good." She was referring to her short sword that she'd named Sticker.

Kisha continued, "We are about five miles south of Zora's Crossing, by the river. Vlad here and I saw them kidnaping those three women. Where're you from?"

"Jovan. It's a small village. I've never heard of Zora's Crossing," Jelena answered, fear growing within her.

"Never heard of Jovan either," Kisha replied, watching carefully Jelena's reaction. "Shit, you're lost now, aren't you?"

Fighting from crying, Jelena answered meekly, "Yes. We have to get home, but which way? How far?"

"Oh hell!" Kisha swore, and then calmed a little. "We'll take you into Zora's Crossing with us. Perhaps, someone there has heard of this Jovan place. Hey, Vlad, you ever heard of a village called Jovan?" The brawny fighter shook his head no, sinking what tiny hope Jelena still had.

"Didn't think so. Vlad claims to be a prince, but he has no idea where his kingdom is located. I call him Prince of No Where. He's a fighter, not too bright, mind you, but honest. You can count on him. Can she be moved? We ought to get back into Zora's Crossing before the Magus Slaver comes checking on his slaver fighters here."

"Yes, give me a hand. Let's get her into the wagon," Jelena answered. The women lifted the unconscious Nia up and carried her to the wagon. Jelena wrapped her in several blankets. A few minutes later, Vlad joined them, but bringing six horses with him, along with what gear the two intended to take back with them to sell. Kisha had already rounded up their two mounts and tied them to the rear of the wagon.

While Vlad led the string of horses, Kisha drove the wagon. As they rode along, the other three rescued women chatted quietly with Kisha. Jelena overheard them, though. "We don't have much, but we will give you as big a reward as we can afford. Thank you for saving us from the slavers. Isn't it awful? They're taking women right out of the towns now, in broad daylight. What's the world coming too?"

"It's all men's fault. They're just beasts disguised as humans," Kisha retorted. In a softer tone, she added, "Whatever you can afford is fine with us. To be honest, we came after them to retrieve my necklace that one of them stole from me. Never steal from a thief! That's a death sentence, but he didn't listen to me. Should have, but then you know men."

Another woman explained, "My Yeva is a good man. He's a blacksmith. I'm sure you can get a fair price for these slavers' things from him."

It was past midnight, when the wagon rolled into Zora's Crossing. One by one, Kisha dropped the three rescued women off at their homes. However, Yeva, highly animated that his wife had been rescued, said, "Please, bring all the things by in the morning. I'll give you top silver for them. That's the least I can do for having saved her from the slavers."

"Hold you to that, Yeva. Cya in the morning then," Kisha replied. Now that it was just Vlad and her left, she asked, "So Vlad, you want to take the horses with you to the inn? Meet up with ya around nine, and we'll hold Yeva to his word?"

"Yah, that be best. So sleepy. Cya Kisha." He led the horses off down a different street. Kisha turned back to Jelena. "So what do I do with you two? Got any silvers to pay for an inn?"

Jelena's heart sank. "No, we were out collecting herbs and roots when the Slave Wind caught us by surprise. It came way early this fall. Please, can you help us?"

"Oh hell! I can't just toss you out onto the street. Men, now they would likely do just that. Okay, for tonight, you can stay at my place. See she doesn't bleed all over the place, and don't mess with any of my stuff!"

"We won't. Thank you, Kisha, thank you." Kisha slapped the reins and the horses began slowly ambling down the darkened street once more.

Her place turned out to be a ramshackle, waddle and daub building on the edge of Zora's Crossing. It consisted only of two rooms, her bedroom and her combined kitchen, dining room, and living room. "Sorry, but you'll have to sleep on the floor. Bring in all the blankets we salvaged. They'll make a mattress of sorts, I suppose."

A short while later, the two half carried the unconscious Nia into the small living room, and laid her onto the pile of blankets. A bit later, satisfied her patches were still holding, Jelena laid down beside her friend, falling into a deep sleep almost immediately.

She awoke to the smells of griddlecakes and sizzling meat. She rose and rubbed the sleep out of her eyes, tossed her blonde hair back, found the chamber pot, and then went to see if she could help any. "Nah, got breakfast about ready. How's your friend?"

"Still sleeping. That's a good thing for now. Say, is there a good witch in Zora's Crossing? I'd like her to look at Nia and make sure I did everything right," Jelena asked. "I'm only an apprentice witch."

"Sure several, but I think Zuzana is the best. We'll take her there after I get done with Yeva," Kisha answered. She was in better spirits, Jelena surmised, probably because she was about to sell off the slavers' gear and make some silvers. She wasn't wrong.

While Kisha was gone, Jelena worked on her patient, re-cleaning the wounds, noticing they were healing well, at least she thought so. These were the worst wounds she'd ever had to heal thus far. When Kisha returned, she was in good spirits and tossed Jelena a large linen blouse. "Here, put that on her. She's got to have something to wear. How's she doing?"

"Good, as far as I can tell," Jelena answered, adding, "Thanks. How did it go with Yeva?"

"Really good. Vlad and I made out far better than I ever expected." She hefted a small money pouch. As Jelena sat me up to get the blouse on me, I finally woke up.

"Oh, the grey void is still here. I hurt some. Jelena? The cavern has now turned into a room, I think. When will the hallucinations end? I'm hungry and have to pee pretty soon. If only this room would materialize better out of this infernal grey void. I keep getting lost in it."

"Hey, it's over, Nia. The Slave Wind is done. We got captured by those slaver men who took refuge in our cavern.

They ripped your arms off. I've got the wounds healing. We are in Kisha's house right now. Can you stand up?"

"Huh? All over? My shoulders are throbbing some. I can stand. Why does the room keep slipping and sliding into and out of this grey nothingness? Am I going mad now?"

"Don't know. Let's get you up and to the chamber pot. Want some help with your pants?"

I think my face flushed quite red. That's the last thing that I wanted the world to see — my privates. Yet, mom or dad always helped me with my jeans. I never could unbutton them or button them, though I could wiggle into them. With their steadying arms, I got to my feet. "Just unbutton me, please. Where's the toilet?"

"Sorry. What's a toilet?" Kisha asked. "Oh, you mean the chamber pot?"

I flushed again. No toilet. Still somewhat disoriented, I bit the bullet and allowed the two to pull my pants down and then my panties. I ignored their gasps and made good use of the chamber pot. Done, I looked up at their startled faces. "I'm a woman, as you can see. Just glad it's not my period right now. I know. I've got a man's thing too." I think my face must have been quite red by then.

Unabashed, Kisha asked, "Does it work? I mean, like a man's does?"

I was just glad that there were no men about. "Yes, it does. My doctor told me I can impregnate myself or any other woman with it. I know — it's really weird."

Jelena added, "She comes from a Sky Ship. We saw it coming down from the sky. She's Sky People."

"Hey, I'm the only woman like this on our ship. Mom and the other women are just like you. It's just me that's different. Born this way. Don't know why. Please, can I get something to eat? And how soon is this grey fog going to go away? I keep drifting in and out of it." No one answered me. Not good, I thought.

They got me redressed and to Kisha's small table. "Do we have to feed you?" Kisha asked, slightly annoyed with that notion.

"Of course not. Just slide the plate over," I replied,

30

annoyed she had to ask me that. I picked up the copper fork between my right toes and dove into the griddlecakes. "Um, really good!" Kisha finally smiled at the compliment, though she was staring at me, fascinated, I suppose, with how I managed it. Jelena gathered up her things while I ate.

After sipping the hot tea, again impressing Kisha, I watched as Jelena, finished with her packing, sat down beside me and explained, "Nia, as soon as you are done, Kisha is going to take us to visit a really good witch. I want her to examine you and make sure I've done everything properly. Then, we have to figure out what we're going to do. You see, I've no idea where we are at now. No one seems to know where my village is, and I don't know where Zora's Crossing is at — that's the town we're in here. We've got a really big problem, Nia."

"Crap! Well, it looks like I can't just use our ship's medical machine to heal me up quickly. Okay, then, we best have this woman check on my shoulders. By the way, thanks for helping me, Jelena. I think I was bleeding to death back there, but I couldn't really tell. Too much grey void. Thanks for letting us stay in your house, Kisha."

"Let's get going. I told Zuzana you would be dropping by," Kisha changed the topic. She didn't like others thanking her, I noticed, or perhaps it was that she was wholly unused to such politeness.

Zuzana was in her forties and had a very kindly demeanor. While she listened to Jelena's tale, she carefully examined my shoulders and changed Jelena's dressings, so that she could get a good look at them. She also gave Jelena a pot of healing salve to put on the wounds at night. "You've done a very good job with these wounds, Jelena. There are no signs of infections, and it is already healing rapidly. You show great promise as a witch. Your mother should be proud of you." Later, Jelena asked her if she had heard of her village of Jovan. She hadn't.

Just when I though she was done with me, Zuzana checked my eyes. "Hum. Jelena, this is not good at all. While her physical wounds are doing well, she's in big trouble because of the Slave Wind. Look here, at her eyes. She keeps

31

seeing the grey void. You can see why."

"What's wrong with my eyes? Am I going blind or something?" I nearly panicked. If I were blinded, then I would be in very serious trouble!

"No, that's not it at all. She's turning into a magus, if I'm not off my mark," Zuzana pointed out. "This is serious. The grey void isn't going away, not without help. Jelena, you need to get Nia here to a magus and very soon! If you don't, she could well go utterly mad and kill many, quite by accident."

Both Jelena and Kisha cursed, but I merely panicked. "What do you mean? I'm crazy? What magus?" I fumbled about, trying hard to think properly. That I kept fogging out didn't help.

"There's old Magus Triska at Sana Falls. She's the closest magus I know of, but Sana Falls is two hundred plus miles south of here," Zuzana replied. "Pretty rough country between here and there too."

Jelena sighed, "Somehow, we'll have to make it there. Can you draw me a map of how to find this Sana Falls? I don't know where we are at all. I'm totally lost."

"Sure dear. Say, Kisha, you ought to take them there. After all, you rescued them from the slavers."

"Yes, but they don't have any silvers, and that's a long trip. No profit," Kisha commented.

"This young girl's life is in your hands, whether you admit it or not, Kisha. All right," Zuzana sighed, "if you do this, then I'll owe you a big favor."

"Deal! Draw up the map," Kisha replied, very thankful for a gracious way out of the mess. She knew she ought to have already volunteered to take us to see this magus herself. Once more, she'd spoken out of turn, worse, mentioning monetary gain. Though a thief by nature, if ever she spoke the truth, she was never truly interested in money, but was interested in showing that she was more able than most men.

A half hour later, the trio walked back to Kisha's place. Zora's Crossing was rather large, some five thousand called this place home. I looked at the houses; some were adobe brick, some were waddle and daub. All were single story affairs. "Thanks for taking us to Sana Falls, Kisha. I hate to be imposing on you, but I'm really at a loss," Jelena commented.

"That's okay. Back there, I didn't really mean I only do things for money. Say, Nia, can you ride a horse?" Kisha asked.

"I don't know. I've never seen them before last night. Is it hard to do?"

"What? How do you get around? Do you walk everywhere or just use wagons?" Kisha asked.

Jelena answered for me. "She's Sky People. They fly around in this big, silver bird. I saw it landing not far from our village."

I doubted Kisha believed what Jelena was saying. She rolled her eyes around. "Okay, if we have to go by wagon, that's going to take a whole lot longer. Zuzana said we should hurry, so let's see if we can use horses. It's dangerous country down there. I'll see if I can get Vlad to come with us. We can use a good sword this time. Besides, he's got little else to do. He's as lost as you both are. Worse, he doesn't even remember the name of his lands only that he is supposed to be a prince. I doubt that, but I think he suffered a bad knock on his noggin."

"Did he get wounded in a battle?" Jelena asked.

"Think so. I found him unconscious some miles from here. Brought him back to Zuzana's, but I think his mind is still goofed up somehow. He keeps thinking he's a prince, but he can't remember what or where his lands are. He keeps wandering around — has been for the last three years. Good fighter, though. Hey, we're going to need to get Nia something better to wear on the trail. It gets cold at night. Fall's nearly here."

"But we don't have any silvers," Jelena countered.

Kisha sighed and stopped walking. "Look, I should have split the silvers with you two — the silvers that we got for all the slavers' things. After all, if Zuzana's right and Nia here is turning into a magus, then it was she who killed the other slavers, earning her the right to share in the profits. I'll cover the cost of a descent leather dress for Nia and cloaks for the both of you. Come on; we best find Vlad and start making our preparations. Two hundred fifty miles by horseback is going to take us at least a week, maybe more."

A bit later, Vlad commented, rather hopelessly, "Whatever. Sure, I'll come with you. I don't suppose this Magus Triska at Sana Falls will know where my kingdom is located, though. That would be too much to ask. Still, maybe I will recognize my lands if I see them. Could I be from down there? Probably not."

Chapter 3 On the Road

"Always mount from the left side," Kisha instructed me. I was now properly attired, that is, I looked like everyone else. Kisha had kindly purchased me a leather dress, similar to what she and Jelena wore. Unfortunately, I had to relinquish a bit of my independence, since I could not yet figure out how to put it on or take it off by myself. I swore to myself that I would experiment and learn to do it somehow. I just needed time and to get rid of this highly confusing grey fog that kept floating over me, like some dog that refuses to give up the scent.

I had watched Kisha making her preparations — rather amazed actually. She had more concealed weapons than I could imagine places for them! While she kept her short sword strapped to her leather belt, she had two throwing daggers in a harness across the top of her back, in easy reach for throwing. She strapped another pair of daggers, one on each leg, along with a pair of knives. Then, she had other smaller items, whose natures were currently unknown to me, stuffed into all manner of strange locations — one being in her hair. She tied a bow and quiver to her saddle and stowed an axe across the back of her saddle. Yet another bag contained more throwing daggers, which she stored on one of the packhorses — all this before she even got to the bedding, cooking gear, and food supplies. An amazing young woman, I thought, always prepared. Indeed, I was soon to learn that was her motto: be prepared for anything, for it's highly likely to happen.

Vlad led a pair of packhorses, while we three each rode ours. I admit, when I first saw the horse that was to be mine, I flinched. She was quite tall, though I noticed later she was smaller than the others were. Knowing nothing about such beasts of burden, I knew I had to learn and learn fast. If only this damnable grey fog would dissipate! I put my foot in the stirrup and heaved upwards, swinging my leg over. I'd made it up without disgracing myself too badly.

"For now, Jelena is going to lead your horse, so all you have to do, Nia Elain, is sit and not fall off," Kisha explained. I nodded and began to observe how they rode theirs. I needed to learn fast, but as we began to ride through the streets of Zora's Crossing, I experienced a whole new concept of motion. I knew this was going to take some getting used to, if I was ever going to master riding a horse. Still, as we rode along, I paid close attention to the others and how they did it.

We wove along the twisted streets. I concluded the people just constructed their homes wherever they desired, without any plan or design for the town or someone's passage through it. Adobe homes predominated nearer the center of the town, the richer folks I presumed. Cradled on a hill overlooking a wide, but shallow river, Zora's Crossing got its name from the ford below the hill. As we ambled past the blacksmith shop with smoke curling from his hearth, Yeva waved good-naturedly. Kisha waved back. I could only nod. Sweat dripped from his brow, but I was chilly in my new leather dress. Fall was here, and I didn't want to experience winter. Crazy thoughts tickled my consciousness, as I drifted in and out of the grey fog, even riding through the town.

When we reached the southern edge of the town and began descending towards the ford, I could see more wattle and daub homes, similar to Kisha's. To the west, I saw fields of glowing, waving amber. Kisha pointed them out. "Yonder lies our breadbasket. Wheat and barley fields. Lots of farmers in and around Zora's Crossing."

Jelena asked, "What lies beyond? We have a small wheat field in Jovan."

Kisha responded, at least a little. "Rus country, mostly. I've been as far south as Millers Town, mostly hills and forests between here and there. According to the map, it's about a third of the way we have to go. It's the only town for close to a hundred miles south of here. We Sud's are farmers mostly. My folks moved to Zora's Crossing when I was a baby, least that's what they told me. Up from the far south, looking for good farmlands. But the Rus range all through these southern woods. They are fierce hunters. We have to be alert for their hunting parties on this trip. They don't take kindly to us farmers; we don't take kindly to them either. That's why we've got Vlad along with us."

"Yah," the big man commented dryly, "probably have to fight some of the Rus along the way. Might even get killed ourselves. Whatever."

"What do the Rus look like?" Jelena asked, growing a bit more worried.

"You can't miss them," Kisha answered. "Imagine a wild man, and you've got them. Long, tangled hair and beards. Dirty, greasy, smelly, and wild, but keen fighters. Guess they have to be, if they are depending on hunting bear and deer. Some have weapons they've stolen from us Suds, but most have stone weapons. Mind you, a stone spear point will kill you just as dead. Here's the ford. Only place we can easily cross the Hill River for many miles. It comes down from yonder mountains to the west and goes mostly eastwards for a hundred miles. After that, who knows?" She shrugged her shoulders, but Jelena focused on leading her horse and thus mine into the shallow, rapid waters of the river.

As my horse waded through the flowing waters, creating various hypnotizing swirls and eddies, I drifted into the grey fog once more. The lurching of my mare, as she climbed up the bank on the other side, jarred me back from the grey mists. I cursed silently for having drifted off yet again. Would this nightmare ever end?

Once on the other side, the forest closed around us, again dimming down the world, but adding that special fragrance that screams loudly "woods!" With trees and brush growing everywhere and bits of gnarly rocks rising up, as though unwilling to be replaced, I was instantly lost once more. In contrast, Jelena took a deep breath. "What a wonderful, old woods," she exclaimed.

Kisha grumbled, "Dangerous woods, if you ask me. Witch, if you got any woods sense, alert us to troubles."

Unfazed by Kisha's sour tones, Jelena replied, "Sure thing. These are old woods, great trees. Many are hundreds of years old. Such stories they tell." Kisha rolled her eyes, but didn't say anything. We ambled slowly along, and I drifted into and out of the grey mists. It was hard to remain focused on the forest, for it, too, seemed, to my eyes, to be one vast void.

Thrice Jelena called a brief halt. Twice to allow a distant

37

bear to amble on its way, and once to allow a wild boar to grunt and snort at us, before trotting off into the brush. We were following a pair of ruts made by wagons. Jelena pointed them out to me. Once she had, it was obvious, and I wondered why I hadn't noticed them myself.

When we made camp beside a small creek smack in the middle of the forest, Vlad commented, "This should be a defensive site, for all the good it'll do us. Probably all get killed in our sleep."

"Oh, cool it, Vlad," Kisha countered. "You'll scare our strangers. Still, Witch Jelena, if you have some kind of protective spells or something that can alert us to troubles in the night, that would be welcome. We're on our own, if you hadn't noticed. In towns, I'm at my best, but out here, I'm not in my element, if you take my meaning."

"Okay, I can do that, I think," Jelena replied, somewhat conservatively. She took out some powders and sprinkled them in a giant circle around our campsite.

Me, I just tried to get my legs back. I'd gotten off the horse easily, but the second my feet hit the ground, they collapsed. Mush. I had mush for legs! Kisha giggled, "You'll soon get your horse legs, Nia Elain. Everyone's like this when they first go for a long ride. Vlad, how far do you think that we've come today?" I was grateful for the change of topic. He was handling the horses, hobbling them, and tying them into a line roped between two scraggly oak trees.

"Oh maybe thirty miles. Whatever. Does it matter, Kisha? We're not there. Probably won't get there either. If we don't get lost, the Rus may get us."

"Is he always so gloomy?" Jelena whispered to Kisha.

"Pretty much so. I think it's because he can't remember things," she replied, while setting about making camp. "Probably that knock on his head." I now saw the purpose of the axe she had tied behind her saddle: wood chopping. I felt miserable. Everyone set about camp duties, but I could do little more than stand and watch. True, I was out of my comfort zone. Hell, I've never been camping like this, so utterly crude and yet so quaint. I found myself enjoying the experience, even though I wasn't actively able to pull my own weight. Still, I observed and began thinking of ways I could help later on. Poignantly, my own deficiencies were being pointed out to me in rather stark images. I began to realize just how isolated my whole life had been to date. In the Eagle's Seed, I could manage well enough, but out here in the real world, it was quite another story. I fought hard from breaking down and took comfort in the grey void that continually seeped into my mind.

Later, I was able to feed myself and dry the dishes for them, a very little something. While I was finishing them up, a small, brown and black striped ground squirrel came into the camp. Sitting on a small tuft of grass, it observed me closely, and I, it. "He's just saying hi and is curious," Jelena whispered to me, as she slowly sat down beside me to watch him. "Lots of friendly animals in the woods."

Three days on the trail found us entering Millers Town, the farthest that Kisha had ever been in this direction. In many respects, I found it quite similar to Zora's Crossing. We did stop at a pub for an ale, Kisha's treat, and for news. "Well, Kisha, long time no see. Yah, Rus have been active 'tween here and Deercreek," the pudgy, but friendly barman answered Kisha's query. "Be warry."

His conversation was the very least of my worries! As we entered this quaint adobe pub with its rather garish sign of two semi-naked ladies tacked into the bricks over its door, I began to hear voices inside my head! *I don't suppose he'll have any real news. That would be too much to ask.* Was that Vlad? It sounded like his dreary comments. But more voices came at me, some nearly simultaneously. *Who are these strangers? Look at that set of knockers! Hey, I've seen her before, but where? If I don't get my ace, I'm broke again. Rus? Sure hope they stay away until I get my harvest in. Wonder if Branka will smell ale on my breath again?* Am I going crazy? Mad? Like Jelena said? She did say that people go mad after the Slave Wind is done. My head is splitting!

I don't remember sitting down or ordering an ale. I've never drank alcohol before, but I downed the ale quickly. "Thirsty, eh? Good stuff, best stout in these parts," Kisha explained to me. I noticed her now. I belched, and my group chuckled. Someone refilled my mug. I felt a hot sensation in my stomach, then a dullness. Ah, that lowered the volume of the voices in my head, so I drank more, until silence came at last. I hadn't noticed that many had left, including the four who were playing a card game in one corner. Now, I finally observed the rough-hewn planks that formed our table and the crude bench we sat on. I belched again and smiled, self-consciously, wondering if they had noticed my madness and hoping they hadn't.

"We best keep a sharp eye out for the Rus hunters," Kisha advised as we headed out of the pub to resume our journey. Do they need to keep an eye on me? Am I going to be doing dumb, ridiculous, or dangerous things? I don't want to hurt any of them; they're my friends. What's happening to me? *She sure gorged herself on that ale. Well, if I were in her shoes, I'd probably do the same.* Who's saying that? Kisha? Did I hear her? Oh god, I am going mad!

I tried to focus on the world around me. As we rode along, we entered a dense forest of oaks. Their gnarly bark, twisted limbs, and great girths suggested we were the intruders into their timeless world. I tried to listen to whatever they might be saying, but unlike Jelena, I heard only the wind and the squirrels, whose chatter told me we were not welcome here. I longed to be back on the Eagle's Seed! There, my world had been orderly, if boring. I got by very well in our ship. Yet, as soon as I thought of the ship, like a thunderbolt, pangs of loss struck me. I had no idea where the ship was located or if anyone there was still alive. I was lost; worse, I was lost in a grey fog and now likely going mad. I tried to recall how long Jelena had said some of these Slave Wind victims lasted before being put down, but I couldn't focus well enough — maddening in and of itself. The day wore on.

That evening, we all sat around the campfire. Dinner and dishes were done — the latter, my only real contribution. "So how much danger are we in if we run into these Rus?" Jelena asked. "So far, we've not had them up in Jovan."

Kisha answered slowly. "I think they are the first settlers around these parts. You can't mistake them. They look like barbarians. Wild, long hair, though the women sometimes braid theirs. Fierce fighters, even the women. They use wicked blades that are more sickle-shaped, with a hook on the end. When they hit you with that, the hook really tears a nasty wound. Theirs are bronze weapons, though they've stolen some of our iron blades. Our people don't always win, you see. The one thing we've got going over the Rus is that they are clan oriented. You'll almost never see more than around fifty together in any one spot. I think the clans also fight among themselves. Still, we don't want to run into them, if we can avoid it. Jelena, don't forget to put up your protection spells, please, witch."

Jelena chuckled, "Already done, Kisha. I don't want to have my throat slit while I'm sleeping either." Kisha smiled, and we turned in for the night.

It must have been midnight, that's my guess anyway. A birdcall roused me. I wiggled to sit up and saw that Jelena was already awake and rustling Kisha. The ruddy embers of our campfire still provided some illumination. That's when I saw him, a Rus!

He wore animal skins, though I couldn't tell what creature they came from, only that it was furry and probably warm. His hair was long and stringy, probably hadn't been washed in months. I didn't want to smell him, I concluded. As I watched him, I detected mostly a feeling of curiousness coming from him. His strange weapon was slung across his back, and he was merely looking at us. As Kisha woke and sprang to her feet, while drawing her short sword, the Rus backed up, nodded to me, turned, and melted into the dark forest. I heard not a sound from him.

"Damn! That was a Rus! Probably a scout. We best post a guard from now on. Good going, witch!" Kisha exclaimed. "I'll take first watch. You go back to sleep." I laid down and did just that, the image of the barbarian Rus burned into my mind. That's when I realized if Jelena hadn't cast her alerting spell, we might all have been killed in our sleep!

Sometime later, I calmed down and drifted into an ill sleep. The grey fog beckoned to me, but I fought against it. Did I sleep? Can't say, but I felt exhausted when Jelena brought me a tin of breakfast. I think I was grumpy this morning, but it only got worse as the day wore on.

After we stopped for lunch, I began to feel better. The air had a crispness to it, rather pricking my senses, pulling me out of the greyness that seemed to be continually calling me into it. As we then rode on, Kisha guessed we were about halfway to this Deercreek town. That's when it all happened. So fast. One minute, we were just riding long, and the next, we came upon a battle. Okay, the others were alerted to it long before I was cognizant of it. I can blame it on the grey fog again.

Just ahead of us, two fighters were battling what, to my eyes, seemed like a host of black-clad fighters. The two were valiantly defending themselves, their backs to each other. Five of the enemy men were down, a pair of whom were frantically dealing with sword cuts to arms and legs. As we came upon the battle, Vlad called out, "Hey, twenty to two is not fair odds."

Kisha yelled, "Those are slavers — the men in black. Best give the two a hand or we'll have them attacking us next." She rapidly dismounted and took up her bow, while Vlad charged into the left flank of the men, who were mostly waiting to get their chance at the two fighters. His horse trampled one, and he chopped into a second, before executing what I can only describe as a flying dismount. Kisha hit one with an arrow, dropping him. Jelena hastily gathered up our many reins. She wasn't about to enter the fight, not armed only with her long knife. Me? I dismounted and stepped forward to see better. Pain equals fire — that went through my mind.

While I was partly in the grey fog and partly witnessing the battle, the dull throbbing in my shoulders kicked in hard, reminding me that I was being threatened yet again. So many trees were in the way. I fought hard to stifle the thought of fire, imagining igniting the whole forest by accident. But there were lots of rocks and small boulders lying around, along with some dead wood. Stop the pain, that was my only real thought.

The pair of back-to-back fighters was taking their toll, two more men fell, but another pair took their place. Each was fighting three men. Poor Vlad was being surrounded. Worse, another six ran towards Kisha, who continued firing off her

42

arrows as fast as she could, emptying her quiver in short order. In seconds, they'd be on us two and poor Jelena, who was struggling with trying somehow to hold all of our horses. I stood just behind and to Kisha's right, facing the charging men.

As I now understand what happened, I acted, but at that time, it was all rather hazy and surreal. Boulders rose up and smashed four of the oncoming men in the backs of their heads. They dropped like stones, but the boulders flew on over to three men that were coming at Vlad's backside. They too dropped. Next, a hail of the stones flew upwards like inverted rain. That is, they rose up from the ground and flew into the mass of men surrounding the two back-to-back fighters. Several dropped to the ground, others, in surprise, turned to face their unseen opponents only to get more stones flying at them. Some ducked in time, but others took them head on. Those did not fare too well at all.

Kisha was not a fighter. I noticed she lacked the skill of the man who finally reached her and engaged her. She'd dropped her empty quiver and bow, drawing her short sword just in time to parry a deadly thrust her way. I saw a boulder near that man's right foot. The next instant, the boulder rose up and smashed him in his head, dropping him. By this time, the second fighter finally closed upon me.

I can't imagine what that fighter must have thought. With deadly sword in hand, he charged into a young teen, armless and bearing no visible weapons. I sensed his blood lust, however. He didn't care. Killing was his sole thought. Kisha pivoted to protect me, drawing a throwing dagger with her free hand, but we both knew she would be too late to stop him from striking me. I acted. Memories and years of training kicked into action in one single instant. No thought, just coordinated body movement. As he swung his deathblow, I ducked, pivoted, and raised my left leg. As he lunged forward off balance from his miss, my foot found its mark. Even Kisha heard the snapping, crunching sounds of his neck vertebrae, as they broke or shattered. He died on his feet, in slow motion, his body dropping to the ground before me. I think I screamed and charged into the fray.

Stunned by what she'd seen, Kisha paused a moment before racing after me. Later, she described me as a wild banshee, whatever that is. I never did get a satisfactory definition of that creature. I dropped three more men, though I will say that I took them from behind. Kisha took another by surprise, stabbing him in his back. Together, we relieved both Vlad and the other pair of fighters. With only four of the black-clothed men still unwounded, they chose to flee the battle, racing into the woods as fast as they could. The battle was over in a flash. As I began to learn, sword fights are swift things. The aftermath is also bloody.

As soon as the four fled, Vlad moved systematically to each of the fallen, wounded men and finished them off with precision swings of his large blade. With a number of dead bodies lying between Kisha and me and the gasping and bleeding pair of fighters, I watched the two lean on their blades, panting, gasping for breath. The man said, "Hail and timely well met!"

While I stared blankly at the strange pair, Kisha had the presence of mind to act. "Kisha Mila out of Zora's Crossing. Vlad is cleaning up the fallen. Come back to our horses. Our witch will see to your wounds, sir." Sir? Her form of address seemed archaic or foreign to me. "Here, lean on me. Nia, you help the woman back to Jelena." That was an order. Mechanically, I complied, moving close to the bent woman, who continued to gasp, leaning heavily on her sword, a rather large one, I thought. She reached out. I felt the strong downward pressure of her left arm upon my shoulder and knew she needed a lift up. I felt my leg muscles tense, but they bore her full weight as she rose up. Together, we began stepping over the fallen bodies, moving back towards Jelena.

As the battle approached its end, Jelena had had the presence of mind to tie the horses to various tree branches and had already begun removing her healing pouches. By the time we four reached her, she'd already begun to collect bits of deadwood for a fire and had a small pot out, along with one of our water skins. Her mind told me she wanted boiling water. Without thinking about it, I saw the deadwood suddenly ignite, surprising her and everyone else. Jelena took that burst of flames in stride, placing the pot and water on it.

"Okay, sit them down here on this patch of grass. Who is cut the worst?" Jelena asked professionally, as though she had dealt with just such injuries everyday of her life. I knew from her thoughts she had done no such thing.

"Please, witch, cure this gallant ranger before me," the man answered.

I had a moment to glance at each of them. Both were bleeding from several sword wounds to their arms and legs. Silly me. I thought they both were in pretty bad shape. Jelena's keen eyes and wisdom came to the fore. She handed Kisha a rag and said, "Here, hold this tightly to his left leg wound until I can get to it." She did as instructed, but not until she helped him sit down, though a controlled collapse was more like it.

"Here Nia, you hold this rag on her right leg. Lots of pressure, while I get this nasty arm cut of hers handled," Jelena ordered me. I sat down, kicked off my new moccasins, and did as she asked, while watching her and the woman. In the background, I could hear Vlad mechanically going about his duties and also the pleading thoughts of the wounded men that he put down. Strange symphony of sounds, visuals, and thoughts.

The woman was extremely attractive, with rich, raven hair. She had trimmed bangs that nearly touched her thick eyebrows, an oval face, a rounded nose, and thick lips. Her eyes were bright, but maybe that was from the pain she was enduring. Strangely, I felt my male organ rousing and vainly tried to think, "Not now! Please, not now!" She was probably six feet, a little taller than I was. Her arms and legs were well muscled, highly toned, though my own legs were a bit thicker and stronger. Her arm muscles were nearly double those of Kisha's or Jelena's, though with the latter, that's not saying much. I noticed she wore some kind of leather-like armor, which Jelena had to remove to get to the many wounds, most of which she ignored for the moment, dealing with the two worst ones first.

Just as soon as the water boiled, Jelena began her real work. "Fraid this is going to hurt some. I have to sew up the bigger cuts, ma'am. Here, bite on this rag. Nia, keep up the pressure." I watched while Jelena began stitching the flesh in her upper arm back together. To her credit, the woman barely grunted, though I could occasionally feel her leg tightening in reaction to Jelena's needle. Once she'd put in six stitches, she tied it off and wiped it again with the hot water and rag, before covering it with her salve. Now, she had me move back. I watched as blood quickly began seeping out of her leg wound once more.

Jelena allowed it to bleed a little more. "Let it clean itself a bit. There," she explained, and began stitching this one up, using ten stitches this time. "Okay, the rest can wait a bit." She moved over to the man and began working on him.

"Kisha, I've taken care of the others," Vlad commented dully. He'd come up behind us. "I suppose you'll be wanting more water."

"Right. You hurt?" she replied.

"Don't think I'm dead this time, Kisha. Never know. Lightning might strike anytime. Say, where did those rocks come from? You throw them?" he asked, suddenly remembering the flying projectiles.

"Nah, probably Nia's doing. Get me double the amount of water and give her a good drink, will ya?"

Now, I could see the man better. He was covered in a cloak of tiny metal rings. How strange, I thought. Then, as Kisha helped him remove it, I realized this was what Vlad called ring mail. It had stopped the worst of the sword blows of the enemy, far better than the woman's leather had. He also wore a similar set of leather armor below the mail. I picked up his thought: padding. God, am I hearing their thoughts now?

An hour later, Jelena finished patching up the two, and she set about fixing lunch for everyone. During this time, Vlad had also rounded up the pair's four horses and thirty-six of the black-clad slaver's mounts. He'd done a thorough search of some thirty-two dead men, forming a pile of their valuables, along with what he thought that they might be able to sell, once they got to the next town.

The hot meal brought the pair back to life. "I must thank you all for coming to our aid. I am Sir Dmitri Vana, knight of King Jereni the Bold. My tracker, Ranger Danika

Jereni, the king's daughter," he said formally.

"Pleased to meet you, sir," Kisha replied for our group. "I'm Kisha Mila, good thief out of Zora's Crossing, up north a ways. This is my friend, Vlad Zelimir. He claims to be a prince, but when our paths met, he'd taken a blow to the head. He's forgotten everything, but how to fight well. This is a pair of strangers we rescued from the slavers. Nia Elain Compton and Witch Jelena Kish of Jovan. Both women were caught in the Slave Wind and taken by a slaver magus. By chance, have either of you heard of this Jovan village?" I detected Jelena's keen interest in what they would answer. Alas, I sensed their reply before they gave it.

"Sorry. I've never heard of this village," the knight replied formally. Danika shook her head no as well. "Say, who is the magus here? Those boulders were quite timely, though in time, I do believe Ranger Danika and I would have killed them all. Slavers! Scum!"

Kisha hesitated a bit. "Well, we think it might be Nia Elain here. She's still going in and out of the grey void. I took her to see a witch in Zora's Crossing, and she said that to save Nia, we have to get her to see a magus in Sana Falls. We're on our way there now. Are you sure that you could have killed all those slavers?" she asked quite pointedly, doubting that very much. *The man has a big ego.* I picked that thought up from Kisha.

Ranger Danika spoke up, "Not really, Kisha. We are in your debt, and yours, Witch Jelena. Tell them the whole story, Sir Dmitri, or I will." She tone was accusative, and I sensed a bit of rivalry between the two. Danika looked like she might be a couple of years older than me, but Sir Dmitri was in his early twenties, a handsome knight, though rather battered up at the moment.

He glared at her briefly, but complied. "I left the king with a company of a dozen fighters and Ranger Danika here. We were charged with removing the slaver bands that have been raiding the towns and villages of King Jereni's kingdom. While she and I were getting some additional supplies back in Deekcreek, these despicable men raided our camp and killed my men — all of them. She and I swore revenge and tracked them to this glen, where we set upon them. Too bad four of them got away. As soon as I get my strength back, I'll go after them. The swine!"

"You'll do no such thing," Jelena spoke up. "If you do much of anything during the next couple of weeks, you will rip those stitches out and bleed to death. Your body needs time to heal or I won't be responsible for your life, Sir Knight." She stood over him with her hands on her hips, glaring down at him. I picked up her thought: *Foolish man!*

Ranger Danika countered him, "She's right, Sir Dmitri. We have to heal up some. Don't be so darn headstrong. Besides, we need to get some more fighters from dad, unless you want to take on the army of slavers by yourself. If so, leave me out of your suicide, please. On top of that, we owe these people for coming to our aid."

His boisterous manner evaporated for a moment. "Alas, you are right, Ranger Danika. Yes, forgive me in my enthusiasm. We owe you. We should see you safely to Sana Falls."

"That's better. Say, what happened to you, Nia? Lost both arms. God, how can you survive? I can't believe you took out several of those fighters with only your feet," Danika finally asked what had been on her mind for some time now.

"She's Sky People," Jelena answered for me. "She was born without them. I think something must have gone wrong in her mother's womb. That can happen, you know. The Sky People gave her new baby arms before she landed near my village, though such magic is beyond me. We were out hunting herbs, when we were captured by the slavers, during the Slave Wind. You see, her arms were really tiny things, but the slavers accidentally pulled them right off of her shoulders. She heals fast though, which is a good thing, I think."

"Sky People? Who are they? Another nearby village?" asked Danika.

I finally spoke up, "I and my people come from another world. We landed in a spaceship. She's right. I only got my new arms a few months ago. They were very tiny, and about all I could do with them is brush the hair out of my face, so they aren't any big loss, you see."

"Don't see, but I'll accept that," Danika replied. "Do all of you Sky People have such large bosoms? Yours are impressive, Nia."

I think perhaps I flushed. "No, I'm unique." What else could I answer? I had to change the subject, so I blurted out, "You are welcome to come with us to Sana Falls. That way, Jelena can look after your wounds. She's a really fine healer." Why did I want her to come along with us? Once again, the thing in my pants was reacting! But reacting to a beautiful woman! I felt awfully warm again.

"After you risked everything to help us, nothing's going to stop me from seeing you all safely to Sana Falls," she replied with some spirit and a big smile. That was the first time that I melted. Her smile — like a breath of warm air in a chilly bed — a radiance vying the magnificent gaseous nebulae I so love. I must have smiled back. "Kisha, we'll see you all get a fair price for the horses and gear when we get to Deercreek. Also, Sir Dmitri, you can send word to dad about these slavers and ask for replacements. That would be wise."

"Yes, I believe you are right, Ranger Danika. I should let King Jereni know what we've accomplished, though I regret the loss of his dozen soldiers," he replied, ceding the point to her. Via Kisha's thoughts, I also saw that, while he thought of himself in charge, he held the king's daughter in high regard, but not because she was his daughter. I wondered what that meant.

Vlad spoke up, "Whatever. We should just leave the dead for the carrion birds. It'll take me all day to bury them. Probably those that got away will return with more and kill us all before I can get them buried."

A perplexed look came over Sir Dmitri's face. "Vlad, while the honorable thing to do is to bury them, at the moment, I m not in a position to help you. In good conscience, I cannot ask you to do this. Regrettably, we must leave them for now. When I get more replacements, I'll return and bury what's left of them." He seemed satisfied with his pronouncement. Now, I picked up what had to be Danika's thought: *Saving face again, Sir Dmitri?* I wondered what that meant.

A short while later, we gathered up the horses and prepared to head on to Deercreek. Vlad tied the long string of horses together, "I'll bring them, since no one else can."

"Sorry, Vlad, I'm not up to helping you," Sir Dmitri quickly admitted, but he and Danika came over to me, thinking they'd at least lift me onto my horse.

As always, Jelena was holding the mare's reins. "No, I can mount. Honestly, I really am not helpless." As I mounted, I saw Danika watching me very carefully. For once, I mounted very well. A surge of pride swept over me.

Suddenly, I had memories of mom flooding my mind. "You are showing off again," she teased me. I had just cleaned up my room in record time; everything was now in its proper place. I remember grinning back at her. I recalled why I'd wanted to show off for her. The night before, I'd overheard her and dad talking about me, and whether or not I would ever really be truly independent. I wanted to show her that I was. Now, here I was doing the same thing for Danika. *Why do I want to show off for her? I dare not say because she's gorgeous!* I watched her mount. She swung up in the saddle like a graceful swan! I couldn't help but give her a smile.

We rode on down the barely visible track through the forestlands. My heart fluttered a little. Danika moved in beside me and began chatting. "You are really impressive, Nia Elain. I'm my father's son. You see, dad always wanted a son. As a rule, kingdoms are handed down to the first-born son, but alas, he got me instead. Something happened to mom after I was born. She can't have any more children. So dad's treated me like his son all these years. I suppose one day, I'll take over ruling our kingdom from him. The Jereni Kingdom lies south of the Sana River. We're up here, trying to drive the raiding slavers out of our realm and its borderlands. I'm a ranger. What's your story? You don't really come from the sky do you?"

"Actually, I do come from another world, Danika. We've got something in common. I'm dad's son too. You see, mom had an awful accident just after they were married. She was hit with a lot of radiation that left her sterile. So they adopted me. I was supposed to be a boy, but I'm not, obviously." Shit, it wasn't obvious. I hoped she wouldn't press the issue.

No such luck. "How come they didn't look at your body before they adopted you? One glance ought to have told them that they weren't getting a boy," Danika perceptively picked up on this detail and asked.

My face flushed — at least I think so. How the devil do I answer this one? Hell, as soon as I take a leak, she's going to see. "I've got both male and female organs," I replied softly and a bit hesitantly. At least, Sir Dmitri didn't hear me. He was up with Vlad, riding point.

"What? Both? Does it work? Like a man's?" she asked. I looked at her. She was genuinely interested, but not in a derogatory or discriminatory manner.

"This is so embarrassing. Yes. I have my periods, just like all women, but the other thing is there too. It also works. The doctors say I could even impregnate myself, but I don't want to do that." There, at least I was totally open with her.

"Wow! I've never met someone like you. It's a shame about your arms, though. I can't imagine getting along without mine. How do you do it?" she replied, genuinely interested.

"I do things my way, with my feet mostly."

"That I can see. I can't believe you took out those fighters with just your feet. Impressive, Nia Elain," she praised me.

I grinned. "Yes, mom and dad wanted me to be independent. They made me take martial arts lessons whenever we were planet-side. I can be very deadly with my kicks, but until I got here, I've never killed anyone before. I don't think I like doing that, but I didn't have any choice. The man was going to chop me to pieces with his sword."

"I don't like killing either, unless there is no other way. Sir Dmitri doesn't share our views. The only good slaver is a dead slaver — that's his motto. I couldn't talk him out of going after those men, once we buried his dozen fighters a couple days ago. Thank the gods you came along when you did. Just between us, we would never had survived that battle without your help, Sir Dmitri's claims aside. He's a good man, just strong willed. So don't you really miss not having arms like everyone else? It must be awful for you."

I found myself reciting my usual line. "You can't miss what you've never had." I felt a little silly. "I never had them. Mom and dad just encouraged me to find my own way to do things. Now, it doesn't bother me much, except I still hate the stares I always get when I am around strangers. It's worse than the men staring at my monster breasts. At least all women have them."

Danika tossed her shoulder-length hair back a little, while smiling. "Nia Elain, you should be proud of them. Mine are so small. That bothers me. Men are always teasing me that I'm really a man, because mine are not very prominent. That's nearly as embarrassing."

"But you are about the most gorgeous woman that I've ever seen," I protested.

She laughed. "I know. I am just that. Often, I use it to distract the men I'm fighting, giving me the edge I need. This is a man's world, or so the men all claim. A woman's place is in the home, having babies, canning food, sewing, and cooking meals. Hah! Not this woman. Thanks to dad, his 'son' is a better fighter than most men are, and this ranger never gets lost. There's a whole world out here, so much to see and do. Why should men have all the fun, eh?"

"Right. But what's a ranger?" I asked.

"A fighter, but also one very skilled in tracking and survival in the wild. A ranger has a perfect sense of direction and is seldom taken by surprise, even in the woods. I love the woods. I know how to use a lot of weapons and can track just about anything. That's why Sir Dmitri demanded I go with him on this trip — to track the slavers after they slaughtered his dozen new recruits. He would never have found them. I led him straight to them, you see. Still, I'm glad you all came along when you did. What's happening?"

I was drifting into that grey fog once again. The warm, early fall sun was lulling me into a stupor again. I mumbled something about the grey void. She said, "Nia Elain, snap out of it. Fight it, if you can. Don't lose yourself in it." Her pleading voice, so full of concern, did pull me out of it a little bit. I think I smiled. "Come on; tell me about flying among the stars. What's that like?" In hindsight, she did the right thing — kept me talking and focused on the present, the here and now. Honestly, that helped enormously. We made Deercreek the next evening.

Sir Dmitri took charge, as we rode into the forest hamlet, home to a couple thousand. "Okay, Ranger Danika, you get us some rooms at the inn, while Vlad and I get the horses and gear sold. Meet you there."

"Aye, Sir," she replied formally.

We stopped at an adobe inn; the Tree House read the hand-painted sign. It wasn't writing, per se, but rather a clever pictogram — a tree and a building connected to it. As we four walked into the inn, Danika saw how I used my head to toss my long, thick hair over my shoulders, hiding the fact there were no arms present. She smiled at me and nodded knowingly. "We'll take two large rooms."

"Ah, Ranger Jereni. Back from your hunting expedition already. Looks like you saw some action," the innkeeper commented, accepting her silvers and noticing her many bandages.

"Aye, we eliminated a band of thirty of them. Hopefully, they'll think twice about bothering Deercreek again," she replied. "We'll be wanting hot baths and supper as well. For six." She handed him another couple of silvers. We had rooms two and three. Even I carried some gear in the large collecting bag that Jelena had given me.

Once in our room, a young teen came by with kettles of hot water, filling up two washtubs though making ten trips. I suspected she might be the daughter of the innkeeper. She had his eyes. Jelena advised, "Okay, don't get your two big wounds wet. We should wash her."

"I'll do her back," I offered. We three set to work on Danika, carefully avoiding the two large, salve-covered wounds. Now that I got to see her naked form, I was even more enamored with Danika. She was beyond gorgeous. Her arms were very well defined, though more muscled than either Kisha or Jelena. She was right; her breasts were small, but perky, but her body form was extremely well proportioned. A goddess, I thought. The numerous small cuts didn't detract from her appearance. However, I did spot two large scars, one on her upper left calf and one across her lower chest, battle wounds. Well, she'd now have two more, I thought.

Once she was out and drying off, it was my turn. "Can one of you tie up my hair? If it gets washed, it'll take all night to dry. It's not that smelly yet." Jelena giggled and did so. While Jelena and Kisha had already seen my unusual privates, Danika hadn't. Still, I did spot all three taking a very good look.

I decided not to try to hide it. I turned. "Take a good look. It's really strange and unusual, isn't it?"

Kisha replied, "No kidding. I don't think I could handle having it. If it were me, I'd just cut the damn thing off!"

"Ouch!" Jelena flinched at such an idea. "Why? It's there. It's part of nature, Kisha. Perhaps, having it gives her a benefit that we don't have."

"How could it possibly benefit her?" Kisha asked. I found myself wondering the same thing, thankful that she'd asked it. I was too embarrassed to ask such a thing.

"She has double the chances of finding a mate," Jelena answered, quite unabashedly.

"Huh? You mean she could — with a woman?" Kisha finally picked up on Jelena's thought.

"Yes, if it works, like she says it does. That gives her twice as many possible mates as we have," Jelena explained.

"Oh it works," I added, but very unwilling to demonstrate.

"So are you attracted to women as well as men?" Danika asked softly.

I burst out laughing. "Yes." I kept it simple, but couldn't resist teasing them. "So you three had best watch out; Nia Elain is on the prowl." All of us burst out laughing, breaking the somewhat restrained atmosphere.

After the men returned and had bathed as well, we six went out into the common area for supper. Only a few others were dining there, and we had the place mostly to ourselves. For once, I didn't hear too many conversations in my mind. Apparently, with the recent activities of the slavers, the number of travelers was down at this time. I could see why. The best news for us was that Vlad and Sir Dmitri had gotten quite a bit of silver from the horses and gear. Combined with the valuables that Vlad had taken from the fallen men, quite a pile of silvers and a few gems lay on the table to be divided up. Both Danika and Sir Dmitri insisted we four take it. Neither wanted or needed the silvers. For the first time since arriving on this world, I had my own money pouch with a hundred silvers in it. I felt elated. Now, I could pay my own way, at least for a while.

"In the morning, we'll head for Sana Falls, first thing," Sir Dmitri declared, sliding his wooden plate away from him, while reaching for his mug of ale.

"I've a map that the witch gave me," Kisha explained. "We follow this track down to the river, and then follow the Sana River into the foothills. She says we can't miss it."

"Aye, but that's the slow way to get there," Danika advised. "If we cut across country, we can cut both the distance and time in half. Be there in three days, not a week."

Kisha frowned, "Maybe so, but we'd get lost and miss it completely."

"Not with a ranger guiding you. Besides, I've been to Sana Falls several times. Going to see Magus Triska?" Danika countered and asked.

"Yes. Do you know her? Can she really help Nia Elain?" Jelena asked politely.

"If anyone can, Magus Triska can. She's rather old though. I think she must be at least fifty by now," Danika explained.

Just as soon as she mentioned the woman's age, Sir Dmitri hastily said, "May the gods grant her a long life." Danika quickly echoed it, as did Jelena and Kisha.

I looked at them curiously. Vlad explained, "Superstition. Mention someone's age, and you have to say that or else you could be hexing them, cutting their life short. Don't suppose it makes any real difference, you know. If she's fifty, then the gods have already granted her a long life. Can't see saying that will do her much good. Whatever."

"How old do most people get?" I asked, somewhat startled but this sudden vocalization of protection.

"If you live to fifty, you are really most fortunate," Sir

Dmitri explained. "Though we fighters, we knights, usually don't make it that old. Occupational hazard, you see."

Jelena asked, "So how old do your Sky People become?"

Oh brother. How do I answer this one, eh? I decided to tell the truth. "Around eighty or so, sometimes more. Of course, we do have a Rejuvenation Machine that allows one to become young once again. Those who can use it often live a hundred fifty years or more, but to do that, you have to really have a whole lot of silvers to afford the procedure."

"Good god! Who would want to live that long?" Kisha gushed. "That's three lifetimes!"

"I suppose they must have good reasons for wanting to live that long," Jelena replied, rather conservatively, as was her nature.

"Whatever," Vlad mumbled. "Not for me, unless I can find my kingdom again. Might change my mind then, but maybe not."

Danika looked at each one of us and then softly said, "May the gods grant all of us a long life. It's best to play it safe, don't you think?" Kisha nodded in complete agreement with her, along with Sir Dmitri. I said nothing. What can anyone say against superstitions? I figured this was what was real to these people and left it at that.

Chapter 4 The Observatory

As agreed, we left Deercreek early the next morning, heading southwest, cross-country, depending upon Ranger Danika to guide us to Sana Falls. Right away, I could tell we were not following any kind of trail. Kisha was a little nervous about not following the obviously well marked map, but Sir Dmitri didn't seem to mind, and Vlad didn't care in the slightest.

Three times, Jelena asked to stop, while she gathered some medicinal herbs. "I've used up most of mom's salve. I think it would be wise for me to gather some more ingredients, don't you all think? If we run into more trouble, that is." Danika agreed with her and allowed her to stop whenever she spotted what she desired. Sir Dmitri grumbled, but said nothing.

Me? I had the strangest feeling that we were being watched or perhaps followed might be a better concept. Remember, I was way out of my league at this time. Things only got stranger, however.

Late that afternoon, we came upon an entire clan of Rus. Men and women were dragging everything they owned behind them. Two long poles with a sort of wicker cradle between them were pulled along — the bottom two ends dragging on the ground. All manner of goods were piled onto the cradle, but furs and hides hid most of what they carried. A few women also carried their young children.

The forest was quite dense, which was why we had little warning of their coming. Danika moved her horse off to one side, allowing the group of perhaps forty adults to pass us by. Since the Rus men didn't draw their weapons, neither did she nor Sir Dmitri. I got a very good look at them. They wore clothes made of furs, though their moccasins were quite similar to mine. Most had either brown or black hair, long, uncut I'd wager. The men's looked rather stringy and in dire need of a good washing. However, what struck me the most was the close resemblance these Rus had to the Sud. I'd been led to believe that the Rus were stone-age savages, but I swore if you cleaned one of the Rus up and dressed him in Sud leathers, you couldn't tell the difference between them. How curious, I thought. Perhaps, the Rus were the ancestors of the Sud people.

As they walked slowly past us, dragging their loads behind them, I caught snatches of their conversations. As I said before, I speak quite a lot of languages — thanks to the language disks on our ship. I was able to pick up a number of words, just as I had with the Sud. While the Sud language was a derivative of a Slavic language, the Rus language seemed to be a derivative of Russian. Unfortunately, I didn't make the obvious connection at that time: both were languages spoken at one time or other within the Federation of Planets, not the Imperium of my world and universe.

I picked up what one woman was saying: Ceri are coming. Hence, I decided to try my hand with their language. "Hello. The Ceri are coming?"

She looked up at me, rather startled. "You speak our language? The Ceri are coming. Flee for your lives. Go east, far east, or the Ceri will get you."

"So you are moving east to get away from these Ceri?" I asked.

"Yes. You must flee too or die. Must hurry." Unfortunately, she was now moving well past me, and I didn't have the chance to ask her anything further.

Just as soon as the last woman and her poles past us, Danika asked me, "What did she say? You can speak Rus?"

"Not well, it's similar to another language I know. Her clan or group are fleeing to the east. She urged me to flee too. Something about the Ceri are coming, and that they will get us if we don't flee. What's Ceri?"

Danika touched her right temple and then her left, as if warding off some evil spirits. Only then did she speak. "Ghosts. No one can see them, but when they come, people die. It's just a fairy tale my mother told me when I was little. Obviously, such things don't exist." I noticed Sir Dmitri and Kisha also touched their temples in the same pattern.

"Fairy tales. Just fairy tales. Leave it to the Rus to flee from fairy tales," Sir Dmitri barked accusatively. Of course, he then touched his temples again. We rode on until near dark.

Just as the sun was setting over the tall western peaks of the distant mountains, we halted for the night. Nothing could have prepared any of us for what we saw as we reined in at the base of a green hill beside a welcoming stream. The hill was barren of trees, as we know them. Instead, stone trees rose up, giant fingers pointing to the sky. How very strange! Stone trees.

While the others setup camp, I stretched my legs and walked up the green hill to inspect the stone monoliths. Imagine my surprise when I reached them, only to find that most were twenty feet tall, three feet across, and half that thick. A cross stone lay on top of each pair and the pairs formed a giant circle. In the very center was a strange, three-foot tall, pointed stone. I walked to the center to examine the pointed one. Eerie. No question of that, but what was this place?

I spotted the three moons of Metcalf-4. They were just rising and fairly close to each other in the sky. One was bluish; one was a sort of blue-black, and one was rather a pale green in color. I stared at them for a while. As I said earlier, I thought they were positively cool.

Suddenly, I sensed the presence of another. I'd heard nothing, but then that's not unusual. I was still having trouble slipping into and out of the grey void that always seemed to be following me. I turned to see a Rus man standing silently beside me. He had no weapon drawn, and I relaxed a little. He could have killed me, had that been his objective. Since I'd already figured out some rudiments of the Rus language earlier, I said, "Hello." Then, I realized he was the same Rus that had entered our camp at midnight, days ago. He must have been following us!

He looked startled. "You speak our words?"

"A little. I'm Nia Elain. What is this place? It's really spectacular."

"Rus built it. Observe sky, moons. See." He bent down on one knee, aligning an eye with the point of the three-foot pillar with one of the more distant arches. I emulated him. The three moons seemed to be framed by one of these arches. He continued pointing. "Orya, Dessa, Platon." I guessed these were their names for the moons. Orya being the blue one; Dessa, the blue-black; and Platon, the pale green.

He added, "Stones predict. Soon, all three will be together. That's when Ceri come. Must flee before then. No one wants to die." Note, he wasn't really speaking so brokenly, rather, I was piecing together what words I could from his language. While similar to Russian, it wasn't precisely the same.

Then, he turned and faced me squarely. His eyes swept over me, like some mechanical Imperium scanner. To my amazement, he pulled a small, carved stone statue out of a pouch. It looked like a woman who had big breasts, but no arms. Even the legs were rather stylized, but visible. "You come. You save us. Micha has vision. Carve likeness. You come, just like Micha sees. You save us from Ceri." He fell to his knees and I swear he was worshiping me!

Just then, Danika called out, "Supper's ready. Oh gods, a Rus is with her!" She drew her sword and began running up the hill.

"Micha go now. You see. You save us from Ceri." He rose and slipped off into the growing darkness.

When Danika got to me, she apologized. "Sorry, we were not keeping watch. Are you injured? Did he attack you?"

"No, that was really strange. Come on; I'll tell you about it." As we headed down the hill, I did just that.

"So the stones are some kind of observatory? The Rus built it? How? Those stones are monsters," Danika asked, quite taken aback.

We discussed this unusual construction and the Rus over dinner. Afterwards, we all walked up to the center pointer stone and looked around. Now, the three moons were arched between a different set of pillars. I knew that our astronomer, Roger, would have loved to spend days here, working out how it worked. Was he even still alive? Wrong thought. I felt pangs of grief and worry over my parents, wondering if they were living or if they'd gone mad during the Slave Winds.

Back at our cheery campfire, Danika asked, "So this Rus thinks you are here to save them from the Ceri?"

60

"Yes, that's what I got out of him. He was the same Rus who spied on us some days back. Remember, around midnight. He's been following us ever since. Even stranger, he had a carved stone figurine that looked sort of like me. He claims I'm the one to save them from the Ceri. Apparently, the Rus believe the Ceri actually exist."

Just then, Danika picked up a small pebble and without looking, she tossed it behind her. Hastily, Sir Dmitri and Kisha followed suit. "You can't see the Ceri ghosts. Toss a stone behind you is supposed to scare them away from you, kind of like telling them that you can see them," Kisha explained. "I know, it's silly, but if it helps. . ." She didn't finish her sentence.

"Still, we ought to stand watch from now on. I'll take the first watch," Sir Dmitri ordered. "Vlad, you relieve me; Danika, you relieve him. Best get some sleep." We did just that, though I thought about the day's events for some time before drifting into sleep, among the greyness around me, still hearing the soft sounds of an occasional pebble landing on the ground, tossed by Sir Dmitri, as he watched over us.

I recalled mom drilling into my head that people don't do things without a reason. The larger the action, the bigger the motivation, she'd once told me. This megalithic stone observatory, of which I had no doubt, must have been an enormous task to build. Who knows where they found the stones — let alone cut them, transported them, and set them into place? Their motivation, their reasons, must have been gargantuan. No doubt of that. But what was that reason? Prediction. That seemed to be the only reasonable explanation to my way of thinking. But predict what? From Micha, I suspected it had something to do with the three moons, but I had little more to go on and wished I'd paid more attention to our astronomer, Roger. I filed this in the back of my mind and drifted into sleep.

The next morning, we rode around the hill, not daring to trespass on this sacred mound, but we got a good look at the circle of standing stones. "Surely, the Rus didn't build this," Kisha whispered. "How could they? Those stones must weigh tons. How could they get the stones up on top? How do they know just where to place them, for that matter? No, the Rus must just be using it," she concluded. I had my doubts about her opinionated conclusions. Micha had seemed very well informed.

This second day of this leg of our trip brought me more alertness to my surroundings. I began to notice that the trees were changing from the oaks with their seemingly endless supply of squirrels to various pines. Even the air felt chillier than it had. Then, I noticed that the horses were gradually gaining elevation, the land was systematically rising. From the crests of some hills where the pines didn't block my view, I caught fleeting glimpses of distant mountains. To my eyes, they looked tall and rugged, but with white, cloud-like puffs at their peaks. Snow. I finally got it. I was seeing the first signs of winter.

Almost as if reading my mind, Danika called out, "Another week and the trees will bring forth their autumn beauty. It's winter on the tops of the distant Melor Mountains, Nia Elain. Don't worry; it won't snow in these parts for at least six weeks yet." She added, "Me, I love to wander about during the fall, just to see the spectacular colors. Of course, by spring, I've just got to get out to see the return of the pale green. I get cabin fever bad." She chuckled a little.

"So how do you know the right direction to go to get to Sana Falls?" I asked her.

Danika flashed me a disarming smile. "Easy. It's cradled in the foothills at the southern edge of the Melor Mountains ahead of us. See that last really tall peak far off? Sana Falls is about twenty miles due west of that peak. Can't miss it."

I asked, "So where is your hometown from here?" I just wanted her to continue talking to me.

"About a hundred miles southeast of here. Pudislava. That's our town. Got close to ten thousand there now. It's even got a tall wooden palisade around it. Keeps us all safe at night. The slavers cannot get inside," she explained in time with her rocking motion in her saddle.

"So what do the slavers actually want?" I asked. To my way of thinking, there were three distinct populations on this world: the Rus, the Sud, and these slavers. "Where do they live?" I suspected the Rus hunters wandered around the land, while the Sud were agriculturally oriented and thus fixed to specific locations — their towns. But where were the slavers? Who were they, and why did they want so many slaves? I had a lot of questions. The grey fog was not swallowing my mind this crisp, fall morning. I could think, but had no answers.

"Don't know and don't know," she replied. "They just appear and do their dirty work." Well, that wasn't helpful, I thought, as we continually gained elevation. While we did go down a hill, the subsequent crest was always higher.

That rising upwards reminded me of the time when I was thirteen and at Lou's Martial Arts back on Descartes-3. There were a dozen of us practicing away, when an earthquake struck. A tall bookcase leaned and then fell, almost in slow motion, as I recall it now. Unfortunately, it conked the Master on his head, knocking him out, before it fell on his legs, pinning him beneath it. Naturally, we students tried to lift if off him, but it was too heavy. We had some lumber nearby that was destined to be cut into two-foot sections for us to practice breaking with well-placed foot blows. I had the stronger boys move one of the concrete blocks over to the edge of the heavy bookcase, while the rest helped me carry the long board over to it. After I instructed them where to insert the board beneath the bookcase and over the block, I sat down on the very end of the board. My weight raised the bookcase up enough so the stronger boys were able to pull our Master out from beneath it. We'd raised the bookcase up, though it weighed far more than any of us. As I said, I make good use of physics.

"What're you thinking about?" Danika interrupted my memories. I flushed and related what had happened back then. "Good thinking," she replied, with one of her electrifying smiles.

"Thanks. Probably the Rus used something like that to raise those heavy stones in their observatory. It's not as difficult, as you might imagine," I finished up, receiving another of her grins.

Late that afternoon, we made camp beside a small creek, whose banks were dotted with pine trees on the northern side and two giant oak trees on its southern shore. We pitched camp between the oaks. "These are great oaks, Nia Elain," Jelena explained to me, while setting up our bedrolls. "Hundreds of years old. Such stories they are telling me. This is a wonderful place to camp. Can you sense just how alive they are?"

I strained my senses, but couldn't "hear" the oaks. "I guess I'm not suited to be a witch," I admitted. Jelena didn't seem to mind that and continued going about her chores, leaving me to sit back against one of the oaks and watch. There was little that I could really do to help them. While I could have done a few things, they were all going about their actions swiftly. If I had jumped in, I would only have slowed them down considerably. It takes me a long time with my alternate ways to execute some of their actions.

As I sat there, from the corner of my eyes, I thought I saw a glowing form, shaped something like a human body moving out of the second oak tree. I quickly focused my gaze directly at the yellowish form. It vanished entirely, as though it had never been there. Strange. I looked back at my friends. Again, from the corner of my eyes, the glowing, shimmering form was still there, right where it had been. Am I hallucinating again? Oh god, I hope not!

Safe. Somehow, that single thought appeared in my mind. That we were safe camping here between these two giant, ancient oak trees — white oaks, Jelena had said. Again, I glanced directly at the second oak and its shimmering yellow form. As before, nothing was there, nothing was visible. Again, I looked back at my friends and our camp. Once more, the form appeared at the very edge of my peripheral vision. It seemed to be looking at me.

"Are you seeing something?" Danika called out. She'd seen me looking about and instantly became alert to potential trouble.

"I must be hallucinating again. I thought I saw a yellowish thing over by the oak. Obviously, not," I replied. She glanced that way and then tossed a small pebble over her shoulder and touched her temples for good measure. "Jelena, you sure that this is a safe place for us to camp?"

Jelena looked up, focused a moment, then smiled. "Yes, very safe place, Danika." Danika accepted her declaration — this pronouncement coming from a proven witch, though not before she nervously tossed another small pebble over her shoulder a second time.

This wasn't the only time that I saw these yellow, ghostlike forms. While I perhaps could have used my toes and leg to toss a pebble over my shoulder, I had no intention of doing such a superstitious thing. In the first place, I'd come to fully trust in Jelena's observations, especially when they dealt with the forest. I had no doubt she was somehow able to be in rapport with Nature. Once dinner was finished and everyone lay back on their bedrolls, again I began to see these ghostly, shimmering forms.

Now, there were two of them — one beside each of the two oaks. They were clearly visible, but only at the very edges of my vision. Even the slightest attempt at a more direct look caused them to vanish completely. Yet, in the growing dark, their energy glow was quite visible to me. Neither did more than just watch over us. Long I stared indirectly at the pair. Were these actually the Ceri? If so, then there were four races in conflict on this world: the Sud, the Rus, the slavers, and now the Ceri. After watching them for what must have been a half hour, I convinced myself that they were real and must be the Ceri. I began to wonder how I might be able to communicate to them, but I fell asleep before I reached any conclusion. When dawn came and I awoke, I didn't see them again.

Spirits ran high this morning. According to Danika, we ought to reach Sana Falls before nightfall. I could sense the relief emanating from both Jelena and Kisha, who desperately wanted me cured of my Slave Wind madness. Well, I did too, for that matter. Rather, my mind was preoccupied with the Ceri I'd seen yesterday. I was convinced they did in fact exist, but that they were some entirely new species and certainly not human at all!

In hindsight, this is the aspect that most intrigued me — an alien, human-like species. Across the vast Imperium and its thousands of worlds, there is no such example. Habitable planets have always been discovered to contain the homo sapiens species. True, there are all manner of strange, indigenous plants and animals, but no true intelligent, alien species has ever been discovered. In fact, I knew linguists have had a ball piecing together the overall language families these humans speak. Rare indeed is the truly unique language spoken on a newly discovered world. Usually, that language is some kind of derivative of an already known one, such as I myself discovered with the Sud and then the Rus here on Metcalf-4. It seems an inescapable conclusion that at some distant point in the past, we homo sapiens had colonized all these habitable worlds that we are just now rediscovering. I've no idea how that could have happened, though. My curiosity was aroused, that's for sure.

Late afternoon, I spotted Sana Falls in the distance. Danika was right; you couldn't miss it. Cradled in the rugged, high foothills and not far from the Melor Mountains proper with their already snow-capped peaks, Sana Falls was the largest town I'd encountered, home to perhaps five or six thousand. Just south of the outer wooden palisade, the Sana River roared over a hundred foot, rocky gash between hills, a spectacular water falls, as far as I am concerned. A foamy mist rose above the bottom pool, where the river continued on its easterly flow, no longer inhibited by the rough terrain to the west.

Here at this higher elevation, the trees were in full autumn colors, breathtaking. My eyes took in the reds, yellows, oranges, browns, and darker colors — all brought into a striking relief with the grey stone of the distant mountains, the dark umber of the hills, and the lighter browns of protruding fingers of stone, now sprinkled with dry, colorful leaves. The smell? I've no way to describe it, save a somewhat refreshingly dry odor. We came in from the northeast. From our vantage point, we could see the low stone fences outlining the many cultivated fields that lay primarily east and close to the river itself. Already, harvest time had passed. Men and women were out burning thatch and plowing the remains into the fields.

As we headed down this last hill into the valley before

Sana Falls, a company of six soldiers hastily rode up to us, challenging us. "Halt," one barked accusatively, before recognizing Danika and Sir Dmitri. "Ah, it's Ranger Jereni and Sir Vana."

"Hail, Captain Alexi," Danika called out. "What's happening? Guard duty?"

"Aye, we've only had to repel three slaver attacks this past week. For some reason, they keep wanting to raid Sana Falls, but we've stopped them each time. You'll find six patrols out guarding the periphery. Can't have our farmers bothered just now. Too much field work to do," Alexi replied, sheathing his sword. I noticed he too wore ring mail armor, but his companions only wore leather, similar to Danika's. I guessed the six were in their mid-twenties.

"Wonder why? We've wiped out a band of three dozen slavers just beyond Deercreek," Danika explained. "Didn't think that they ranged this far west."

"Hey, who knows what goes on in the slavers' minds? Where ya headed?"

"To find Magus Triska. Can you point us in the right direction?" she inquired politely. Alexi responded with directions, and we continued heading down this last hill, joining up with a dirt road, leading to one of the heavily guarded city gates. There we were accosted a second time, but allowed to enter. That both Danika and Sir Dmitri were well known here certainly appeared to eliminate entry hassles. With three attacks in one week, I could appreciate their extra vigilance.

Sana Falls had a somewhat better arrangement of streets than any town I'd encountered thus far. The outer palisade was roughly circular. Just inside, a low mound of grass-covered earth rose up to the walls. A wide walkway was attached just below the top, where the defenders, archers I assumed, could be positioned to repel attackers. Many ladders provided access to the walls. An open space some twenty feet wide allowed horses and men to move freely, while defending. The first buildings were stables and barracks for the soldiers. Granaries came next, and then the multitude of shops and homes. In contrast, Sana Fall homes were primarily single-story wooden constructions.

The streets were filled with children dashing about playing games and women doing their frequent shopping. A few men visited the various trade shops. Several blacksmith shops were present, but unseen. I could hear the distinct sounds of hammers on anvils. The air was filled with the odor of burning wood from hearths. I took an instant liking to this town.

Chapter 5 Magus Triska

We halted before a large, two-story building, quite large in comparison to the surrounding buildings, here near the heart of the town. The Pig's Head Inn was a block to the south. Danika advised, "We should take some rooms at the nearby inn and then check out the magus. While you are visiting her, I've got to get my armor repaired and send some messages to dad." A few minutes later, we had our rooms, quite plush considering the inns I'd seen thus far. I insisted on paying my own rent, five silvers for the week, including meals, but not ales.

After settling in, Kisha and Jelena accompanied me the short block to call upon the magus. If I had fingers, I would have kept them doubly crossed. I knew I must be going mad. The grey fog still partially clouded my mind and thinking, but seeing all the hustle and bustle of Sana Falls helped keep me more alert than I might have been. As we walked up to the front door, there was no doubt that we'd found her. A wooden sign over the door read: Magus Triska Sana — actual writing. Jelena knocked, and I waited with baited breath.

An old woman answered the door, but not until Jelena's sixth round of knocking. Her hair must have once been black. Traces still showed through the grey. She wore it tied back in a ponytail, giving her weathered face a rather stern appearance. She wore soft leather pants and top, devoid of ornamentation. Rather, her eyes commanded my attention. I've never seen such coloration! Animated reddish swirls that seemed to pierce one's mind missed nothing! Yet, I sensed her annoyance at having been disturbed from some important work by our appearance.

That slight rise in hostility rapidly gave way to intense curiosity, as her eyes drilled into mine. Jelena spoke up, "Excuse us, Magus Triska, but my friend and I got caught in the Slave Wind up north. Nia Elain is really bad off. A witch in Zora's Crossing told me I should bring her to you and that you could help her. Please, can you help Nia Elain? Oh, I'm Witch

Jelena Kish, our friend, Kisha Mila. Also, we are lost. Do you know where our small village of Jovan is located?"

Magus Triska was slightly shorter than I was, but far more fragile. She extended a bony hand towards me, but quickly moved it over to Jelena and shook her hand. "Come in. Mind you, do not touch anything, if you value your lives. This way, my reception room." She eyed me closely, perhaps verifying I really didn't have any arms. I still sensed curiosity emanating from the sorcerer. The room was just off the entrance hall. I spotted an oak staff lying close to the door, as I followed her. The small room contained one moth-eaten tapestry on the windowless inner wall and a number of chairs. I took one.

Magus Triska pulled a chair up before me and sat down barely three feet from my face, making me a little uncomfortable. Her eyes ran up and down my form, as though searching for something. At last, her eyes met mine. "Yes, you have been changed by the Slave Wind, Nia Elain. You have suffered a tragic accident? Both arms? Are you sure you don't want me to just put you down? Relieve you of your suffering?" Well, this is not how I had expected this discussion to begin.

Jelena spoke up before I could. "She's Sky People. She was born this way, though she had some baby-like arms when she first came to my village, Jovan, but the slavers that captured us ripped them off. She has all sorts of ways of doing things, and she can fight well. She has killed many slavers already. Some, I think with fires and rocks, but I saw her kill several with her feet when they attacked her with their swords."

I added, "She's right. I just want this infernal grey fog or void thing to go away. It's driving me mad."

"I see. Sky People? Perhaps, you should begin at the beginning and tell me your story. Just who are you, Nia Elain?" she asked quite sternly.

I began at the beginning, with the landing of the Eagle's Seed here on Metcalf-4. I decided that I ought to spare no details. If somehow this magus could help me, I simply had to have her cure me of this interminable grey fog. If not and if I couldn't find our spaceship again, then maybe I ought to be put down before I accidentally harmed one of my new friends. I left out nothing, even telling her about the Rus observatory and the Ceri I saw from the corners of my eyes. In hindsight, I think the fact I was able to see the Ceri broke the ice between us. Certainly, she became intensely interested in me by the time I finished my story.

Then, she spoke, "So you admit you are an alien to our world?"

"Absolutely. Is that important?"

"It may well be. Fascinating indeed. Okay, first of all, I have never heard of your Jovan village. Sorry, but right now, that's the least of our problems. Second, I can help you overcome the grey fog, as you call it, Nia Elain, but whether you like it or not, you have become a magus yourself. You will need to be trained immediately. Are you staying here in town?"

"Yes, we just took rooms at the Pig's Head," I answered.

"Good place. Okay, Jelena, Kisha, you may leave now. I'll send her back to the inn later today. In the morning, you best take her to Kolina's and get her and yourselves some winter clothing. It will be snowing soon. Nia can return here once she's been measured for some new apparel. Now, be off with you two. Nia and I have much work to do."

"How long will this all take?" Jelena asked.

"Can't say. Learning cannot be rushed," she replied, in a quite non-committal tone. She rose and led the two to her door, while motioning for me to stay seated. Shortly, she returned. "Follow me, please." I rose and followed dutifully after her, noticing she moved slowly. I guessed her joints probably ached. If only I could get her into our medical machine, I could heal her.

We climbed a wooden stairs, though she held onto the railing. I sensed her pain. I'd never been able to do such a thing before and wondered what was happening to me. At the top of the stairs, she took me into her private study. Wow. Books, scrolls, and all manner of esoteric items lay strewn around the room. Three oil lanterns added to the light coming in from a mica-sheet window, casting a warmish glow to the room, which smelled like lamp oil and the musty odor from the parchments. She motioned me to the only other chair in the room besides hers, which was behind a crude desk, filled with all manner of objects.

She positioned her chair before mine and again looked me squarely in my eyes. Magus Triska was silent for a time. "Yes, you are quite the anomaly, Nia Elain, quite. Well, let's begin, shall we?" I nodded, though wondering what precisely she'd meant by this.

"The grey fog, as you call it, is your own mind, the seat of power for us magi. It is your reserve of energies and is nothing to be feared. It is always under your control, if only you discipline your mental powers. Close your eyes. Good. Now, can you see the grey void?" I nodded. "Good. Now embrace it, for it is yours and yours alone. Accept it, as you would accept your head, your foot. It is always under your control. So let's get it to do what you wish. Let's begin by making it appear, say, yellow."

I strained a bit, but nothing happened. She had me keep at it. Soon, it did just that. It turned yellow. She had me change its color several dozen times. Next, she had me make it seem positively enormous, followed by making it seem like it was pea-sized. Time passed. Finally, I was able to make it become any size I desired. Once I had this mastered, she had me move it around, above my head, behind it, to my right, to my left, below my feet, and so on. At last, I did have total control over the grey fog, and I decided to keep it pinkish and above me, where I considered it to be obvious and out of my way.

"Well done, Nia Elain. Now, you are no longer a threat to your friends. Yes, I can read your thoughts, as you can mine. Let's go over just what your new magus powers are. You see, all we magi have certain abilities in common and a host of powers that are uniquely our own. First, we can read other's minds, their thoughts. Just think of the person, visualize them, and decide to listen to their thoughts. Let's try it now. Think of Jelena and see if you can hear what she's thinking right now."

I flushed. I thought of Danika instead. I can't tell you how surprised I was suddenly to pick up her thoughts! *I probably should get myself a suit of ring mail. Hell, the way*

Sir Dmitri has been acting this trip, he's going to get me into more trouble than I can handle. But is this the best armorer in Sana Falls? I wonder. If I ask him, he's likely to say yes, whether or not he is. Maybe I ought to ask around some, before committing. I broke the connection that I'd just made. "Er, I picked up Danika instead. Is that all right?" My face felt hot.

Magus Triska chuckled. "Yes, dear. Quite. See, you can do this. When you are not here with me, you should practice doing this. She then outlined the basic rules of thought-reading, which was her term for this action. Later, I decided it was really telepathy, quite rare throughout the Imperium.

She continued, "Now comes the hard part, Nia Elain, learning the ritualized actions that can be executed, though to non-Magi, they are perhaps better thought of as spells. We magi usually are limited in what we can bring about. I am a master of fire-based spells, the fire elemental forces. Others are masters of water-based, air-based, and earth-based forces. In addition, there are a catalogued set of standard other actions that most can do, such as the Torus of Teleportation, which you've already encountered with the slavers' magus."

"How do you know what ones you can do?" I asked innocently, yet somehow sensing this was a very important detail.

"The eyes tell. Look into mine. What do you see?" she commanded. I did so. I saw the strange, seemingly swirling patches of red. I told her about them.

"Precisely. Red is for fire. Blue swirls, water. Brown swirls, earth, white, air. Here. Let me hold a mirror so you can see your own eyes." She held a small mirror up so I could look at mine. I was floored. I saw little moving swirls of red, brown, blue, and white.

I managed to utter, "All of them?"

"Precisely so. All of them. This alone is quite an anomaly. You are the only known magus who appears to be able to use all of the elemental forces. Perhaps, this has come about because you were constrained from using fire forces during that second attack, and used earth and air instead — the stones. Who can say? Certainly not I."

73

"Oh my."

"Indeed. What I usually do next, is have the new pupil copy my master Spell Book, that large volume with the leather cover there, into their own book. Then, I have them practice doing them. Right now, though, I don't have the time to copy all of them for you."

"I can write well enough, though I am a bit slow at it," I answered.

"How? Dear, you haven't hands."

"Feet. Where can I get a blank book and something to write with?" I asked, hoping to get my feet into this one. Her book, I guessed, would hold many answers I desperately desired.

"When you come by tomorrow, I'll have them prepared for you. It's late. I best let you head over to the Pig's Head Inn. Tomorrow, I believe we'll have much to discuss. Can you show yourself out?" I picked up she didn't want to endure the pain of going back down and then up the stairs. I thanked her and did so, letting myself out, though I had my usual trouble with the door latch.

I had quite the story to relate to my friends over supper and ale. The next morning, we visited the dressmaker's shop. Kolina was rather intrigued with making outfits for me — no sleeves. I ordered three tops and three pants, along with two pairs of fleece lined leather boots that I could easily slip on and off by myself. Additionally, I ordered a heavy, warm cloak and a fleece-lined cap. At least, I didn't need gloves as my friends did. I was rather proud that I could pay for these from my own money pouch.

Around ten, I knocked on Magus Triska's door. *Come on it. Up the stairs. Same room as yesterday.* I smiled. This telepathy thing was proving quite useful. Using my foot, I let myself in and headed up to that mysterious room, which held all the answers I so desperately desired.

There was a new, thick, leather-bound book waiting for me, along with a number of quills and a pot of ink. Those, I spotted at once. Of course, I would need them placed on the floor, though. After showing them to me, she suggested I begin making my copy. After slipping off my shoes, she saw I would need to be sitting on the floor. "Well, this is as good a time as any for you to master your first spell. You need to have your new book lying on the floor before you, Nia Elain. I can see that now. So in your mind, very carefully work out just what you want to have happen, and then decide that it is so. The key is to be very confident and quite precise in your postulates, your decisions, and your thoughts. Go ahead and try it."

Carefully and slowly, I envisioned the heavy book lifting up off the work table and lowering to the floor before my feet. Once I had its motion worked out, I felt a slight tug from my grey-pink energy mass, and the book did just what I'd decided it would do. I let out a cheer. This was amazing! Then, I did the same thing to her precious spell book and then the quills and inkpot, being very careful of the latter. Magus Triska smiled for the first time. "Well done, Nia Elain. Well done indeed. Start at the beginning and copy everything precisely as you see it."

Thus began my "education." It began with such simple tasks as cleaning up a mess or sewing a tear in my leather dress. Magus Triska watched me closely. I sensed she hadn't truly believed me when I said I could write. No, rather it was that so very few of Metcalf's inhabitants could actually read and write! She smiled at me, as I picked up this thought from her.

I guess the turning point came the next day. When I showed up just after breakfast, Magus Triska was waiting for me. "I've taken the liberty of finishing the copying for you, Magus Nia Elain."

"What? You didn't have to do that, but thanks. It takes me so long to write," I replied, somewhat taken aback. I didn't quite know what to make of this. Was she feeling sympathy for me? If so, that would instantly rouse my hostilities. I don't want or need pity and sympathy. I looked at her and didn't sense that was her motivation. Somehow, I managed to restrain my budding rise of emotions — a good thing, as it turned out.

"Yes, I need your help. I've come across some things that are bothersome at the very least and might be critical at most. Let me begin by asking you to level with me. You come from another world out there?"

"Yes, we came here exploring new worlds, prospecting for minerals that the Imperium needs. There are thousands of inhabited worlds of the Imperium, billions upon billions of people," I answered truthfully.

"I can't imagine, but I accept this, which leads me to my next question. If your people fly among the stars and worlds, surely you must know a great many things," she continued.

I wasn't sure if that was a question or not. Deciding it might be, I spoke up, "Yes, we know quite a lot, but I'll admit we know nothing of these magus spells or even Jelena's witch spells and things. But we do know lots of other things."

"Then, I'm not wrong in my hunch. Nia Elain, earlier this spring, some miners south of here made a startling discovery. Thank heavens they had the good sense to bring it to my attention right away. I've been studying the find ever since then. I also think this discovery is why the slavers have been hounding Sana Falls this summer. Even though we kept this find relatively secret, somehow someone must have alerted the slavers to our discovery. I think the best way to proceed will be to take you there and show it to you."

"Okay with me. I'll do anything I can to help out," I answered, sensing she needed some encouragement along this line. She flashed me the briefest of smiles; I'd hit the mark.

"Good. Could we have your companions accompany us — for protection? If not, I'll get some town guards to tag along. The threat of these slavers is quite high," she asked, very serious. Her aged face crinkled as she spoke. I didn't need telepathy to know she was more than a little afraid.

"I can ask them. I'll run and see," I replied, fully prepared to dash the block back to the Pig's Head, hoping to find them still there.

"Use your magus skills, Nia. Focus on one person. Get them firmly in mind. Then, place the thought to come here in his or her mind. Remember, you must have no doubts or suggestions that it isn't going to work," she countered. Her voice was soft, but full of intention.

Intention. That was the secret, as I began to master the gifts I'd received from the Slave Winds. I focused on Danika first, not Jelena as I had intended. I might have flushed as I did so, but Magus Triska didn't comment, allowing me to continue. An image of the gorgeous woman appeared in my mind. I placed the thought as best I could. That done, I moved on to Jelena, then Kisha, Vlad, and finally Sir Dmitri.

"Okay, that's done," I said, opening my eyes. Now, I wondered if it would actually work.

"Good. Wait here for them. I need to get my cloak and put on my warmer boots." I heard some of her joints creaking a little, as she rose and left the sitting room, leaving me looking at the solitary tapestry on the one wall. It was a rural farming scene, probably harvest time. Figures were cutting wheat. Others were thrashing the kernels from the shafts, while a few were scooping up the grain into sacks. Quaint, but crude, I thought, recalling one of the monster machines I'd seen working a huge field on Descartes-3. Before long, my friends arrived, Danika first.

"Is something wrong, Nia Elain? I had this strange thought you needed me here," she said, as I opened the door.

"Hi. Yes, that was me sending you the thought to come here. We need you and the others. A secret mission or something. Magus Triska is going to take us there. She want's our help. Thanks for coming," I explained. Of course, I had to repeat that a few more times, as one by one, the others arrived.

Magus Triska timed it perfectly. Just as Sir Dmitri arrived, looking somewhat confused, she joined us, wearing her heavy, traveling cloak. "Ah good. Magus Nia Elain summoned you. I have asked her for some help." She explained about the spring discovery, and that the slavers wanted to get their hands on this find. "So you see, I would like your protection while we visit the site. Probably nothing will happen, but with the sheer number of slaver attacks we've had ever since this discovery, I can't count on it. Will you come with us?"

"Magus Triska," Sir Dmitri spoke formally, "my sword is yours to command!"

The others nodded. Danika asked, "Do we need to bring horses? Food supplies?" She was ever the practical one, I noticed.

Magus Triska smiled briefly. "No, I will open a Transportation Torus to the site. It is safer this way. We cannot be followed. Magus Nia Elain, pay attention. You need to learn how to execute this powerful action. I did, but still had no idea how it was done. Somewhere in that giant spell book lay the answer, if only I could have the time to study it.

A golden, glowing, yet undulating torus appeared right there in her sitting room. Its top touched the ceiling, while its bottom lay upon the wooden floor. "Follow me. Just step through the torus." She took her slow steps and vanished. I followed her, marveling at how great this spell would be, if only I could learn how to do it! The others came behind me.

I stepped out into the cold, frosty morning. Fall was definitely here. Most of the trees had already lost their leaves. I stepped onto the colorful remains of what had once been green, while around me, the barren stick trees raised their naked branches to the blue sky filled with puffy white clouds. Two old oak trees still held onto their leaves, as if unwilling to face yet another winter, just like me. I was not looking forward to the cold weather. I'd once been in the snow and hadn't liked it, but that's another story.

Once we all got oriented to our new surroundings, Magus Triska explained, "We are about a hundred miles southwest of Sana Falls, very close to the southern edge of the Melor Mountains. Sir Dmitri, if you will be so kind as to pull that canvass covering aside. Yes, that's our way of camouflaging the tunnel's entrance. We've been trying to keep this discovery a secret. A pair of miners discovered this entrance in early spring." She then spoke a command and a light appeared at the top of her oak staff. Now, I realized she'd brought it along, the very same staff I'd spotted near her door. She leaned on it for support and entered the tunnel. "Please slip the cloth cover back over the opening, once you are inside, Sir Dmitri. We don't want to get surprised by slavers when we exit."

The tunnel was low and narrow, yet not long. Barely twenty feet inside, it opened up into a metal-skinned world! She cautioned us, "Be careful, there are a lot of very sharp metal edges in here."

I recognized what we were in — it hit me like a flash. A spaceship! "This is a spaceship, but not in very good condition," I exclaimed, without thinking.

Magus Triska turned to face me and thus my companions, who looked quite startled at my sudden declaration. "Ah, then it is as I concluded: a flying ship of the skies."

"Yes, but it's in really bad shape. The metal is all corroded. It must have been here a very long time. It's all so bent up too. Did it crash land?" I asked.

"That's why I need your help. I've examined every inch of this metal monster. I concluded it must have fallen from the skies, but there were people onboard as well. There are some skulls the miners found before they contacted me. Don't worry, we've re-buried them," she explained.

"Come. I will give you a tour. Magus Nia Elain, do you recognize anything? Is this perhaps one of your Imperium's ships?" she asked, hoping to gain far more information from me.

We stayed close to Magus Triska and her light, while moving slowly around the interior of the ship. Occasionally, we had to use extreme caution navigating around sharp, ripped edges of the corroded metal walls, bulkheads, I presumed. The ship was huge. My guess was it once might have held over a hundred people. However, the more I saw of it, the more I was convinced it was not an Imperium ship.

That was confirmed when we finally reached the command post, near the front of the ship. Here, the damage was quite extensive. My guess is it had crash landed, pretty much bow forward, burying itself into the ground. For sure, from the remaining bits of instrumentation, I knew this was most definitely not an Imperium ship and said so. "No, this isn't one of ours. Perhaps, it is an old Federation of Planets ship. From its size, it was a large one, perhaps carrying a hundred passengers. It looks like it's been stripped of almost everything that might be useful."

"Ah, that agrees with what little I've been able to work out, Magus Nia Elain," Magus Triska replied. "I've searched this flying ship very thoroughly. I discovered some writings, a log, I've determined. However, I've not been very successful at translating those written words. I found it lying there on what is likely a seat." She pointed to what I would think was the pilot's seat.

"Okay then, that's all there is here to actually see. I've the log back at my place in a secure location. Let's head back. Magus Nia Elain, I'd like to see if you are able to read it better than I am. I'm sure it contains very valuable information. Plus, I would also like to share something else I've discovered, something that may well mark the end of our world." Her tone sounded very sinister indeed. My sober group followed her and her light, quite fearful of being left inside the eternal darkness of this dead ship. I spotted the others making many gestures, warding off evil spirits or such, touching their right temples, followed by their left temple. Superstitions explained much of what was so far beyond their reality. Ancient flying ships were not in their sphere of knowledge or awareness. I couldn't begin to imagine the thoughts racing through their heads, save Jelena, who had at least seen our Eagle's Seed.

A half hour later, we reached the twenty-foot long tunnel. Ahead, dim sunlight could be seen, barely piercing the woof and warp of the cloth covering the tunnel's entrance. I heard Vlad and Sir Dmitri heave sighs of relief upon seeing that pale glow just ahead. I was glad they didn't have claustrophobia. As we approached the covering, Danika raised her hand, cautioning us. "Voices!" she whispered. As we froze, I distinctly heard swords being drawn. Slavers! How the hell had they found us here?

"Karsh!" Danika whispered, an utterance I took to be their local curse word.

"I need time to construct our return Transportation Torus," Magus Triska whispered.

"Vlad, Danika, form a line around me. We'll teach these bastards a lesson!" Sir Dmitri commanded. "Kisha, Jelena, you stay behind us and protect the magi." As soon as the two moved up to his side, the trio drew their swords. At his signal, Kisha and Jelena pulled the cloth covering aside, and they stepped out to face the enemy, with the rest of us just behind them.

I spotted nearly a hundred men wearing leather armor and with drawn swords rummaging around the general area. A great, glowing Transportation Torus glimmered in the sunlight around two hundred feet ahead of us. A man wearing robes stood at its edge, seemingly directing the searching men. The instant we made our sudden appearance, all hell broke loose.

Six of the nearest slavers rushed forward to engage our three fighters, while a veritable swarm of men ceased their searching and began running to join them, dodging around boulders and trees. Just in front of me, Kisha tossed a pair of throwing daggers, thudding side by side into the forehead of one onrushing fighter. He dropped like a stone, while five clashed into our three fighters, steel upon steel echoing the otherwise stillness of the autumn morning.

I sensed the enemy magus was about to drop a wall of fire upon us. I had to act. Wind. Wind and leaves. Those were what I saw in that brief instant of time. A veritable wall of leaves rose up from the forest floor, obscuring the vision of everyone just beyond the five fighters, who were trying to kill Sir Dmitri, Vlad, and Danika. At least, my quick thinking stopped the horde of other fighters from joining their comrades. More importantly, my action confused the opposing magus, whose spell detonated. A raging inferno ignited all the flying leaves, forming a blazing wall between them and us.

Danika dropped one of the fighters before her. Shortly, Vlad and Sir Dmitri did the same, leaving only two enemy fighters left. Both tried to back off, but they were caught between our three fierce fighters and the blazing wall of fire. Their momentary confusion was all the aid Sir Dmitri and Vlad needed. Two thrusts and they too dropped to the ground, just as Magus Triska's torus appeared. "Run!" she commanded. Our fighters didn't hesitate, dashing forward, followed by Jelena and Kisha. Magus Triska and I stepped through last, arriving back in her sitting room, the odor of burning leaves accompanying us.

"Anyone hurt?" Jelena asked the moment that the torus vanished.

Gasping slightly, Danika replied, "All okay here." She looked at Sir Dmitri and Vlad.

"Just a scratch," Vlad commented, looking at a seeping patch of red flowing down his left arm.

"Let me look at it, Vlad," Jelena insisted.

"Whatever," Vlad replied, sitting down and removing his leather shirt. "Ruined my new shirt. I ought to have known that would happen. Why bother getting new clothes anyway?" he complained somewhat apathetically.

"How did they find us?" Danika asked what I thought was a far more important question.

Magus Triska frowned. "Spies? I don't know, but we've been having quite a lot of trouble from the slavers, ever since the ship was discovered this past spring. They seem to know what we are planning to do, even as we work it out. Thank you all for risking your lives. Wait here while I fetch that log and my notes," she added.

"It doesn't need stitches, Vlad," Jelena said, having examined his wound. Kisha had already headed for the kitchen to boil some water for her.

"Perhaps not, but my new leather shirt does," Vlad lamented.

While Jelena patched up Vlad, Magus Triska returned with her find. The log was ten inches by twelve and one inch thick. It had a logo embossed on its cover, but I'd never seen it. If I was back at our spaceship, I could scan it in and have the massive Imperium computers do a search on its origin. Alas, I was still lost. She placed it on a table, while we gathered around it. The first page contained figures and writings. Everyone else merely shook their heads. "Can you make anything of this?" Magus Triska asked me.

I reasoned if this had once been the pilot's log and assuming all pilots logged essentially the same type of data, then these first pages most likely reflected dates, times, and durations of flights. I noticed a proper name at the top of the first name: Igor Konstantin. This was definitely an ancient Rus-type of name, but definitely not that of the Rus dialects I had studied on the Imperium language disks. I sounded it out and it sounded quite similar to the Rus dialect I'd heard spoken here by the Rus, who had pointed out their observatory to me.

"It looks like a pilot's log with dates and times on it. Flip some more pages, please," I answered. She did. More of the same appeared.

"Okay, now look at these entries, much later on," Magus Triska suggested with growing interest. I sensed I was validating the conclusions that she'd reached.

"Ah, a total change in entry styles. This looks like some kind of running log entries that have nothing to do with flights," I pointed out, noticing the pages now appeared to contain running script. The symbols looked strange to me, but I quickly discovered that by sounding out the words, they began to make some sense to me. This ancient Rus dialect was not all that diverse from the spoken Rus that I'd become familiar with. Or maybe, it was just me speaking in Imperium Rus that made the words make sense to my ears. Sorry, I am not a linguist per se.

Over the next hour, slowly, the story of these ancient people began to become clear to me and thus to everyone else. Magus Triska quickly pointed out that she'd done some extensive research and had come up with an estimate of the date of these writings. Converting it to the Imperium Standard Calendar, the date was around the year 1000, almost four centuries ago. Depending upon how I translated one word, this had been a colonizing ship or an exploration ship with one hundred twenty-three people onboard.

It had smashed or run into or had a collision with a "rock" — here, I'm not sure of the exact word. They lost "functions" or possibly power or navigation capabilities, and attempted to put down on the nearest inhabitable world. This much made perfect sense to me. I had to explain the dangers of space travel to the others, however. Certainly, the ship had made a hard landing, that is, it crashed.

They'd lost all ability to communicate back to their home world that much was clear, though I was unable to translate the name of that world. As I suspected, they then set about establishing a colony here on Metcalf-4. Many pages were devoted to the success of this endeavor, along with a list of native flora and fauna.

Nearing the end of the journal, I came across an entry

in capital letters with a box drawn around it. I carefully sounded out the words: We are not alone! I tried to read further, but the handwriting became highly agitated. I could make out some words: ghosts, can't see directly (or something similar), and Ceri. As soon as I said that last word, everyone suddenly jerked erect and began paying close attention to my fumbling efforts to read and translate the entries.

On the next page, the entries became even more confusing — something about a triple conjunction of the three moons and an impending disaster. Magus Triska whispered, "Please, take your time. This part is vitally important, Magus Nia Elain."

Several pages back, the writer had run out of ink and pencils. I noticed that now, he or she was making do with locally found dyes made into ink, which had not aged so well. Compounding the problem was the acid in the paper of the log, which nearly matched that of this homemade ink. I remember reading about special processes that can be applied to bring out latent images and thus make the writing more legible. However, I didn't have access to such at this time. Okay, I did the best that I could. (I'd like to see you do any better under such primitive conditions.)

I will admit I found my background in physics coming in handy once again, though not as you might expect. I pieced fragmentary pieces together. The key word, assuming I was translating it properly, was perturbation. Already I knew the names of their moons: Dessa, Orya, and Platon, though just now I wondered who had named them, since the Rus names for these moons were the same four centuries ago. If what I was deciphering was correct, then based upon what that Rus had told me at the observatory, we were in big trouble.

I looked up and summarized. "Look, I can only partially make it out. My best guess is the writer was saying something like this. 'Physicist Matvey's observations of Platon prove that during the triple conjunction, Orya and Dessa's perturbations on Platon has critically altered its orbit. He predicts Platon will hit this world within one month. We face utter extinction in less than thirty days.' This isn't good. That Rus fellow at the observatory suggested this triple conjunction is about to occur again."

"Karsh!" Magus Triska cursed, a rare show of emotions from the old woman.

"May Orya protect us!" Danika whispered what I took to be a prayer. I wondered what powers these people ascribed to the moons. Others echoed the magus' curse.

Magus Triska sighed, "My own observations confirm this, at least in part. You see, ever since I was a little girl, the three moons have so totally intrigued me. I've spent much of my adult life making observations of them. I believe this triple conjunction, where all three moons are in a complete line with each other, occurs once every hundred-twenty years. It's about to occur now in 1375 (I am converting her years into Imperium Standard dates), and has occurred in 1255, 1135, 1015, and 895, and probably even earlier. The reference to the destruction of our world may well be quite real."

"How so?" Sir Dmitri asked. "Surely, we can prevent such from happening. After all, it's just a tiny moon. Our world is huge; it's small."

Silly primitives, I thought. That moon only looks small to you because it's so distant. Metcalf-4 is about eight thousand miles in diameter. As I recalled Roger's chat, the three moons are each about a thousand in diameter. If Platon's orbit brought it close to Metcalf-4, the tidal forces alone would destroy the world. If it actually collided, well we'd all be very dead. I wondered if I ought to explain all this to my new friends.

Magus Triska continued, saving me from having to make that decision right now. "I've invented an arc-measurement tool. It measures the angular size of the moons. Orya and Dessa have remained pretty much the same arc-size over the last forty years that I've been observing them. On the other hand, Platon's size has been ever changing. Forty years ago, it was five units across. Mind you, I've no idea what that actually means, save it is small. Within the last ten years, its size has increased rather significantly. It's now four times what it used to be, upwards of twenty units, almost equal to that of Orya and Dessa's arc-size. If Platon is somehow moving closer to us, then that would explain its increase in size."

She went on, "So this notion that the triple conjunction is going to somehow pull Platon down onto our world is not so farfetched. In fact, that's what I began to believe was happening, though, mind you, I have no way of knowing for sure. Nia Elain, you are from the stars. Is this possible?"

I was on the spot. How do you explain physics and gravity to primitives? Well, perhaps Magus Triska wasn't so primitive after all. "When we first spotted your world, we took some measurements. As I recall Roger's briefing to us, this world is a sphere about eight thousand miles in diameter. Each of the three moons is only one thousand miles across, quite large, but they appear small to you because they are so distant from you."

"Oh, I see what you mean," Sir Dmitri interrupted. "Danika, it's like how riders appear small in the distance and steadily get larger as they approach us. So this Platon is as big as the other two moons?"

"Precisely so, Sir Dmitri. Here comes the hard part. Every object in the universe exerts a force on all other objects. We call it gravity. The more mass, in your terms, the heavier the object, the stronger this force of attraction is. The gravity pull of this world is what pulls us to the ground. Of course, as far as we are concerned, only really huge objects have any appreciable gravity. While the gravity force of your body is pulling on me and everyone else here, Sir Dmitri, that force is really undetectable, far too small to even be noticed. No, it takes really massive objects, or super heavy ones, like this whole world or the moons to make a measurable difference. Are you following me?"

"Sort of. So we are pulling on each other, but it's too small to notice," Sir Dmitri struggled to grasp the concept.

"Right. The weight of the world or mass to be precise is the dominating force acting on everything here," I went on trying to think fast. "For us, there are only five objects whose gravity is important for us. The sun that we Sky People call Metcalf is the strongest, because it is hundreds of times heavier or more massive than our world here. Our world and the three moons come next."

"Wait," Danika interrupted me, "If the sun in pulling on

the world and the world is pulling on the sun, why haven't we been pulled into the sun and been burned up?"

"Both are pulling on each other," I tried my best to explain it. "Our world is moving around the sun in roughly a circular orbit." I wished I had a computer or paper and pencil so I could show them better what I meant. I had to make do. "Okay, let me show you. Sir Dmitri, you stand up here and pretend you are the sun. Danika, you stand up here and pretend you are our world." I used my body to sort of push them into the center of the sitting room.

"Okay, here we are at one instant of time. Sir Dmitri's gravity is much stronger than Danika's and he wants to pull her towards himself. Danika wants to go this way," I walked at right angles to the line between them. "Okay, Sir Dmitri, with your arm, which is going to be your gravity pull, grab hold of Danika's arm. Danika, you keep on trying to walk at right angles from the line between you." She tried to do so, but ended up walking in circles around him. Now, everyone caught on to the idea of an orbit.

After we sat down, I continued, "The force of gravity is highly dependent upon the distance between the two objects. Whatever the force is going to be, it is divided by the distance between them twice. So if two moons move to a position that's twice as close to each other as they were before, then this gravity force isn't just doubled, it's quadrupled. That's what's happening now. As Platon draws closer to both Orya and Dessa, their gravity pull is going to increase drastically. I'm afraid that's going to force Platon to come crashing into our world. It's as if Kisha joined up with Sir Dmitri and also began pulling on Danika. Together, they'd pull her into them."

"Karsh! We're all going to die?" Danika gushed. I knew she and the others now fully grasped the significance of this dire prediction.

Magus Triska spoke up. "Like I said, if these predictions are correct, this triple conjunction has occurred at least five times in our past. Somehow, someway, we've been spared."

"But how?" Danika asked.

Magus Triska suggested, "Magus Nia, read on. There is a bit more from the log that is decipherable, perhaps."

"The writing is fading out rapidly, but I'll try." I strained my eyes, but could only discern snatches here and there. "Panic — dig — tunnels — storing food below — Ceri come — bright, glowing beam — visible in daytime — touching Platon — from Tikhon. That's about all the words that are still visible. I'm afraid it doesn't make a whole lot of sense to me. Perhaps, they dug tunnels and moved their possessions and themselves underground to protect themselves from the widespread destruction. That would make sense, perhaps."

"But the Ceri — they are ghosts and not really real," Danika protested, "children's tales."

Magus Triska spoke up, "Perhaps, the Ceri are real. What fascinates me is this glowing beam, which I believe must have somehow prevented this disaster from happening. Where does it come from? Who did it? Magus Nia Elain, do you aliens have such a thing — that could push the moon back to where it belongs?"

"I suppose so, but that's rather beyond my education. If dad or some of the others are still alive, they might know," I answered, but the pangs of their likely deaths from the Slave Wind once more struck me hard. I fought back my tears.

Sir Dmitri declared, "Well, where is this Tikhon place anyway? It sounds like the answer lies there. Has anyone ever heard of it? It's a Rus name, isn't it? Not a Sud."

Once more, Magus Triska had a partial answer. "I've been searching for this place all summer and early fall. I'm convinced it does not lie anywhere in the western half of our world. Look," she unfolded a crude map of the world — at least the continent on which we were at. The continent was roughly rectangular. The Melor Mountains to the west and the Leonid Mountains to the east, both ran north-south, dividing the continent into roughly thirds. The Hill River, which began just west of Zara's Crossing, ran eastward across the middle lands between the two mountain ranges, before it arced to the south, eventually emptying into the ocean at a port city of Duscha in the Kingdom of Gavril. The Sana River began at the Melor Mountains, about halfway down the continent and ran eastward, joining the Hill River at the giant bend, close to the Leonid Mountains. Danika's kingdom lay just south of the

Sana River. While there was no indication of scale on the map, Danika pointed out that her kingdom was about a hundred miles square. I judged the rectangle was about seven hundred miles tall and several thousand wide.

Based on her description, we could perhaps rule out nearly two-thirds of the continent. The far north, the Leonid Mountains, and the lands to the south of there and to the far east remained possible locations for this Tikhon. Magus Triska added, "Based on my observations of the moons, we have less than twenty-nine days to find this Tikhon place and figure out how to save our world from annihilation."

"Count me in," I spoke up at once. Hell, if I am going to be stranded forever on Metcalf-4, I want to be able to live, not die some horrible, flaming death. Wouldn't you?

"I pledge my honor, my sword, my skill to this worthy goal, Magus Triska," declared Sir Dmitri. He spoke formally and a great pride, though I suspected he had not the faintest notion what was going to likely be involved.

"You'll need a ranger, so count me in too," Danika added, casting a dirty look at Sir Dmitri, who had beaten her to the punch.

"I'll come too. You always need the healing hands of a witch or so it seems," Jelena said with a wry smile. "But we should be careful. If you get too badly wounded, I might not have the skills necessary to save you. There are a lot of slavers out there."

"Whatever," the morose Vlad added his voice to the mix. "I might find my missing kingdom. Then again, I might not. Probably won't. So whatever."

Kisha found herself the last to commit to this adventure. For once, she thought before she spoke too hastily. "I'll come. We might just come across something of great value. Besides, if we don't succeed, I'd rather die with my friends than alone in my tiny home up at Zara's Crossing. What have we got to lose, eh?"

"Thanks, everyone," I replied. Looking at Magus Triska, I added, "You've got all of us to help you now. Where do we begin?"

Magus Triska visibly relaxed. "This is almost too good

to be true. Thank you all. Where to begin? Well, I think it wise for Magus Nia Elain to learn how to cast more of her spells. We still have some time, so let's allow her another week to learn as much as she can. Meanwhile, Sir Dmitri, Ranger Danika, we'll need good horses and quite a lot of supplies. You see, I can't create a Transport Torus to places I've never seen. Alas, I've never been to these other lands. The furthest I've been is to Duscha and only once when I was far younger. I don't trust my memory to open a torus to that kingdom. We'll ride east, following the Sana River. However, I caution you all, this will be a very dangerous trip. I believe the slavers make their home somewhere east of the Hill River, but no one knows precisely where. My guess is it will take us a week to get to the areas that must be searched for this mysterious Tikhon place."

"Shouldn't we leave at once then? Give ourselves more time?" Jelena asked in her conservative manner. Several others nodded.

Magus Triska answered quite solemnly. "Ordinarily, I would agree with you, Witch Jelena. In this case, Magus Nia Elain really does need time to learn her craft. I feel it in my aching bones; her skills are going to be tested on this adventure. Let's give her a few days to learn what she can."

"That makes sense. I'll visit the witches here in Sana Falls and lay in as many healing salves as I can afford," Jelena replied.

"Hey, use some of my silvers to help pay for them, Jelena," I hastily spoke up. My pouch was bulging with silvers. I couldn't think of a better use for some of them. Quickly, Sir Dmitri, Danika, and Vlad concurred and offered her some of their silvers as well. Begrudgingly, Kisha also counted out some of hers as well, pleasing Jelena immensely.

The week passed swiftly for me. A bond formed between Magus Triska and me, rather like a surrogate mother. I worked hard, and she was a good teacher. I learned how to create spell after spell, including the Transportation Torus, which I really loved to cast, though it was one of the more difficult ones to master.

Meanwhile, the others set about obtaining our needed supplies. That winter would soon be upon us only made things more difficult. We would need far warmer clothing and more food, as well as some grain for the horses. They explained to me that horses ate grasses, which died off during the winter months. They also insisted on doubling their weapons. Kisha explained to me that their iron blades often broke, though not as frequently as the Rus' bronze blades. At last the day of our departure came.

Chapter 6 In the Hands of the Slavers

The air was crisp, filled with the odor of burning pine and the dead leaves of fall. Wearing my heavy cloak and sitting on my mare, I was able to get a good view of Sana Falls, as our party rode out to the east, following the Sana River. Kisha led my horse, since I had not yet figured out how I could control the mare. Jelena, who I discovered had a golden touch with horses, brought our string of packhorses behind her. Up front, Danika led the way, with Sir Dmitri and Vlad right behind her. Magus Triska was riding at my side, her oak staff stowed in a leather tube behind her saddle.

To my eyes, the world seemed at peace. Yet, if we failed, everything could well be utterly destroyed when Platon came crashing into the world. I wonder if they would even know what was happening to them if that should happen. I doubt it. As superstitious as they were, they'd probably just figure some unseen god had it in for them. Still, Sana Falls was picturesque, quaint in its rustic nature. A hard life, though, as Magus Triska bore witness to. Only in her fifties, she was considered to be quite old. The average lifetime is barely fifty, quite a contrast to those in the Imperium worlds, even ignoring our Rejuvenation Machines.

Once clear of the town's walls, I spotted wagonloads of chopped wood creaking along towards town. I tried to imagine how much wood one might need to keep warm during the winter, but couldn't. No experience with it, but it must be a lot, considering the number of wagonloads coming into the town. The neatly fenced agricultural plots now appeared quite barren, awaiting the first snows and then later spring planting — quite the contrast.

Billowing white clouds dotted the sky, but the setting three moons, so close to each other, looked ominous to me. We had until they finished this new cycle of their phases. When they reached new moon, some twenty days from now, gravity would begin our doom. We just had to succeed, though if you asked me how, I couldn't have answered. We were searching for the proverbial needle in the haystack. Nothing like starting off without sufficient data to know just what you are supposed to do, and yet knowing failure meant the death of the entire world.

What would I have liked to do? Find Jovan and our ship, then search for my parents and any other shipmates who might still be alive. Now that my mind was finally clear from the grey fog, I hadn't forgotten them. I gave the location where we landed considerable thought, especially at night when I lay down to sleep. I'm certain of what I saw out of the view port windows as we landed. Tall mountains lay just to our left. We landed in the foothills to the right of the peaks. However, I didn't know which way was north. Thus, I reasoned, we could have been coming in from the north, so hence our landing point may be to the west of the mountains. Or we could have been coming in from the south, in which case, it would be reversed; we'd have landed to the east of the peaks.

Additionally, I do recall the tall peaks didn't continue far off into the distance. My conclusion was we'd landed near one end of the mountain range. If I trusted Magus Triska's crude map of the continent, then there were two such mountain ranges, giving me eight potential locations to search. I ruled out one of these, near Sana Falls, because Magus Triska had never heard of Jovan. I also decided that just to the west of the mountains opposite Sana Falls was not our likely landing point. Surely, she would have heard of the village if it were within a hundred or a hundred-fifty miles of her town.

As we rode along on this pretty day, I also got to thinking about what Magus Triska had told us. The slavers made their base of operations somewhere to the east, near the Leonid Mountains. I reasoned the village of Jovan must not be anywhere near the slavers, because Jelena had told me the slavers were seldom found around her village. If the slavers' town was near the southern edge of the Leonid Mountains, then I could rule two more areas out, leaving me with only four real possibilities where we had landed the Eagle's Seed.

I tried recalling everything I could, trying hard to remember just what I had seen from that view port. Then it hit me. The mountains had ended near the ocean. Smiling, I realized I only had four possible landing sites. Duh, stupid me. Make that two possible landing sites. If we were heading for the northern edge of the mountain range, that could only mean we landed to the right or east of the range. The Eagle's Seed was either to the east of the Melor Mountains or to the east of the Leonid Mountains!

Funny how one breakthrough leads to a flood of ideas. As soon as I realized this, I also realized I was being stupid. I could now cast the Transportation Torus. Like Magus Triska, I could only open the portal to a place I was quite familiar with — duh, like Jovan! Laughing, I called out, "Jelena, I can get us back home anytime now. I just ruled out all possibilities but two. Silly me, that doesn't matter now. I'm very familiar with your village. I can open up a Transportation Torus to Jovan anytime we want."

"That's the best news ever, Magus Nia!" she turned in her saddle and with a big, relieved grin on her face. I could sense relief flooding out of her. After all, how would you feel if you suddenly found yourself in some distant land where no one had ever heard of your town and you had never heard of theirs — lost and with no way to find home? Scary? Frightening? Forget maps. They didn't have such things on this primitive world. I had no idea just how critical my realization would become!

By this time, I could no longer see Sana Falls when I turned around in my saddle. We'd gone quite a few miles. Once more, the stark trees and rugged, rocky ground looked utterly foreign to me. Perhaps that's why I began thinking about what Danika had told us, as we were leaving the town. "I have the feeling we're being watched and even followed. Best be on high alert." I didn't give that much thought, as we were leaving the large town. Who would launch an attack so darn close to thousands of people, many of whom might well come to our aid?

Now, we were out in the middle of nowhere, at least as far as I was concerned. No one was nearby to help us if trouble came. I realized just how much I was depending upon the others, particularly Sir Dmitri, Danika, and Vlad for protection. I think Magus Triska also had similar thoughts. As we continued our relatively rapid progress, I kept seeing armed men behind every tree and every large boulder! Of course, they weren't there.

Perhaps, it was because I was so keenly alert for a slaver attack that I suddenly spotted one of the ghostly Ceri from the corner of my eyes. Startled, I turned to look directly at the form. Of course, it vanished, only reappearing when I diverted my eyes once again. As we slowly rode past the creature near an old oak tree, I continued to study it using my peripheral vision, which I found rather annoying. Magus Triska whispered somewhat nervously, "What are you seeing?"

"A Ceri. Over by that oak tree. Can you see it too?" I replied, keeping my voice low. Hastily, the others touched their temples, warding off the ghosts, unable actually to toss a pebble back over their shoulders while on horseback. Weird. Only I was able to see this creature. How very strange. Still, Magus Triska believed she might have seen something, but she wasn't sure, because her eyesight was not what it had been. Only now did I learn she was going blind. I vowed silently to get her to our medical machine and get her eyes healed, once we finished this mission. If we failed, then it didn't matter; we'd all be dead.

When we broke for lunch, over dried rolls and jerky, Danika explained, "I doubt they will try to ambush us like they did back at the tunnel entrance. With two magi, they won't risk an open attack, unless they are incredibly stupid. If I were them, I'd attack us in the middle of the night, when we are most vulnerable. Don't worry, we'll stand watch each night."

When we stopped for the night, Magus Triska had a difficult time. Riding all day, her joints not only ached, but she could barely walk. Still, she stoically endured and didn't complain, though she leaned heavily upon her staff whenever she had to rise or walk. At least, she had an excuse for not being very helpful setting up camp and preparing our supper. As cold as it was, I was pretty much useless, which annoyed me more than I dared to admit at that time. I nearly froze my toes off trying to eat dinner, and there wasn't any snow on the ground yet. Thankfully, we all turned in very early, just as twilight ended.

Sir Dmitri and Kisha took the first watch. Danika and Vlad were supposed to relieve them halfway through the night. Jelena also cast her witch protections around our campsite. She would be alerted if someone or something tried to sneak into our camp circle while we slept. I quickly fell into an ill sleep.

I was rudely awakened by the attack. It had come before Danika was to relieve Sir Dmitri and Kisha. Jelena's alarm triggered, waking her, as well as alerting Kisha to impending trouble. She tossed several branches onto the fire, while Sir Dmitri roused us. Magus Triska apparently was a light sleeper and awoke at once. She immediately caused our campfire to rise in a blazing inferno, casting much needed light out in a hemisphere some two hundred feet, centered on us.

Kisha had an arrow notched, pointing it one way and then another. The three fighters dashed around, forming up a defensive perimeter, swords drawn. By the time I got to my feet, I could see just how outnumbered we were. After that last encounter with the slavers, they'd sent at least a hundred men after us. Worse, Magus Triska pointed out three enemy magi. They were standing back, just barely visible at the extreme edge of our campfire illumination. All were protected by a dozen fighters, who stood in front of them. This would be a magi battle, my first, and not a sword fight.

An electrical bolt of lightning shot towards Magus Triska. As I watched, she chose to absorb it with her staff, having the charge flow down the staff and into the ground. Good move, I thought, regretting I had no staff at hand. Another pair of magi cast a very strange spell! They animated the roots of the large oaks around our campsite. Suddenly, twisting roots pierced upwards from the ground, encircling the legs of Sir Dmitri, Danika, and Vlad, pinning them in place. Magus Triska shot a bolt of lightning back at the magus who had tried to kill her. I decided to do something to free our three fighters.

I know. Hindsight is wonderful. I should have gone after the enemy magi instead. However, I didn't want anyone to harm my gorgeous Danika, who was pinned to the spot, unable to defend herself, should these hundreds come at her. I acted, countering the roots, driving them back into the ground where they belonged. Meanwhile, Kisha dropped three fighters, but had used up her quiver's arrows. While she had brought along three more quivers, they were not at hand.

Another magus fired off a swirling cyclone, a mini-tornado, whose winds were howling fiercely. Picking up leaves and twigs, the grayish form moved in towards our three fighters, who were finally free from the entanglement of the tree roots. Again, I acted to counter this one, lifting it high up into the air, where it rapidly dissipated, much to the annoyance of the magus caster. Magus Triska shot a wall of flames at one of the magi, who tried to dodge it, but his robes caught fire. The many fighters around him took the flames full on. Even the dry leaves caught fire, adding to the confusion around us.

Looking back on the fight, I realize now the magi were being extremely careful not to physically injure us with their spells. Otherwise, they could have dropped three walls of fire right on top of us. With all the dry leaves around us, we'd have most likely been incinerated.

Their next pair of spells rather did us in, I'm afraid to admit. First, we all got hit with a hurricane-force wind, designed to knock us off our feet, which it certainly did. Second, a cloud of some type of noxious gas settled on top of us, as we struggled to get back onto our feet. We never made it up. I had just gotten to my knees, when I felt all the strength seep out of my legs. My body no longer obeyed me. My mind went dark. I must have fallen back onto the ground along with everyone else. My last thought was: We are being defeated; this can't happen, not now!

Daylight. I felt warm sunlight on my cheeks. Slowly, I came too, but panicked, as I recalled we had just been in a huge battle. I tried to move my feet to get up, but they seemed tied together, as they had been when Jelena and I first got captured by the slavers during the Slave Wind. I looked around. I was lying on a crude bed, whose mattress was a bag stuffed with straw. I was inside a building, a wooden one. A crude wooden table and some chairs occupied the middle of the room, some ten feet from me. I spotted eight other beds up against the walls encircling this room.

Struggling a bit, I sat up and looked around more carefully. There were my friends, asleep on five other beds. We were all covered in a woolen blanket, but we still wore our warm leather clothes. I noticed our fighters' armor was lying in piles near their beds. At least, they hadn't confiscated the ring mail, I thought. Quite why I thought this eludes me. Perhaps, it's because I was still quite disoriented. Where were we? What was going on? I was about to yell out to my friends, when I heard footsteps coming up to a door to this room.

A large man wearing leather armor and carrying a sword, sheathed, walked into the room. He was not quiet about his entry. His deep bass voice bellowed. I wish he'd used far less volume. My ears throbbed with his every word. "Okay. Wake up time, slaves. Wake up!" He came to my bed and tossed back my blanket. He moved on to each of the five other beds in succession, tossing back the blankets, as one by one, my friends awoke to this new nightmare.

Cries, gasps, curses flew from our mouths the moment we finally understood our situation. Now, I could see why my legs felt immobilize. They were. Three sets of cuffs held them together. One set was above my knees; one just below my knees, but a chain connected them, ensuring that neither could slip down. A third set were around my ankles. Each set consisted of a three inch wide band of iron that went completely around the leg. At my knees, the opposite bands were fastened together by a one-loop chain link, which permitted only the slightest of movements. The second set just below my knees were similar but had two links connecting them, allowing for the natural outward curvature of my lower legs. The set at my ankles had only one link, forcing my booted feet tightly together. That's the point at which I suddenly realized I was completely helpless!

"Come on, slaves. Up and onto your feet. If you haven't guessed, from now on, you walk by hopping, just like all the other slaves around here. Come on; get up or I'll yank you to your feet!" the bass voiced man barked, wholly unsympathetically. I tried desperately to do as he asked. I couldn't help but recall the last time I was bound and jerked to my feet. I'd lost my baby-sized arms.

"My arms!" Danika cried out, joined by Jelena and Kisha as well. Now, I saw their arms were similarly chained behind their backs. The three inch bands were positioned just above their elbows and with only one link connecting them, forcing their elbows to touch together behind their backs, but leaving their lower arms free but darn near useless. "My shoulders are aching. Get me out of this," Danika pleaded with the man, who only laughed at her.

"Okay, come on. Hop after me. The boss wants to greet you all personally. Hop or I'll give you a push," he barked loudly.

I did as asked, taking small hops and being very careful to keep my balance between hops, made all the more difficult without arms to flail around. Stoically, Jelena attempted to follow my lead, swinging her arms this way and that behind her, as she tried to keep her balance. Humiliating. That's the best way to describe all our feelings just now, as we had no choice but to hop after the man. At least, the three men fared better. They still had full use of their arms, unlike Jelena, Kisha, and Danika. Then, it hit me! Where was Magus Triska? I was about to ask, when the man walked through the door to the outside world, and I was instantly distracted.

We were in some town. Wooden buildings stretched in all directions. I spotted around a dozen guards standing idly at various locations around the streets. What so shocked me were all the other men and women. They were all chained just as we were. The men carried picks and shovels, as they were hopping off to work, led by a guard. I spotted three such groups of men. I spotted a well, and at least twenty women, all hopping along just as we were. Their elbows were pinned together behind their backs, just as Kisha, Danika and Jelena's arms were. Several were carrying water buckets and hopping towards the well. There must have been at least fifty of us hopping along.

I was shocked, and I swore I would somehow rescue all of these victims. Admittedly, I had no idea how I could do that. I heard my friends cursing under their breaths, but the guard either didn't notice or didn't care. He just kept on leading us through the streets. Now, I spotted even more men in groups of six to ten, all carrying shovels or picks, heading off as a work gang. Another fifty women, at least, were also out, hopping, but to where, I couldn't tell. Later, I learned they were hopping to the food supply building to get their day's rations to cook.

Slowly, I became a little more comfortable with hopping along on this level, dirt street. Ahead, a large building appeared, twice the size of all the others, which now that I reflect upon it, all looked the same, and which in fact, they were. A sign over the porch read Arnwald. At this moment, I didn't grasp the significance of the language in which it was written, but I soon would. Our guide bellowed, "Okay, nearly there. Hop up the one step. Try not to fall down, cause I sure as hell ain't going to help you back up."

Being in the lead of our small group, I made the attempt first. I reckoned if I could do it, the others, who had a little more ability to maintain their balance, could as well. It was still scary. I bent my knees and did my best, over shooting it a little. Only a Herculean amount of wild wiggling on my part kept me from falling down! My heart was racing, as I hopped closer to the door, which the guard now opened, motioning for me to enter. As I did, I heard Danika crashing into the porch floor, and I did a frantic hopping in place turn around to see what had happened. She'd not made the jump and had landed on her shoulder rather hard. At least Sir Dmitri, who followed her, was able to use his hands to help her back up. Her eyes were wet, and I could sense she was suppressing a good deal of pain.

I did another hopping sort of turn and continued into the room. I spotted a long, wooden bench against one wall and a chair against the other. Two closed doors were on the other two sides. I figured we were to sit on the bench and hopped all the way to the far end, hoping to make it a little easier for my friends. When Danika finally made it inside and saw the bench, she nodded to me, and I knew I had been right. It was all she could do to make it to the bench before collapsing down on it rather hard.

Soon, we seven sat in a row on the bench waiting what was to come next. Where was Magus Triska? Again, I desperately wanted to know that. Our guard knocked on one of the doors and hollered out, "Boss, they're here." He moved back to the main door and stood before it, blocking any attempt we might make to escape. Ha. Chained as we were, what did he think we would do? Fly away? I was pissed, but knew I had to bide my time. And time was what we had the least of!

The door opened, and a relatively short man marched into the room. What got my full attention was the Imperium d-gun strapped in a leather holster at his side! He was in his sixties at least, but wore a fine leather local outfit. His boots were Imperium soldier-issue, that much I knew from Net images I'd often seen. His hair was black and bowl-cut, giving him something of a monkish appearance. He was far from holy, that much I knew. His eyes met mine, and I saw the telltale reddish swirls. I knew at once that he was a magus and a master of fire elemental forces. He blinked when he saw mine. Rightly so, for I was supposedly a master of all four elemental forces.

He slid the chair over and sat down ceremoniously before us seven. He began by speaking in Sud, since my six companions were all Suds. "Welcome to Arnwald. I am Commander Arnwald Berend. You are now my newest slaves. As you have seen, you are tightly chained and will remain so until your death. If you take a moment to examine the chain rings, you'll notice there is no way to undo them. So my pretty thief, forget trying to unlock them," he looked Kisha squarely in her eyes. I guessed he figured that out from the gear, which she had carried.

"Here's the way it works. You three men will be put to work in my mines. Picks and shovels. As long as you work, you'll receive free room and board. All the food you can eat, and all the women you care to bed. If you don't work, then your arms will be bound as the women's are, and you'll be put to more domestic chores. Don't worry; nothing you can do will get you killed. I know, so many who come here have that as their first goal — to die and get out of working for me. Let me assure you that's not going to happen."

"Now, you women will be assigned to a home where you will handle the daily domestic duties, fixing the meals, keeping it clean, fetching water, and so on. At night, men will bed you. Have to keep the men fully satisfied. A satisfied worker is a happy worker, you see. That's my motto around here. We have to keep your arms pinned behind your backs so you can't resist the advances of the men when they bed you. You'll find if you help each other, you can manage to do your chores, even with your elbows pinned behind your backs. Alone, I highly doubt it. So remember to work together, ladies."

Danika spoke up, "My shoulders are throbbing; it's ripping my arms from their sockets!"

"Tisk, tisk, Danika is it?" he said covertly. "Don't worry, soon your shoulders will go quite numb, and you won't feel them after that. Can't have you using those powerful arms of yours keeping men from bedding you, now can we?" If a glare could kill, hers would have!

"Where's Magus Triska?" I ventured to ask.

"I'm truly sorry. She didn't make it. She died during the attack. I wish it wasn't so, for I so wanted to talk to her about her discoveries, but now I have you. My army was instructed to bring you all back here alive and well. As I understand it, this Magus Triska was aged and long overdue to die. She was given a proper burial, befitting a magus. We are not animals," Commander Arnwald explained in a rather fake, kindly way.

"Now then, that brings me to you," he addressed me. However, I was surprised. He spoke in Imperium Standard! My suspicions were instantly confirmed. He grinned, "I see you can understand me, just as I guessed. I'll speak in Sud so the others can understand us." I nodded, still shocked.

"Our deep space transport had to make a crash landing on this world back in 1320, about fifty-five years back. Our comm system was shot to hell, and our fuel supply was exhausted. At least, the pilot managed to land the transport on vapors. Without any way to contact civilization, we found ourselves stranded on this backwater of a world. The only saving grace is my late geologist did find large deposits of raw psi-crystals. We both know that given enough of the crystals, in theory, we could refuel our ship, and depart this god-forsaken world."

I protested, "But they have to be refined."

"Bright teen. Yes, they do. And just where on this world would we find the technology to refine the ore into the fuel we need to escape? Nowhere. The only recourse open to us is to make use of what resources are available to us. Hence, Arnwald, Slave Town. My men began capturing local savages and putting them to work mining for the crystals. Next, we needed metal ores from which to make a crude refinery. You see, our only goal here is to make enough fuel to get off this dump and back to civilization. Over the years, we've had to continue to add to our slave labor force, scouring this world."

I butted in, "But you haven't yet gotten the fuel, right?"

"Observant. Precisely, the refinery is still not operational. Over the years, most of my crew has died off. If only we had brought along a Rejuvenation Machine. Ah well. At this point, Arnwald is a thriving city. I have six hundred or so slaves working the various mines, and an equal number of women to cook and satisfy their sexual needs. Plus, we've built up quite an army, replete with five magi and two witches. You seven will fit right in here nicely."

"However, I did detect your deep spaceship high overhead, far to the northwest. I sent out my soldiers to try to find you. I was planning to beg you to rescue your fellow Imperium citizens, but that's not going to happen now. That damned Slave Wind killed off most of your crew. Yet, I nearly had you at that time. Lord knows how you escaped my men, but you did. I've been on your trail ever since."

"Of course, I got a lucky break when you surfaced at Magus Triska's place. For months, I've been trying to find out what she discovered. Although we were able to trace you when she took you to that spaceship site, we underestimated your resolve. However, we did discovered what she was hiding from us, another crash site. It was stripped, just like the one we discovered south of here. What I want to know is what did she find there? Unless, Magus Nia Flain, you want me to begin torturing your companions, you will tell me everything she discovered or removed from that site."

Danika cried out, "Don't tell him anything!"

Whatever else this sadistic Commander Arnwald was, he was observant. I think my facial reaction gave away my feelings for Danika. He countered, "Ah, I see. Wouldn't have guessed you care for her. Figured it was for the knight fellow. Anyway, if you don't start talking, I'll have my men start carving up the ranger here, starting with her arms she has been complaining about. Don't forget; we have a medical machine here. I can hack off bits and pieces with complete freedom. What will it be, magus? Should I remove her arms and make her like you? Wouldn't you just like that?"

"You wouldn't dare. What kind of a beast are you anyway?" I retorted.

"The kind that always gets what he wants. So, you going to spill it and hand over or tell me where she's keeping what she's found in that ship?" he glared at me.

Danika stuck up for us, "Don't tell him. We'd all rather die."

"Yes, you bastard. I'll find a way to kill you! You are nothing but the lowest, vilest scum on our world!" Sir Dmitri swore, clenching his fists so tightly, I thought a vein might pop right there.

Vlad got in on the action, displaying some uncharacteristic anger. "Whatever, beast-man. I hope you drown in your own piss!"

Jelena, who had been totally silent all this time, added, "Why are you such a beast? You are less than a man. Even the Rus are more honorable than you and your slavers."

Not to be outdone, Kisha spoke softly, but with no less conviction. "You do this to Danika, and I swear no matter where you go, I'll find a way to follow you across the universe, until I can slit your gut open like the rotten, slimy fish that you are!"

Commander Arnwald laughed and belittled her, "Hardly, thief. I'll remove your arms too for good measure. Let's see you use your knife then. You are all pathetic primitives! You don't seem to realize your lives are utterly worthless. I'm doing you all a favor by making you my slaves! At least here, you can count on square, nourishing meals and a roof over your heads. That's a hell of a lot more than you can scrape together in your primitive towns and houses of mud and barbaric farming methods. You have no conception of just how pathetically primitive you really are." I expected Kisha would be cowed by his threat, but she wasn't. She simply glared back at him, though she wisely held her tongue.

He raved on, "What's your life expectancy? Answer that one, if you dare. Hell, that magus what's her name was what, barely fifty years old, and practically on her deathbed. Even I could tell her body was battling a severe case of arthritis. Just ask Nia Elain here how long we civilized Imperium humans live. Eighty, ninety at least, ignoring our Rejuvenation Machines. With them, we can live to a hundred and fifty or more, triple your life expectancy. We fly among the stars, while you ride your filthy beasts, which consume more of your grain than you people do. I'm far older than I appear to you; I used the Rejuvenation Machine before we left on this ill-fated mission."

Jelena surprised me. She spoke up, softly but firmly, "But we are more human than you and your men. We treat others with dignity and respect, not with brutality and slavery. You can have your wonderful Imperium. If those people are like you, go back to them, and leave us alone."

Once more, Commander Arnwald Berend laughed sadistically. "Leave you alone. Yes, perhaps that is the wisest course to follow. I should let you all get used to your new lives for a few days. I can see you are just like those wild beasts you are so fond of riding. They have to be broken first, before anything can be done with them. Okay, I'll have the guard take you back to your new home. You women will find everything you need to prepare meals in your new kitchen. Of course, you'll have to draw your own water from the central wells, and you will need to visit the PX to be given your daily rations of food supplies. Meanwhile, you men will be put to work in one of the many mines. You see, I've found it necessary to have iron and silver mines as well. Primitives seem to desire silver as a means of exchange. So utterly primitive. Credits works so much better that there's no comparison. We'll talk again in a few days. By then, you may be more conducive to telling me what I want to know. I'll send a guard to check on your well-being once each evening. That is all. Return them to their home, and see that the men are issued picks and shovels. Put them in whichever mine needs the help."

With that, he turned sharply on his heels and left the room, shutting the door behind him. The bass voice guard barked, "You heard the boss. Up and hopping. Back to your quarters. Pay attention. I'll point out the nearest well and where the PX is located. If you want anything to eat today, you best fetch your water, food supplies, and cook. Your men will return at suppertime quite hungry and in need of a good meal. In the morning, when you hear the bugle call, get yourselves up, and get the men their breakfast quickly. If the food isn't ready by the time the work crew foreman comes by for the men, they'll get no breakfast. Men, you can bed whichever of these women you desire each evening. That's the rules. Now come on, hop."

We had no choice but to stand and hop towards the door, which he held open for us. I found hopping down the single step far easier than going up it. Still, we were all panting from the exertion by the time we were close to our new home. This PX place, where they doled out the food, was two blocks from our building, which had a wooden placard over its door identifying it as #102. The well was two blocks in the opposite direction. During the trip back, we only spotted around twenty women struggling with heavy water buckets. We saw no sight of the work crews, which were presumable now at the mines, working as slave labor.

As we approached our new dwelling, the guard said, "Okay, ladies. You know what you have to do. Men, come with me. I'll get you your digging tools and take you to your mine. Action. Time's a'wasten."

I continued hopping up to our door, but was stopped by the closed door. Danika followed me up to it. "I can't open it," I whispered.

"I can't feel my hands anymore. My shoulders have gone numb," Danika whispered back.

"I got it, I think," Kisha came up behind us, hopping up to the door, and doing a bit of a hopping turn in place. While looking back over her shoulder, she maneuvered her lower right arm a bit and got the door opened. We all hopped inside.

"Thanks, Kisha. My god, do I ever have to pee. Can

someone help me?" I asked, feeling utterly miserable. Now, I was truly helpless, dependent upon the others for everything.

We all had to use the commode, and Kisha and Jelena were able to help each of us in turn to accomplish this necessary task. Yet, both Danika and I saw just how hard it was for them to manage it. "Let me look at your shoulders, Danika," Jelena then suggested.

We sat down on the beds, while Jelena hopped and twisted around to get a good look at her shoulders. She and Kisha had to remove her leather top just to get a look at her shoulders. "How bad is it?" Danika whispered, fighting hard to keep from breaking down completely. "I can't feel anything in my hands now."

"Not good. They've turned black and blue. I don't know what that means," Jelena replied. "Perhaps, it's like he said. In time, you'll get used to it. At least, Kisha and I are flexible. Still, what are we going to do now?" The two struggled to get her top back in place. I found that at least I could give them directions. They had to work with their heads mostly looking backwards.

I suggested, "He's right about one point. We have to get some food in here along with water and get something cooking. The men will be utterly exhausted and in dire need of a meal when they return. If we don't keep up our strength, we're going to perish rapidly. Time is not on our side. We still have to find this Tikhon place. Damn, we can ill afford this delay."

Jelena added, "I know we must. We owe it to Magus Triska at least to try to finish her work and save our world. Even if this vile man doesn't care about us in the slightest, he's going to die right along with all of us, if we don't."

"Ah," Kisha grinned, "so we're going to get the last laugh. The bastard. Men, they're all alike, a self-serving lot of sadistic ego maniacs!"

"That's rather a harsh condemnation of all men, don't you think," Jelena countered. "After all, Vlad isn't like that. Sir Dmitri is a bit bossy, but he's a kind heart, don't you think?"

Kisha grimaced. I could tell she hated to be corrected when she was wrong. "Well, perhaps not all men, just most," she modified her curse.

I took control again. "Come on; we have to get to this food distribution place and then get some water in here." Valiantly, we four rose to our feet. Taking a deep breath, I led the way, hopping carefully to our front door. Again, I cursed silently because I had no way to open it. Worse, Kisha had to do it from a most awkward position. She had her back to the door so she could use the limited mobility of her hands, craning her neck around to see over her shoulders. Again, I found I was able verbally to direct her somewhat.

This time, we found relatively few women hopping on the streets. I figured they were now back in their homes struggling to prepare meals. God, what a nightmare Commander Arnwald Berend was inflicting on all these people. However, upon entering the building with the PX sign above its door, we got another shock.

Hopping inside while Kisha held the door open for us, we saw what I would describe as a warehouse. A low wooden counter top sitting on a barricade blocked off most all the room, which was filled with floor to ceiling shelves. Each shelf was packed with food supplies of all kinds. Several men stood behind the counter, filling the daily orders. That was not what so shocked us. Rather it was the ten other women who were standing before the counter waiting for their daily supplies to be given to them.

A third of them were like me, completely armless, while the others had lost their arms at their elbows. Each had either a large sack slung over their heads which were being filled with their supplies or they had a dual basket system resting over their shoulders and affixed to their necks, a pair of baskets hanging from each side, also being filled with groceries. Several did a hop-in-place turn around to see us.

A pair of nearly identical twins turned to face us. They were the closest women to us, as we entered. Both were tall and thin, with the lightest brown hair that I'd seen, wavy and quite long. I thought they were quite attractive and were likely my age, around nineteen perhaps. They each had sacks around their necks, empty just now. One spoke up, "Oh, you must be the new arrivals. We saw them bringing in all of you last night.

I'm Jovanna Darvan. She's my twin sister, Jana. We were going to come over to your house, as soon as we get our supplies, and lend you a hand. Well, help anyway, since we lost ours."

Their leather tops had short sleeves, allowing them to make use of their stumps, as much as possible. I saw at once the thin, conical ends of their upper arms and knew precisely what that meant! An Imperium medical machine had been used on their arms, preparing their stumps for prosthesis, which of course Commander Arnwald never provides. I replied, "Hi. I'm Nia Elain." I introduced the other three.

Standing beside the twins were two armless women, each with the dual baskets fastened around their necks and resting upon their shoulders. The two were not much older, perhaps twenty at most. "I'm Tesla Niko. My friend, Anya Pavel. We're coming over too to help show you what can be done, Nia Elain." Tesla had very blonde hair and pale blue eyes, while Anya was more robust with raven hair and eyes. I guessed right away that Jovanna, Jana, and Tesla were of Sud origins, but that Anya was likely Rus.

Tesla continued. "Jovanna's right. We saw them bringing in all of you last night, but we were shocked to see that they'd already removed your arms, Nia Elain. Usually, that doesn't happen for several days after they pin your arms together behind your backs."

I picked up on her thoughts immediately, probably because of the pain and numbness that Danika was having. "I was born without any arms. The slavers didn't do it. But what do you mean about several days? Danika here had bad pains in her shoulders when we woke up this morning, and now her whole arms are numb and black and blue."

As I said that, all of the women here turned to look at us quite sympathetically. I had a sickening feeling in my stomach. Tesla explained, "Oh, that's not good, Danika. We were like that. All of us here."

Jana broke in, "Hey, a quarter of all women here are, Tesla."

Tesla continued, "Right, at least a quarter of all us captured women got excruciating pains in our shoulders when they pinned our elbows together behind our backs. Not every woman has that kind of flexibility in her shoulders. It's not good, Danika. When the pain subsides, your whole arms go numb. You can't feel anything with them or move them. When that happens, you have to tell the guards about it. They will take you to their witch."

Jana broke in, "Doctor, Tesla, they call that man their doctor. She's right. You have to tell them. Yolinda didn't, and she died within a week. If you are lucky, you only lose your lower arms like us."

"If they can't save them," Anya continued, "they take all of them off. It doesn't hurt. Tesla and I didn't feel anything when they removed ours. They put us in a strange machine."

Jovanna continued, "Right. None of us felt anything at all. You see, these metal bands and chains cannot be removed. We've watched them putting them on others. They use some kind of machine. Jana, what did they call it? I forgot."

"A forger, I think," her sister replied. "We're the lucky ones, but Tesla and Anya are almost as lucky. At least, we now have full use of what is left of our arms."

"Yes, but we don't. And it's a bitch being like this, but you must already know that, Nia Elain. Still, we are the really lucky women," Tesla explained.

"How in hell are you lucky?" Kisha asked, angrily. "These wicked bastards!" This last, she uttered softly so that the men who were busily filling orders didn't hear her.

"Cause we are left alone and not raped like all the other women are. You see, the men return at night and rape us, once they are fed," Jana explained, quite rapidly.

"Right," Tesla added, "but the men don't want anything to do with us. The guards have moved all that are like us into our own houses. So now, we are safe from the men. We're left mostly alone to fend for ourselves. That's why we four decided that we'd move in with you, Nia, to help you newcomers out. But Danika, we had better get you to the doctor fellow soon. I think if they get to you soon enough, you won't have to lose all of your arms, just part of them. Take it from us, that's a whole lot better."

Danika nearly passed out. I pressed my body against

hers and up against the wall, steadying her as best I could. I tried to keep from screaming, "Can't they take these damned bands off of us?"

All the women sighed, very nearly together. Anya replied, "There's no way to do that. Once they forge them onto a person, they can never be taken off. We've been here what, two years? Tesla? We've never seen anyone having them removed."

"She's right," Jana added. "We've been here nearly two years now. They even bury those who die with the bands still on them. I've chatted with some of the guards who have been here for years. No one has ever had them removed. They say it can't be undone. So unless you want Danika to die, you've got to get her to this doctor fellow soon."

"She's right," Jovanna broke in. "Once we get our day's food and water drawn, we'll help you take her to the doctor man."

By now, the other eight women had been handled and they made their careful way past us and out the door. While the men filled up the four's two sacks and four baskets with their daily rations, one man fitted me with one of the basket contraptions. It locked around my neck and a padded wooden arm rested across my shoulders. Two baskets hung from either side. They hung a large sack over Danika's head. When it was our turn, we hopped up to the counter, and the men began doling out our supplies. Thank god, the men had the good sense to keep the weight in my baskets balanced!

A few minutes later, we four hopped out of the door, while Jana held it open for us. "We're coming with you to help," she explained. We eight began our careful hopping back to our new home.

"See, Nia Elain, you can carry things in these baskets, just like we can," Tesla chatted, while we did our best to keep from falling down. "At least, they feed us really well. The only real problem is in the winter, when the ground is covered in snow. Hopping is really hard then. We fall very easily. Still, we have a warm home. They always keep us well supplied with wood to burn. Honestly, life is more comfortable here. I was married to Anya's brother, before we four were captured. Both our husbands died last year. I don't think the miners live too long." She continued chatting, until we reached our house. Jovanna used her stumps to open the door, much to the relief of Kisha, who was struggling to carry her sacks in her hands behind her back.

I was amazed at how well Jana and Jovanna managed to unload the supplies on the kitchen table. In fact, they were better at it than Kisha and Jelena, who finally just stood still and let them do it all for us. Jana explained, "Okay, always remember to get water last, Nia Elain. That way, your two water buckets can dry out before you get food tomorrow. Also, since we can't easily carry water and since you have two buckets, your job is to carry the water for us. You see — we all work together to help."

"Right, we're the water bearers," Tesla explained. "We carry more water than the normal women. They really struggle with fetching water. Since there are three of us with the buckets, perhaps we can make two trips, and Kisha and Jelena can rest up here."

I followed the four back outside, heading for the water well. I hated to leave Danika alone. God, the thoughts that must be going through her mind right now! Still, I had to make a decision. Soon! Did I get her to this doctor fellow right away? If so, she'd surely lose part or all of her arms. For the fighter-ranger, this would be devastating. Her life would be ruined. Or did I dare wait. Wait for what? They said these bindings were somehow forged onto us and couldn't be removed. Surely, they would have removed them instead of chopping off arms, if they could have. Yet, this commander considered these people as mere animals, not human beings. Hence, I figured, even if there was a way to remove the bands, he'd not do it for that very reason. One could always capture more "animals." What to do? That question occupied my thoughts as we fetched the water.

At the well, I was amazed at how the twins managed to operate the crank that raised the water bucket and filled up our six buckets. The weight of both full buckets was almost more than I could handle, while trying to hop my way back. Still, if Tesla and Anya could manage, so could I. After all, I'd just seen this was one of the few ways the armless women had to help everyone survive.

When we returned, Jana and Jovanna took charge in the kitchen. Kisha and Jelena worked with them, learning the ropes, so to speak. Tesla and Anya hovered around them, doing what little they could, mostly trying to stir the pots with spoons held in their mouths. Me, I sat on a bed beside Danika, trying to figure out what to do.

Finally alone, at least partially, Danika sobbed, "My life is ruined. I'll be a helpless cripple now, just as they are. Nia, I'd rather die. Can't you do something to kill me? I beg you."

"Danika, I love you. I can't kill you. Look, I've gotten by all my life like this. It's a royal pain at times, especially hobbled like we are now, but I've gotten by."

"But I'm a fighter, a ranger," she protested, tears trickling down her cheeks.

"You'll still be a ranger. Danika, we have a mission before us. Somehow, it is up to us to prevent Platon from destroying every living thing on the world. I need you, Danika. I can't do this without you. Besides, I'm madly in love with you." There, I finally really admitted what I'd been feeling for her, almost from the first moment I set eyes on her. Funny how love is. I'd gone eighteen years without the slightest attraction towards any man or woman. I get one look at Danika, and the arrow struck me hard. I can only ascribe this to the fact I've got dual sexual organs, but perhaps I'm only justifying my feelings with that.

"What? Love? Me? Really?" she asked, taken aback by my intense admission. "But I'm about to become a hopeless cripple. You heard what they said — all the men now want nothing to do with them. We're outcasts, unwanted cripples. We'd be better off dead." She began crying once more.

I was getting nowhere. Then, I realized something. Danika was a fighter, a ranger. For whatever reason, she'd adopted a man's role in her society, so totally different from Jelena, who was a caring, loving, nurturing young woman. I took a different approach, hoping reason might carry the day. "Look, Danika, you chose to be a fighter and ranger." She nodded. "So when you did that, didn't you also know one day you might get badly wounded and lose an arm or leg in some fight?"

She sniffled. "Well, yes, that's an occupational hazard. Many fighters get badly wounded. Some die, but yes, you're right, some lose arms and legs, becoming hopeless cripples for the rest of their lives."

"So," I countered, "you knew the risks, and yet you chose to be a ranger and fighter, helping those many others, who could not defend themselves, right?"

She sobbed a bit more, then admitted, "Well, yes, but I always figured I was better than most men and wouldn't get badly hurt, or that I would be killed in an honorable, worthy battle, not like this."

"Battles come in many forms. I think we are facing one huge one right now, my love, and we must rise to the challenge. Look, I'm even more helpless than the others are, but we can't give up. Look at all these people, these helpless men and women who have been kidnaped and so brutally mistreated. We have to put an end to all these slavers, once and for all. Perhaps, fate has chosen us, Danika, to rid our world of this hideous scourge."

"Our world? You aren't planning to leave us?" she asked, taking me completely by surprise. That's not what I had anticipated her reaction would be.

"No, I'm not leaving."

"But won't you leave just as soon as you can find your people, those that are still alive? Won't you be heading back into the stars?"

It came to me in a flash! She fully expected I would leave Metcalf-4 at the first opportunity that came my way. If so, how could she possibly commit to me or even allow herself to have any deep feelings or attachment to me? Hell, I don't know what I intended to do either. Beyond the Eagle's Seed, I really had no life out there in the Imperium. That was mom and dad's world, not mine. I grew up in a stupid spaceship. Here, I was part of something much larger, a whole world. Besides, I figured they were all dead by now.

"Danika, I'm not leaving. This has become my home now, and I want to share my life with you, always. No matter what happens, I'll always be true to you," I admitted and committed myself.

For the first time, she leaned her body into mine, resting her head on my shoulders. I knew then that was just what she absolutely needed to hear. "Okay," she whispered, "we best get this done. If I can still have a bit of my arms, that would be so much better, I think. I do love you too, but I was scared you would leave me."

"Never, Danika, never. Be the brave warrior I know you are. We'll surmount all barriers and pull this off, together." I kissed the side of her head that I could reach, like a mother to her daughter. A memory of my mother kissing me while comforting me came to mind, unbidden.

Sometime later, Kisha called out, "Soup's on. Come and get it. Jana and Jovanna are really good cooks and can handle this much better than we can, that's for sure."

Eating became our next hurdle, after hopping carefully to the table and bumping the chairs around such that we could sit down on them. Kisha and Jelena had a terrifically difficult time trying to feed each other. Finally, we all decided just to allow Jana and Jovanna to feed the rest of us. While they were incredibly awkward, holding the spoons between their conical stumps, they were able to raise bites up towards our mouths. We, in turn, wiggled and maneuvered our mouths to meet the spoons.

"See, we work together, and it all works out," Jana declared, rather proudly. I praised them all and thanked them repeatedly.

Once we finished, Jana and I took Danika off to see this doctor. He was a bespectacled man, probably close to seventy years old. "Ah, Jana, is it? Well, let's see what we have here." He removed Danika's leather top. I grimaced when I saw the black and blue shoulders. It looked really bad, but then I'm not a doctor. "Not good, not good at all. But that's to be expected. Not everyone is able to have their elbows touching behind their backs. Let's see what the medical machine can do for you." With an arm around her, he forced her to hop into another room, leaving us to sit on chairs, waiting and fretting.

A half hour later, he helped Danika up out of the

medical machine. "Well, that's that. You are alive and well. You didn't feel anything, did you?"

Danika gasped. Her lower arms and hands were gone. Her upper arms now ended in small cones, about an inch in diameter at her tips, but the black and blue bruising was gone. She fought hard to keep from screaming or bawling, "No, nothing." She dare not say more for fear of losing what tiny bit of composure that remained to her. Meanwhile, the doctor proceeded to shorten the sleeves of her leather top, allowing a few inches of the ends of her upper arms to remain uncovered.

"There you go. Now you can use them as your hands, just like the others." He proceeded to force her to stand and hop on out to the room where we were waiting.

When I saw her coming, my stomach knotted, but I stifled my reactions and got to my feet, as did Jana. The aged doctor commented, "Jana, you got her to me just in time. Another day and I would not have been able to save any of her arms." He opened his door for us, a signal we were dismissed without further discussions.

Once outside, Danika wanted to let out a shriek, but suppressed it. Soon, though, she commented, "I can keep my balance better now. I've got some arms to compensate."

Jana smiled, "I know. We have it lots easier than everyone else does. We best make sure Nia Elain doesn't take a fall."

Once we returned and Kisha's swearing died down, Jana stated, "Don't worry. We will always be with you. We all have to work together now."

Kisha grumbled, "That's fine, but I've got to find a way to get these off of me. We've got a mission to fulfill or we are all dead — the whole damned world."

Tesla picked up on her declaration. "What mission? Can we help?"

I decided to tell our four new friends about everything we knew and had planned to do. My decision to brief the four turned out to be extremely fortuitous, not only for us but also for the survival of the whole world.

Anya spoke up, "Oh, I know where Tikhon is at. It is an island just off the extreme southeastern coast. I think it is about three or four hundred miles southeast from here. I know the way. Nikolai and I once hunted way down south. Strange island, but very close to the shore."

The more we chatted, the more I realized that we needed these four women with us, once we somehow handled the slavers. Although it was only early afternoon, we again set about making a large supper, figuring our two men would be ravenous when they returned. Besides, doing even these tiny things was quite a challenge. On the bright side, Danika now found she could really help Jana and Jovanna. The three did most all of the cooking.

Late afternoon, our two men finally returned, as filthy and exhausted as we anticipated. At least they were able to feed themselves, but not before Sir Dmitri swore a dozen curses over what had been done to Danika. After they finished eating, the two took turns feeding the rest of us, which we greatly appreciated. We were just finishing when a guard came by to check on us, making sure we fed our men properly.

Feeling a bit restored, Sir Dmitri outlined how their day had gone, dismal beyond words. They had to hop a long way to the mine. "Just try using a pick and shovel when all you can do is hop about. God, that was horrid. We heard rumors most men don't even last a year in the mines! We have to escape soon, Nia. Ideas?"

I was about to tell him about our new friends when someone knocked on the door and let himself inside, saving one of us the hassle of hopping over to the door to let him in. I guess he already knew that. The man was one of the Commander's magi! After shutting the door, he looked at us rapidly and moved over to Vlad, who was now sitting on his bed, completely exhausted.

"Vlad? My prince? Is that you? I thought I recognized you last night when they brought you in. I thought you had escaped," he said rather animatedly, but in a hushed voice. Vlad looked apathetically up at him. I expect to hear him say another "whatever," but Vlad was silent. "It's me, Bo. Magus Bo Chesna. Don't you recognize me?"

Vlad finally spoke, "I think I know you, but I'm not sure."

Kisha defended him. "He took a very bad blow to his head. Lost his memory. He says he's a prince, but he can't remember where his lands are or even its name."

"Damned Vlad! This is bad," Magus Bo replied. "You are in it now. The Kingdom of Zelimir. Years ago, the salvers moved in and took it over. They killed his father, King Damek Zelimir. I got Vlad out of the kingdom just before the slavers came for him. He was supposed to raise an army and come back to free us. Being a magus, Commander Arnwald has been using me and didn't turn me into one of his slave miners. Damn, Prince Vlad. Now there is no hope at all!"

"Can't anyone ever get these cursed bonds off of us? If so, we can fight," Sir Dmitri exclaimed.

"Sorry. In all these years, no one has ever had them removed. The dead are buried with them still attached," Magus Bo answered.

I decided to pump him for more information. "So what is the Commander really trying to do, Magus Bo?"

"He's got what he calls a flying ship. Apparently, it crashed around here many years ago. He's been using the iron that the miners dig to rebuild it. Now, he's trying to make fuel for it. He claims that once he has fuel, he'll take off. He's promised to take a number of us with him, his new crew, as he calls us. I don't think that's going to happen anytime soon, though."

Suddenly, Vlad spoke up, "Bo? Bo, is that really you? I'm starting to remember things. I see flashes. Fighting. Men dying. Fleeing. A hilltop fortress."

"Yes, My Prince. It's me, Bo, your best friend. We were losing the battle, and I opened a Transportation Torus to allow you to escape. You were supposed to raise an army."

Vlad sighed. "I got waylaid. Hit on the head, and I forgot everything. It's slowly coming back to me now. Is dad dead?"

"Long dead."

"That means I'm the king," Vlad muttered. "King Vlad of Nowhere."

Magus Bo had no idea how to respond. Instead, he said, "I have to go before anyone gets suspicious. If anyone asks, I was just checking up on you new arrivals." He rose, bowed to Prince Vlad, and left.

Kisha looked at her friend in an entirely new light. "Well, Prince Vlad, you are finally remembering things. That's really good."

"Yah, but what's the use? I've found my kingdom, but it's been overrun with the slavers. Nothing left. Whatever," Vlad at least grumbled this time.

Jelena, ever practical, suggested, "I think we should get ready for bed. We're all overly tired and physically exhausted. We need as much sleep as we can get."

There weren't enough beds for everyone, now that the four women had permanently moved in with us. However, Jana slept with Tesla, while Jovanna slept with Anya. Jana explained, "You see, with our short arms, we can help Tesla and Anya."

Danika took the hint and slept with me. For the first time, we lay close beside each other, and I felt I was in heaven, particularly so when Danika gave me our first passionate kiss.

The next day, the men helped Jana, Jovanna, and Danika rustle up what little food was left. We all ate a hurried breakfast. Neither man wanted to work all day on an empty stomach, and neither wanted us to have to struggle to feed ourselves. Just as they were about to head off to work, a guard came, "Boss wants to see you all first thing. Come on; up and hopping. Not you four. Just the newcomers," he resisted the efforts of our four new friends to tag along.

Jana called out, "We'll fetch today's rations for you."

Chapter 7 Escape and Revenge

A half hour later, we had hopped to the Commander's building and were again sitting on the long bench. His solitary chair faced us, as we awaited his arrival. I knew I had to take positive action this time. We couldn't survive much longer. If Kisha's arms started turning black and blue or Jelena's, we'd be in far more trouble. Yet, I wasn't sure just what I could do, not just yet.

He marched pompously into the room, this time carrying the precious log that Magus Triska had found. "Well, I see Danika's shoulders are no longer aching. See, we have a nice medical cure for what ails you," he teased and taunted me. I could not help but remember his threat yesterday. Well, it had happened, but for a different reason.

Commander Arnwald continued. "I've all your things stored in the back room. Been going through them yesterday. Now this," he tapped the logbook in his hands, "is precisely what I wanted out of you yesterday. This is ancient and comes from that downed spaceship. No use denying it, Nia Elain." I didn't, sitting stone-faced before him.

"Now after having spent a day getting used to your new lives, are you more willing to discuss things with me today?"

"Like what?" I responded.

"Like what else did Magus Triska find in that ship? Fuel? Devices? Blasters?"

"If she had found a d-gun, I assure you we would have had it with us and used it on your men. No, the ship was stripped of anything remotely useful. It was just a smashed shell. The metal isn't any good either. It's pretty well corroded now," I replied.

"Hum, that's what I expected, but I had to be sure. You can appreciate my position here. I have to get my ship operational and get off this unbelievably primitive world. So, what's the log say? Anything useful? Or was she unable to read it? Hell, we all know these primitives can't read."

"I read it. It talks about their crash landing and

attempts to survive on this world. I believe they were the original Rus people," I answered, withholding the mention of the Ceri and the impending disaster. If he didn't know about that, the better.

"Makes sense. You might be interested to know that twenty years back, we uncovered another shipwreck, south and a little west of here. Found it stripped too, damn them. Wish we could find where they took all their components though. Might have been useful; might have found spare parts we could use. Corroded shell was about all that was there, along with this log." He waved a second logbook I'd not noticed, having paid more attention to the Rus log.

"Can't read it either. Here, see if you can read it, Nia," he almost tossed the logbook to me before he caught himself. "Oh, you don't have any hands to catch it or page through it. No matter. I'll have a guard hold it for you. I'm curious if you can read any of it."

I wondered why he couldn't read it. Shortly, a guard entered, and I found myself staring at the handwritten pages. Quickly, I was able to ascertain it was another Federation of Planets ship that had crash landed here, some hundred seventy-five years ago. The language was a derivative of the Sud spoken by my friends and the agrarian peoples of Metcalf-4. I found it interesting the modern-day hunter-gatherers were so closely related to the farmers, but neither knew that fact or even suspected it. This ship had crashed around the year 1200. Further, it had been a colonizing transport, destined to establish a new colony on another of the outer rim worlds. Hence, at least they had the means to begin farming, that is, the seeds and animal stock.

The log did mention their warlike encounters with the indigenous hunter-gatherer peoples. Further, towards the last entries, it mentioned the ghosts, the Ceri, but nothing about the triple conjunction and what that represented. For that, I was thankful.

"Excellent, Nia Elain. See how cooperative you can be? And I didn't have to cut off everyone's arms to force you to speak. Now then, where is your ship? The one that brought you here. We've been unable to locate it."

"I don't know." I lied. Well partially. Until recently, I'd not worked out where our landing site was located with respect to where I was at or Jelena's village for that matter.

"I see. We did find a number of dead bodies, victims of the Slave Wind for sure. Probably, they all went mad and killed themselves. No matter. Now then, I need to move up my timetable for departure from this hell-hole world."

"Why is that?" I probed a bit. Did he know about the triple conjunction and what it meant?

He didn't say anything for at least a minute, but just stared at me. I didn't flinch. Finally, he did. "Okay, I'll level with you. Have you noticed how close the three moons have gotten?"

"Yes."

"Well, when the new moons come, they'll all be tightly aligned, very close together. It's known as a triple conjunction. One or more of us must have reacted, but it wasn't me, and I couldn't see who had. "Ah, I see you know about that. Well, we've been plotting their motions. I'm afraid I've bad news for the natives. Because of this conjunction, the pale green moon, the one they call Platon, is going to be tossed out of its orbit and will come smashing down onto this world. You know what that means? Kaboom. No more world. No more nothing here." I think I blinked though.

"So you see, I've been forced to move up my timetable. I have to get enough fuel refined so I can at least liftoff this pathetic, doomed world in time," he laid bare his plans.

I saw my opening and took it. "You need fuel, right? That's all you need to take off and leave this world forever?"

"Clever magus. Yes, I lack only the fuel. If I have to, I'll work every damned slave to death to get enough fuel refined in time," he answered frankly. I didn't doubt his threat.

I knew I had him! "I think perhaps we can make a deal, Commander."

"What deal? You want me to take you with me, just because you are from the Imperium?"

"Hardly. Suppose I could give you a full fuel cell," I hinted.

"A full cell? That would be a miracle. Hell, we could get

a very, very long way from here on that much fuel. Compatible with all standard Imperium ships?"

"Of course, compatible. Is there any other kind?" I taunted him. We both knew the Imperium had long ago standardized every spaceship engine to use a single type of fuel cell. This resulted in vast credit savings, since one size fuel cell could be used in all types of spaceships.

"You have such a thing?" he asked, very much interested, perhaps even drooling, at least figuratively.

"I believe I can get one, but it'll take a couple of days, no more than three, to get it here."

"Ah, you must know where your ship is located. I could torture that information out of you."

I had visions of him cutting off the arms and legs of all my companions, just to get me to reveal that location. I knew what I said next could well result in the mass mutilations of my friends. I chose my response carefully. "You've already destroyed the life of the woman that I love here. The others are just traveling companions of Magus Triska. So you can only torture me, rather what little is left of me. I assure you that will do you no good at all. You'll be stranded here and have to face the coming doom along with the primitives. We both know darn well you'll never be able to refine psi fuel quick enough. So you need my help."

"That may be, but if you don't want me to fly you off this rock, what is it that you want? To have the metal bindings removed? Sorry, that can't be done. They are made of a unibody, fusion construction. Even if I wanted to remove them, which I don't, it cannot be done, not without cutting the arms and legs off along with them. I don't think you want to become merely a torso and head," he taunted me. Danika, who was sitting beside me, flinched visibly.

"Obviously not. I give you a full fuel cell, and you give me complete control over your entire slaver operations here," I declared flatly.

Commander Arnwald laughed. "So you can run the profitable operation until the moon wipes everything out, eh? That's your plan? Stupid woman. You can't free the slaves or yourself. I don't see why you want this."

"Hey, you made out okay with the operation. Why not me? Maybe the moon won't hit us. Then, I can have a wealthy future. I'm willing to take that chance. How about you?" I tossed it back into his plate, knowing full well he certainly didn't want to take that gamble. He was convinced the moon would come crashing down and soon.

"I plan to take a number of my field commanders along with me. You won't have too many men left to oversee the operation," he explained.

"I figured as much, but then I'm a magus."

He was silent for a minute. "Okay. I'll agree to turn the operation over to you, but only if you produce this full fuel cell, and only after I take off in my ship. I can't guarantee you the fighters and magi will obey a crippled and hobbled up magus, though. That's your problem, not mine."

"Then, I believe we have a deal. I'll need some of my companions to come with me. Obviously, I am rather severely limited in what I can physically do," I played my last card.

"Well, you can take your precious Danika with you."

"Thanks, but I'll need hands, don't you think?" I retorted, but thankful he suggested her. I didn't want to leave her alone, not right now, not after just losing both her lower arms. She was too vulnerable.

"Take the dim-witted Vlad with you. Plus, I'll send along one of my men. He can carry the cylinder back with you."

"Agreed. However, when I return, if any of my other companions is harmed in any way, I'll disintegrate the cylinder and cancel the deal. Agreed?" I countered.

"Agreed, but if you fail to return within three days, I'll have the other two women's arms removed and the so-called knight's too, just for good measure." I nodded. "Don't be late."

"But we can't even walk," Danika whispered to me a little later. She, Vlad, and I were standing out in the street, just beyond the Commander's building, ready to depart.

"We'll have to hop and make this work somehow, my love. Be brave. I really need you now," I countered. The guard who was to accompany us finally walked up behind Vlad. The Commander and the rest of my group stood on his porch,

124

watching us. I also spotted several of his magi standing around as well. I knew his magi were going to try to follow us, that his real objective was to find the Eagle's Seed, and probably steal it. No way was I going to let that happen.

Carefully, I focused, just as Magus Triska had taught me. I whispered to Danika and Vlad, "When we start hopping, don't stop hopping until I tell you to." They nodded, and I activated my Transportation Torus, not a large one, but just big enough to handle us. Once the translucent, undulating lines of the torus appeared, I took a deep breath, focused, and began hopping carefully into the torus. I appeared just where I had planned, and focused a second time, opening another torus. Danika and Vlad, with his supporting arm around her, came hopping right behind me. The instant they reached the streets of Sana Falls, I closed the torus, keeping the guard from joining us. My second torus appeared, and we continued hopping. I kept the distances short, naturally. We appeared on some rocky ground. Unfortunately, I couldn't keep my balance and took a nasty tumble. Likewise, Danika and Vlad fell upon arriving. Rough ground wasn't suited for our hopping. The torus closed at once.

"Damn! That hurt," Vlad complained. He struggled to his feet, then helped Danika get up, and then helped me to rise. "Where are we?"

"Not far from where we left our spaceship, Vlad. I recognize this place. Come on; it should be just up ahead. God, hopping here is a nightmare."

"Hold on. Let me get my arms around each of you," Vlad suggested. His support, as feeble and wobbly as it was, helped Danika and me make it to where the ship was supposed to be at, where I had last seen it. However, it wasn't visible! For a moment, I panicked! Had dad or another survivor taken off, leaving me behind? Calm, calm, think, I told myself.

"Keep on hopping. It has to be here somewhere." We hopped a bit further and ran smack into an invisible barrier!

"God! The ghosts have us now!" Vlad exclaimed.

"Hell, I can't toss any pebbles over my shoulder! I'm doomed," Danika gushed, quite frustrated.

I laughed. "It's the ship. Someone has turned on the

cloaking device, making it invisible. Now, all we have to do is find the entrance entry pad. Crap, I don't have hands to feel for it. Vlad, I need you to use your hands and feel along here. We are looking for a small box thing about a quarter of an inch out from the skin of the ship."

An hour later, just as I was about to give up hope, he found it. Now came the hard part. I felt around with my nose, until I had the pad's dimensions firmly established. Using my nose, I punched in the code to open the bay doors. The hissing sound of the seals cracking and the low hum of the synchro motors lowering the doors was the finest music I'd heard! The two saw a gaping hole appearing, as if in the middle of nowhere.

The lights were on, but the ship was deathly silent. I called out, but no one answered me. We carefully hopped on up the ramp, but once inside, I used my nose to close the doors once more. "Look," I explained, "I know they are trying hard to follow us and to steal this ship. No way am I going to let them get this ship!"

"What now? If we could walk, I'd love to see your ship," Danika whispered, fearing the deathly silence.

"Follow me. We have to get to the supply section, near the back. At least, we won't have to negotiate any stairs. We've got elevators," I replied, but then realized neither of them knew what an elevator was. Well, they would soon find out. As I hopped along the hall, I fought off waves of homesickness. I can't believe I actually missed this ship! Well, it had been home to me for eighteen years.

By now, you are probably wondering if I was really about to give that sadistic butcher a working fuel cell, allowing him to escape. Hardly. I admit, my mind sometimes follows devious pathways. It was doing so even now. Our engineer had discovered one of our new fuel cells had a fatal manufacturing flaw in it. Arthur was meticulous about his engines, and he always microscopically inspected every fuel cell that came onboard, to say nothing of the engines, which were his "babies," as he always told me.

A half hour later, I found the faulty cell. Now, all we had to do was to get it back to the slavers. It was very heavy, posing a severe problem for us. Had we been able to walk, I think between Danika and Vlad, they might have been able to carry it, but not hobbled as they were. This, I had to work out; and I had time to figure out just how I could free us from these damnable metal bindings. Ordinarily, I'd just rummage around the engineering section, opening this and that drawer with my feet. Now, I could only hop and had to have Vlad be my arms. I can't begin to tell you how frustrating that was for me!

I had only a vague notion of what I wanted to find. Regrettably, I had not paid much attention to various engineering devices. It took me three hours finally to find the right tools! Arthur had this tiny cutting device, which operated much on the same principles as the d-guns. These, however, focused the disintegration beams into very tiny and precise beams, designed to cut a fine line through the densest of materials, pursuant to applying a welding patch to the hull in case of a dire emergency. Well, this was one, if I ever heard of one. But would it work and without hurting us? That, I did not know.

I explained how it worked to Danika and Vlad, who was very eager to try it out right now. I thought better of that. "Look, if we go back there with our bindings removed, Commander Arnwald might go back on his deal with me. We have to make him live up to the bargain. Once he and his men take off, we can then free ourselves and as many of the others that we can. There are six of these cutters. Let's see if you can hide them on our persons. Make sure they can't fall out if we take another tumble, Vlad."

He took a while, but managed to conceal the six devices on each of us. I had one stuck between my mammoth breasts, a good hiding place. That handled, I now needed a way for us to carry the heavy cylinder with us, as we hopped through the Transportation Torus. Vlad commented, "If I had my feet free, I could drag it through the torus."

Danika was near tears. She knew she had been very strong, and that between Vlad and herself, they could have carried it, but not now. Not ever for her. I could sense her grief mounting and had to act. "I know, Danika. Life has changed us. So now what you and I need to do is find alternative ways of doing what we used to be able to do."

"But how?" she whispered, afraid her voice would crack, if she spoke any louder, and that she'd break down completely.

"We drag it," I replied. Okay, I admit I just made it up on the spur of the moment. I'd not really thought it through; it just came to me. An hour later, Vlad had the cylinder securely bound in some thick ropes. He tied three others around our waists and fastened the other ends to the ropes around the fuel cell. Together, we tried to pull it along as we hopped.

Only barely. That was the result. We three began laughing at the absurdity of our predicament. By leaning forward and pulling as hard as we could while trying to manage a tiny hopping step, we did move it. We didn't stop laughing for ten minutes. Now that I think of it, that's the first time I ever saw Vlad laugh!

It took us two more hours to get the cylinder outside the ship and the bay doors closed once more. After taking a few minutes to catch our breaths, I focused and created a Transportation Torus, opening it onto the street just where we had left, some ten feet from the Commander's building. Once more, I created it as close to us as I dared. Then, we strained our leg muscles to the limit, as we pulled the cylinder while hopping forwards barely an inch per hop. I was never so glad to be through a torus, as I was that late afternoon. The instant the cylinder cleared the torus and arrived on the street, I canceled the torus. Several guards came running up to us, swords drawn. However, they quickly sheathed them, as we posed no threat whatsoever.

Presently, Commander Arnwald stepped out of his building and looked down at us. A perverse grin formed. "Well, that was fast. I figured I'd be amputating arms and legs before I ever saw you again. That was a nasty trick you played, leaving my man behind. Where the devil did you go?"

"To get you this full fuel cylinder, as agreed upon. Now unhook us, and get your ship ready to go as soon as possible. Don't forget your part of the bargain," I reminded him, figuring he'd try to double cross us. Why did I think that? He had the cylinder now and didn't need me any longer.

"Guard, escort them back to their house," Commander Arnwald ordered, stepping down to inspect the cylinder personally. We had little choice but to hop on back to our house, where the others were anxiously awaiting us.

"What happened? Did you get it? Are we going to be free?" Kisha asked the instant we hopped into the house.

Danika was very pleased to tell everyone what she'd seen and what we'd done. They were just as eager to hear all about the inside of a real flying machine. Me, I was thankful Jana and Jovanna had a hot meal waiting for us, and that they were quite willing to use their short stumps to feed us. However, as I had insisted, she didn't mention the six cutting devices we brought back. The time wasn't right. No telling what this Commander would do next. I doubted he would live up to his bargain. However, once he was gone, we could make our move, at least I hoped so.

That night, just in case of a double cross, I had Vlad hide the four cutters he had on himself in various places around the house. As it turned out, that was a wise move. In the morning, the guard came and forced Vlad and Sir Dmitri out to continue their mining operation. Meanwhile, we women worked together to get the day's rations, the needed water, and meals prepared. Our personal hells continued into the second day. By the second night, I could tell the awful toll this work was having on our two men, ignoring our own plight. I wished the Commander would hurry up and take off!

That day, I had also learned a shocking tale. I'd innocently asked Jana where all of the babies and children were being kept. After all, with all the men raping the women on a nightly basis, surely there must be loads of them around. "Oh no. When a woman gets with child, after three months, the doctor removes it."

"What?" I exclaimed. This twist took me by complete surprise.

"They called it their stem cell replacement project, whatever that may mean. No one knows what that is," Jana explained. "But honestly, what woman here wants to bring a baby into this life? We can't care for them, and what kind of a future would they have? No, perhaps this is best." I couldn't believe what I was hearing, but as my anger subsided, I understood why. The doctor was using the babies as a replenishment source for their medical machine, which used stem cells as part of its healing process. I'll admit that is the extent of my knowledge of these machines.

That night as we were again preparing for bed, particularly since our two men were unbelievably exhausted from working in the mines all day, suddenly a glowing torus appeared in the middle of our main room. Almost at once, Bo stepped through, and it vanished as suddenly as it had appeared. "Sorry for taking you by surprise, but they are watching us all closely. I came to warn you all."

"Have a seat. Thanks, Magus Bo," I replied, and he pulled up a chair.

"Okay. Tomorrow morning, they're planning to depart. The ship is located at the edge of our town, close to the mound of refined stuff the miners have been digging up for many years. He's taking twenty of us with him, two magi and eighteen fighters. This afternoon, he held a meeting with all of the rest of us who are not leaving on his ship."

"What treachery has he planned for us?" Kisha spoke acidly.

"Plenty. He told us about the bargain he made with you, but we already knew about it by word of mouth. After that, he said, 'After we take off, I don't care what you do. If you want to have that helpless, hobbled cripple leading you, that's fine with me. If you don't and if I were you, I'd remove some more arms.' Everyone took that to mean the rest of your group, Magus Nia Elain. It gets worse. One of the majors complained they couldn't do that, because they wouldn't have access to the medical machine any longer. Another complained after he was gone, they'd no longer have a way to bind new kidnaped victims to work the profitable mines."

Bo elaborated further, "I was surprised by Commander Arnwald's answer. He said, 'No problem. I'm leaving both the Medical Machine and the Binding Fabricator behind.' He said something about weight limitations, and that he wanted to take as much gold and silver with him as he could. That appeased many of the majors, who oversee much of the daily operations. He also is training two of them to be able to use the machines, claiming they are so easy to use that a child could operate them. Don't know about that, though."

"So I came to warn you all. You are not standing alone. I've made some discrete inquiries. I think some two dozen guards will be on your side. I'm sure the miners will be, but hobbled as they are, they won't be much good if it comes down to a fight. King Vlad, how do you want to handle this?" Bo finished up.

Vlad grimaced and looked at me. I answered, "We have to play it by ear. Don't take any action until you hear from us. Give us time to figure out what the situation winds up being."

Bo nodded. "As you wish. I best be off before anyone becomes suspicious." Once more, he conjured his Transportation Torus and stepped through it, leaving us with much to ponder.

The next morning, we rose earlier than normal in order to fix what little of yesterday's food remained. I thought it wise for us to eat something before the day's action commenced. This turned out to be a wise move, because a guard came by a little earlier than normal. "Okay rise and shine. The boss wants you to come and witness his departure. Come on; up and get hopping. Now," he barked, adding, "yes, you four too." By that, he meant Jana, Jovanna, Tesla, and Anya.

By the time we got out of our house, the streets were rather packed with men and women. It seems everyone had come outside to watch the "boss" and his chosen men take off. Well, I could see that. These people had been forced to work for this day for years, and now had only one opportunity to see this spaceship actually take off. On the downside, we had to hop at least a half mile to get to the site. Vlad and Sir Dmitri muttered this was nothing. They'd had to hop a couple of miles. I couldn't imagine how much they'd endured. A half mile had pretty well done me in, as well as the other women with me, except perhaps Danika.

At the edge, we spotted the rebuilt deep space transport. It looked more like a patchwork quilt of mis-matched metal patches, crude by all Imperium standards. Still, it looked to me like it could fly as long as it had fuel. Fifty guards and five majors, accompanied by five magi stood between us and the town. To our right was a giant pile of psi-crystal dust, laboriously mined and pulverized into a fine dust, ready for the final refining process that would have converted it into the fuel used to power all the vast Imperium's spaceships.

Commander Arnwald stood before his new crew, consisting of the aged doctor, two other old men, presumably from those who had originally crash landed here, and the twenty "chosen" ones. Of those, two were magi, and the rest were majors and captains, presumably the most loyal of his followers. Once we all hopped to our appointed place, Commander Arnwald spoke rather loudly. "Today is a glorious day. All these years of toil have finally paid off. We are going to depart this world now. As everyone knows, I'm officially turning over the operation of Arnwald to Magus Nia Elain and her group standing there. I bid you all adieu."

With that, he turned and marched triumphantly up the bay ramp, followed by the others. Shortly, the doors closed and we waited. Then, I heard the telltale hum of the engines firing up, a very good sign. If I had fingers, I would have kept them crossed, hoping and praying the damned ship would actually liftoff. All I could do now was wait patiently, along with everyone else. I was acutely aware of all the guards and magi standing between us and the town. I knew damn well they would not accept my leadership. Trouble would follow soon after takeoff.

At last, the ship began to liftoff, shooting out exhaust gases, rather furiously. That in turn had a side effect. The winds whipped up the finely pulverized dust. My group was suddenly inundated with the dust, causing us all to cough like mad. Fortunately, the guards were just beyond the pile and weren't impacted by the back flow as we were. Over the noise, I heard Jelena cry out, "That's the Slave Wind! It's come again!" From her frightened tone, I knew we were in trouble again. However, I doubted very much this was part of the Commander's plan. He had never indicated he had any idea what caused the magi to get their powers. I now did, and I didn't like what was happening to us.

Before long, the silverish ship rose far above us. The dust cloud began settling down, but not before we had all inhaled far too much of the stuff. All eyes were strained skyward. Many were shouting and pointing at the rapidly receding ship — all in awe, dutifully impressed with the great flying machine. No one moved, even as the ship became barely a tiny silver dot in the blue sky. When it was finally almost too small to be visible any longer, one of the majors shouted something and over fifty swords were drawn. The rebellion against us had begun. However, the timing could not have been better. At that instant, a blinding explosion rocked us all, a brilliant white light expanded outwards from where the spaceship had last been seen. I smiled; the micro-fracture in the fuel cell had ruptured from the intense vibrations of the takeoff, just as our old engineer had speculated it would. Way to go Arthur, wherever you are, I thought.

"Never mess with Nia Elain Compton or her friends," I said in a low voice, but loud enough for my group to hear.

"You did that?" Kisha gushed.

"Yep. You didn't think I'd let that evil sadist get away, did you? Not after what he's done to my Danika and all of you, let alone all the countless others, now did you?"

"Damn! You are one powerful magus!" Kisha replied. "Impressive. Guess I won't have to try to follow him and slit his gut after all."

"That's fine with me," Vlad replied. "Looks like trouble over there though."

One of the majors shook off the explosion and yelled to us, "Okay, now that he's gone, we are taking over, not you pathetic slaves. Guards, march them back to their quarters. Give us any trouble, and we'll kill you." The armed guards, swords still drawn, as if we could possibly have the slightest effect on them, surrounded us, and ordered us to start hopping back.

As we approached these new leaders, the same man said, "Tomorrow, we are going to come by, take those two women, and remove their arms too. That way, you can't give any of us any trouble. If you two men try anything, we'll remove your arms too. Now march or hop, rather," he fumbled and had to correct himself. As we passed them, I noticed that Bo was watching me, looking for any sign. I was careful not to give him any.

Back on the streets, the other slaves were talking about the explosion. Most had rightly concluded the evil boss had met a fiery end and were quite pleased. Still, they obeyed the guards' orders to go back into their homes, though they did say the women could go obtain their daily rations and water in an hour. I was really pooped when I finally got back to the house and collapsed onto my bed, Danika landing beside me.

Jelena whispered urgently, "Nia, Nia, that was the Slave Wind! We got exposed to it again!"

"I know. Okay, everyone, listen up. If you start having delusions or seem to be in some kind of mental fog, let me know at once." I had Jelena outline all of the symptoms she knew about.

"Are we infected?" asked a very worried Jana. Her three companions were just as nervous about having been exposed to the wind that drove people insane.

"Very likely, but Magus Nia Elain may be able to cure you, if you get it," Jelena advised. Me? I cringed, trying to recall all Magus Triska had said or done with me. Meanwhile, I had further problems. If I did nothing, in the morning, Jelena and Kisha would be armless as well. I refused to allow that to happen. The question was: would they force the men back into the mines yet today? I decided to take a gamble.

"Vlad, retrieve one of my cutters. It's time to see if we can free Kisha's arms at least, before they come to drag you and Sir Dmitri off to slave in their mines."

He was only too eager to oblige. "Anything to free my little Kisha!" I was surprised. He'd just expressed some fondness for her, and she also noticed it. Gone was his perpetual apathy. He had his memories back at long last.

Now came the uncertain and dangerous part. While I knew well the operation of the cutter, I couldn't use it, even if my legs weren't bound. Vlad, who had no such knowledge, would have to use it to free Kisha and without harming her arms in the process. I knew I would have to give him very simple and precise directions. First, I had him take a few cuts out of the wooden bed plank. When I though he was ready, I sat on the bed against the wall where I could see well. Kisha sat on the edge of the bed, pivoted at an angle. Vlad sat beside her, such that he could get a good angle on the chain. He cut through the chain that held her elbow bands together in less than a minute, freeing her arms, though the metal bands were still tightly around her leather sleeves.

Spontaneously, cheers broke out. No one was more relieved than Kisha, who massaged her shoulders, before rising and hopping over to the next bed, while Jelena hopped to take her place. A minute later, she too was massaging her shoulders. That was the immediately critical action. Now, if they took the two men off to the mines, Kisha and Jelena could work on the rest of us. I decided not to press our luck and had Vlad hide the cutter once more.

A few minutes later, our guard entered, ordering Vlad and Sir Dmitri out to the mines to work. Dutifully, both obeyed, and the man closed the door. "Okay, we best get our food rations before we try anything else. Kisha, Jelena, I think it will be best if you stay here and let us get the food." I was right. The fact their arms were free would have been noticed immediately. We had to endure yet another torturous morning obtaining our rations and then many buckets of water. Once more, I was pooped out, considering I'd already hopped to the edge of town and back.

This time, Jelena began doing all the cooking. She had no trouble; her hands were free. Meanwhile, Kisha practiced with the cutter and then used it to cut through all of the links holding our leg bands together. Before Jelena had our lunch ready, all eight of us women had our legs free. However, the metal bands around our legs and their arms remained. Somehow, I needed to get them cut off us as well, but without cutting into our flesh.

Kisha proved a quick study. She soon discovered a setting, which severely limited the depth of the cut. Although it was still thicker than the metal bands, she accurately estimated the thickness, holding the cutter precisely at the right distance from the bands. Before long, she had the six bands cut off my legs, with only a few cuts into my leather pants. After lunch, she worked on the others and herself. Hence, by the time that the exhausted men returned home for supper, we eight were wholly free of the bindings.

While the two ate greedily, Kisha first freed their legs and then, one by one, cut through their bindings as well. That she was becoming quite adept at this greatly pleased the little thief. Now we were free, but Vlad and Sir Dmitri had no armor or weapons. They were presumably still in the Commander's building.

I had a hunch Magus Bo would drop by this evening and was right. Shortly after dark, the torus appeared, glowing in the center of our room. A moment later, Bo stepped into our house, and the magic vanished. Yes, he was taken by complete surprise. "King Vlad! You are free of the bindings! How is this possible?" he exclaimed. I had to explain, but briefly, knowing he really would not comprehend the physics behind a cutter. The most understandable concept, I discovered, was to say it worked like the Commander's d-gun, which many had seen in operation, mostly disintegrating people.

Magus Bo spelled out the majors' plans for the morning. "Early morning, once the men are marched off to the mines, and the women have gotten the daily rations, they are going to come for Kisha and Jelena. So what do we do?"

That was the problem. What to do. Bo pointed out that twenty-five guards would fight for King Vlad, along with himself and another magus. I reasoned we'd take them on once the streets were clear. I didn't want the hobbled or crippled prisoners getting hurt in the crossfire. Plus, Bo pointed out that more than half of the guards would be off overseeing the many miners, leaving the three magi and perhaps twenty-five other guards to handle us.

"Okay, here's my plan. When the guard comes to take you fellows away, I'll kill him quietly. Hopefully, he and you two won't be missed in the morning rush. Then, when they come for Kisha and Jelena, we'll attack. Surely, they will not all be present at one time, and we can pick them off, as they come out to join the battle."

"Yes, but you are forgetting one detail," Sir Dmitri spoke up. "We've no swords."

Bo hastily spoke up, "Leave that to me. I'll get them for you later tonight." The knight grinned. I could read his mind. He wanted to teach the guards lessons that they'd never forget. I couldn't blame him. Bo also suggested he and his fellow magi, Magus Burian, would take up positions on opposite sides of the street, where they could get the other magi in a crossfire of spells. Our plans were really just by the seat of your pants plans. Okay, we were winging it. What else could we realistically do?

By morning, things took a turn for the worse. All seven women had begun hallucinating, rather wildly. They all had gotten ill from the Slave Wind, which I finally concluded came from inhaling the psi-crystal dust from which the Imperium manufactured their fuel. The two men had been far enough from it to inhale only a small amount of the dust. The only positive thing was Sir Dmitri and Vlad had their weapons and armor back and were wearing them, ready for battle. Poor Danika was beside herself. Here was a worthy battle, and not only could she not fight, she was seeing all manner of creepy things crawling the walls of our room. Whenever I got her to see that the bugs were not there, she saw the men ready for battle and broke down, bawling like there was no tomorrow. Every time she saw her own weapons and armor, she was acutely reminded she'd never be able to even lift them again. Her grief was acute and quite real.

I knew the guard would soon come for the men, instigating the battle for control over Arnwald. Yet, all I could do was move from woman to woman, trying to get each one into the present time and out of their current hallucination. By the time I had gotten to each one, the first was smack into another hallucination, just as I had endured some time back. I was gaining no ground whatsoever and then the guard entered.

Sir Dmitri executed the guard before he ever knew what was happening. Quickly, he and Vlad dragged him into a corner out of the way. The two began closely watching the street just in front of our house, peering through a couple of cracks in the wood that they had cleverly enlarged, claiming they didn't want to be taken by surprise. They had bought me a few more minutes to deal with the seven hallucinating women.

After making yet another round of trying to calm each one, the first was back to smashing her stumps onto the bed, trying to kill imaginary bugs. I was getting nowhere with this approach. It didn't help when Vlad called out, "Get ready, here come a dozen men." I had no choice but to leave the women to their hallucinations. I moved quickly to the door. The two fighters were already there, nodding to me.

Vlad opened the door. He and Sir Dmitri stepped outside, and I stood just behind them. I can definitely say our appearance took them by complete surprise. Sir Dmitri wanted to rush them, taking advantage of our surprise, but I held him back. Why? A dozen could swarm the two from all sides. Standing close to the house in a pyramid formation gave us the best defense, and I could prevent more than two attackers on each of them at one time. Besides this point, per Magus Bo, some of the guards were on our side, and I didn't know if some of these twelve were part of those who wanted to help us in the fight for freedom or not. I calculated any guard who chose to charge us was our enemy.

The dozen did charge us, and I reacted at once, dropping a conjured wall of flames on the back half of the charging men, taking six completely out of the battle. Steel met steel, as both Vlad and Sir Dmitri hacked into the first men who reached them. I spotted a major dashing out of the former Commander's building. I concentrated and shot a bolt of electricity at him, knocking him off his feet. His body went flying backwards ten feet. One man tried to sneak his way around Vlad's flank. I reacted with a circle kick, snapping his neck. Another on the other side backed away. He didn't want to test me further. His face was one of complete disbelief. Two minutes later, the first skirmish ended. The dozen were no longer living. The odor of burning flesh filled the air. Cautiously, we backed up into the house and closed the door.

"Well, that's shaken them up a bit," Vlad commented dryly.

"Aye, now comes the real fight. They'll hit us with all they have," Sir Dmitri replied. "Best get ready."

The seven women were mostly hysterical at this point. I

had to do something or they all would go mad, if it wasn't already too late. I tried to recall what Magus Triska had done for me. The more I thought about it, the less I saw she actually had really done for me. Mostly, she had convinced me what I was seeing was my own mental powers, now greatly magnified. Okay, enormously magnified.

Sometimes bright ideas just come in a flash. Perhaps, it is female intuition, if I truly am female. Hell, at that moment, I no longer knew or cared. I had to do something and I did. I focused and joined my mind with all seven of the others! For an instant, I was literally overwhelmed with their insanity. Yet, I knew it wasn't that. They were merely seeing very vividly old memories or nightmares.

I refocused and sent them all calming energies. *You have all become magi now. All these things are just your own imaginations and memories you are magnifying a hundredfold. Focus on me. Yes, like this. You are powerful. Feel the waves of energy you command. You are not ever going to go mad. You are all fighters. Focus on what you want to have happen and allow your energies to make it happen. The secret to all this is to be very specific and precise about what you want to have occur, and it will. Do not doubt yourselves. You can do this. Soon, a wall of guards and magi will be coming for us. We must stop them. We must put an end to these slavers.*

My thoughts were interrupted by Sir Dmitri. "Here they come. My god, look at all of them!" I broke my connection with the seven briefly and looked out the door. A hundred guards were swarming down the street towards our place. I spotted two smaller groups off to the right and left, suggesting they were on our side and were staying back, until they were needed. I also saw the ten majors who had retaken control of the town from us. They were standing back of the wall of men, along with their three magi.

The attack came swiftly. The three magi dropped walls of fire onto our house, hoping to burn us all out. I focused and a giant wall of water rose up out of a well and drenched the fires. A mountain of steam rose up above the house, but I was told this later on by the many witnesses. Just then, I heard my

Danika scream, "You bastards!" She'd come up behind me, focusing all her hatred, grief, and rage at the three magi. If you think she would have shot fires back at them, you don't know my Danika. Oh no, not fire. She blasted them with a wall of pure physical force, similar to the force behind a heavy sword strike. The magi died instantly — their chests were utterly crushed. Later when we saw their bodies, their torsos were but a few inches thick!

Kisha got into the action as well. One of her daggers was tossed, but she then added her own mental energies to it. Shocking everyone, her dagger flew through the air, dodging guard after guard who was in its path, flying unerringly directly towards one of the distant majors. At the last instant, he saw the dagger coming at him, and he tried to dodge it. Amazingly, the dagger's trajectory altered, finally striking him right between his eyes. "Exit one major. Never mess with Kisha!" she cursed and drew another throwing dagger.

For a minute, I just watched the effects being created by my seven new magi. Jelena's action was to levitate one of the distant majors high into the air, releasing him when he was at least fifty feet up. He too died, screaming at the top of his lungs. Kisha tried her dagger trick a second time. It had the same effect as before. Meanwhile, the twins, Tesla, and Anya dropped sheets of fire down onto the charging horde of guards.

As Sir Dmitri explained to me later on, "There comes a point in any battle when one side's morale breaks, and the army routes." With their powerful magi dead, a third of the ranks of guards aflame, two majors dead with daggers between their eyes, and another two dropped to their deaths from high in the sky, the remaining majors fled the town as fast as they could run, abandoning everything. The guards who were not on fire did the same, fleeing down all four possible streets from our place. The battle was over.

"Damn! I was just getting started!" Kisha complained bitterly. "Hey, I like my new skills. What did ya think of that, King Vlad?"

Vlad still stood before the door with his sword raised. He'd not even gotten in one swing. In awe, he turned to Kisha. What he said took everyone by surprise. "What do I think of that, Kisha? Marry me. Become Queen Kisha and protect me for a change!"

"What?" several of us echoed the same thought.

Kisha actually blushed, taken aback by the wholly unexpected marriage proposal. "Well, what say you, Kisha dear?" Vlad asked again.

"Oh, you for real?" He nodded. Kisha then said, "Well okay. You're all right, Vlad. That's saying something." He grinned from ear to ear. He grabbed her, twirled her around, and gave her a passionate kiss.

"You are deadly," Jana commented to me. You actually kicked that guard to death, even when he was coming at you with his sword. We saw it."

"I know. You can be just as deadly too. Just takes a lot of training, Jana. I can teach you all. I have to teach all seven of you and soon. You've all got great powers now," I replied.

I glanced at Danika and saw that radiant smile of hers, one I'd not seen since we had been captured by the slavers. "Dear, I'm pretty good now, don't you think?"

"Better than me, love. Better than me. Well done indeed." She stood tall, her self-pride returned.

Magus Bo and Magus Burian finally arrived at our door. Both appeared rather awestruck by what they'd just witnessed. Bo said formally, "King Vlad Zelimir, may I present Magus Burian."

"I'm honored that you are with us, Magus Burian. I will not forget your contributions towards freeing all these people and restoring the Kingdom of Zelimir. Gentlemen, may I present our new Queen Kisha Mila." She stepped forward a bit and grinned broadly. He added, "Did you see her two incredible dagger throws?"

They had and quickly the men began discussing the battle. Me, I just sat down on my bed, exhausted. The adrenaline rush was gone, and I was starving. Danika now sensed what I was feeling. She came to my side and put her short arms around me. She whispered in my ear, "I love you too. Thank you for saving me." I flashed her a smile, but she planted a passionate kiss on my lips. We both sensed my arousal. "That's going to take some getting used to," she whispered into my ear. I flushed.

One of the guards brought our day's rations to us, while another kindly brought in several loads of water. Jelena quickly set to work cooking up a hearty stew. She too was famished. When it was ready, I sat down and proceeded to use my foot to feed myself. "Look at Nia Elain!" Tesla exclaimed to Anya.

"I see, but I don't know how she can do that. Come on, Tesla; let's try it."

"Takes practice, but you can do it," I validated their fumbling efforts. Then, Jana and Jovanna decided to try it my way as well. Not to be outdone, Danika also took off her boots and took a stab at using her toes. Soon, we eight were laughing at their clumsy efforts. "Practice, ladies, practice. You'll soon get the hang of it."

Danika teased me, "Yes, but Nia dear, you've had a nineteen-year head start on us."

While the others laughed, I countered, "Only seventeen. The first two years don't count. I was a baby then." Now, they roared. Laughter did us all a whole lot of good. Emotionally, they were all a shambles. I call it a triple whammy. First, they had been kidnaped and physically bound in terrible ways, ignoring the raping that had gone on, though they'd escaped that bit of men's nastiness. Second, they'd suffered the loss of part or all of their arms, something I'd not wish on my enemies — lives are devastated by such things. Third, they'd been forever changed by the Slave Wind and its induced madness, which I'd only barely relieved. None had any grasp on what this change had really done to their minds and potential abilities. Laughter, however brief, over their pathetic attempts to accomplish utterly minor actions they'd taken for granted all their lives, only provided a minuscule respite. Long, hard, upsetting days lay ahead for the five, though Jelena and Kisha also now faced the aftereffects of the Slave Wind on themselves as well.

Yes, I could well have just stopped everything and spent our days helping these women learn to live once more, but I couldn't. The triple conjunction was only two weeks away. After that, Platon would come smashing into our world, wiping out all life, everywhere.

If this wasn't enough to handle, I also knew we had to deal with all of the other bound prisoners and the awful lives they were forced to live, from which we had only just extricated ourselves hours ago. I had six cutters and hundreds of others to free from their metal bindings. This ignores the enormity of the problem facing King Vlad, the restoration of his entire kingdom, which had been pretty much destroyed by the slavers.

So I too laughed along with my friends. Either that or cry and feel sorry for myself and everyone else, especially for Danika. I knew her old life was gone forever, but would that also take away what I so loved and admired about her? With my new gift for getting into the minds of others, I had already sensed the enormity of the loss that Danika both had and felt, and now with these other four new friends as well, though they'd been suppressing nearly everything for many, many months. So yes, I laughed along with them all.

After we finished eating, King Vlad brought us all squarely back to reality. "So how do we proceed? We have to get these new magi trained, as we did with you, Nia. We have these hundreds of other hobbled victims to free. We have to get things organized fast, if we're to survive the coming winter snows. Plus, we've what? Two weeks to stop our world from being destroyed? Where do we begin?"

"Obviously, we have to get everyone free of their metal bindings," Kisha answered without hesitation. "Look, if we're all going to die, at least we can give them their freedom of motion back before then."

"I've only got the six cutters. I don't know if there'll be enough energy in them to free everyone from the metal bindings," I cautioned everyone. "She's got a point. We have to free them right away. We should cut the elbow chains off all the women immediately. At least, that will give them back the use of their arms."

Kisha broke in. "Right. That's the easy part. After that, I'll cut all the leg chains apart, doing the women first and then the men. After that, I can cut the metal bands off of the women's arms and then their legs. If the cutters are still working, I can then do the men's leg bands." I could not help noticing she was dealing with the men last. Well, that was Kisha. Just now, I didn't disagree with her proposal.

"Okay, Kisha. Take the six cutters and have at it. Jelena, go with her. If anyone gets cut badly, let me know right away. Commander Arnwald did say he left his medical machine behind. I can use it to heal any bad cuts, that is, if it is still in working order. I will focus on training Danika, Jana, Jovanna, Tesla, and Anya, though I also need to train the both of you as well. Still, we need to head south very soon."

"Good plans. I'll see about organizing things here," King Vlad decided on his role. A few minutes later, I was left alone with Danika and the four other women. Now to their training, I thought. Without the hands of Jelena, I struggled mightily to get my copy of Triska's spell book out of my large sack. While the five looked on, I sensed their overwhelming sense of loss and grief flooding back into their very beings. When I looked up, I saw a trace of tears on Danika's cheeks. She so wanted to help me retrieve the spell book, as she always had done for me, but now she was as helpless as I was.

Silly me. I sat on the floor and used my feet to open it to the first page. That done, I suddenly realized none of the five could read! Neither could Kisha or Jelena! For an instant, I panicked. What good would this massive spell book do for them? Nothing. No, I would have to read it to them and help them grasp it. At least, I wasn't going to have to make copies for everyone like Magus Triska had done for me. Slowly, I began explaining every detail to the five eager women.

Kisha and Jelena made a good team. Magus Bo knew the total layout of the homes and the prisoners. One of his duties had been to keep accurate records so the Commander could replace those who perished. Naturally, Kisha visited the two houses that held the other women who had already lost part or all of their arms, freeing their legs completely. Jelena kept an accurate count by using hash marks on a paper. Twelve women were armless and eleven has lost their lower arms. They had divided roughly in half so those with upper arms could assist the less fortunate women. Of course, what was going to happen to these two dozen women had yet to be decided.

The six cutters ran out of charges by the end of the third day of operations. All of the women had been completely freed of their bindings, two hundred six. Three dozen were also in the first trimester of their pregnancies. There were four hundred ten men. Only half had their metal bands removed, but at least the others no longer had to hop.

The fact that not one needed the medical machine's cure was a fitting tribute to Kisha's skill with those knives. A few had minor cuts, which Jelena easily handled without a single stitch. If we could ever get out of crisis mode, I knew I'd have to go back to the Eagle's Seed and figure out how to recharge the cutters. The job had to be finished one day.

On the positive side, King Vlad discovered he now possessed one gold mine and two silver mines. With winter close at hand, he made a bargain with the freed men and women. If they continued to work the mines during the winter, the men and women could keep half of what they mined. That would give them a large nest egg when spring came, and they could finally return to their own lands and homes. On the other hand, if they wanted to remain here, he promised them royal wages for life.

As the days slipped by, I began to grow more worried. The moons were spectacular, but terribly close. Now, they were in their third quarter phases and even closer together in the sky, almost overlapping. We just had to get on with our trip. Until now, I hadn't been too worried, since Anya knew where this Tikhon was located. I figured I could somehow get a Transportation Torus up, getting us there rapidly. Worse luck. We had the first snowfall of the season. The others took the cold, wet stuff in stride, commenting upon how much easier it was to walk in the snow than it had been by hopping, but I didn't like the cold, slippery, wet stuff.

A week before new moons and the triple conjunction, the men had our horses saddled, our gear stowed along with ample food supplies. It was time to depart. Anya and the others were not yet skilled enough to construct the torus. I did the next best thing, rather obvious. I joined my mind with hers and used her memories to construct the glowing, tall torus.

Vlad insisted he and Kisha come along. "Look, you need many more hands on this trip." I couldn't disagree with him. Besides, the five were now nearly in a panic over how to ride a horse without their hands and arms. I knew precisely what they were feeling, been there, done that. Doesn't mean it isn't scary!

Fighting back tears, as she watched the men saddling her stallion for her, Danika was emotionally upset once again. She'd practically grownup in the saddle, and now she couldn't saddle her own horse. Still, the ranger insisted on mounting by herself, using her upper arms as best she could. Once mounted, she had the men tie the reins in a knot. She then held them between her two upper arm stumps. It just barely worked.

Hesitantly, Jana and Jovanna emulated her, but looked positively terrified, as did Tesla and Anya, who merely had to sit in the saddle, while others led their horses, just as they did mine. "Nia, I can't hold on!" Anya cried out to me.

"I know. Just do your best. It's frightening," I admitted, sensing a good deal of relief. If I thought it was scary, then their fears were justified, at least a little. You might also be saying I was crazy to take five equally helpless women along with me on this adventure. Look, I needed Danika's skills; she's a ranger with a superb sense of direction. Besides, Anya has been there once. These were my friends. The four had taken it upon themselves to hop over to our house to help us when we really needed their assistance. I just could not leave them behind. It wasn't fair to them. If the world was going to end, I wanted to die among my new friends.

Chapter 8 Tikhon

Danika and Sir Dmitri rode through the torus first. Jelena, leading me on my horse, followed them. Vlad, leading Anya, came through next, followed by Kisha leading Tesla. Jana and Jovanna brought up the rear. As I appeared on the other side of the torus, the roar of ocean waves crashing on the shore competed with the calling of many sea gulls. The air was humid, though chilly. We were on a low, grass-covered hill just above the beach below. I was thankful that it had not snowed this far south yet, though the chill in the air told me it would soon come.

To the southeast and southwest, the blue-green ocean swept off as far as my eyes could see. The day was slightly windy, and I could see small whitecaps on the waves as they rolled into the shore, only to break up and sweep swiftly up the brown sands, before dying out and seeping back from whence it had come. Picturesque, yes. More importantly, due south lay a low lying island, Tikhon, or so Anya claimed. I hoped this was the "right" Tikhon.

Behind us, a few trees dotted the horizon. Likewise, a few also grew on the island. From our vantage point, I could not see the southern edge of the island. Later, I learned it was roughly triangular, with its curved base facing us, some twenty miles long. More importantly, a rather imposing stretch of water separated the island from the mainland. Our hill ended in a rather steep cliff, dropping seventy feet to the brown sands below us. Other than the crying sea birds, the area was totally deserted.

As we sat on our horses surveying the landscape, I retold what little we knew about this place and what theoretically had happened here in the past. I pointed out, "Look, take it from me, this skyward shooting beam of light just has to be some kind of repulsion beam. That means there must be some alien machine somewhere around here, rather large I would expect, that activates every hundred twenty years to push Platon back into its normal orbit, keeping it from smashing into our world here. Trust me; it takes quite a lot of force to push something as massive, as heavy, as that moon must be. That much force must require a rather large piece of alien machinery. Hence, we are looking for some kind of large, foreign-looking equipment around here somewhere. It should be plainly obvious, once we spot it."

"Perhaps there are some clues on the beach," suggested Kisha. Sir Dmitri and Danika scouted along the eastern side of the hill for a way down, while Vlad and Kisha did the same to the west. Both found an easy way down to the beach about a mile on either side of our position. A half hour later, we rode along the sands, stopping just below where we'd arrived. Here, the cliff's edge had been eroding over time. A large chunk of earth had somewhat recently collapsed, forming a mound that covered the sandy beach.

"Maybe it is on the island. That would keep most everyone from finding it," Kisha volunteered.

"But how do we get across the waters?" Danika asked. "I don't know how to swim. Besides, even if I did, I can't now."

"A torus," I replied quickly, before the others began reacting to their inability to swim, if they had been able to before. I never could swim, though I enjoyed being in the water, as long as it wasn't too deep. I focused and conjured another torus. Minutes later, our horses walked out at the other end on the sandy beach of the island called Tikhon. A number of gulls on the beach protested our arrival rather noisily, but didn't stick around to see if we'd leave.

Danika continued studying the ground here, just as she'd done first on the hill and then on the beach. "No signs of any people having been here or horses either," she reported. "It's just a desolate stretch of coastline. Perhaps this machine is inland."

Tikhon was fairly flat with a few trees. The ground was rather rocky, but a hardy grass insisted this was its home too. The horses appreciated that, munching while we decided what to do next. At last, I took Danika's suggestion that we split up and search the island. Half went around the western sides, while the other half traveled the eastern edges. We met at noon at the southern point of the triangular island. Jelena and

Kisha kindly fixed us some lunch.

We'd no more than finished when a thunderstorm hit us full force. Most of us were soaked before those with hands got the cloaks on those of us without them. Cold was the rain, made even more so by the chilling effect of the strong winds. To be expected, winter was almost here. After it passed, miserably cold and wet, we rode together down the middle of the island. Once again, we found absolutely nothing at all, save a few trees. Late afternoon, we decided to make camp here in the middle of the island, where most of the trees were growing.

While Vlad, Sir Dmitri, Kisha, and Jelena handled the horses and made camp, Danika insisted on scrounging around for firewood. I watched as she determinedly dragged a dead branch into camp, her upper arms clamped awkwardly around it. I didn't need my magus skills to sense her intense frustrations and grief. All her life, she'd been the outdoors woman, and now she could only barely manage to drag some driftwood into camp. Still, Jana and Jovanna watched her and volunteered to help her find more.

"We can't do anything to help, can we?" Tesla whispered to me. She, Anya, and I were sitting with our wet backs to a tree. I sensed both women's huge sense of loss and their feelings of complete helplessness.

All that I could say was, "I know. I can't either, but we can light the fire once they are ready for it." All of us spent a rather miserable night.

The next day, once more hopeful of finding something, we began searching again. Alas, by noon we were back at the northern edge of the island, having found no trace of anything at all, except sea birds and turtles.

However, as we rode out on the sandy beach, disheartened somewhat, all of us were shocked to see that the beach had nearly doubled in size! "How can this be? I thought the waters began about here?" Danika protested. "Has the land risen or the ocean sunk overnight?"

"Wait! Tides. I forgot about them. The sun and moons cause tides. When the three moons are close together, they ought to pull more water towards them, making really high tides and also very low tides later on," I rattled off, not knowing if these people even knew about such things as tides.

Danika gave me a funny look. "The moons pull the water up?" she asked incredulously. "Well, I can claim ignorance on this one. This is the first time I've ever been to the ocean." So I explained a bit.

"Ah, so it is a really low tide now?" Sir Dmitri grasped the concept swiftly.

"Right. And perhaps more importantly, a really, really low tide at the time of the triple conjunction. Probably the lowest and highest tides the coast has during a hundred twenty years," I explained.

"I get it," Danika gushed out. "Perhaps then, what we are looking for is only visible at such times. Like that incredible mound of collapsed cliff across the waters. Look how much the cliff has slumped down."

Kisha asked, "Can this alien machinery thing operate from underwater?"

I frowned. "Well, who knows about alien things, but if it were an Imperium device, the answer is no. Water and electricity don't mix."

"But," Danika persisted, "if the ocean goes lower, it might make the alien thing be above the water. Then, it could work, perhaps."

"Good idea. You might be on to something. Maybe we should camp near here and keep an eye on the water level." I didn't know what else to suggest. My biggest fear was we were in the wrong place entirely. If so, this would be all for naught, but I didn't dare tell them that.

Everyone was pretty much in agreement that this spot or better just below the cliff was the likely location. Once more, I opened a torus, and we walked over to the mainland beach. We set up camp just above the sandy beach, where the grasses began. Why? We figured the high tide would not reach the grassy area, but stay on the sands. "Twenty-four hour observations, gang," Danika ordered, taking charge as she used to do. "We'll keep our lanterns going all night and keep watch at low tide times. Something must happen within three days. That's how long we have." We all glanced up at the moons, visible here in the daytime, just east of the sun, tiny crescents. A few more days and they would be nearly invisible, new moons. Only this time, all three would be having their new moon phase at the same time and almost at the same location in the sky, though not necessarily that close in space. Still, Platon would be close enough that the gravity pull from the other two moons would distort its orbit, sending it crashing into our world.

Anya and Jana gave us the next morning report. Anya explained, "Gang, the low tide was even lower last night. More of that mud from the cliff was exposed. We think we might have seen something else down there, but we couldn't be sure. It was too dark and the lanterns, not bright enough."

Sir Dmitri grumbled, "You know, it might be nice if we had some way to predict the times of high and low tides, but I admit, such things are way beyond me." The others chuckled at the impossibility of such predictions, though I knew some of the crew on the Eagle's Seed could have worked that out for us. Thinking that, I felt a pang of grief over their deaths. Doesn't grief ever end? Time heals all, it's said. Why wasn't it working with me? Answer that one, if you can.

All day long, we kept watch, milling around, and occasionally glancing at the shoreline, waiting for the waters to recede further again. Most of us sat on the sands, which grew warm as the day progressed. The men foraged for more firewood, giving them something to do. Waiting was not something Sir Dmitri was particularly skilled at, and King Vlad had many other things on his mind. Me? I kept oscillating between fear we had the wrong place and fear we'd not find it in time to save the world.

Late afternoon, Anya suggested, "Hey, I think the ocean is going down again. Look, that mound wasn't there the last time I looked." We all got up to take another look. I think she was right. The ocean was going down again, but would it reveal anything useful, I wondered.

Reveal. That was the key word just then. While we stood peering into the mud from the cliff subsidence and the receding waters, from the corners of my eyes I spotted Ceri! Not one, but many! I was not alone; the others also saw these yellowish, glowing forms, humanoid in shape only.

151

"Karsh!" exclaimed Danika, "I can't even toss a pebble over my shoulders to protect myself any longer! The ghosts are going to get me!" She made rather pathetic waving motions with her upper arms. Both twins were doing pretty much the same thing, waving their stumps about, warding off the "ghosts." Anya and Tesla couldn't even do that much. Both somewhat nervously stamped their feet up and down on the sands, as if they were about to dash off any second. However, Kisha, Vlad, and Sir Dmitri grabbed some pebbles and tossed them over their shoulders, muttering to themselves.

I didn't see the pebbles had any effect on the dozen glowing forms. Rather, they didn't seem remotely interested in us. It's hard to see anything with great clarity from the corners of your eyes, but I'd say they were also looking at the same mud pile that we were carefully watching.

As I stood there, my senses alert, I was acutely aware of many conflicting emotions. Anya and Tesla were bordering on terror, hugely exacerbated by their sudden sense of complete helplessness. All they could physically do was nervously shift their weight from foot to foot. I felt way too keenly their emotions and frantic thoughts, notions I'd never really experienced before. I was born without arms, so I never had them to depend upon or use. They had and were once more re-experiencing the utter fright of not having their arms when they most needed them. I found this a rather unusual sensation. They were now true magi with enormous other powers, far beyond normal human beings, and yet they were wholly unaware of this, focused entirely on their tragic loss and the helplessness that they felt without their arms and hands to protect themselves. In a flash, I finally understood Anya and Tesla, and also Jana, Jovanna, and Danika as well, who were radiating similar thoughts and emotions, but to a slightly lesser extent, since they still had upper arm stumps to wave about, for all the good that did, next to nothing, which is precisely what the three thought about the actual worth of their stumps to their lives.

While these emotions and thoughts were by far the strongest that I was sensing, they were by no means all I was being deluged with. No, I sensed another loss, and I began to zero in on it, quite curious about it. Something was lost, gone, and it had to do with the mud pile that was slowly appearing at the shoreline! Now I began zeroing in on those thoughts. They were coming from several minds, of that I was certain. Each mind has its own unique feeling about it. I found it rather chaotic, mingling with the terror, grief, and hopelessness from my friends.

It's gone. We can't get in there now. We're all doomed. What can we do? Don't know. This is really bad. What happened here? The entrance is gone. Is this finally really the end? We're never going to get off this planet.

Right there, I decided these Ceri were real, and that they must be some type of alien life force that had not been encountered in the vastness of the Imperium. A life force. My instant conclusion, based mostly on my intuition, was they were sentient beings. I was still just getting used to hearing the thoughts of my friends and had even less experience at placing my thoughts into another's mind. Unable to actually view these Ceri directly, let alone speak or hear their voices, assuming they even had such a thing, I decided to make an attempt at communication. Why not? We had somehow to figure out this strange machine the ancient Rus log had suggested always seemed to save the world from Platon's smashing hit. Superstitions or not, I wasn't about to flee for my life. Thus far, they didn't seem remotely threatening, and I certainly am not afraid of "ghosts," mostly because I've never seen one.

Hello. I am Nia Elain Compton. We've discovered some ancient logs that suggest some kind of energy beam comes from around this location every hundred-twenty years, when the triple conjunction of the three moons happens. The pusher beam moves the Platon moon away from its perturbed orbit, which threatens to smash into our world. Do you know anything about this? Can you even understand me? We can sort of see you.

Talk about instantaneous confusion! Apparently, my thoughts were received by these Ceri. Further, they were both shocked and totally surprised that one of this group of primitive humanoids was sufficiently developed and intelligent enough to actually be able to communicate intelligently with them. They were aware that such humanoids could sometimes just barely perceive their forms.

Could these primitive humanoids have sufficiently evolved? Another countered. *Well, they have had eight hundred fifty years to do so, since we got here, well not quite that long. We had this place to ourselves for the first five hundred years.* Another added its thoughts. *Perhaps we should attempt to reply. I believe one or more of them are picking up what we are thinking.* The first added, *Perhaps we should warn them.* The second countered, *But they already seem to know what is about to happen.* The third suggested, *We are all going to perish, so why not see if they can understand us?* The second said, *Then, you do it. I don't want their slimy energy over me.*

While they were thus engaged, I sent calming waves over my group. Then, I sent, *Hey, these Ceri might be willing to talk to us. They aren't here to harm us. Join with me and listen in.* One by one, I felt the intimate touch of the women struggling to join me. I've no words to describe this feeling.

This is a surprise. You may call me Andarin. You have evolved sufficiently to communicate with us. How amazing. What are you doing here at this location?

Hi Andarin. I am Nia Elain. We are here trying to make sure that Platon gets pushed back to where it belongs and doesn't come crashing into our world, wiping out all life.

I see. How do you know about this location?

We found some ancient logs of the Rus people, who crash landed their spaceship here around three hundred seventy-five years ago. It spoke of a beam of light that rose from Tikhon up to Platon, pushing it back after Orya and Dessa pulled it out of its orbit during the triple conjunction, which happens only once every hundred twenty years. However, we can't seem to find its precise location.

You are well informed. Alas, we are all doomed now. As you can see, the cliff has subsided and has buried the secret entrance. No longer can we get inside to run the equipment. This time, there will be no stopping the collision with this world.

154

Can't we dig out the mud?

We are unable to do such a thing. The Ceri have evolved into nearly pure energy beings. Long ago, we forsook flimsy humanoid bodies. We, along with all of you, are now doomed.

I see. So the mud just has to be removed, is that it?

Yes, but the volume is more than your humanoid bodies can move. Six of you do not seem even to have the appendages for digging any longer. It is hopeless. We shall die together. Besides, entrance can only be gained at the lowest tide, which will be in another twenty of your hours.

What if we can remove the mud in time? Can your people then run the machinery to prevent this disaster from happening?

Yes, of course, but there is too much mud and dirt and so little time. With only four of you to do the digging, it cannot be done in time.

We must try. Let us see what we can do. I broke the connection. Now, we had something specific that we could do.

"The ghosts are real!" exclaimed Anya, quite shocked by what she'd just heard.

"He didn't sound like he wants to harm us," Tesla ventured, although still rather hesitant.

"They are still scary," Danika whispered. "How can we move all that dirt and mud in time? Most of us are helpless, Nia."

"You are all forgetting our magi powers. I know. I've not yet gotten you remotely trained, but we can do this. We use our powers to push and shove the mud off to the western shore, away from the collapse spot," I suggested.

We seven walked to the edge of the landslide zone. "Watch what I do and see if you can do it too," I suggested. "Magus Triska told me not everyone can do the same actions. So don't worry if you can't do it. I think we'll be using earth elemental forces and maybe a bit of water elemental too, not fire or air elemental forces. Let's give it a try. Somehow, someway, we must open this cave-in back up so the Ceri can save our world."

I focused and began creating a sort of scooping action.

Small quantities of the dirt rose up, moved some twenty-five feet further on down the shoreline, and landed there. Back and forth I went. My attention was fully focused on the task at hand. Tesla soon managed to emulate my actions, while a half hour later, Anya was able to master it as well. Danika didn't, but found another way to help. She created a force push, much like a bulldozer blade, pushing small mounds up and out of the hole and over to the ever growing pile.

As the mound grew, the amount of water also being moved and already in the mud caused the pile to start oozing back into the hole we were steadily making. At this point, Kisha, Jana, and Jovanna saw a way to help. They dropped small walls of fire on top of the pile, while Jelena kept a steady breeze blowing across it and out to sea. Steam clouds rose and floated off. I couldn't help but smile. We were a team.

Near dark, Andarin contacted us all. *You should stop now and wait for the lowest tide to come. You are amazing. We Ceri believe there is hope that we can avoid the collision. The Ceri had no idea the humanoids on this world were so close to evolving into higher beings!*

Most are not like us, I must honestly admit, Andarin. Can you let us know when we need to dig some more? He agreed. Only then did we seven realize just how fatigued we actually were. We'd used up an enormous amount of mental energies. All of us were too tired to even make an attempt to feed ourselves. Perhaps, Andarin and the Ceri also realized this and stopped us in time.

Sir Dmitri and Vlad had not been entirely idle. They'd procured more firewood and had a crude stew and hot tea waiting for us. They teased us a good deal, though, while they fed all seven of us. After that, they helped each of us get into our blankets. I swear I was asleep before I hit the ground.

Morning came way too soon. I just wanted to sleep in, as I often did as a young child. However, the smell of bacon made my stomach demand otherwise. With sleep in my eyes, I got up, but once more saw dozens of the Ceri surrounding our camp. Of course, they were just barely perceptible at the periphery of my vision. Sitting before the campfire, I slipped off my boots so I could eat breakfast. "Damn, it's cold. I'm freezing my feet off."

Sir Dmitri chuckled and proceeded to lend me a hand. "Cold on hands too. It's going to be today. We live or die. Strange. I could see some great battle between two struggling armies that decide our fate, but this? Well, it depends on these ghost-like creatures we can't hardly see and their strange machines. Aliens. Our lives are in the hands of these aliens, not good, strong fighter hands."

Danika had just gotten up as well. She'd come over to us and overheard him. His last words started another flow of tears down her cheeks. "I'll never be able to wield my sword again, and I was a good, strong fighter, Sir Dmitri. I was dad's heir, and now I'm so useless I can't even feed myself, let alone fight to protect my kingdom or our world."

Sir Dmitri's face turned quite crimson. He knew he'd put his foot into his mouth this time. I sensed this knight had considered Danika his best friend and picked up his surface thoughts indicating he had trusted his life in her hands many times. Now, he was being forced to totally reconsider their relationship. A rough and tough personality, though honorable, he knew only fighting. Dealing with us six was totally foreign to him. He knew he'd blundered, had significantly upset Danika, and felt ashamed.

I picked up additional thoughts from him, not good ones from our point of view. Apparently on this world, losing a limb or two in combat was rather commonplace. I spotted his internal conflict. Those who had become "disabled" were subsequently considered worthless, and, as a result, he'd disassociated himself from them, sometimes abandoning them to their fate, even though they'd once been considered a friend of his or at least a fighting buddy. The latter action I took as being somewhat less than a "friend."

Ranger Danika had been his closest friend, but now in his eyes she was a mere helpless woman, dependent upon him for everything, something a fighter could ill afford. He wanted to disassociate himself from her, and yet he could find no honorable way to do that. The situation was made even more acute, since he was the sworn knight of King Jereni, her father. Worse, she could well become the new ruler.

I intervened a little. "Sir Dmitri, you have to give Danika and the others some time to learn new ways to do things. They have immense potential powers, but need time to learn how to use them. In time, they'll be quite impressive in their own way."

"You don't have to stick up for me, Nia," Danika sniffled sadly. "It's so humiliating. I didn't even get a chance to fight back. If I'd lost them in a battle, I could handle that, at least I think so, but not this way, not as a helpless victim. I can't be a victim. I have fought against that my whole life, and now I am one and will be one for the rest of my worthless life. No use pretending otherwise, Sir Dmitri. That's just the way it worked out for me. Be better for everyone if I would have just died."

Sir Dmitri wanted to say, "Don't say that." However, even as I picked up his intention to say that, he thought better, saying instead, "I'm truly sorry, Danika." He wisely said no more.

You can't argue or reason with grief and tragic loss. The victim isn't rational, no more so than trying to hold a rational discussion with an angry man. If you don't believe me, try it some time. Reason is the furthest thing from their thoughts. Time is supposed to be the Great Healer. I seriously doubt that philosophy. The loss will never just "vanish." For these women, the loss would be with them every second of every day for the rest of their lives, a constant reminder.

Instead of plying my love with sympathetic platitudes, which I personally passionately hate to receive, I changed the topic. "Well, if we are not successful today, then we don't have to worry much more about it. We'll all be quite dead. Let's eat up and get ready for the action."

Chapter 9 The Triple Conjunction

Around noon, the ocean level had really sunk, far below what it had been yesterday. I didn't need the Ceri to tell me now was the time. However, Andarin did so anyway. *Can you dig the last bit out now? We have only a few hours to do this.*

Tesla, Anya, Jana, and Jovanna were still very nervous about the presence of so many aliens around them. Well, so were all of the others, for that matter, but they could toss pebbles over their shoulders to ward off the Ceri. That thought caused me to smile. A whole lot of good that superstitious action actually was. If the Ceri wanted to, I'm sure they could do something nasty to us humans. In all probability, a pebble did absolutely nothing to them. If they were more energy than matter, a pebble was akin to a dust particle hitting us humans. Nevertheless, we all set to work on the remaining muddy slope at the bottom of the cliff.

An hour later, we could see bedrock. In fact, there was a tunnel carved into the rock below the cliff, just opposite Tikhon. As we all assembled there, I noticed the rock surface showed distinct signs of having been melted. How very strange, I thought. As we peered into the dark tunnel, the Ceri moved close around us, spooking the four rescued women more than the rest of us. Again, I picked up their thoughts — they felt particularly vulnerable.

Andarin sent to us all, *We have decided you ought to get a chance to see what is inside. You have earned this much. Do not touch anything and stay in the center of the chamber.*

Magically, lights turned on. The walls themselves provided a strange, but strong lighting. It wasn't phosphorescence, but some kind of electrical fixture, alien in nature, but akin to our usual fluorescent lights. What was going on here? As we moved into the rather large oval chamber, I spotted a large control panel ahead. With averted vision, I spotted a number of Ceri hovering over the knobs and dials. What kind of chamber was this?

Then it struck me. This was a control room of a

spaceship! It wasn't an underground chamber filled with electronics. I sent, *Andarin, when did your spaceship here crash on this world?* I didn't call it Metcalf-4, because they likely didn't know it by that name. Neither did the inhabitants for that matter.

He replied, *You are very observant, Nia Elain. Yes, our exploratory ship crashed landed here in the year 500.* (Note, I've converted the year to the Imperium Standard Calendar year for your benefit.)

So your people have been stranded here for eight hundred seventy-five years? I asked pointedly.

Andarin replied simply, *Yes.* I didn't press the issue. Instead, we all watched as the control panel became alive with flashing lights. A low hum could also be heard coming from what must have been another room beyond this one.

It was at this point in time that I began to pick up emotional and troubling thoughts, not from us, but from the Ceri! *Too low on power. Might not have enough power to stop it! Have to try.* Again, the thoughts came from several minds, and I grew worried again. However, I decided to let Andarin relay any word to us.

Perhaps a half hour later, Andarin sent, *We are ready to fire it up. You should leave and stand back on the shore, well away. The electrical energies might harm your bodies.*

Okay, but will it work? I asked.

The ship is about out of energy. We are not sure if there will be enough to work this time. I will let you know. I sensed he was being honest with us. Quickly, we hustled out of the spaceship, down through the tunnel it had made during its crash landing. Once on the shore, we decided to move a thousand feet away, just in case. Now we watched.

"Look! You can see the new moons," Sir Dmitri pointed up close to the sun, which was low in the sky. I admit, it was an incredible sight. Sunlight reflecting off of Metcalf-4 bounced back to the dark sides of the three moons, which in turn reflected some of it back down to us. We could see the faint glow of the three moons. What was so striking was their movement. Ordinarily, one would have to watch the moons over hours to see their slow movement against the background stars. Now, they were almost overlapping. You could see them moving over each other, partially eclipsing each other.

I tried to figure out which moon was which, but in the very faint light, I just couldn't tell. Danika did. "Orya is covering Dessa now. Platon is moving in towards both." As I watched, Orya completely covered Dessa. The now faster moving Platon moved over both of them. For a brief instant, only Platon could be seen, but it soon moved apart, far more rapidly than I'd suspected. I realized the moon had just undergone the slingshot effect. I recalled our astronomer, Roger, explaining that a common trick to increase speed when not in hyperspace was to use the gravity of a heavier body. "Fly close and use it's gravity to slingshot you around the other side, traveling much faster." I rather wished Roger was alive and could see this in operation.

Just then, a yellow energy beam shot up from the buried spaceship. It streaked in a straight line, hitting Platon squarely in its center. For a second, I thought I could see some light on the moon where the beam struck it, but that was mere suggestion. It was definitely a pusher beam. The rapid movement of the moon began to decrease. It was working.

Just as we began cheering, the beam fluttered twice and vanished. "That must not be good," I said to no one in particular.

"Hey look! The ocean is coming back!" Vlad pointed out. I looked down and saw the ever in-rushing waves were now moving very close to the tunnel! The tide was coming back in. If the Ceri didn't come out soon, they would be buried under tons of water! "Can you see the Ceri yet? They'll be trapped if they don't get out soon."

We all turned out heads this way and that, trying to catch a glimpse of the yellow ghosts. As the waters rose higher, I spotted them running out of the tunnel, then over and through us. For a moment, I wondered what it would feel like if one of them bumped into me.

I was about to try to reach out and contact Andarin to find out how it went, when he touched my mind. *Nia, I have most difficult news. Our machine is out of energy, and there is no way to recharge it. Alas, there wasn't enough to push*

161

Platon back into its original orbit. We have around thirty days before it comes smashing into the world. I am so sorry, but we have failed this time.

Thank your people for trying, Andarin. At least, we have thirty days to try some other approach to push it out of the way. If we could get a hold of many Nuclears, we could maybe break the moon into many smaller pieces. When those hit, the damage might be smaller. If only Platon wasn't so massive, I could even try to pull it back with our deep space transport.

He thought to me, *It is time for you to get your people and horses way back from this area. We are going to blow up what remains of the buried ship. It is of no use to us any longer.*

We did as asked. Shortly after that, a large blast came shooting out of the tunnel, preceded by a giant shot of water. The ground shook. Not surprisingly, the edge of the cliff rose up a little and then slumped down even more, burying the destroyed spaceship once more.

"Well, that's that," Sir Dmitri concluded. "We're all going to die in a month. Wonderful!" His sarcastic tone said it all.

Andarin, we can't just give up. There must be other ways. I reconnected with him. Him? I just assumed that the Ceri had sexes.

We can see no way to avoid it. They've already made the decision to self-dissociate soon.

What's that? It didn't sound like a positive step.

We consist more of energy than of matter. When we dissociate, our energies return to the universe at large. It is equivalent to your humanoid body deaths.

But you can't just give up and die. There must be other ways to get Platon out of the way.

We can see none.

Okay. Where did you all come from? At least you ought to tell us something about your race. Are there more Ceri out there? If we somehow survive, are there other Ceri that we can contact and tell them about you? I decided if they were bent on self-destruction, then perhaps they'd tell us their story. I was curious. The Imperium had never encountered a non-human race before, at least as far as I knew.

We are an ancient race. Our worlds are in the globular clusters in the halo that surrounds the galaxy. Your people populate the spiral arms, where all the younger stars and planets are located. The stellar birthplace is our term for the arms with all their gases. The distances to our clusters are vast, and your race has never ventured that far above or below the arms. So there is no one for you to contact. Our own communications were destroyed long ago when we crashed. I am ashamed we were unable to save your world this time.

There is no shame, Andarin. I just think it is a bad idea to give up so soon. We still have a month to move Platon out of the way. Surely, we can put our heads together and figure something out.

Alas, we have no other ways, Nia. Perhaps, you should pray to your gods, if you have any, and prepare yourself for the end of all things, much as we are doing now. It is no disgrace to choose the time and place in which to end your existence. It is your life and no other's.

Well, I ran out of persuasive arguments. I did agree with him, that it is our own life to do with as we choose, but I wasn't about to just quit and give up, not until the very end. Tenacity. That's what makes us humans. We've a tenacity to life that other species do not. That's how I see it.

That evening as we sat solemnly around our campfire, we could not help but see the Ceri dying. Like large fireflies, a yellow glow flared up very brightly, and then was gone, that spark never to return. Although we'd only known these ghosts, the Ceri, for such a short time, we all felt somber and saddened with their deaths. No one spoke, but we all watched the extinguishing sparks.

In the chilly morning, once more the four with hands took care of those of us who didn't. Still no one spoke much at all, until we sat back to enjoy the rapidly cooling tea. "So now what do we do? Head home and wait for the collision and death to come?" asked King Vlad. "What a waste! I spent years trying to find my home and kingdom. Now that I've finally found it and found the woman of my dreams, is it all for naught? I can't believe this is really the end of our world."

"Will it hurt badly?" asked Tesla, rather innocently.

"Should we warn my village?" asked Jelena, who was starting to get homesick.

"Tis a battle we cannot win, eh Danika?" Sir Dmitri suggested. "Perhaps, we should return to the king and tell him the world is ending in a month."

I picked up her thought. *I can't face dad! Not like this!* She raised her stumps illustrating her unspoken thought. He took her gesture as non-committal.

"I suppose I ought to let the people in my kingdom know that we've failed," King Vlad joined in, sounding very disappointed.

"But I don't want to die," protested Jana, shaking her head. Jovanna nodded just as vigorously as her twin did. "Isn't there something that we can do about it?" The twins looked at each of us, questioningly.

I sighed and said, "I need time to think. We didn't endure all this just to die in a month."

"Couldn't we do it in someplace warmer?" Kisha suggested. "We're awfully exposed out here, besides it could snow anytime." I agreed and opened a Transportation Torus back to Arnwald. Once there, Vlad and Sir Dmitri headed off to consult with Magus Bo, while Kisha and Jelena handled the unpacking of our horses. Once more, the six of us were unable to do much to help them. Instead, Jana and Jovanna clumsily prepared us some hot tea. Me? I just sat back down on my old bed to think.

At least we six were now able to handle our physical needs. The house was warm, and we could use our feet once more. I knew without a doubt that I didn't like cold and snow. As I sipped my tea, I knew everyone on this world was going to perish in less than thirty days. None of them had even the remotest possibility of handling this moon catastrophe. No, as I sat there sipping, I knew if Metcalf-4 was to be saved from this catastrophic disaster, I would somehow have to do it. There wasn't any other choice. I could sit back, watch it happen, and die myself, but I'll be damned if I was going to do that.

I'm not stupid. I know what I know and what I don't. Planetary orbital motion is not one of them. Roger was our astronomer. He would have known just what would have to be done to Platon to avoid the coming disaster. I admit I do not. But Roger was lost, just like all the others of our crew, including mom and dad. At least, I had found no sign of them when I was at our Eagle's Seed. I needed a place to start and chose our ship. Was there any chance any of them had survived the Slave Wind? If so, they could help me.

What if they really were dead? Then what? That thought bothered me. While I could easily go visit the ship, if no one was there, then what? The only thing I could think of was to call someone for help.

Ah, but who? Again, I silently cursed myself for never having paid any attention to the comm center and who dad's boss was. Other than my martial arts master back on Descartes-3, I knew no one else on the Imperium worlds. Right then, I realized just how sheltered a life I'd led, flying among the stars with mom and dad in search of new planets. I decided I could just send out an emergency broadcast and contact whoever was listening in, hoping for the best. Having made up my mind, I told the other women my plan.

Just as I finished my explanation, the men returned. From their sour faces, I knew something else had gone wrong. Sir Dmitri just slumped in a chair. King Vlad took off his heavy cloak and sat on the edge of the table. "Bad news," he began. "Bo and some others took a trip to Zelimir City, about a hundred miles northeast from here, my old town. Evidentially, the Commander didn't tell Bo and us everything. Our grain supplies come from the farms up there. Guess what? The Commander made a second, even larger, slave town out of my hometown!"

After several curses from some of us, he continued, "Damn him. He's enslaved nearly everyone there, bound them just like the men and women were here. Only there are a whole lot more in Zelimir City than there are here! I can't begin to tell you how bad it is there. Bo's report was dismal. He estimates there are five hundred guards, magi, and majors running the farming city. There's at least a thousand bound men working the fields and handling the butchering, and over fifteen hundred women bound just as you all were. We've only touched the surface of the Commander's slavery."

He added with a huge sigh, "But maybe it won't matter. We'll all be dead in a month anyway." Kisha went over to him and gave him a supporting hug. Our mood changed drastically. Our great victory seemed pale in comparison to what else lay just northeast of us. All that we had done, all that we'd accomplished seemed to evaporate like water on desert sands.

At last, I spoke up. "Gang, I'm going to return to my spaceship and try to call for help. Maybe I can get someone to come and help us get the moon away from us. We should deal with Platon first. That's the most critical one. If we don't, nothing else matters. King Vlad, I promise you if we can get the moon out of the way, I'll lend you a hand in freeing your people."

"You are right," he replied soberly. "If we don't do something about Platon, then nothing else is really going to matter is it? We'll all be dead, one way or the other."

I added an afterthought. "Say, if the doom does come, I can take a bunch of us away from here in the spaceship! None of us has to die."

That brought a spark of life to the group. "How many can you take?" Kisha asked.

"Probably thirty or so, but I really don't know. I'll have to see if I can find out how much weight the ship can handle. In the meantime, be thinking of who else we want to take with us, if we can't stop Platon from smashing into the world." In hindsight, I managed to give them some hope and something to consider. They began speculating on who the other twenty-one people might be.

Since the hour was getting late, I decided to make the trip first thing in the morning, right after we had breakfast. "No, we travel light," I explained while eating Jelena's pancakes. Sir Dmitri had wanted to take our horses. "Anything we might need is in the ship. It's warm inside too." That brought a smile to several faces.

We did don our heavy winter cloaks. After all, it was

cold outside and snowing giant flakes. Winter had come. While the others were used to the snow and cold, I wasn't. I grimaced as I stepped outside into the white street. Focusing, I opened another torus and led our group through the portal. We arrived close to the ship. To my surprise, it was visible now, covered in the white stuff. So much for a cloaking device. I guess the inventors had not considered the effect of having the ship covered in snow, making it visible. Unlike the previous trip here, I was able to find the keypad quite readily. It stuck out in the snow over it. Using my nose, I punched in the numbers, and the bay doors opened, much to the excitement of everyone else. Most had never seen a real spaceship.

I had Vlad and Danika give the others a tour, while I headed to the control center, where the comm system was located. Now, it was up to me. I tried to recall everything I'd ever seen or heard about its operation. Slipping off my boots, I used my toes to turn it on and adjust it. I had no idea what frequency to use or who to call. For a moment, I cursed my silly ignorance. Instead of listening to countless language disks, I ought to have been learning how to use the comm system.

"Hello. Anyone out there? Mayday. This is an emergency. I need help badly," I spoke in Imperium Standard into the microphone. I repeated this several times. I was about to give up and try some other settings when I heard a voice replying! Thank the stars!

Chapter 10 Unexpected Assistance

A woman's voice came over the speakers. "Hello. This is Marisol Blackwater. Who are you? What is your emergency? Where are you? Over."

"Thank god! I am Nia Elain Compton. I'm on Metcalf-4. The star is a yellow main sequence one, known in the Imperium catalogues as #149325. It's in the very outer rim. I'm only nineteen. Everyone else on our ship, the Eagle's Seed, is dead, at least I think so. We were exploring new worlds for the Imperium. The people on this world are rather primitive by Imperium standards. Anyway, one of the three moons is about to smash into the world. It's going to happen in about thirty days, unless someone can come here and help us. It will wipe out all life on this world. Please, can you help me? Over."

"Okay. Can you switch to video feed? Over."

"What's that? Sorry, I'm unfamiliar with the comm system. How do I do that? Over."

I received some instructions and flipped a switch. Now, I could see the woman with whom I was talking. "Okay, that's better. I'm taking control over your outer cameras so I can see the world just outside of your ship. Oh, Nia! You've lost your arms? Over."

I saw a pretty, black haired woman sitting at the controls of her comm system. Her hair was quite long and very wavy. She was quite attractive, I thought. "No, I was born without them. Please, can you help us? I've made a lot of friends on this world, and we don't want to die. Over."

"Hang in there, Nia. I'm using your ship's outer cameras now to look at the world. Meanwhile, my friends are looking up your location on the star charts. What?" She was obviously suddenly distracted by some unseen person. "Oh sorry. We've located Metcalf. Really, it isn't too far from us. We're on Ashford-5. What can you tell me about this moon? How do you know that it is about to ram into the planet? Over."

I admit I probably overdid it. I chatted on for over a half

hour, outlining everything that had happened to me since I got here, paying particular attention to the Ceri and their repulsion beam, which had failed to push the moon out of the way. While I was explaining all this, the others wandered into the comm system room, gathering around me and staring at the image of the pretty, young woman on the monitor. Of course, Marisol also saw them via the video camera, which was pointing more or less at me.

After I finally said, "Over," Marisol replied. "Okay, Nia, you and your friends stay there on the ship for now. I'll get back to you in say six hours, and let you know what can be done about the impending moon-planet collision. I think would be near your suppertime. Will that be okay for now? Over."

"Yes, thank you, thank you. Over."

"Until then. Over and out." Her image vanished from the screen.

"So who was that?" Danika asked. "She's really very pretty, such lovely hair."

"Someone with a long name. Marisol something. She is on Ashford-5, wherever that is. Come on; let's see if we can figure out where her world is located," I suggested. I took them to the navigator's room. After we all squeezed in, I used my toes to operate my favorite "toy," the galactic projector. A three-dimensional representation of the galaxy appeared, hovering in space.

"Wow! What is that?" asked Anya. I realized none of my friends had ever seen the galaxy before. I patiently explained, while using my toes to type in Ashford. The galaxy swirled and began zooming in on one section of the spiral arm. It stopped with a star highlighted in red, far out near the rim of the galaxy.

"That's where this Marisol is located, on a planet circling that small reddish star there. Now let's see where we are," I explained, typing Metcalf into the projector. Shortly, another star was highlighted in yellow. It was even further out in the rim, but not all that far from Ashford, which I thought was very encouraging. They would not have to travel too far to get here.

169

Danika commented, "So the fuzzy streaks in the nighttime sky are really this arm thing?"

"Precisely, Danika. Clever of you to spot that. Yes, the streak is the arm looking edge on. Here, I'll rotate it so that it looks like it does from here." I fiddled with the controls a bit and presto, they saw the galaxy as seen from Metcalf-4. I further backed the view out, and soon all were able to recognize what they always saw in the very dark sky. All were most impressed.

Danika then asked, "So what are all those brown dots and the tiny white dots? Are they stars too?"

"The white ones are dying stars, called White Dwarfs. They are very old, tens of billions of years usually. The brown ones are called Brown Dwarfs. Those are stars that didn't quite make it into becoming a real star. They are quite small too."

"Gosh Nia, we really are primitives, aren't we? We know next to nothing about all these things and this ship. Everything is so foreign," Danika commented.

"Not really. You all know quite a lot. It's just there is a vast amount to know. I admit I know so very little of what there is to know. But right now, I could use a good, hot bath. Come on; let's use the showers and the clothes cleaner machine," I suggested.

I showed everyone how to use the showers, and for we women, how to use the electro-static hair dryer that I so missed all these days. Danika tried it out on her lovely black hair. The drying machine literally separated every strand of her hair, dried it, and settled the hair back down, leaving it magnificently combed, both full and straight. "This is ten times better than a good brushing, which I can't do any longer!"

"I know. I miss this machine. There, what do you think of mine?" I asked, as the machine finished up with my hair. My waist length hair was parted in the middle, falling luxuriously and very full to my waist, hiding my shoulders, just the way I liked it.

"You look gorgeous, Nia," she praised me and then tentatively gave me a passionate kiss. I responded in kind, and she gently rubbed her short arms over me. I shivered all over and my extra organ activated. We both laughed at that. For the first time ever, I didn't feel ashamed of having it.

Danika whispered, "Have you ever done it?"

I flushed. "Never, but I'd love to now."

We were still naked from our shower. The next thing I knew, Danika had me lying on my bed. Nature took her course, but we both had the most intimate experience ever. Later, I learned we'd gone into a total rapport with each other, almost a shared, single beingness. When we finished, we needed another shower and to use the electro-static hair dryer once more.

Meanwhile, the others, following my directions, had our clothes cleaned. Most were leather, and the machine did an excellent job of cleaning them. When Jelena helped Danika and me into ours, the clothes smelled like fresh leather. Later when we all met up in the galley and dining room, everyone chatted quite enthusiastically about the showers, hair dryer, and clothes washing machine. Sir Dmitri commented, "We need one of these washing machines back at your dad's fortress, Ranger Danika!"

She laughed, "No, I'd rather have one of those hair drying machines. Just look at our hair — so full, so straight, no tangles. Picture perfect." We women chuckled.

Next, I used my toes to operate the food dispensary. While everyone ate what I fixed, everyone, including myself, greatly preferred "real cooking and real food." I laughed, "No kidding. This is slop compared to what you all eat. See, we don't always have things that are better than you have. I'll take your food any day to this stuff!" Everyone roared. They began to see that even though I came from a highly advanced world, not everything was "more advanced" than what they had.

Our hunger satisfied, many decided to take a nap. Kisha, Danika, and I took the six cutters and headed to the engineering room. I had to find a way to recharge the cutters. If I couldn't, then thousands would be bound for life in their chains. I made a mental note to ask whoever came how they could be recharged, if I couldn't figure it out on my own. Alas, I couldn't, but the others had a grand time examining all the tools and equipment in the large room. I had my hands full trying to explain them to the pair. Okay, figuratively, all right?

After we gave that up, we three headed off to take naps ourselves. Later and refreshed, I decided to start teaching them all how to read and write. After all, the new magi just had to learn to read if they were ever going to master all the spells in the large volume that Magus Triska had given me. I thought this beginning lesson went fairly well, all things considered.

I kept careful track of time though, and we were all sitting or standing around the comm center when Marisol's call came through, right on time I thought.

"Marisol of Ashford-5 calling Nia Elain of Metcalf-4. Come in if you are there." She repeated it twice before saying, "Over."

"We're here. Hi Marisol. I hope you have some good news for us. Over," I replied very anxious. If I had had fingers, I'd have kept them crossed. Instead, I crossed my legs. Superstitious? Okay, a little. So much depended on her response to our desperate plea for help.

"We are sending a transport to you now. They will be leaving shortly, bringing along people who can evaluate the situation and recommend ways and means to deal with the moon's impending collision. They should be at your location around nine tomorrow morning, your time, assuming it is late afternoon there. Please stay with your ship until they arrive. Over."

"Fantastic! Yes, we'll be here. Thank you, thank you!" I exclaimed forgetting to say "over." It didn't matter. Her smiling face told all. We signed off, and let out a collective cheer. Naturally, my friends asked me if these people could actually move Platon out of the way and if they too were godlike. I had no good answer, save to keep on hoping they could somehow save us. I could see how they thought of Sky People as godlike.

After supper, I needed to find everyone quarters for the night. Since my old bedroom was way too small and though I felt a little funny about it, Danika and I took my parent's room. One nice thing about being onboard the Eagle's Seed here in the wintertime, it is warm, unlike the nearly unheated and drafty wooden homes I'd been in thus far. Instead of sleeping in our clothes just to keep from freezing, we stripped.

All rooms on the spaceship had nighttime lighting. That is, from dusk to dawn, the ship automatically turned on floor-level, dim lights. This allowed anyone to see where they were going, in case of an emergency. "Nia, you are incredibly shapely," Danika whispered to me. We were both standing, having helped each other undress. My thick, long black hair draped down my shoulders to nearly my waist, outlining my mammoth breasts, tiny waist, and wide hips. Her cute, black hair with their enticing bangs over her forehead was only about half the length of mine. As far as I am concerned, Danika is the sexiest woman I had ever met, and I was eagerly anticipating climbing into bed with her.

Just then, Tesla, Anya, Jana, and Jovanna slipped quietly into our room. They too were naked and ready for bed. The twin's long, light brown hair was nearly as long as mine and looked rich and thick, thanks to the elector-static dryer. Tesla's long and very blonde hair contrasted with Anya's black hair. In the dim light, all four looked incredibly appealing to me as well. I sensed Danika was also feeling aroused by them as well, and I felt less embarrassed about my own feelings. Then, I flushed, remembering all we magi could easily sense what another was thinking or feeling.

Tesla spoke for them. "Nia, we have to stick together. We're scared too."

"Come on it. Let's sit on the bed," I answered softly. They didn't need any further invitation. While Danika sat on my left, Tesla quickly perched on my right, while Jana sat beside her. Anya gracefully sat down beside Danika and Jovanna squeezed in beside her. "So what are you scared of?" I asked, preferring not to probe their minds directly. While I could do that — any of us could do such a thing now — I preferred not to do it. It didn't seem right to probe another's private thoughts.

Tesla leaned her head towards my shoulder. "We four have been talking a lot about us and our future. We just wanted to find a kind man, get married, and raise a family. Maybe help him work the fields and put up food for the winter. You know, we just wanted to be ordinary wives."

"Tesla, there's nothing wrong with wanting to be a wife and raise a family. That's a vital part of life. Without children, there is no future," I replied, not quite grasping what the four were so concerned about. I soon would.

"We know. We're not fighters like Danika or Kisha. We're not healing witches like Jelena is. We're just ordinary young women," Tesla continued, choosing her words carefully, I thought. "But now, all that's been taken away from us." I frowned, and she hastily went on, "Like we four are and you two as well, no man is ever going to want to marry us. Why should he? We're almost helpless. Besides, after what we've all been through, we don't want a man anywhere near us — I mean in bed, that is." She fumbled for words.

Anya backed her up, "She's right about that. Go on, Tesla. Tell her."

"We know that now we six have to stay close together at all times so we can help each other with everything. None of us is independent anymore. We can never be truly independent again, so we have to stick together," Tesla explained.

"I know. We really do need each other's assistance," I admitted.

"But we still want a family and to have babies, Nia. You can give that to us. We know it for sure. We couldn't help but sense you and Danika doing it. We want us to be one big family and have you help us have children too. We don't want to break in on the love you two share, but we want to share it too. Please, don't deny us this one last chance to become what our hearts most greatly desire: to be mothers and raise a family. Look, if we six are always together, we can help each other out with the babies. I know Anya and I will have a hard time with them, and you will too, Nia. Jana, Jovanna, and Danika can help us too. We want to be a marriage of us six, though we know Danika will always be number one with you. Please, you just have to help us with this. We all promise always to be with you, no matter where you go or what you do. We really don't want to live alone, not as we are now. We can't, not really. What's the point of it, if we can't have and raise a family?"

"Please, Nia," Anya begged. "You've rescued us, but if

we can't be together, helping each other survive, and have children, what's the point in rescuing us? We've nowhere to go. No one will want to take us in. We're a total liability to them. Please, you must. We all promise to give you as much pleasure as we can, and all our help and love. Please."

Jana added her viewpoint to the mix, rather startling me with it. "Look, Nia, you are the most unique woman in our world. No woman here is like you. You are very, very special. The gods have sent you to save us and our lives — to give us a way to be real women again. You can't deny that. Just look at we five. We don't have what you were given by the gods. Surely, you have been sent to us by the gods to help us women. In return, we all promise to always be with you, to give you all our love, and to give you all the help we possibly can."

Behind their pleadings, I sensed a huge volume of suppressed grief. Yet, their resolve to do this was quite strong. Further, I sensed something else, something ghastly. In a flash, I knew if I did not go along with this — their only solution they had to their lives — then they had no more reason to continue to live, and would likely find ways to end their lives! This thread of hope for the future was the *sole* consideration that was keeping them alive!

Me? I had no such thoughts. I've never had arms to depend upon and to later lose. I had no such feelings, though I knew damned well my body was totally different from all other women and men, in more ways than one. Still, it was mine, and I was content with it, having known nothing else. Now, the stark reality these five were facing struck me, as though someone had taken a hammer to my head.

Further, there was no use in denying I was highly aroused by Danika and head over heels in love with her. Plus, I was also quite attracted to these other four young women as well. Maybe they had a point. Maybe this was why my body was the way that it was — to help other women who had no other alternatives in life. Suddenly, I had a purpose, a reason that my body was the way it was. Until this instant, I'd always looked upon myself as being something of a freak of nature. I'd met no one who was remotely like myself, body-wise, that is. Perhaps, just perhaps, this was the reason for my body's existence.

Just then, I remembered something my mother had told me a long time ago. We were sitting on my bed, and she was brushing out my hair before bed. "Nia Elain, you are a very special girl. God made you different from me for a reason. One day when you grow up, you will see that for yourself."

"Why mommy? Why am I different?"

"God has a unique role for you, my darling Nia, a very special role. I don't know what that maybe, but you must always trust in him. One day, you will know what that is to be. Surely, I don't know, but it must be very, very special for him to have made you so different." I took comfort in that back then. Now it seemed I'd finally found what God's plan for me actually was! Spooky. Where was this God? Who was he? I knew I had no answers for such speculation and tossed them from my mind.

"Okay. I do love Danika, but I also admire you four as well. If Danika doesn't mind, perhaps we can all work and live together as a large family. There are things I don't have any way of doing, obviously. Together, we'll find ways to do them for ourselves," I answered.

The relief that Danika and I felt from the four was intense. Danika spoke up, "Nia, they are right. In our world, no man will want *anything* to do with us. We're helpless cripples, constrained to begging for handouts to survive. But together as one, we might be able to get by. Certainly, we're never going to find a man to love us. On that, you can count! Wherever we go, we can expect to be more or less shunned by everyone. I dread returning to dad and the Kingdom of Jereni. We'll be stared at as freaks and shunned by all, pitied too. We might be able to use their pity to get some food and shelter out of them, though."

I didn't like her summary of what our life on this world would become. Surely, people would not be as heartless as she was making them out to be. Mom, dad, and everyone else on the Eagle's Seed weren't like that. But then, they were not "primitives" eeking out a marginal existence either. I will admit up front, that at this point in time, I'd forgotten completely about our magi abilities. They didn't seem to matter much at the moment.

"Okay. From now on, it will be we six together, always. I don't think I can do it five times in a row though." The five laughed heartily, embarrassing me.

Danika explained, "Even the heartiest of men can't do that either, despite all their bragging and boasting." I grinned sheepishly. She added, "But we'll need a much larger bed." We all giggled and crowded into the bed made for two. As I finally drifted into sleep, I felt the short arms of the others resting on me, reminding me of the comfort that I once had from my mother. Security, safety, and love. I think the five finally got a very good night's sleep and for the first time in a long time for four of them.

In the morning, we wiggled into our clothes. When Jelena came into our room to help us dress, she only had to handle the ties. With renewed hope, we headed off to breakfast. Kisha's cooking filled the halls of the spaceship. With breakfast done, we donned our heavy cloaks, slipped on our fleece-lined boots, and headed outside to await the arrival of our rescuers.

Punctual. Their ship arrived precisely on time, rather amazing, I thought. We spotted the silver bird high in the sky overhead, slowly descending, growing larger and large by the minute. "Sky People come!" Jelena exclaimed, pointing out the ship. She was the first to spot it. Outside, it was both cold and snowy. An inch of the white stuff covered everything. I found myself thinking why can't it be spring or summer?

I recognized their ship's type as it grew closer: a deep space transport, not even half the size of the Eagle's Seed. Well, they aren't going to be able to use that ship to push Platon out of the way, I concluded. The ship landed not far from us, and eight men and women walked down their bay ramp — three men and five women. Compared to us, they were strangely dressed. All wore heavier pants, warm boots, and thick coats, warm I guessed, wishing I had one of them. They appeared to be in their mid-twenties, though I later learned they'd used the Rejuvenation Machine and were in their mid-seventies.

"Hello. I'm Doctor Andy Hammil. My wife, Doctor

Mindy. Can you understand me? What language should we use?" He spoke in Imperium Standard, which only I could understand.

"Hi. I am Nia Elain. They don't understand you. Their language is a derivative of Slavic. Do you know that one?"

"Ah, sort of. We've been listening to the language disks on our short trip here. Let me try it again, though we'll sound pretty crude. I'm Doctor Andy Hammil. My wife, Doctor Mindy." He observed everyone now smiled and nodded, though his words were sounding like pretty poor Sud. "This is our physicist, Theo Hammil. Our astrophysicists, Diego and Ann Valen. This is Maggie Childa. Lisa and Lissi Laag-Hammil." They all had quite unusual looking yellow eyes.

I quickly introduced my group of ten. "Let's go inside where it's warm," I then suggested. They followed us up the ramp, and Lisa shut the door for us as she entered. We went to the planning room, the largest space on the ship. When they took off their heavy winter coats, we all got quite a surprise! Until that moment, I thought I was unique in the universe with my mammoth breasts. Even I stared at these eight, who all had knockers as large as mine! Even the men!

Doctor Andy spoke up. "I see explanations are in order. However, I think it best that Theo, Diego, and Ann take off, inspect this problem moon, and see precisely what the situation is. Will that be okay?"

"Of course. Please, you have to find a way to keep it from destroying the world," I replied. The three nodded, put their coats back on, and left us. Meanwhile, Dr. Andy continued his explanation, which all of us really wanted to hear.

"Nia, you are not alone. We eight are also victims." He began a lengthy explanation of the genetic agent or bio weapon that had been unleashed on the Imperium almost a hundred years ago. After all these years, I had a name for my type of body: hermaphrodite. Further, these men also had female organs as well as their own. We all found it hard to believe that these men had had a number of babies themselves. Yet their mammoth breasts were convincing in their own right. Even more curious for we six women was the fact that Lisa and Lissi were married and had raised a large family, with each giving birth to five children over the years.

I also learned this terrible genetic weapon had caused many other genetic defects, most all of which had been cured by these two geneticists and others. More importantly, I learned the first real clue about my own origin. Many of these victims who had children had no choice but to give them up for adoption. I now had several likely planets on which I might have been born and where my birth parents lived.

Tesla asked, "So it is not strange that two women can marry and have babies?"

Lisa chuckled. "No, not at all. Back then, there were more of us women than men. Normal men didn't want anything to do with us. Luckily, Lissi and I fell in love with each other. So it all worked out perfectly, right Lissi?" Her mate grinned and nodded.

Dr. Mindy then said, "Nia, we took the liberty of looking up your medical records from Descartes-3. You were given the genetic cure that should have regrown your arms."

"Yes, but it didn't work out," I explained, going into a lengthy tale of what had happened in the Slave Wind and our subsequent capture by the slaver men, one of whom had literally pulled them off my shoulders.

"We are both doctors, Nia. We would like to take a few minutes to examine everyone's health. Would that be acceptable?" Dr. Mindy asked.

"Jelena is a healing witch and a good one. She's healed me up fine, but perhaps it would be wise for you to check us all out," I replied.

"Okay, do you have a medical machine on this ship?" she asked. Of course, we did. Though that room was only large enough to hold four, we all crowded around and watched, as one by one, she and Andy gave each of us a complete checkup. Meanwhile, I continued our long tale of what had happened, picking up where I'd left off, when I came down with sickness caused by the Slave Wind and continuing to the present, including our episode with the Ceri.

King Vlad added, "But we've found another slaver's encampment. They've taken nearly my entire city's people captive, binding them just as they did us. If you can stop the world from being destroyed, then we have to rescue all of them."

"Right. First things first, good thinking, King Vlad," Andy replied.

Dr. Mindy asked, "Tell me more about becoming a magus. Just what powers does a magus have?"

I began in again, outlining all that Magus Triska had taught me, and what effects we had executed thus far, including being able to pick up other's thoughts and emotions. "I think I know what is causing people to get sick from the Slave Wind." I explained about the Commander's giant pile of psi-crystal dust that he was planning to refine into fuel. "During his takeoff, the exhaust covered us all, and we inhaled a lot of it. They all came down with it right after that. Plus, Jelena said it was the same odor she always smelled when the Slave Winds blow. Somehow, this dust must be causing it. I think it killed my parents and the rest of our crew last fall when it got me."

I continued, "So now I'm trying to train them in how to use their magi powers, but first I'm teaching them to read and write." I elaborated on this, explaining about Magus Triska's spell book that she'd given me. I had a fascinated audience, that's for sure.

When Dr. Mindy finished checking on Danika's health, she announced, "Congratulations, Danika. You are pregnant."

"What? Really? Oh!" she exclaimed. "We only did it yesterday." She flushed red and so did I.

"Yes, come July you will likely have a daughter. Congratulations."

"Oh, Nia! It does work. I'm going to be a mother! I'd given up all hope of that," Danika exclaimed, still shocked by the news.

Tesla added, "See Nia. We are right. We can still have families!" All four nodded and hovered around Danika, who didn't quite know what to think of all this unexpected attention or the fact that she was pregnant.

By the time the doctors finished our checkups, the other three had returned. "Good news and bad news," Diego reported to everyone. "The good news is Nia is correct. That moon passed too close to the other two during the triple conjunction and its orbit was perturbed. It is going to keep getting closer to the planet here until it collides. But the tidal forces will wreak havoc long before the two actually collide. We have less than a month to fix it."

"Can you help us? We don't want to die," I asked.

"We're certainly going to try, Nia. If we can't, then we can bring a whole lot of transports to Metcalf-4 and rescue all of the people, relocating them to another world," Diego explained. "So don't fret, you're not going to die, but we have lots of work to do. How's everyone's health?"

"All are fine, including Nia's shoulders. Evidently, the slaver's used a medical machine to remove arms and lower arms," Doctor Andy answered formally. "I think we should hold a conference to work out how best to proceed here and check in with Queens Linda and Rael and Governor Misty. Nia, if you don't mind, we'll return to our ship and contact our bosses. Will you and your people be all right for a while? Do you need us to do anything for you?"

"No, we are fine. Please, find a way to save our world," I replied. They agreed, donned their heavy coats, and left us for a while.

Once we were alone, Sir Dmitri commented, "Danika pregnant! I never thought you would be having a baby. Nia is it?"

She flushed, "Yes, so what of it? I'm a woman, after all. Did you think I'd not want to have a child one day?" She got quite defensive.

He flushed, "Well, not so soon I suppose."

"Well, I can't do much else now," she replied testily. "We both know the fate that awaits a fighter who loses their arms or a leg."

"Occupational hazard. We both know that," he justified. "Still, your father isn't going to abandon you, is he?"

"We both know dad," she countered. He grimaced.

"But how will you all live?" he asked, growing more flustered.

"We six can get by. We help each other," she countered.

He salvaged his blunders. "Well, I won't toss you to the wolves. Let me know when I can do something for you, all of you." That eased the mood, and I suggested it was time for tea.

Back in their ship, Dr. Andy said, "Okay, make sure your mental barriers are up. We have eight wild telepaths in that ship. What they call magi are what we call *mentales* gifted! They've no training whatsoever and only rudimentary notions of what their power are. Worse, they've all suffered tragic losses. The emotional state of five of them is precarious at best. We've got a real mess on our hands."

"They are all in dire need of Basic Therapy. Plus, they know about the psi-dust as being the cause of their magi gifts. Nia is no dummy," Dr. Mindy added. "Lord knows how many more of these magi are out there. Do you have any ideas about how the moon problem can be handled?"

"We should compare notes and call the queens and the governor," Theo advised.

Shortly, Queen Linda, Queen Rael, who were married, and Governor Misty Childa-Bellweather appeared on the large monitor. Theo spoke first. "We've got a real mess here. Nia is right. One of their moons is on a collision course with the planet. Less than thirty days before this world is annihilated. We need a few more days of observations to pin the exact trajectory down. That's the least of our problems. Here, I'll let the doctors fill you in on the worst of it."

Dr. Andy relayed their basic findings. "What's really going on here is a variation on our own *mentales* gifts. Here, they call it the Slave Wind, because it usually causes insanity. Those that survive are called magi or sorcerers, since they have a range of actions, similar to ours. Nia has already figured out that inhaling the psi-dust is what is causing the change. Plus, there are areas in the mountains where this dust is prevalent, picked up by certain winds and spread over some of the surrounding lands. Right now, including Nia, there are eight untrained telepaths here. Lord knows how many more of these magi are out there. We've a real problem. Over."

Queen Linda replied, "Well, so much for our peace and tranquility. If word gets out that there are telepaths on Metcalf-4, there'll be a race to see who can get there first and kidnap them."

Her mate, Queen Rael added, "We need to prioritize actions. First, we'll need to deal with this moon. While that is happening, give Nia and the others Basic Therapy. Once that's done, they are all going to need official tower training."

Linda interrupted her, "But how, dear? Send some of our tower's members here? That's not going to fly. Besides, that will only alert others to what's going on there. We have to keep this a secret."

Governor Misty took her turn before the camera. "I have two ideas. Give me twenty-four hours to work on them. Meantime, get all the observations you can of this errant moon, particularly its mass. Also, gather all the data you can from them about this new, alien race, the Ceri. That is vitally important as well. Over."

Theo replied, "Okay. Will do. Twenty-four hours then. By the way, we're having a hard time with their language. According to Nia, it is a variant of Slavic, not found much in the Imperium. Nia believes these people are descended from two crash landings of Federation of Planet ships. The Rus are hunter-gatherers, while the Sud are agrarians. The two only get along marginally. Apparently, Nia believes the Rus came first, around three hundred seventy-five years ago, while the Sud are more recent, a hundred seventy-five years ago. These slavers definitely were from the Imperium. Check on a Commander Arnwald Berend. He was the one responsible for bringing human slavery to this world and in a big, sadistic way. Find out about him, if possible. Over."

They agreed and the connection was ended. Dr. Andy suggested, "All right. I'll work with the two men. You ladies can handle the women, at least to start with. Perhaps, Kisha and Jelena will allow me to work on them, after I finish with the two men. We best get started now."

Lisa added, "I have dibs on the ranger, Danika. She's cool, but buried in grief. She'll be a tough case, I suspect."

A short while later, our tea was interrupted by their return. "Good news," Theo announced to us. "Our scientists are working on a way to get the moon out of the way. We must make more observations to determine the moon's mass and path. We'll know far more in twenty-four hours, I promise."

"Meantime," Dr. Mindy picked up where he left off, "on our world, we've developed a powerful mental therapy that helps a person erase all of the mental and physical trauma they've suffered. If you have no objections, we're going to start giving that to all of you starting now. I'll take Jana. Lisa will take Danika. Lissi will handle Tesla, while Maggie does Anya. Andy is going to do King Vlad and then Sir Dmitri."

"I've no idea what you are talking about," I complained. "It's not going to hurt them, is it?"

"On the contrary, Nia. You will see. It's going to help restore life and vitality to them," she answered.

"Only getting my arms and hands back can do that," Danika protested, fighting back her emotions, which once more threatened to surface. As a ranger, she had long suppressed them. She had to.

Dr. Mindy answered her and the rest of us, for that matter. "We can genetically reverse what was done to Nia's body, but it only works once. Since she's lost the regrowing arms, she, like the rest of you, is going to have to live as she is. Imperium medicine has yet to perfect a way to regrow limbs that have been lost. I'm truly sorry about that. Still, Andy and I continue to work on that problem. One day, we hope to be able to regrow lost limbs, but that's in the future. Now, let's get started, shall we?"

In a private room, Lisa began working with Danika. "This isn't going to amount to anything, Lisa. Around here, losing both arms is a death sentence. Honestly, you should all just put the six of us out of our misery. The others think we can work together and make a go of it, but who's kidding whom? We're as good as dead, the walking living."

"I understand, Danika. Close your eyes. Good. Now let's return to when you were first captured by these slavers. What are you seeing there?" Lisa began, nudging Danika into her nightmare experience.

Two hours and a bucket of tears later, Danika shrieked. "That doctor tells me it doesn't hurt — that I won't feel anything. I didn't, but now I do! This hurts worse than getting cut by a sword!"

"I understand. Please continue, what happens next?" Lisa was correct in her observations of the women. Their huge loss was right here in the present time. Insufficient time had passed for them to bury the trauma sufficiently. Even with the others who had lost their limbs a year or two earlier, they still felt their loss acutely. Their continuous nightmare hadn't ended, until Kisha had cut them free of their leg bindings. Still, she knew the process was likely to take days to erase this particularly nasty trauma in the women.

Kisha and Jelena fixed a hearty supper for the group. They enjoyed experimenting with the onboard food processor, putting a little of this and that into the mix. While both would have preferred to cook with their own local food supplies, they were intrigued with the alien machines and the "food" that it produced on demand. Unable to read the menu items, they punched in tiny quantities of this and that, tasting what came out. If it suited them, they added more of that into the mix. Finally, Jelena stumbled upon the bread-making machine. Both made good use of it, serving up freshly baked bread to go with their "stew."

"Hey, smells good, Kisha, Jelena," I praised them, when I entered the dining room. As usual, I used my toes and the other five tried to emulate me, as they continually did. Wisely, our alien guests allowed them to make their awkward, fumbling attempts to deal with eating.

When we finished, Dr. Misty suggested we all get a good night's sleep. "Therapy takes a good deal out of you. Get plenty of sleep and good food. Tomorrow promises to be an important day. We should hear back from our scientists too." Filled with some hope and an admonition not to talk about what had gone on in therapy sessions with others just yet, we did as asked. I think she also knew we needed more time to get ourselves ready for bed than normal people did. She was right about that.

The next day was awfully boring for me. Tesla, Anya, Jana, and Danika spent most of the day in their therapy sessions, along with Vlad. Kisha, Jelena, Sir Dmitri, and I began poking around the personal possessions of my parents and the crew, storing them into shipping crates. I decided if we couldn't find any trace of them, I'd ask these people to see the crates were returned to their relatives, probably back on Descartes-3, though in fact I honestly didn't know just what planet they had all called home world, other than mom and dad.

On the positive side, at breakfast, I asked Theo if he knew how to recharge the cutters. He didn't know what I meant, but Kisha proudly showed him one. "Ah, those. Sure. Let's drop by engineering, and I'll show you." Kisha was elated to hear that bit of news. Of course, they needed a full day to recharge, but this meant we had a way to rescue the thousands of other prisoners later on.

Late afternoon, all the sessions ended an hour before supper. Why? They expected to hear back from their bosses. Meanwhile, we hung out around the galley chatting. I sensed the four women were feeling more alive and cheerful, though they followed their therapy giver's advice and didn't specifically talk about it. "Have to wait until we're done," Danika said. "Then, I'll tell you all about it. I do feel better, that's something."

In addition, that afternoon, some of the villagers from Jovan came to see the new Sky People. Jelena met with them and returned to her home for a brief visit. When she returned, Jelena reported her mother was delighted she was still alive. They'd lost three villagers to the unexpectedly early Slave Wind. However, they'd not heard from the other Sky People since that time, confirming my suspicions they had perished.

Onboard their transport, the group anxiously awaited the return call from the queens and governor. At last it came. "Hi all," Governor Misty began. Once more, the three women appeared on the monitor, sitting beside each other in the queen's comm center. "Got a lot of news, all good. I discussed this situation with our new Emperor Bino Sanguro. He agrees with our assessment. Metcalf-4 is a potential powder keg. His solution is to admit Metcalf-4 into the Ataro Empire, as the fortieth world. He has already put that motion before the Senate and expects to hear back in a few days. You know how slow senators are. Anyway, he's also sending a battleship to you. It should arrive in two days. If your mass calculations require more than one battleship, let me know as soon as possible. Over."

"Okay, we'll run the calculations through the computer tonight and let you know. Annexed into the Ataro Empire? Wow. Sneaky move. Over," Theo replied.

"Here's the tricky part. We're going to need to bring the 'magi' back here to Tierra to be tower trained and to sign the Articles of Annexation. Also, they'll meet up with their new queen at that time and bring her back with them at that time. Over."

"But they'll be insisting on fighting the slavers who hold some thousand plus prisoners and horribly bound. Over," Theo countered.

"That does pose a problem, doesn't it? Well, see what you can work out on that one," Governor Misty tossed the ball back to Theo. "Just make sure that Nia and the women magi know how vitally important it is for them to come here to get their tower training and sign the annexation papers. Keep us posted. Over and out."

"We will do the calculations," Theo suggested to Andy. "You get to convince them they need to come to Tierra."

"Ah, give me the hard part," he jested. "Just don't mess up the calcs. I don't want to get crushed by some moon."

"Hey, it's already creating giant tides," Theo explained. "We took some images of a port town down south. The ocean is now rising over their wooden docks. It's only going to get worse before we can get this moon handled."

"Wow! Platon is noticeably larger," I commented to the others. After Theo told us what he'd learned, we headed outside for a quick peek at the moons.

Once we were all back inside, Dr. Andy began his lengthy explanations. "Okay everyone, I've lots of news. On our world of Tierra, we have had the same problems as you are having here. While you call it the Slave Wind, which makes magi out of those who survive, on our world, we call them the *mentales* gifted. The ability to hear other's thoughts and to send yours to another is called telepathy. It is critical that you who have this gift learn to block your thoughts and to dampen out the sometimes myriad thoughts of others. Failure to do so can lead to madness, which may be what happened to Nia's parents and the others on her ship. Additionally, each person who has this gift can do many powerful things, such as creating the walls of flames that you've described and many more. We've a huge catalogue of things that we can do."

"Like you, those of us who possess this gift have yellow eyes. Here, your eyes have the four colored swirls in them. What we would like to do is to have you eight who have this gift return later on with us to Tierra for a few weeks. During that time, our people will fully train you in blocking your thoughts from others and from being overwhelmed by the thoughts of all those around you. Plus, we'll train you in all the special skills or actions or spells, if you prefer that term, so that you will be all set. When you return, you will be able to give others here the training in turn."

Kisha interrupted him. "Wow! We'll get to fly in the sky like Sky People and see another world!"

"Right, Kisha. That you will. Yet, there is a bad aspect to all this. You see, in the vast Imperium out there, telepaths, such as yourselves, are exceedingly rare and highly desired. Unscrupulous men and women will go to nearly any length and means to kidnap telepaths, and force them to use their skills and spells for their monetary gains. Shortly, the Imperium is going to become aware that Metcalf-4 has natural and powerful telepaths on it, you magi. There will be a mad dash to come here and kidnap any of your magi they can."

"Crap!" I exclaimed. Others swore their own curses.

"Ah, but we've worked out a way to protect you and all your people from that. You see, not all worlds want to harm you or steal your people. There is a group of us, known as the Ataro Empire of the Wasps, which believes you should be left alone to develop as you see fit and protected against the unscrupulous of the other worlds. The leader of the empire is called Emperor Bino Sanguro. He's willing to accept Metcalf-4 as the fortieth world in that empire, protecting your entire world. This is the best protection we can provide. He is protecting our world, Tierra, as well."

"What does he want of us?" Danika wisely asked. I wish I had thought of that question.

"He will send along a queen. Her job will be to settle disputes and prevent wars and conflicts. In time and according to your wishes, trading can be worked out. Primarily, education is the most important thing he can offer you. Knowledge is the only real and lasting power. We on Tierra are taking full advantage of this, you see. All of us got our education from one of their schools. So this is a win-win situation for all of Metcalf-4."

"So this emperor fellow — he rules over us?" asked Sir Dmitri.

"Not at all. Your people continue to rule as they always have."

"Oh, that's much better. You'll never get the kings to give up their thrones," he replied.

"And we certainly don't want that, except in the case of these slavers. They have to go," Theo added.

"Right!" Sir Dmitri exclaimed rather vehemently.

I broke in, "But we can't go until we free all those who are enslaved in King Vlad's city."

"Right," Theo admitted. "I didn't think I could get around that one. We'll do what we can to help you with that."

The next few days passed slowly for some of us, and a bit hectic for those getting their therapy. Each evening, we checked on Platon. It was obvious to everyone that it was growing steadily larger. No one who looked up could have missed that fact. I just hoped and prayed they would be in time and be able to save us.

After that, a giant Imperium battleship arrived, though we could not see it in orbit. Theo, Diego, and Ann took their transport up to discuss ways and means of dealing with the moon. I was mostly in the dark, but then I won't pretend to understand such things as orbital calculations. The next day, Ann returned and began giving me my Basic Therapy.

"I don't think I've much trauma to handle," I explained to Ann, as we sat down in a private room. We chatted a while, and before I knew what was happening, I was going over some of the times I was acutely aware of the difference between my body and everyone else's bodies. Honestly, those incidents weren't much at all, mostly a child's curiosity un-quenched.

189

Then, she again asked me for something that was similar and earlier in time.

"But I can't recall anything before around three years old," I protested. She gently nudge me and kept me looking. That's when I ran smack into my birth! It wasn't particularly pretty and pain-free, for that matter. Rather, what fascinated me was the opportunity actually to see my real birth mother! Let me tell you, I paid darn close attention to her and to the place where she was! Yes, I was looking for clues. What world was this? What was she like? Who was my birth father?

Just when I thought I might get some clues, I found my little body being taken away from her. I'm in a bassinet and people are looking down at me. That's when I recognized mom and dad. They'd visited me shortly after my birth and adopted me when I was barely three days old! As we went over it, I picked up my birth mother's speech. I recognized it at once as that which was spoken on Aquila Prime, a world on which this genetic genocide had been unleashed. I knew about that from mom's history lessons. I admit I was quite elated to uncover these details, which meant more to me than the birth trauma and everything else.

In fact, it meant more than what we discovered in subsequent sessions. Yes, I discovered I had lived before. That is, I'd had other bodies, which had their share of trauma, and I was obviously an immortal spiritual being. But none of that compared to having seen what my mother looked like and the world from which she had come. As I was still going over this one last time, I suddenly heard her voice. The sonic was finally totally clear, as if I was right there in that hospital room!

"Oh my god! Ann, mom was dad! I didn't have a mom. Dad gave birth to me! No wonder he gave me up for adoption! Besides being in that assisted living home, he had no idea how to care for a baby. Besides, he didn't have any arms either. That's so funny, Ann. My mother is really my father!" I roared with laughter. In fact, I couldn't stop laughing all day. Even the next day, someone would say some little thing that set me off on another round of laughter. Ann quietly said I was done with my Basic Therapy, and she set to work on Jovanna.

When the full Platon moon occurred, its size was more

than twice the size of the other two. Further, Theo reported massive tides along the coast. In fact, the next morning, he took us all onboard their small transport so we could see what high tide looked like down south. "My god!" I exclaimed. The waves were inland. An entire street close to the wharf was under water. Waves had actually destroyed some buildings and was threatening those a street further inland. I had no doubts at all; if they didn't get the moon moved, this world was doomed!

The next day, the real action began. Theo explained they'd landed on the moon and surveyed it to determine the possibility of splitting it into pieces, which would be more manageable. That wasn't feasible. At this point, the giant battleship hooked its tractor beam onto the moon and began trying to pull it out of its collision orbit. Theo explained what would be happening.

"You see, the moon is so massive that the battleship can't just pull it way like it could another spaceship. Instead, they are applying maximum thrust applied continuously over several days, moving it a little each day. Expect a cumulative effect over the next several days. Don't worry; if that fails, there is a more dangerous backup plan in place."

"What's the backup?" I asked growing rather curious.

"Break it up with bombs. That's the last resort, since some of the pieces could well land on the planet. Keep your fingers crossed, Nia," Theo suggested.

"Would if I had any," I replied, bringing a grin to many faces, including his. He'd set me up for that one, and I chuckled along with him.

Now, we watched the moon closely after it rose later each day, at least those of us who were not still getting their therapy sessions. At first, I detected no change, but then I realized this was positive. It had been getting steadily larger in size each day. This meant the battleship was at least holding it stable in its orbit. As it approached third quarter, I swore it looked smaller. The next morning, Theo and Diego confirmed my observation. "It is working, albeit slowly. We are working out a permanently stable orbit for Platon, one that will prevent this from ever happening again."

"From what physics I know, isn't this really a four or five body problem and thus very difficult to solve?" I inquired.

"Smart woman. You're right. It's taking up massive computer time on the battleship's main computers to work it out, rather empirically, since a precise math solution has never been created," Diego pointed out.

By new moon, I knew this was going to work. Platon was back to appearing to be the same size as Orya and Dessa. Disaster was no longer imminent. I began to relax really for the first time since the Ceri's failed attempts.

Perhaps even more wonderful, one by one, the other five women finished their Basic Therapy. My own success with it was unique and just what I'd always wished to know. However, with Danika, Tesla, Anya, Jana, and Jovanna, in my humble opinion, the results were spectacular and life-changing. Gone was that massive mound of suppressed grief I'd been sensing. While it's one thing to be minus something, it's another to have something back. In this case, these five radiated both vitality and life! I was more than a little impressed; rather I was shocked at the change in them. They laughed; they were vibrant; they were happy and content; they were full of life! I praised and thanked Lisa, Lissi, Ann, Maggie, Mindy, and Andy repeatedly. I think I must have embarrassed them by my enthusiastic praises.

Later that night, I cornered Lisa and had a long chat with her. "As you know, I've known my body is different since I was little. Thanks to all of you, I now understand what happened to my dad and how my body is what it is. But I've lost my mom and dad, and I don't really have anyone I can talk about such things with anymore. Can I ask you about such things?" She readily agreed to be my surrogate mother.

"Danika and I want to be married, but the others, Tesla, Anya, Jana, and Jovanna also want me to be the father of their children too. They want us all to live together as one large family. I can see why; we are able to help each other do the things, which must be done. But is this an okay thing to do? Can we have a family of six of us?"

"Nia, love is what matters. Love, admiration, respect. As long as you share these feelings for each other, you six should do well together. I won't say otherwise, but you six really do need to work together unless you can find the right men in your lives."

"On this world, men won't have anything to do with them. I can understand why. It's not like the civilized Imperium worlds. Here, survival takes quite a lot of work on everyone's part."

Lisa replied. "Yes, I suspected that would be the case. Yet, after you come to Tierra and get your training, you eight will be vastly more able and powerful than you ever suspected. Trust us on this detail, Nia." She then added, "I can have Theo marry you, if you like, or arrange a group union as well. He's our ship's captain. We can worry about getting your new Imperium ID cards when you get to Tierra. If you marry all five, they will get dual citizenship, that is, they will also have Descartes-3 citizenship, which might be a good thing for them. They could have a far better life there, if things don't work out for you all here."

I agreed and promised to ask them about this tonight. I had a lot to ponder. I knew from my own life that we would all fare much better on Descartes-3 than we could here on Metcalf-4. Yet, this was the five's home world. Everything would depend, I decided, on how we were ultimately accepted, and if we could find ways to survive well.

In the morning, Captain Theo married us six. Considering my unique anatomy, I was listed as the dominant member with the others technically logged in as my five wives, though with everyone's agreement that Danika was my true love. Per the short ceremony, the four agreed to honor her in that way. Further, I now realized the five were truly my responsibility. I was considered by Imperium law to be the major bread earner. However, Lisa suggested I would soon inherit some credits from my parent's estate, once that could be settled back on Descartes-3. Hindering that was the lack of bodies, which would prove their untimely demise.

I also have to give these women from Tierra a heart-filled thanks. Knowing what we were doing, they rearranged the largest of the bedrooms on the Eagle's Seed. Somehow they got several beds joined together to form one large one, big enough to hold all six of us. We had quite an experience on our wedding night, a very memorable one.

Chapter 11 Handling the Slavers

With the coming of December and more snow along with the first quarter moons, officially Platon had been moved into a vastly more stable orbit. Diego did tell us that in several hundred years, the process would need to be repeated, since it was still being impacted by the gravity of the other two moons. Apparently, Platon's mass was significantly less than that of either Orya or Dessa. Still, as far as I'm concerned, the deadly problem was solved. Yet, we received even more news, encouraging news for sure.

Captain Theo relayed the news. "First, Nia, the Eagle's Seed now belongs to you. It seems your father owned this ship outright, paid in full. It is worth millions of credits, should you wish to sell it. Second, as soon as the legal proceedings are finished, you'll inherit everything they had. This includes the small home back on Descartes-3 and their bank account, which currently has around fifty thousand credits in it. Third, both your parents carried million credit life insurance policies that pay double in case of accidental fieldwork deaths, which this certainly fits. So as the primary provider for your wives, you should do extremely well in that department. Congratulations. You are a very wealthy young woman, though I know you'd rather have your parents back."

Okay! I admit it. Theo's news shocked me utterly! Honestly, I never knew they had so much money. I guess discovering new worlds for the Imperium paid very well indeed, if they could afford to buy the Eagle's Seed.

Theo also explained the insurance policies were routine for all deep space explorers. "It's a risky business at times." He continued, "Now that the immediate threat has been neutralized, we're going to launch a search for your parents and the rest of the crew. May and Lelos Heilwig are on their way here now. He's an archaeologist. Both have the *mentales* gifts like the rest of us. His unique gifts allow him somehow to see traumatic incidents that have taken at some spot. Don't ask me how he does it, but I swear that it's downright uncanny. May's a top-notch linguist, and she's going to study the Sud and Rus languages here. Hopefully, she'll be able to make good language learning disks in short order."

After thanking him for helping me, he then became far more solemn. "Now for the bad news. It seems this Commander Arnwald was quite the criminal. He was wanted for very serious crimes on ten worlds before he apparently vanished without a trace. I think he and his crew must have crash landed on this world while fleeing the authorities back in 1320."

"Well, he certainly was a sadistic egomaniac. So why is this bad news? He's dead. I saw his ship explode on takeoff."

"He left quite a large criminal organization behind. Others have taken over his top position, calling themselves the Commander. Of course, a few of his successors have been caught and sentenced. However, every time the Imperium forces capture the current Commander, another one rises to take his place. This mob of criminals calls themselves The Righteous, and they operate on many worlds, but usually in secret. As fast as the ID division gets a line on them, they seem to vanish, only to pop up on some other world."

"What's The Righteous got to do with me?" I asked.

"You can count on them having heard the legendary Commander Arnwald was living on Metcalf-4. Word of his death has made the Imperium newscasts. The ID Minister suspects they will be sending agents here to see just what Arnwald was up to on this world," Theo explained.

I still didn't get what this had to do with me. I frowned. Theo picked up my uncertainty and explained further. "You can count on the fact they will discover this world has magi. In short order, they will figure out that magi are also telepaths."

Now I got it. "So they'll start kidnaping the magi of this world?" I asked.

"Would not discount that, Nia. Still, the emperor is going to do all that is humanly possible to protect this world from such scum. Just play it safe and be alert," he finished up. I found this troubling.

As we finished our chat, King Vlad cornered us. "Isn't it about time we rescue my people in Zelimir City?" In fact, it was.

Theo helped us out. Taking King Vlad and Queen Kisha with him, he flew reconnaissance over Zelimir City. The transport kept a high altitude, and Theo saw no indication it was spotted from the ground. Through the magnifying optical system, which projected the images onto a giant monitor, Vlad and Kisha saw the city, once home to some five thousand or so. Its outer wooden palisade was distinctly visible as a brownish black line encircling the hilltop city. Beyond the walls, rectangular farm plots and patches of forests formed a patchwork quilt for several miles surrounding the city.

Captain Theo knew he was on thin ground by helping this local King Vlad. Imperium rules were quite specific when dealing with Closed Worlds, a designation that Metcalf-4 would soon have. On the other hand, if there were some of these Righteous criminal organization members down there either running the slave camp or assisting the locals run it, then the Imperium could take decisive action, but only in rounding up the criminals. Based on the tales Nia and her group had told them, combined with the corroborating data from their therapy sessions, Theo felt compelled to help free these thousands of bound men and women.

There was one physical problem though and that dealt with the nature of the "male" hermaphrodite bodies. While their voices were still male, they no longer had that testosterone drive. Not one of the many male hermaphrodites was a physical fighter. Their mixed set of hormones tempered such drives rather significantly. Some philosophers suggested this was a good evolutionary change, while others predicted the doom of mankind, as the roles between men and women in society began to blur. Neither Theo nor any of the other men with him were fighters.

Nevertheless, he and his group felt strongly they should help King Vlad retake his city and free the poor victims. Considering the ground was snow-covered and quite cold, the how became the major problem. King Vlad insisted the walls and homes not be damaged, if at all possible. More information was needed. Hence, I opened a Transportation Torus to Arnwald, and accompanied Vlad and Kisha on their visit to Magus Bo. Unfortunately, he had little more direct information on Zelimir City. Here, life was getting back to normalcy and spring promised a rebirth. We took hope from that much and returned to the ships.

That evening, we held a planning session, thanks in part to Theo, who had printed off one of the overhead images that clearly showed the layout of the buildings and streets. Theo suggested, "I can land this transport here in what must be a city market square. It's large enough. That will get you inside the walls without a fight."

"Perfect," Vlad exclaimed. "We can take them by surprise. They've never see Sky People and their ships before, so they won't know what to expect. Sir Dmitri and I can charge out and deliver my surrender or else message. You magi can stand behind us and do your thing again. If these majors and magi are like those at Arnwald, they are cowards and will prefer to stand behind a host of their guards."

"Dear," Kisha spoke up, "You can't stand against five hundred guards! We can't kill that many, even with all of our spells."

Theo spoke up. "There might be a way around that. Officially, we've not received word that Metcalf-4 is a Closed World. Officially, we've not received word that there are not a bunch of The Righteous here running things. So, what if we put a PDS on King Vlad and Sir Dmitri?"

"Theo, you clever dog you," Diego replied with a wry grin. "That might work well."

"A Personal Defense Shield?" I asked. I'd heard of them, but never seen one. The others of my group looked confused with no idea what he was talking about.

Theo explained, "Our Imperium soldiers have a personal defense shield that they wear when they go into serious combat situation. The shield is a force field that would protect you against being harmed by swords, arrow, and any kind of strike. The only way through the shield is by moving slowly. Someone could come up to you, move his hand slowly inside the field, and then harm you, but that's not likely here. We've got two, so both you men could be protected from the guards, but you would still be able to use your swords."

I spoke up, "We should try to minimize harming the guards. Some of them may well have been pressed into service and took it to avoid being bound like the others, forced to hop everywhere. Besides, it's those in charge and the magi that we need to handle. Once the leaders are taken out, the guards will surrender."

Vlad agreed with me. "She's right. Once the leaders are taken out, the magi will flee, and the guards will route or surrender. While I won't thereafter trust them, we'll need able bodied men to help us with the thousands of poor victims. We just need to be particularly careful of fire. If one of the buildings catches on fire, there'll be no able bodied men to fight the fire. That's the worst thing that can happen. All of the homes are wood and close together. If one goes up, the whole city could well burn down." That was a sobering thought.

While we discussed additional issues, the plan stayed the same. Because Captain Theo continued to insist some of us had to return with them to Tierra to get trained, sign the papers, and pick up the new queen, thereby making everything official, we decided to launch the attack in the morning, but it got delayed one more day by the arrival of another deep space transport, bringing May and Lelos Heilwig here to help out.

Jelena and I took May to her village, where Jelena's mother welcomed the older alien woman. May planned to stay here for a time, learning the Sud language and preparing computer learning disks for others, who needed to learn the local language, well one of them at least.

Lelos had Jelena and me tell him all that we knew of the area and where my parents and the rest of the crew were last seen. He did promise me he'd do his best to discover what had happened to them.

The air was clear and cold. A thin layer of frost covered the roofs and wooden palisades. The deep space transport slowly descended into the central market place of Zelimir City, located on a large hilltop, commanding a wide view of the surrounding countryside. The Great Manor where Vlad and his parents had lived was at the very top, the largest building in the city, and ten blocks from our landing spot. Those few who were out on the snow-covered streets, namely a dozen guards and a few hopping men and women, got the sight of their lives. The silver transport slowly descended straight down from the blue sky above. As anticipated, it caused quite a stir.

By the time we landed, many doors had opened. From some, guards issued forth like small grains of wheat spilling from a bag. From others, men and women hopped out, staring up at this unearthly sight. These people will surely have something to tell their children and grandchildren, I thought. Funny how on the eve of a battle, strange thoughts come unbidden.

As we neared touchdown, we could see some of the probable leaders and potential magi coming out of the Great Manor. That they were in charge soon became evident. Marshaling their guards, they ran towards the Central Market. Meanwhile, Diego strapped the small PDS devices to the two fighter's waists. "Okay, press this button to activate it, but don't do it until you are clear of the ship. Press it again to deactivate it."

King Vlad and Sir Dmitri proudly walked down the bay ramp, each pushing the activation button after stepping off the ramp. Both had their swords drawn. Kisha followed just behind them. Danika, Jovanna, and Jana followed next. Tesla and Anya walked behind them, and I brought up the rear. My objective was one of protection. Since I had the most experience with all of the elemental forces, I was to extinguish any fires that might be set and to provide protection from enemy magi spells. The others were going to attack directly the leaders and magi, while the two fighters would keep the multitude of guards from us. That was the plan anyway, and I sincerely hoped that it would work.

As Vlad anticipated, the guards, magi, and majors formed up lines on the streets approaching the square, but all were most hesitant to get too close, fearing this strange metal beast, descending from the sky. Had gods come down to earth? I could sense fear — strong fear coming from all around me. Rightly so, they were facing totally unknown and vastly superior machines far beyond their reality.

However as expected, when King Vlad and Sir Dmitri became more visible, they became the focus of everyone's attention. When he thought the leaders were close enough to hear him, King Vlad bellowed as loudly as he could. "I am King Vlad, and have come to free my Zelimir City. I give you majors, you leaders, and your magi and guards one and only one chance to surrender to me now. Otherwise, I'll unleash the wrath of the gods upon you. Surrender now or die!"

Danika and Kisha, along with Jana, Jovanna, Tesla, and Anya, paid very close attention to those in the rear, where they anticipated the leaders and magi would have positioned themselves. They ignored the many guards who formed up the front lines on the square's four connecting streets. I kept an eye on them and on the two fighters. If they were smart, they would surrender.

For a minute, I thought they might just do that, surrender. But then, some leaders in the rear ranks ordered the guards to charge the fighters. Those orders were not well obeyed. Too much fear. Too much uncertainty. Too much strangeness. A few foolish guards cautiously approached the men, who stood their ground. As a couple of them swung their swords at Vlad and Sir Dmitri, both did little more than reflexively parry the strokes, not entirely trusting the strange alien devices around their waists. However, quickly, they saw their enemy's blades shattering when they struck the invisible force fields that surrounded the two men.

That had the right effect, I thought. Fear turned to terror. The few who had unwillingly pressed the attack following orders turned tail and beat a hasty retreat. The other guards, who were moving towards the fighters, stopped about fifty feet from them, hesitating. They'd seen four swords shatter before their eyes. While their crude iron swords often broke, not four at once.

As I watched, six magi took the action. Two shot electrical bolts at the two fighters. The result was quite a show. Brilliant electrical sparks cascaded down them outlining the force shield quite well. For an instant, the two men looked like a glowing bell jar that I'd seen in a physics book. Another pair tried to drop two walls of flames on the entire area. Now I acted, raising all the snow on the ground rapidly upward, sort of a reverse snowstorm, rather a cool effect, if I do say so myself. Steam and a white cloud obscured the view for a minute, before drifting off us and on south.

At this point, both Kisha and Danika's spells flashed. Once more, Kisha had thrown one of her daggers, guiding it unerringly to its target, the forehead of one of the magi, instantly killing him. Danika's spell was one of her mighty thrusts. It caught two magi squarely in their chests, crushing them, just as it had done before back at the battle in Arnwald.

Tesla and Anya dropped walls of flames onto the back ranks of the men near where the magi and leaders were standing. They were careful to keep the flames away from the wooden buildings, thankfully. Chaos erupted. Men broke ranks and fled down all four streets. As I watched, several Transportation Torus spells activated. Jana downed one magus just as he was about to step through his. Jovanna somehow defused a second torus just as that magus was stepping through his. The lower part of his body dropped onto the street, a most interesting effect, and quite unexpected. The others got away.

The battle for Zelimir lasted two minutes, though we waited another five for all the guards to leave the city gates hastily . Just as the streets became completely deserted, another torus opened up and a man stepped out before us, his hands raised, palms facing King Vlad.

"Don't shoot. It's me, Niko, Vlad. It's me." He was short and stout, dressed in a heavy cloak and thick boots. He had a black moustache and eyes with brownish swirls in them. I suspected earth elemental forces were his specialty, as Magus Triska had taught me. I guessed he must be in his late thirties or early forties, an older man for this culture.

"Niko? Niko, is that really you?" Vlad called out.

"Thank the gods that you are alive, Vlad!" Niko replied. "After so many years, we thought you hadn't made it."

"Very nearly didn't Niko. Gang, this is Magus Niko Veth, dad's magus, the one who also helped me out of here when the slavers attacked the city three years ago."

"But what is that thing? That beast from the sky? Vlad, what is it?" Niko finally asked what he'd been wondering about from the moment he saw it descending from the sky.

"Sky People from another world come to help us free our people and save our world, Niko. Such a tale I have for you. Oh, my wife and our new queen, Kisha. Magus Kisha, this is my oldest friend, Magus Niko."

The two deactivated their PDS devices, and we all gathered around Niko for introductions. Captain Theo joined us and retrieved his devices. He could not afford to allow them to remain on our world, and I understood why. Wearing them, the two fighters would be invulnerable and supermen. I sighed, now would come the heart-wrenching part.

Considering that some of the men might well return, Theo suggested we get inside the transport and plan our next move. I was thankful for his intervention. I was freezing. As I said before, I don't like the cold and snow one little bit.

Reminiscing would have to wait. King Vlad had Niko outline the situation here in the city. It was grim indeed. "Alas, half of our people have perished at the hands of these slavers. I've done my best to help the people, but it was never enough. So many have died."

"So how many are left?" Vlad asked.

"I have accurate figures. That was one of my jobs — to keep population counts. There are only one thousand sixteen men left, Vlad. Yet, there is some hope. We have one thousand five hundred sixty women still alive, but barely. Some are in terrible shape. So many have been raped repeatedly. The children, my god, Vlad, the children — they are all gone. Dead. Beyond horrors. An entire generation wiped out."

"The filthy butchers!" Vlad cursed. "How?"

"They bound them, as they bound the others, but as their bodies grew, the metal bindings cut off their circulation. They lost arms and legs and were mercifully slain. There is a huge burial pit just north of the city. So many, Vlad, so many." We all sensed the immense grief that Niko bore. Probably everyone here also bore it as well. I now realized that these thousands also needed the Tierra Basic Therapy, though I could not see how it could be done on such a scale.

Suppressing his grief, Niko continued. "Vlad, the women have borne the brunt of the slaver's evil. You know they bound their arms behind their backs, don't you?" We all nodded vigorously. "Not all women were flexible enough to handle that. So many lost either their lower arms or all of them. The Commander ordered those who had lost them to be housed together and to be the sex slaves for the guards. Beyond horrors, Vlad. But I see you've already encountered it." He glanced at the six of us.

"Yes, we have. Say, how is the food situation here? In Arnwald, the prisoners had to hop to a food dispensary each day to get their rations."

"We're in halfway good shape this year, unlike the past years. Your taking of Arnwald really helped us. You see, they were just about to ship half of our harvest over there when you attacked. Hence, for the first time, we've ample. The guards dole it out a week at a time to the many homes. They have twenty men and women housed per home. They are in the buildings lining the walls — closer to the fields that the men work. But Vlad, there's no way to get them free of their bindings."

Queen Kisha spoke up, "Oh yes we do. You've got your good thief Queen Kisha here now. Er, and Nia's cutters. We'll have them free in no time. Well, it's going to take some days with so darn many. We best get going on it, don't you think? First, we free the women who have lost their arms and hands. Period. The men can come later."

Diego and Theo rounded up four more cutters from their transport, giving us ten of them. However, Kisha insisted that only she cut them free. "Look guys, this is very delicate work. One slight miscalculation and you can cut them badly or even kill them. This is my job, fellows." She was most insistent. Vlad agreed.

While Theo and Diego kept watch using their video cameras on the transport, the rest of us headed off to tackle the immense project of freeing everyone from their bindings. Following Niko, we finally arrived at the first of some one hundred twenty-seven homes. Later, I learned that one hundred two homes held ten men and ten women. Most were husband and wife, though not all. Twenty-five held five hundred four women who had lost arms, but even as we got to them, we found four more had died during the night.

The only positive thing I can say about the first five hundred women whom Kisha freed was that only eighteen had no arms at all. The slavers had learned to spot the telltale signs soon enough to prevent the total removal of their arms. Still, it was a very grim situation, compounded by their repeated rapes. They were in very bad shape, physically and emotionally.

The first thing that King Vlad did was to place each of these women in a home with another healthy woman, who was charged with caring for her needs. But that's getting ahead with the rescue. Kisha spent the entire day just freeing up these women. Jelena and the rest of us took turns cooking up a very good meal and feeding these women. In many cases, we also had to give them a decent bath. We had a very long day of it.

The next morning, after the ten cutters had been partially recharged, Kisha finally consented to doling them out to the others, allowing them to go house to house, cutting the binding chains from the women's arms and then everyone's chains. At least they could use their arms and legs. That second day, nearly all had this much freedom of motion returned to them, exhausting all of the charges in the ten cutters. Theo estimated it would take several weeks to get all of the bindings cut free, perhaps even a month. Still, at least they were able to walk and use their arms again.

That third day, we all met as a group. "Look, we have to get Nia and some of you to Tierra soon," Captain Theo explained. "We can't wait here for another month while Kisha cuts their metal bindings off."

I suggested, "Why don't the six of us go, Theo. Kisha and Witch Jelena can stay. Jelena can heal any of the small cuts that might arise."

"I like that," Kisha commented. "I don't have any desire to go flying off in the sky. I prefer my feet firmly planted on the ground, if it's all the same to you. I do need Witch Jelena, just in case. You six go ahead without us. You can teach us when you get back." After a bit more discussion, everyone agreed on this route. Danika, Jana, Jovanna, Tesla, Anya, and I would accompany them back to this Ashford-5 and deal with what must be handled there, promising to return as soon as possible. Theo suggested it could be three or four weeks at most. He also promised to have Lelos bring the other transport here so that Kisha would have a way to recharge the cutters.

We said our farewells, and I got big hugs from the four of them. In fact, we six all did, but Jelena and Kisha were a little teary eyed to see us go. In spite of her brash words, I knew Kisha would have liked to come with us, but she had vital work to do here, which would take at least a month to accomplish.

When we got back to the Eagle's Seed and the other transport, Lelos had some news for me, pretty much what I had expected. He explained, "If someone inhales too much of the psi-dust, it acts as a poison. In smaller doses, it creates physical changes in human bodies, giving us what we call the *mentales* gifts and what you call the magi gift. I've located quite a few of them, including your parents. I've seen they have gotten a proper burial. I'm sorry, Nia Elain."

"Thanks. It is good finally to know what happened to them. I suspected that they had died for quite some time. Now, I can keep their memories alive in my mind. Thanks," I replied, fighting back the confirmed loss.

Captain Theo wanted to leave as soon as possible, but he waited long enough for May to return from Jovan. "Here you go, crude language disks. Upload them for me, will you Lelos?" she asked. Turning to us, she added, "On your trip, please use the learning disks for both Imperium Standard and for our Midlands languages. That way, when you get there, you'll be able to communicate a little bit. Probably, it'll be a good idea to listen to them for several days after you get there. I'm sending along only the basics of the Sud language, in hopes it'll help the others back home learn yours." While my five wives didn't know what she was saying, I did and promised her that we would.

Considering that we had virtually no possessions, Captain Theo was able to depart just a few minutes later, once we had been escorted to our quarters. "Don't worry. We'll be there in the morning. Watch the view for a while, then hit the language disks. Nia can show you how."

While I explained to them about the disks, he prepared for takeoff. "You put these earphones on at night while you sleep, and the computer plays the language recordings. In the morning, you'll find that you can speak a little bit of these languages. Imperium Standard is the universal language spoken across many worlds, but not everyone speaks it. Midlands is the language of the people with whom we are going to be staying. Don't worry about it. They've got these devices called ULATs, Universal Language Translators. It's a small box that fastens around your waists. It translates into and from your language to whatever language the other person needs to understand you. In this case, May has begun to program the ULATs to be able to handle Sud, but probably not very well yet. So we have to speak their language at least a little. Oh, we're taking off. Come look!" The five gazed out of the windows, watching their world slowly moving away from us.

Tesla asked, "Are they moving the world away? I thought the ship would be flying away." I had to explain about relative motion and perspective. After that, we jumped into hyperspace, and I didn't even try to explain that to them. Instead, I helped them get their earphones on and got us all learning Midlands.

Chapter 12 Ashford-5

Captain Theo was right. We arrived the following morning. I was just as surprised and impressed as the others were to see the dull orange-red sun of Ashford-5, or Tierra as they called their world. Before long, we saw the spaceport coming up towards us. As it slowed, we could see small people moving around, along with many tall mountains. Before long, we landed, and Captain Theo escorted us off the ship.

As we set foot on this strange, new world, I breathed in deeply, smelling the resinous pine, which dominated all other odors. "Oh, it smells like home!" Danika declared. "I like it already. Are all worlds like this one?"

"Hardly. Wonderful, wonderful! It's warm and not cold," I replied, as we spotted several people walking towards us.

For us, it was instant culture shock. Five women came out to meet us. Three of them were as armless as Tesla and Anya, but by now, we were used to seeing such sights. Rather what shocked us were their appearance and lip ornaments, along with their figures. Three had the same mammoth bosom as I had, which I could easily relate to. I guess the best way is to take them individually, though keep in mind we saw them all at one time.

"Hello. I am Governor Misty Childa-Bellweather. Welcome to Tierra or Ashford 5. We meet at long last." She spoke in Imperium standard. I later learned she had little choice in that, because she wore a set of gleaming, golden lip plates, each of which was a foot in diameter. They dropped down, touching her upper chest. The top surface of her upper plate displayed a pair of hands in the process of shaking, which I found comforting. Her waist was so tiny I thought she had been cut in half. She wore strange toe shoes. Only her toes were on the concrete. A tiny metal heel almost touched the backsides of her toes. I soon learned her feet were quite malformed, intentionally in this case. She wore a light blue satin gown, tight fitting, that displayed her prominent curves exquisitely. Black seamed nylons were visible from just below the hem of her gown inches below her knees. I guessed she might be twenty-five. Later, I learned she was seventy-six and had used the Rejuvenation Machine, as had many others. Her hair was very blonde and lush. In gentle waves, it fell to her knees, but a bluebird clasp on the backside of her head held much of it in place. Her eyes were both bright and yellow, as were three of the five women.

"These are our queens. Queen Linda and her mate Queen Rael Valen-Gervasi." They were both armless, but looked much like Governor Misty, including the giant lip plates. Theirs had an image of what I thought might be a castle on them, identical images. Both appeared to be twenty-two, but in fact were seventy-one. Linda had equally light blonde hair falling in waves to her knees, while her mate, Rael, had thick brown hair of an identical length. They wore identical light red satin gowns, almost strapless, but with a tiny strap of satin over their left shoulders. Their waists were also quite tiny, and they too wore the toe shoes with their seamed black nylons prominently contrasting with their gowns and matching shoes.

"This you your new queen. Queen Akira Ayano. She'll be accompanying you on your return trip to Metcalf-4." She too was as armless as Tesla, with a tiny waist, black nylons, and similar toe shoes. She and her companion did not have the monster-sized breasts or the giant lip plates. Theirs were what I called normal. Her gown was a shade of pink. Her hair, very straight and black, falling to near her ankles. She and her companion looked and were twenty-five.

"Her Personal Assistant, Kimi Mari. She cannot speak." Kimi had arms and similar black hair just as long as Queen Akira's. Her waist was just as tiny, and she wore the same style toe shoes and black nylons. Her satin gown was a deep green.

In contrast, we six wore various leather pants and tops and fleece lined boots, though we didn't have our cloaks on since it was summertime here. I thought it a bit chilly for a summer's day, however. Using Imperium Standard, I introduced my five mates and me. "Please speak slowly for their benefit. They have only had a few hours to learn IS."

"And we have only learned a bit of yours. We'll get by. I'm sure. If you'll follow me, we'll get you your new ID cards with dual citizenship, and then I'm sure you have many questions. I can tell you've never seen such elegantly dressed women before," Governor Misty explained. While I'm sure that my mates had no idea what she meant by ID cards, we followed her, hoping for more explanations, especially about the giant lip ornaments. I knew that fashionable women on Descartes-3 wore similar plates, but those were only five inches across. These were monsters. I did have many questions, now that she mentioned it.

The process was swift. Governor Misty explained, "These ID cards contain your personal data and shows that you six have dual citizenship. That is, you are legally a citizen of Metcalf-4, and by marriage to Nia Elain, a citizen of her home world, Descartes-3. This means you can travel freely around the vast Imperium and always be able to return to your home worlds. Now, let's have some tea and chat a bit."

Again, we followed them into a large dining room, very typical of all Imperium spaceports. I instantly knew where everything was located. Such is the benefit of standardization. You can arrive at any spaceport and know where everything is located. Already, someone had prepared the hot tea, and we sat down and took off our boots so we could handle the cups, which had large handles that we could manage with our toes. I think Governor Misty had deliberately arranged for them. We six watched to see how the three with their giant lip plates could possibly drink. They raised their plates up, locking them into a horizontal position. Using spoons, they managed, though the two queens were using their spell powers to levitate and move their spoons, impressing my five mates. Queen Akira's assistant held the cup up to the queen's lips so she could drink.

"Okay. Here on Tierra, all the nobles and wealthier men and women wear these lip plates. It is a status symbol. While we find them awkward at best, to blend in with the locals, we too wear them," Governor Misty explained. She went on to describe much about Ashford-5, including their preoccupation with dressing elegantly. "It is their status symbol, you see.

There is almost no gold on this world, so the wealthy express themselves by dressing elegantly."

She then moved on to the topic of the Ataro queens, allowing Queen Linda to explain in great detail. We learned that in this Ataro Empire, those with the great powers of ruling were always physically restrained to keep them from abusing their immense powers. While I didn't think this was remotely a valid argument, obviously the three queens did. All the queens had their arms removed and wore the incredibly tight wasp-waist corsets. Further, their feet were reformed such that only their toes could touch the ground, forcing them to only be able to wear these toe shoes. Apparently, these styles had caught on here on Ashford-5, I concluded. Hence, we soon had a good picture of the restrictions under which our new queen would be operating. In order to survive, her speechless Personal Assistant would always accompany her. We learned her voice had been removed so she too could not overly influence her queen.

Once we all better understood the queen and her position, Governor Misty brought out the papers that I needed to sign on behalf of Metcalf-4. At first, she was a little worried I couldn't do this action. I quickly signed my name in nice script, bringing a smile to Queen Akira's face. "You have beautiful writing, Nia Elain," she complimented me. I decided against saying anything about it.

"Now everything is official. Metcalf-4 is designated a Closed World, which means that others in the Imperium are not going to be allowed to land and interfere with your people or to bring illegal technology to your world. It's the best protection we can give to a developing world. You are going to be allowed to progress at your own rate, without undo interference," Misty explained.

Queen Rael took over the discussion. "That's done. You'll be staying in my Imperial Castle during your training. I've had a large suite with a very large bed prepared for you. Plus, we should get you women some summer outfits. I'm sure you are all melting in your leathers. Queen Akira and Kimi are also staying with me. They have a suite next to yours. In the evenings, I'm sure she wants to chat with you and learn all about your world. Come on. Let's get you to your new quarters and then see about getting you some dresses."

The tea was finished, and we followed the very, very slow moving women. Honestly, I had no idea how they could even walk in those toe shoes! We took an elevator down to an underground tunnel. From there, we rode two electric cars through the tunnel, and then climbed up a flight of stairs. Along with my mates, I was completely lost. However, Danika still knew which way was which. She had an uncanny sense of direction, which would save our lives later on, but I'm getting ahead of myself again.

We were inside a stone building, of that I was positive. Our suite was huge, warmed by a crackling fire. Giant tapestries adorned many of the walls. Our bed was more than large enough to hold all six of us. Impressive. Queen Akira's suite was right next to ours. We were also shown where the dining room was located, just on down the hall from our room. We couldn't possibly get lost finding it. I admit I was immensely impressed with the sheer size of that room, which could feed five hundred at one time! Later, I learned that was often the case when the queens hosted their official meetings.

After that, we took another short walk, arriving at a place called Elegant Fashions Inc, where we were introduced to Isabel Valen-Franks and her daughter, Marisol Nita. Both women looked twenty-five, but in fact they were mother and daughter. Isabel was in her late seventies. They hovered over us as if we were royalty. I guess in a way we were just that.

I explained I had no credits just yet, but that I might get some soon. Isabel countered, "No Nia. Whatever you wish comes at no cost to you or your mates. Everything is prepaid by Queen Akira. So you six can shop until you drop." I wasn't quite sure what she meant by that last twist of phrase.

We looked through several catalogues of dresses from simple day dresses to fancy gowns, though the emphasis was predominately the latter. A plain cotton dress would have suited me just fine, but Isabel kept on insisting. "A well dressed woman instills confidence in herself and in others." She continued, "Now, I am showing you only the styles designed for women such as yourselves. You see, over the years, we've had a number of women who have lost arms and hands, much as you have. So we've created dresses and gowns that you'll be able to manage to put on yourselves. Now, as you've already seen with our queens, many of the most elegantly dressed men and women go in for the more exotic lines, which require getting body modifications. You know, the impossibly small waists, the malformed feet so they can wear the very popular toe shoes. Oh, and the lip plates too."

"However, I'm assuming you six want none of that. However, you do want to look your best at special times. I would recommend getting some simple day dresses and at least a couple of the really fancy gowns and heels. Oh, about the heels. You simply must get some and practice wearing them. Everyone wears them with these fancy gowns. You'll fit right in on many worlds, such as Descartes-3, for example," she chatted on. When she flipped to the page of the heels, we six gasped.

"Yes, the heels are quite tall, six inches, but take it from me. You and your wives will look and feel extremely sexy in them. Mind you, ladies, poor Nia Elain here is going to get quite aroused seeing you in them, just as will you with her. But yes, it does take a good deal of getting used to them. Everyone says so. Still, we women must look our best." On she went.

As she paged through the many elegant dress samples, I noticed each one came in pairs. One had arm sleeves; the other was sleeveless, as though the wearer had never had arms in the first place. She must have picked up my thought, because she explained, "Yes, these are specially designed for women like you, Nia, Tesla, and Anya. However, I would not recommend the strapless designs, except for you, Nia. They have a tendency to slip down on women who have smaller breast sizes. Nia, you don't have to fear that and would look stunning in a strapless gown."

"I'm sorry, Isabel. We've only gotten here and have no idea what the proper dress code actually is. We are staying at the castle of the queens," I protested slightly, hoping for better guidance.

"Perfectly understandable, Nia, and wise. Let me guide you. I outfit everyone who lives or goes to the Imperial Castle. .

You'll find everyone there wearing the six inch heels or the toe shoes, along with elegant gowns or suits, in the case of the men. However, since you are also going to be getting your training, I would recommend five day dresses and flats for those occasions. However, you best each have five of the fancy gowns and heels for all other times. Seven of each would be far better. That way, you can get by an entire week or more without having to have them cleaned. The queens' staff handles all the cleaning for you, but still having a week or more supply is wise. They all come with the proper undergarments. However, at this time, I would not recommend wearing the fancy black nylon stockings, as sexy as they are. They are difficult for you to put on without tearing them. Now later on, when your *mentales* gifts blossom, you can always come back and get a supply of them."

Finally, we were getting somewhere. First, we all decided on seven day dresses in various pastel colors and matching flats, easy to don. Second, we poured over the fancy gowns, knowing it was obviously expected of us to have and wear them as well. Danika insisted I get a red strapless one, just to see how I would look in it. Mostly, we six chose the more conservative designs, ones that we thought we might be able to put on ourselves, as limited as we were.

What we were not expecting is to be dressed in one right then and there! After Isabel and Marisol Nita helped us out of our leathers, they showed us how to put on the dainty panties. I swear, they thought of everything or had a whole lot of experience. There were big loops that we could catch with our toes, and use our feet to pull them up. Amazing, I thought. Here were panties with me in mind! The gowns had large zippers up the backsides, each with a big loop, which one of us could take between our teeth and pull up or down for the wearer. The matching pumps were also easy to slip on and off as needed. However, as each of us first stood up in these tall heels, we gasped.

"Practice, practice, practice, ladies. Always remember to take small steps. Come; let's practice right now." Both Isabel and Marisol Nita, who also wore similar heels, demonstrated and then had us walking all over her store. She didn't allow us to head back to the castle, until she was sure we could manage in them.

On the positive side, our new gowns were nicely pleated at the waist, flaring out a good deal, but draping only just below our knees. This way, we could handle going to the bathroom by ourselves or even more easily if we helped each other. For this, I was thankful. No way could Queen Akira, in her tight-fitting, long gown possibly have managed that, and we wouldn't be of any use in helping her, for that matter. I guessed my old tank tops were a thing of the past, at least for now.

By the time we walked slowly and carefully back to the castle, Queen Akira met us, explaining that it was lunchtime. We followed her and Kimi on into the dining room, where at least two hundred men, women, and children had already gathered. A quick glance around the room told me that we'd made the proper decision on gowns. Nearly every woman was dressed as elegantly as we were. After we entered, Queen Rael rose and introduced us, slightly embarrassing us.

Once lunch was finished, Queen Rael came over to us. "Your new clothes have been placed in your rooms for you. Each stack is labeled with your first name. Why don't you go change, and then I'll take you to those who'll be training you?"

We found by helping each other as we were accustomed to doing, changing into a day dress and flats was easily managed. Once more, I was pleased with how things were going. We were managing on our own.

Training was difficult. Not only was there a significant language barrier, but the nomenclature differed radically between what Magus Triska taught me and what such things were called here on Tierra. More on the training later on.

The icing came when we finally retired to our suite for the night. Hairbrushes had been provided, along with instructions on the use of their new bathroom. I had no idea that toilets, bathtubs, and showers were brand new inventions on this world. These were somewhat crude by Imperium standards, but easily operated even by us. We took a luxurious, hot bath. The tub was so large that three could bathe at one time with the other three helping from outside the tub.

That done and smelling quite fresh, we sat on our giant bed and worked on each other's hair. What surprised us all was what we found when we pulled back the bedding. Satin sheets! This suite had to be the most luxurious I'd ever been in. We six had a very exciting time before six satisfied women finally fell into a deep sleep. Yes, I slept like a baby. In fact, I can't recall having such a restful sleep in a very long time. This beat my bed on the Eagle's Seed a hundred times over.

We quickly discovered there were hundreds of *mentales* gifted here at the Imperial Castle. Yellow eyes can't be missed. We also knew we were very like them in many ways, only that we had different words. Our first lessons were on handling telepathy. That is, we worked on learning to block our thoughts from other telepaths. Yes, I was quite embarrassed to realize that for days we'd all been broadcasting our thoughts all over the place. Fortunately, no one called us on this detail. Whew. Next, we worked on blocking other's thoughts, particularly from those around us who were not telepathic. Once we passed this test, we were finally given a guided tour of the whole castle and the city named Exchange City. It got its name from being the single location where natives could trade goods with those from other worlds.

After that, they tested us to see where our special skills lay. While we each had certain actions that we preferred, we quickly amazed our instructors by being able to produce each action required of us. They were very much impressed that each of us could create a Transportation Torus, which they called teleportation. Still, among us six, this was my best spell or action. Since there seemed no limits to what new spells or actions we could do, the instructors changed tactics. "Let's work on life skills that you all can use to do far more things."

That was precisely what we needed. We were drilled and drilled on telekinesis, until we could levitate silverware and feed ourselves. Now at last, I understood what the queens were doing when they had their initial tea with us upon our arrival here. Tesla's comment spoke volumes, "You know, perhaps we can get by well on our own now." That was music to my ears. I knew I could or mostly could, but then I had nineteen years of practice.

When we convinced our instructors that we were competent, they then presented us each with a special crystal and helped us to attune it to ourselves. Suddenly, our new innate powers increased many fold! Indeed, we were all very much impressed with these. This then led to a lengthy planning meeting with the queens and several other instructors. Three wonderful weeks had passed.

"Okay ladies, your training is officially complete," Queen Rael began our private meeting. "You are aware how someone who does not have your magus gifts can be made to have them, via inhaling some of the psi-dust. It is your responsibility to see that no unworthy person does that to become a magus. One bad magus can wreak total havoc on your world, as witnessed by the use of magi by the slavers."

"We don't intend to make any," I countered.

"But maybe we should," Tesla argued. "There are five hundred women who have lost their lower arms and who could greatly benefit from it."

"Good point," I admitted, not having thought this through.

Queen Rael changed topics. "Since your world has these rich deposits of the psi ore, the Imperium would like to mine it, and in return for the ore, give something of great value back to your world. As yet, Queen Akira doesn't know what that may be. She won't make any decision on that until she's been on your world and studied your needs. In any event, your world does have something of value to trade with the Imperium at large. So that's good news."

Queen Linda then spoke up. "I'm charging you six to seek out and train the other magi on your world, once you get back. Setup official training schools or any other viable scheme, but see that all telepaths are trained. As you now know, it is vitally so for pregnant women, who have the gift to be properly handled when she is giving birth. I know Nia has the written instructions on those procedures. I urge you to follow them to avoid disasters during child birth, which is one of the most common causes of death on worlds such as ours." We agreed. We now knew how critical this detail actually was and why so few magi ever had children. It was deadly if not handled properly.

I asked about how we could possibly get Basic Therapy delivered to the five hundred women victims, who needed it far more than the other thousands who had survived. Queen Linda agreed to send back with us twenty volunteers who would deliver it, as well as train some of our people on how it was done. The idea was for some of us to become able to deliver Basic Therapy on our own. We loved that idea!

"Finally," she said, "I know Nia needs to visit her home world of Descartes-3 to make financial arrangements and to sign various papers, dealing with her inheritance and the death of her parents. I've arranged for that trip. Once you get back, Queen Akira and the volunteers will head back to Metcalf-4 with you. Good luck and do stay in touch with us." She gave me a contact sheet listing her comm frequencies. With the comm center in the Eagle's Seed, I could call her at any time. Finally, I felt like my universe was coming together very nicely, though I wish my mom and dad were still alive to share it with me.

Chapter 13 Descartes-3

Packing our new gowns and accessories into the shipping crates proved an exercise in diversity. I did it my usual way, one that I'd used since I could walk. Sitting on my bottom, I used my feet to nicely fold the gowns and place them into my large crate. Tesla and Anya attempted to emulate the way that I used, but they became frustrated with it. Instead, they focused and their clothing moved around on their own. Telekinesis can be quite useful. In contrast, Danika, Jana, and Jovanna insisted on using their upper arms to do the work. Looking up from our packing, we all had a good laugh at our various ways of accomplishing the same task.

With only the last minute things to pack, such as our hairbrushes, we went to the castle's comm center and had them bring up the typical clothing styles worn on Descartes-3. In the past when I was there, even though it was only for a few weeks at any given time, I ignored fashions, preferring to wear my jeans and tank tops. Besides, most of the time I spent at the martial arts academy. This trip, I would be dealing with bankers and lawyers. Why that should make me so fashion conscious, I simply can't say. Perhaps, as the head of this family, I felt we ought to make a good impression. Perhaps, it was that we six rather enjoyed wearing very elegant dresses. Marriage does change one's routines. It wasn't just me only now; I had five others to consider.

As I always knew, most of the more fashionable women wore the five inch lip plates. Mom had told me about that, and I had seen some on my previous trips there. More importantly, we six studied the fashions the women were wearing. Breathing a sigh of relief, Danika commented, "Well, they don't look all that different than the gowns we have now, though I do like those simpler looks, the white blouse and black skirts. I think they look more professional somehow, but what do I know about such things?"

"Hey, you've got great taste, love. Anyway, I don't think we'll have to buy new wardrobes when we get there. That's something," I countered. We relaxed about fashions and slept well.

At nine the next morning, wearing our tall heels that matched our various colored satin gowns, we walked slowly out to the commercial transport ship that would take us to my home world. As we walked, I spotted our dozen crates being hauled out to the cargo bay on one of the electric cars. We'd said our farewells, accompanied by volumes of thank you's, and we meant every last one of those. Our lives were so vastly improved thanks to their Basic Therapy, training in the use of our special magus mental skills, and yes, even fashion sense. In a way, this trip had changed us all into modern Imperium women. My five mates no longer thought of themselves as backwards primitive women. They held their heads high, as we walked elegantly to the waiting transport. Yes, I matured a good deal as well, just by being here, around so many others who were just as I was, physically too.

I also made some preparations for this trip. Since not everyone on any given world spoke Imperium Standard, I had us all listening to the language disks that last night and also during the lengthy trip as well. Descartes-3's common language was one of those click languages. I had long ago promised mom that I would one day learn hers. Well, now I was keeping my promise to her. When we arrived, all six of us should be able to speak a little of the local language, as well as understand the speech of others, even if it was only the very basics.

My mates were very excited about this trip, because the transport was going to visit ten other worlds before landing on Descartes-3. They would be able to get a glimpse at ten more worlds, something almost no people on Closed Worlds ever got to do. As we took our seats, Tesla noticed many other people, particularly men, were most definitely noticing her and all of us, for that matter. Several men smiled and gave her flirting flashes. When I noticed such looks, I realized we were being noticed not because of our deformities, but because we appeared extremely attractive to men. This came as a revelation to the five, who had considered no man would ever be remotely interested in them as women. Certainly, I believed that would have been true back on Metcalf-4, but not out here in the civilized Imperium. This promised to be an interesting, educational trip, I concluded.

The small yellow sun of Descartes-3 loomed through the viewport windows. Our approach was right on time. While my mates were all extremely happy with the trip, having seen many intriguing sights, although quite brief during the ten stops, I felt a little strange. I was coming back to the only home world I'd known, even if it was just a few weeks every year or so — coming back without my parents.

Danika brought me out of my introversion. "Well dear, at least, you won't have to spend three weeks practicing your martial arts this time. Where is your city?"

"It's Anlog. About ten miles from the spaceport. When we were here, my parents never did travel far from their ship. We always took temporary housing in Anlog. We'll take a shuttle there."

"It looks so different from our world," Tesla commented. "There's so much stuff." She was referring to the myriad buildings, usually made from concrete and steel here near the spaceport.

"My folks once took me out into the country away from the big city. Out there, it is somewhat like Sana Falls. Lots of farms, trees, and rolling countryside, though it is quite modern. Towns are sometimes only five miles apart. You can tell the heritage of a woman by her lip ornaments. If she wears them, she's from the country. If not, she's a modern city woman. I guess that's not always so true. Lots of wealthy women also wear them as a fashion statement," I explained.

After landing, we made our slow way across the tarmac to the customs checkpoint. Our ID cards were hanging around our necks, easily scanned. My mates took all this in, so new and so inexplicable. They had no idea of computers and what they could do, let alone all of the automation around us. Before long, we found a shuttle to Anlog. Tesla was amazed to see our crates appearing near the shuttle, almost as we arrived. I tried to explain the automated baggage system, but failed miserably. It's one of those things that you just have to see to appreciate.

An hour later, we checked into the hotel, the very one

we used to stay when the Eagle's Seed was planet-side. The doorman and manager did recognize me. As he signed us in, the manager commented, "Well, Miss Nia Elain, you sure have grown up some. A very beautiful young woman. I'm so sorry about your parents. It was on the news, you know."

"Thanks," I replied, not really knowing what else to say. I led them to the elevator, while holding our door key pass between my teeth. Using my nose, I punched 10, our floor, and then had to explain the operation of the elevators.

The view from our suite was that of the sprawling city, which the five ogled over for several minutes. They'd not seen anything like this close up before. Tall skyscrapers, fountains, arches, streets swarming with people, and small shuttles flying about, as if in some kind of mad dance. "So many people!" exclaimed Anya. "I've never seen so many people in one place before. You can get lost in them."

"True. Anlog is home to around seven million people. It's a big city."

"Is that seven thousand thousand?" Anya asked, trying to wrap her mind around the sheer number of people. I told her so, and then we unpacked some of our things.

"Well, first we go to the bank to settle the financial matters," I announced. "It's not too far. We can walk there."

Out on the street, we were suddenly enmeshed in the throngs of people. While most of the men wore business suits or workmen's clothing, the women wore a wider variety. We quickly discovered in our tall heels and gowns, we were treated as elite, wealthy women. Other women wore the white blouses and black or grey skirts, knee-length, but with black nylons showing and perhaps three inch pumps. A very few wore cotton day dresses. At least every other woman wore the traditional five inch lip disks, usually gold or silver colored.

"What are all the women carrying in their hands?" asked Jana.

"Purses. They keep personal things in them, like a hairbrush, their ID cards, keys, makeup and such things. Dresses don't have pockets, like the men's pants do."

"Kind of silly of them not to put pockets in the dresses like we do with our leather dresses back home," Tesla commented.

"Wouldn't do us much good to have purses," Danika added her thoughts to the mix. "We don't have hands to carry them with." We chuckled.

"We're kind of slow, aren't we," Jovanna noted. Indeed, at least two out of three others passed us, walking faster than we could in our heels.

"Yes, but I've been peeking. Some of the men are being aroused by us," Jana whispered. "Wonder why these men do, but back home our men don't?"

"Because here on Descartes-3, men don't need a woman to work as hard as the men do back home. On Metcalf-4, the men depend upon women to work just as hard in the fields and elsewhere to produce enough to survive on. Here, there are tons more possible occupations for women than back on our world. Many of those jobs, all of you could manage to do just as well as any other woman. On this world, we are not at much of a disadvantage as you might think we are."

"So far, I like our world better. This one is kind of sterile and stinks," Tesla added. We chuckled and entered the bank.

We walked up to the receptionist, who was wearing the lip disks. I told her who I was. She replied in her click language, "^ery ^ell. If ^u ^ill ^ollo^ ^e." It took us a second to comprehend her, but she rose and began walking. She wore the professional woman's outfit. That is, a white blouse, probably silk, with a plain grey skirt, nylons, and black patent heels that were about half the height of ours. She slowed down for us, and we soon entered an office that smelled of furniture polish with that new-rug odor.

"Ah, Miss Nia Elain Compton. I've been expecting you. Please have a seat. Cali, bring in three more chairs please." The receptionist did as asked. He was slightly pudgy with black hair and a small moustache. Like all of those from Descartes-3, his skin had a slight grey hue to it. His hair was oiled, and his cologne was a bit strong. Still, he was a pleasant man.

After receiving his sympathies on the death of my parents, he produced a pile of documents that needed my signature. I listed each of my mates as next of kin. This way, they would inherit my fortune if something happened to me. When we finished up, I looked at the total in my account, close to four million credits — a huge fortune!

Then, he took me by surprise. "Do you want to sell the Eagle's Seed? If so, I have a buyer who is ready to pay up front."

"Not at all. I am keeping the ship. Thanks."

"Ah good. Now then, one final matter. As you know, this bank financed the last exploration mission that your father undertook. We've heard that he's discovered substantial psi-crystals on that world. As his heir, would you like to sign over the mining rights to the bank?"

"No. It's officially now a Closed World, a part of the Ataro Empire," I replied, rather shocked that he wanted me to sign over such rights. If I did, the bank would send in many miners and make gigantic profits, none of which would go to the inhabitants.

"Yes, I understand. You can't fault me for at least asking," he quickly reversed course.

I rose and left quickly, avoiding any further protests on his part. I know dad would have signed over such rights, had he not died. Still, these were my people now. I didn't want to see them cheated out of their valuable minerals, with nothing but trinkets in return. I was certain the Ataro Empire would treat us fairly, at least I hoped so.

When we walked back into the hotel lobby, a man I thought I recognized rose from a plush chair to meet us. "Ah, Nia Elain. Remember me? Mr. Kraken. My company sponsors your father's expeditions. My, how you have blossomed."

"Yes, I thought I recognized you," I replied, wondering what he wanted.

"I am so sorry about the tragic death of your parents and the crew," he went on, but I sensed no real grief or sorrow behind his socially polite words. "I understand that he discovered vast psi-crystal deposits on that world, Metcalf-4 is it?"

"Yes," I kept it short and simple.

"Well, your father would certainly want you to sign over the mining rights to me. I've sponsored a great many of his explorations. I make my money from the mining operations and use it to sponsor more such expeditions." He definitely wanted me to sign, but I was not about to do it.

"Sorry. Metcalf-4 is now a Closed World. You can take up your case with our Queen Akira Ayano. She handles all that sort of business. Sorry," I replied, faking sorrow. I sensed a flash of anger building up in him. His fingers clenched slightly, but he kept his sympathetic face on.

"If you wish to reconsider, here is my card," he handed me a small business card, which I was forced to take between my teeth. That annoyed me, but I had no choice, since he wasn't the least bit embarrassed that I had to take it that way. He bowed slightly and left us.

As we walked to the elevator, I dropped the card into the trash bin. An arc flashed, disintegrating it, recycling its molecules. Then, I had to explain about the recycling operations.

Our scheduled return flight to Ashford-5 wasn't for another three days. Over room service and with time to kill, we discussed what sights we ought to see. I'd describe one, and the five would vote on it. Tonight, we decided to visit the symphony. In the morning, we'd take a trip out into the countryside, giving them a different look at Descartes-3. The following evening, we decided to visit the historical museum. We left the rest of the time open, ready to add all manner of other activities. They also wanted to visit a dance hall.

We were well enough dressed for the symphony. After eating, we again headed out, this time taking a shuttle to the giant, egg-shell shaped Symphony Hall. "We fit right in," Jana whispered as we walked into the crowded entryway. Indeed, men wore their finest suits. Our gowns matched well most of the other women, though a few wore strapless gowns, which I didn't prefer, even though Danika loved to see me wearing one. Our heels were just the right height. Hardly a woman present had lower heels. However, most wore the usual black nylons, and in contrast, our bare legs stuck out. Still, we had to be able to use our toes.

While the five had heard local vocal songs, hearing musical instruments was totally new to them. Yes, they were impressed, as I was. I'd never been to the symphony either, for that matter. We six had a thoroughly enjoyable evening, although three times several young men tried to pick us up, completely amazing the five.

It was close to eleven when we finally got back in our hotel room and by midnight, we were sound asleep. That's when it must have happened. Someone unleashed a knockout gas into our room. Much later, I learned that we woke up over five days later!

Ex-Hub Sector ID Minister Martina Wells arrived at the Presidential Skyscraper. Several years ago, she'd retired and moved back to her home world of Descartes-3. Martina had retired upon the death of her long-time mate, ex-Legate Mary Smith, who, along with Emperor Kino Sango, was famous throughout the entire Imperium for having saved the Imperium from collapse during the planetary genocide years, when the unscrupulous had unleashed the terrible bio-agents that genetically mutated human bodies. During those years, she met and became Mary's right-hand woman and mate. Martina took the death of Mary very hard indeed and could not see herself working any further without her mate. Martina was now technically ninety years old, but thanks to the Rejuvenation Machine, she appeared thirty-five.

Like Mary, she had been a victim of the genetic terrorism, but fortunately had had her arms regrown along with many of the other genetic cures. Martina had kept her giant lip plates, partly because of the culture on Descartes-3 and partly to prominently display the fact that she too had been a genetic terrorist victim. She still bore some of the marks. Her waist was still tiny, having had two ribs removed and organs moved to her enlarged pelvis region. Her feet had only been partially repaired, forcing her to wear six inch heels at all times. However, she and Mary had made good use of their hermaphrodite bodies. They had six adult children now, but they were all married and living their own lives. With the death of Mary, she'd returned to Descartes-3. Martina was searching for something, but had no real idea what that might be. She was unhappy.

Descartes-3 was technically just barely in the outer rim third of the spiral arm, while for the most part the Ataro Empire was in the mid-rim section. It was on a Thursday morning that she'd received the secure comm call from the President of Descartes-3, a very unusual call. He'd never called her before, but demanded her presence in his office here in Anlog, the capital city. Martina took a shuttle to the Presidential Office, squarely in the heart of the city.

Her stilettos clicked on the tiled floor, as she entered the spacious reception area and headed to the bathroom. There, she touched up her minimal makeup, re-fluffed her long, wavy blonde hair, smoothed her black skirt, and checked her white blouse. Like her deceased mate, she preferred to look like a professional woman, though the higher heels and larger than normal bosom suggested otherwise. She smiled at the reflection of the embossed image on her top lip plate, which drooped to her chest. Martina and Mary had gotten identical images, a pair of women holding hands, a symbol of their undying love for each other. Yet, Mary had died, and she hadn't. Martina was lost without Mary, or so she considered. Satisfied she looked her best, she exited, and took the elevator up to the fiftieth floor, the Presidential Suite.

As she entered the large suite, the receptionist buzzed the President. "Miss Martina Wells, the President will see you now. That way," she indicated with her hand. Without breaking her slow stride, Martina continued on her way into his room.

As she entered, the President rose from behind his large desk. "Ah, good of you to come. Please, have a seat. You are looking well."

He can't see the bags under my eyes nor the red in them, she thought. A little makeup does wonders for such things. "What's this all about?" she asked politely. Martina was never one to play games. Always immediately get to the point had been her motto when she was the ID Minister and later, the Legate.

"Yes, of course. Time is of the essence in kidnaping cases. We have a politically explosive situation on our hands."

"In that case, why not put it in the hands of the ID

Minister?" she countered.

"Too delicate. Too embarrassing. A very sensitive matter."

"Will you stop beating around the tree and explain what has happened?"

"It's complicated. Recently, one of our deep space exploration ships discovered a new world that is rich in psi-crystals. However, the crew all perished, except the daughter of the captain, one Nia Elain Compton."

"Yes, I heard about the discovery and the loss of that crew. That world is now a part of the Ataro Empire, if the news reports are correct," Martina replied.

"Precisely. However, apparently, this Nia and her five wives — Nia is a hermaphrodite, adopted by the Comptons when she was a baby. Anyway, she and her five wives suffered atrocities on this Metcalf-4 world, losing all or part of their arms. Tragic. Yet, they all are telepaths, Class V from what Governor Misty Childa-Bellweather of Ashford-5 tells me. You see, they went to Ashford-5 to receive training in their telepathic skills, as near as I can tell."

"So what has this to do with a kidnaping?"

"I'm getting to it. Following their training, they were to return and take their new Queen Akira back to Metcalf-4. However, Nia Elain had to come here to her home world to settle the affairs of her late parents. From the data that I have, she's worth around four million credits. We know the six went to Symphony Hall the evening after signing all the documents. The hotel reports they subsequently entered their suite around eleven. They've not been seen since!"

"Governor Misty was notified, when they were not on their scheduled return flight. That was three days ago now. She's threatening to raise all hell if the six women are not found in short order. It's not an idle threat! One call to her emperor and there will be hell to pay for this mess!"

"Damn. But why not bring this to the ID Minister?"

"Because we cannot let it become public knowledge that these six women are Class V telepaths, let alone that there are others like them on this Metcalf-4 world. If this becomes known, the political fallout will force the emperor to take rather drastic actions. It all falls on my head, since they were kidnaped right here on Descartes-3 and in our capital city no less."

"So where do I come in?" Martina asked, growing extremely impatient with his lengthy description and failure to explain directly her involvement.

"I want you to conduct an investigation on the quite — outside normal lines. This way, no one will know the underlying importance of these six women. You were the Hub Sector ID Minister for years. There is no one on Descartes-3 who is more qualified than you are. I want you to do whatever you have to do to find and rescue these women, *before* word leaks out about their significance. Carte blanche. Just find them fast!"

Martina wanted to say go find someone else, but the fact that these were women and likely helpless women at that convinced her otherwise. "Okay. I'll do it."

"Good. Start with their hotel room. It's been left untouched." She nodded, rose, and walked slowly out of his office. She made a side trip to her home, donning her d-gun and PDS belt. Satisfied, she took a shuttle to the hotel to begin her investigation.

For some time, Martina stood just inside the hotel door to the women's suite, studying the layout. There had been no sign of forced entry, but that meant little. Anyone with any electronics skills could bypass the door locking mechanism. A clever person could also fix it so the central computer would not log the fact that the door had been opened. Her initial conclusion was that was precisely what had happened here. That narrowed the spectrum of possibilities considerably. This was a professional hit, no doubt.

She entered the suite and stood observing carefully, spotting a small bit of paper and a discoloration on the carpet just outside their bedroom doors. She squatted down and took a closer look. She recognized the bit of paper as having come from a knockout bomb. Its cylinder was nowhere to be seen. The discoloration occurred as a result of the release of the gas. She'd seen similar evidence before, many times. She made a mental mockup of what must have happened. The women were in bed, asleep. Their gowns and heels were laid out with care on the tops of the dressers. Someone had opened their door and tossed a knockout bomb into the room. That meant they wore gas masks. That also meant the women wore nightgowns or nothing at all, pretty hard to slip them out of the hotel.

Satisfied of her conclusions thus far, she left the room to check on methods of moving six women out of the hotel without being seen. She found no plausible means by which that could have been done. Martina then reentered the suite. The exit point had to be from the suite. She moved from window to window, examining each carefully. "Ah ha," she whispered. "Sealing glass!" The method of egress was now clear to her. A shuttle had hovered just outside this window, while someone carefully cut out the glass window. After the women had been carried out and stowed in the shuttle, he'd used sealing glass to replace the window by re-bonding the cut edges. Mentally, she noted that at least two men would have been required to carry out this action, possibly three. There was nothing further to be learned here at the crime scene, so she returned to her own home.

She fired up her computer and activated several monitoring programs. One would be looking for any "advertising" of telepaths for sale. That was a remote possibility, yet Martina was thorough, just as Mary had been. Another checked for unauthorized shuttle flights. Still another brought up all of the locations of security cameras in the general location of the hotel, along with their angles of view. It was a long shot that the kidnapers had been caught on camera. Pros would be more careful than that. The last one checked all outgoing passenger flights that had a group of six women on it. However, she could not rule out the possibility that they went off-world via shipping containers.

Then, acting on a hunch, she also logged into the Central Bank, using her old ID Minister login. It still worked; so much for their security, she mused. She activated her short program that would isolate and report on all monetary transactions larger than a threshold amount. She paused and pondered the figure she ought to try first. Too low a value and she'd be bombarded with millions of entries. She decided upon two hundred thousand credits and activated the program.

All she could do now was wait. Hence, she made herself a cup of tea and pondered why this kidnaping had occurred. To Martina, the why was often the key detail that lead to solving a crime. She ruled out kidnaping them to become local prostitutes; the details of the kidnaping suggested real pros, expensive ones at that, and well thought out. Since no one had received any ransom note and since the bank would alert her to any transactions on Nia's account, she ruled out kidnaping for credits. These were the two most often motives. Political gain or to coerce someone in power was also rejected, since these women were off-worlders and had nothing to do with Descartes-3 politics or justice.

She was left with two real possibilities. One, Nia could have been kidnaped and forced to sign over the mining rights on Metcalf-4. Those would be extremely valuable rights. Two, the six could have been kidnaped for their telepathic skills. The first, she discounted. Already, it was known that Metcalf-4 had been accepted into the Ataro Empire and was thus a Closed World. Any signed document transferring mineral rights would be null and void now. No, Martina faced the very real possibility that the six had been kidnaped for their unique and exceedingly rare telepathic abilities.

Sipping her tea, Martina settled on the second as the motive. This greatly narrowed the field of possibilities, leaving several potential avenues to be explored, divided along two main lines. First, they could have been kidnaped and sold to very wealthy men here on Descartes-3, either all to one person or divided between six men. Second, they could have been kidnaped and taken off-world to be either sold as a lot of six or sold individually to wealthy clients out there in the vast Imperium. Third, the possibility existed of a combination of the two.

All of these would necessitate a significant transfer of funds. Kidnaping telepaths was very dangerous work, involving great risks. The punishment for such crimes was life in prison as a genetically modified person, who was totally helpless and had to live in an assisted living home. Such criminals were given a dose of that terrible bio agent which mutated their bodies. Hence, she hoped her bank transactions search would yield clues.

Next, she placed a secure call to Governor Misty Childa-Bellweather. "Hi, this is ex-Hub Sector ID Minister, Martina Wells. I've been given the task of finding the missing six telepaths. Over."

"Yes, I remember you. Any leads? How can I help? Over."

"Nothing concrete as yet, other than it was done by pros. What I need is a time frame. How long ago was the flight to Descartes-3 arranged? I'm looking for just how much lead-time the kidnappers had to work all this out. Over."

A bit later, Martina refreshed her cup. While it was common knowledge that Nia Elain would need to return to Descartes-3 at some date to sign all of the legal documents, the when had not been known until two days before their flight departed Ashford-5. The perpetrators could have known that Nia Elain would one day come to Descrates-3 for about a month before she arrived. However, the specifics of her arrival were not known until two days before the flight, which meant that much of the planning had to be done extremely quickly. While no one could have predicted which hotel, let alone which room, Nia would have chosen, Martina's search showed that the Compton's usually stayed at this one hotel. Such info would certainly have been discoverable by the kidnapers.

"So we are looking at a month to come up with the overall plans, but only five days down to one day to work out the specifics. No matter how I look at it, this has to be a rush job. When rushing, mistakes are usually made. Plus one for me." She sipped her tea once more, using a spoon, of course.

Quiet reflection. That was Martina's key to success. As she sat there, lifting spoonfuls of tea into her mouth, negotiating the gap between her lip plates, another recent fact appeared from her memory of the news. The long lost Righteous Commander, one Arnwald Berend, had surfaced on this same world, Metcalf-4. Apparently, he'd crash landed there many years ago. His patched-up shuttle had exploded on takeoff. Could The Righteous have a hand in this, she wondered?

They would have the wherewithal to pull off something like this on short notice, she thought. Martina made a note to follow this line further and went to see if any results had come back on her searches.

It had. Several security cameras were available, and she began to scroll through their files. A half hour later, she had the one with the best angle queued up and began watching the side of the hotel, beginning around eleven that fateful night. Around one in the morning, just as she expected, a shuttle moved slowly up to the side of the building. Martina paid close attention, frame by frame. Suddenly, she paused and tweaked the image. Tweaking the image by blowing it up larger and applying image enhancing software, she got the view she desired.

The shuttle was a very old one but it's markings were visible. She jotted the numbers down and quickly switched to the shuttle registry database to see who owned it. She didn't recognize the company. Still, she had a solid lead. Further checking yielded the fact this shuttle had been scheduled for recycling and had been left at Excore Recycling's field two weeks ago. She placed a call to the company and found that the shuttle was still parked on their lot. She placed a hold on it and headed over there at once, calling in a forensics team who would meet her there.

"I want it dusted for prints, particularly the cockpit," Martina ordered. The six member team and Martina entered the ship. While the team set about their duties, she did what she did best: observe. A glass cutter had been tossed aside. An empty cylinder of glass re-bonding cement lay discarded on the floor, proving her theory. Several long hairs were visible. The women had been brought onboard this shuttle. Now the question she had was where had they been taken before this shuttle was dumped? With nothing further to be learned immediately here, she returned to her home, confident that the forensics team would notify her of any findings, as soon as they had them.

Several more of her searches had completed, and Martina began to assimilate the results. One minor detail caught her eye. A cylinder of the bio agent that was used on Imperium criminals and the more vicious local ones — the very same agent responsible for all of the genetic mutations and planetary genocides — was reported missing, prompting a High Alert among the local Security Forces. Martina's question was: did this have anything to do with the abductions?

She reexamined the ID card images of the six women. Obviously, Nia was a child of one of the genetically modified terrorist victims. However, close inspection of the other five suggested some form of a bad accident, requiring the use of an Imperium medical machine. Why? The inch in diameter, conical tips of their upper arms was a dead giveaway, at least on three of the five women. What bothered Martina was just what would be gained by using the bio agent on them, genetically modifying their bodies? Just to remove what remained of the three women's upper arms seemed pointless.

Yet, the more she pondered this, the more reason she could see for doing this to the six women. They would be severely hobbled up and hence more easily controlled, forced into subservience. Somehow, Martina felt this was a plausible scenario and integrated it into her thinking. She reviewed all of the reported info on the theft of the bio agent. The Security Guard's theory was that it had been an inside job; they were in the process of scrutinizing everyone who had potential access to the cylinders. Nothing to fault there.

Given the data at hand, Martina began to theorize on locations. If indeed the six had been subjected to the bio agent, special equipment would have to be on hand, particularly a bio containment tent or similar apparatus. Such was not easy to acquire. Hastily, she launched another search, looking for all recent purchases of that and similar items. As her program ran, she followed that line of thought.

The containment tent would have to be erected at a location, which simply could not be routinely accessed by normal workers, the public, or even many other people who were not involved in the kidnaping. Anyone seeing a bio containment tent would certainly raise the alarm. Martina now ruled out most all the buildings within any city limits. Why? Building inspectors routinely visited all buildings at random times, checking on electric lines, gas lines, elevator safety, and so on. If they had setup a bio containment tent in one of these buildings, such as an unused or isolated warehouse, they could not be certain that one of the inspectors would not show up for routine checks. The success of something this major could not hang on pure chance, not when professionals had been used for the basic kidnaping.

No, they must of necessity be being kept at an estate far from any city, where such inspections were few, if any. Private estates were almost never inspected, except when being sold. Further, only the very wealthy could afford such estates. Farmland was at a premium. Descartes-3, as a whole, was only just barely was able to fulfill its food production needs, even throwing in vast hydroponics plants and the synthetic goo that passed for food. Centuries ago, the price of prime farmland skyrocketed.

Again, this dovetailed nicely with her evolving theories about the kidnaping. Ultimately, one of the wealthy men or women was likely the instigator, looking to acquire illegally one or more telepaths. She recalled the now ancient cases involving telepaths from Ashford-5 and the extreme measures businessmen had gone to capture and debilitate them sufficiently to force them to serve their needs. All this made sense to Martina, even though she had only the flimsiest of leads at this point.

She returned to her computer and the monitoring programs, bringing up two lists. First, she displayed the wealthiest men and women on Descartes-3. Second, she cross checked those names with the bank logs of the largest credit transactions during the last month. That done, she now had a list of a dozen men, whose accounts showed very substantial funds transfers in this time frame. Martina now had suspects.

It had been five days since their abduction. She took off four days for the time period during which bio terrorist victims werc in their comas, while their bodies were rapidly mutating. That left one day. "So if I am right, today, the six women have awakened from their comas. If they are indeed hobbled up, they cannot have done much with them in so short a time," she spoke to her computer. Furiously, she sent out a request to the

President, asking him to have every spaceship that was scheduled to takeoff from today on carefully searched. If the kidnapers intended to take them off-world, they'd find this avenue blocked, giving her more time to locate and rescue the women. She did not tell him her reasoning, however, not without more proof.

Another search completed. There were six bio containment setups on Descartes-3, plus one recent purchase. Hastily, she contacted each of the six, asking them if their bio containment tents were accounted for. All were. However, when she contacted the company, which had made the recent purchase, she got an ear full. "Look, we've already reported this to the Security Guards. It never arrived here. Company records indicated clearly that it was sent to us, but it just never arrived." The man was quite antagonistic over the loss, though the shipper's insurance companies would take the financial hit and not the maker or buyer. Upon further background checking, Martina verified this company did have a legitimate reason for acquiring such a tent.

This missing and certainly needed bio containment tent only re-enforced her suspicions the six had been subjected to bio terrorism, and were likely helpless victims at this point. That thought caused her to cringe visibly, bringing back her own memories of just how badly she had suffered, because of a similar exposure to this nasty bio agent.

Just then, the forensic report arrived in her email. Quickly, she scanned the results. Obviously, the kidnapers had used gloves. No unexpected fingerprints. However, they did discover a wad of chewing gum and had extracted DNA from it. The person had been identified, a known member of The Righteous, wanted for numerous crimes on several worlds. He was not, however, a known Commander, just a henchman.

This confirmation that The Righteous was involved in the actual kidnaping made very good sense. They would certainly have the means and manpower to pull off such a sophisticated kidnaping. Stealing a shuttle, intercepting a bio containment tent shipment — these would be routine for this band of criminals. While The Righteous always remained in the background, making it nearly impossible for the authorities to locate them — there were a million holes in cities for such rats to hide. Their services, if indeed they had been hired to carry out the actual kidnaping, would not come cheap. Substantial credits would certainly be involved, unless The Righteous had taken the telepaths for their own work or were promised a cut in their sale. Based on her ID Minister background, she ruled out the latter. The Righteous were not known for carrying out very risky ventures without immediate payback.

Martina reasoned that either The Righteous were in this alone, planning to either use the telepaths or to sell them, or that The Righteous had been hired to do the dirty work, presumably by one of these dozen wealthy men. Now, she had to figure out which scenario had gone down. Back to her data gathering she went.

Her next question was: Did The Righteous have personnel who could correctly utilize the bio agent? While it didn't take a rocket scientist to open the cylinder's valve, releasing the potent bio agent, it did take some skill to know the proper dosage and to monitor for ill effects. Quickly, she discovered the authorities had too little information about the nature of their personnel. Dead end.

As Martina sat back pondering this development, another idea struck her, based on her own terrible experiences. Once she had awakened to find her body so horribly mutated, the rescue personnel had to provide her with clothing that fit, very specialized apparel. True, every duplicated crate contained just such clothing and shoes along with the bio cylinder. However, in this case, there were six women to be dressed. Whoever was doing this would have to acquire this unique apparel. She dove back to her computer once more.

Fifty years ago, such apparel was widely available, considering the millions who had been infected and whose bodies had been so horribly mutated. Now, however, the Imperium had put an end to these terrorist attacks, for the most part that is. In today's Imperium, only the modified criminals needed such articles, along with the very few who had not yet received the many cures that the geneticists on

Ashford-5 had created. For a moment, she was distracted by the realization that in all these years, only the geneticists on that world had ever come up with any cures to undo some of the terrible mutations the bio agent caused. How strange, she thought. Says something about that world and its people.

She decided to follow up on this line of reasoning. Martina began making inquiries about where such apparel could be purchased these days. Unfortunately, there were ten supply houses that used Fabrication Machines to make them to fill orders, most of which came from the assisted living homes that housed the modified and helpless criminals. Grunt legwork was going to be needed. She used her authority to request local ID agents to handle this for her. Someone must have ordered at least six outfits and likely far more. A person could not wear the same clothes every day.

She got an immediate reply. One store had been broken into three days ago, and a large number of complete outfits had been stolen. No leads. Martina smiled. This continued to fit her theory about the abduction. The women were now basically helpless victims. Moving them around would be far more difficult. For the first time, she felt a little more optimistic that she might be able to find the women.

However, time was critical. Now that they were out of their comas, they could be moved nearly anywhere, including back into the city. If that was done, she might never be able to find them, but at least if the Security Guards did their jobs properly, the women couldn't be taken off-world.

It was back to following the money trail. With so many thefts in this plan, The Righteous must have charged a hefty amount. Surely, the credits would be laundered to look legitimate. Martina knew she had to try to unravel the financial picture.

Martina toyed with the idea of having the President order raids on the twelve estates, taking their places apart looking for the women. However, the backlash from the other eleven would be political and legal suicide. No, she would have to zero in on the actual culprit before she dared make such an accusation. Wealth had its perks and privileges. That, she could not deny.

Martina was a methodical and visual person. Armed with more information than she had anticipated after only one day at it, she used sticky notes to make a time line of events on the wall behind her computer desk. A red one marked the day and time of the kidnaping. Four subsequent green-tagged days represented their likely coma days. She pasted a yellow marker for this, their first day out of the coma. Then, she added other white-tagged notes above the row, indicating proven data, such as the image of the shuttle hovering at the side of the hotel window. Lastly, using grey tags, she added notes of her theories and potential dates, pasting them below the main row.

The rest of the day, she stared at the financial records of the twelve, getting nowhere at all. Tired, both physically and emotionally, she headed off to bed, frustrated she'd gotten this close to finding them, but had hit a dead end wall. That time was critical for these poor women only increased her frustrations, a good sign she needed sleep. With a heavy heart, Martina turned in, knowing another day had passed, lessening the chances of her being able to find them, but not before sticking another yellow sticky tab, a blank one, onto her time line.

Over breakfast the next morning, another idea flashed into her mind: psych men and their behavior modification. Often on low-level criminals, the psych men attempted to used their behavior modification therapies. On some, it took, and the criminal's behavior totally changed into that of a totally submissive person, easily controlled. Could these people have also made use of the psych men's behavior modifications to make the women go along with whatever they were told, in effect, helpless puppies? Such actions were highly illegal, but that had never stopped some psych men before. Martina cringed even thinking about such a thing happening to these poor women. Still, it was another avenue to pursue.

She checked in with the authorities, learning they'd made some progress. Based on her suggestions, they'd investigated more thoroughly these apparent incidental thefts and discovered either fingerprints or security camera video of at least six more wanted members of The Righteous gang

239

operation on Descartes-3. Martina found this quite encouraging. Perhaps, they could locate some of them and force them to talk, but she knew she could not depend on such happening.

This morning, she decided to play her hunch about the possibility of a psych man being involved. There were one hundred six registered psych men on Descartes-3, anyone of which could be involved. More grunt work, she sighed, sitting back and spooning in her after-breakfast tea. Yet, perhaps not. He would certainly insist on being paid a substantial amount up front for his highly illegal work. She hit the bank records once more.

An hour later, she came across a very unusual pair of entries. A Dr. Akakios had a deposit of a quarter million credits the day of the women's abduction. That same amount was later withdrawn two days later. How very strange, Martina thought. No other suspicious amounts had been deposited in the other hundred plus psych men's accounts. Even more curious, both transactions had been in actual large credit notes. Time for a personal inspection. Grabbing her purse and cell phone, she headed out to her small, private shuttle.

Thirty minutes later, she found the two tellers who had handled the transactions. Martina was more interested in the withdrawal transaction. The teller commented, "Well, yes, this was a highly unusual withdrawal. Two hundred fifty thousand credits in large notes doesn't happen often, so I asked for identification. His face matched his ID card, so I thought it was okay."

"I need to see the security video," Martina requested, biting her tongue a little since she couldn't bite her lips. This didn't just add up. The teller took her to the manager. A half hour later, a technician had the withdrawal date and hour queued up. While she sifted through those series of second-apart images, the man dug up the deposit date's camera recordings. By the time he had that one ready, Martina had found what she wanted, a short sequence of the psych man entering, waiting on the teller, and then leaving with the briefcase full of credit notes. On a second monitor, she spent a half hour finding the initial deposit sequence. Now, she played them both, side by side. There were two clear shots of the man's face, which looked identical on both monitors.

The manager stepped up behind her. "See, we don't make mistakes. It's the same man, this Dr. Akakios. You can see his face quite clearly there and there."

Martina pressed her tongue again against her teeth. Something was wrong, but what? She didn't respond to the manager, but reset the playback loops and watched the two short strips again. Three more times she repeated it. "Ah! Yes, there it is! It was not the doctor making the withdrawal!"

"What? Clearly, it most certainly is. The faces are identical," the manager protested, defending his bank and its reputation. If they'd been conned, they'd just lost a quarter million credits!

"Look at the man entering. See, the real Dr. Akakios has a slight limp. Left leg. Now, look at the imposter who made the withdrawal. No limp. Not a trace of it. Someone has scammed your bank, I'm afraid."

The manager slumped into a nearby chair, crushed by this sudden news and its implications. Martina had seen enough. "Okay. I need a precise listing of just what denomination credit notes were given to that person. I want everything you have on those notes, any forms of identification. Email me the data," she barked, handing him her card. She turned and walked out of the room, her heels clicking uniformly on the tiled floor, her mind racing.

Once back home, she modified her bank search program, based on what she'd discovered with the psych man. It was just a hunch, though. She sat back and pondered the significance of her discovery. Obviously, the man had been paid handsomely for something. Yet, two days later, someone impersonating him had withdrawn that same amount. Interestingly, they had left the man's remaining funds untouched. If this had been a simple robbery, the crook would have drained the account, but had not, only the amount, which had been deposited. Conclusion: whoever made the withdrawal knew precisely the amount that had been deposited and was likely privy to the original deal to pay the psych man for his services. He'd been double crossed.

Her hunch was a simple one. If the perpetrators double crossed the psych man, then they were likely to do the same with anyone else involved in the kidnaping, specifically The Righteous mob members, though those men would be a far more dangerous foe when they discovered they'd been double crossed. Still, she thought her hunch worth checking out. She headed to her kitchen to make another cup of tea.

When she returned, she adjusted the sticky notes, reflecting the two events involving this psych man, Dr. Akakios. "Time to pay this head shrinker a visit," she declared aloud. She looked up his office and home addresses, entering them into her cell. Once more, she headed outside to her shuttle. First stop, the man's office. It was Friday, and he ought to be at work.

A half hour later, she entered the suite and walked up to his receptionist, but could not help but notice a large, handwritten sign. The doctor is unavailable. "Hello. Have you an appointment?" the young woman asked as Martina walked up.

"No. I take it Dr. Akakios is not here? I need to see him."

"I'm sorry. He's not here. I can take your name and add it to the list," she replied, clearly frustrated.

Martina decided to play around a bit. She flashed the receptionist her Sector ID Minister badge, rapidly, so she could not see it had already expired. After all, she was an ex-Sector ID Minister. As expected, the receptionist began to panic. "Yes, he's not here. He's simply not shown up for work for several days. Not answering his home phone or his private cell. I'm just his receptionist." She was on the verge of tears, nervously tapping a pen on her desk.

"Calm down. I'm sure you've done nothing wrong. I need to see his appointment schedule for this week and last. No, I don't need to see patient files," she ordered, adding that last bit to avoid inquiries about needing a search warrant.

A few minutes later, she had what she wanted. He had made two entries on two dates, one preceding the kidnaping. Meet X at 10 at Barak's. The appointment entries for the next day had all been crossed out. Martina asked the receptionist about that. "Oh, he said an emergency had come up and for me to reschedule his patients on another day. I did that. Was that wrong?" she asked worriedly.

"No. You don't know what this emergency was all about, do you?" she asked. As expected, the receptionist didn't. She could add nothing more, except he was rather excited about this emergency. Martina thanked the young woman and headed back home, wondering where this "Barak's" was located. A quick search yielded a restaurant.

Once more, she hacked into their security footage. Knowing the date and time, she quickly queued up the video feed. She spotted the psych man entering and sitting across from a person in a back booth. Whomever Akakios met wasn't visible. His back was always to the camera. She let the feed run for a time after Akakios left. The person rose and left by a back door, still without revealing his face. Frustrated, she rewound and looked for his entry. Once more, the person cleverly avoided having his face caught by the security cameras.

Martina then wasted another two hours, rounding up video feeds from the surrounding buildings, hoping to catch a glimpse of the person coming to the meeting or leaving. The man seemed to know precisely where the cameras were located and thus avoided all of them. "He's good. He knows far more than the average person does. Clever man. Damn," she cursed aloud. She added another sticky tab to her wall time line.

As she sat back spooning her tea and pondering this remarkable event, her mind raced down alternative methods to track this mysterious person in the restaurant. Just then, her cell buzzed and she answered. "Miss Wells, you asked us to report any unusual happenings? You still want them?" It was the local authorities calling.

"Yes, certainly. What happened?" she replied, sitting up straight, looking for her pen and paper.

"Most peculiar. We've just picked up seven freaks down in the red light zone."

"Freaks?"

"You know, the genetically modified. No arms, monster boobs, tiny waists, giant lip plates. Genetically modified bodies."

"What were they doing?"

"No voices. They can't speak and their eyes have been removed. They were crying and terrified, barely able to walk."

"No voices? Blinded? Escaped criminals from one of the assisted living homes?" Martina asked.

"That's what we thought when we brought them into the station. We checked. All prisoners are accounted for. So you asked for weird things. This certainly counts. We don't have a clue who they are and no way of telling."

"Okay, do a DNA test on all seven of them. Make it a super rush job. Send the bill to the President's Office. Let me know the results as soon as they come back," Martina ordered.

"Yes ma'am. Mind telling me what this is all about?"

"Yes, no can do at this time. President's orders. Thank you for letting me know. Goodbye." Martina hung up, pondering this new twist. She had a hunch, which is why she had ordered the rather expensive DNA tests. Now, all she could do was wait on the tests. Back to work, she thought, heading for her computer to see if any further results had come back yet. They hadn't.

Her latest bank runs against the dozen potential suspects finished up. She gazed at the results and shook her head, bothered by them. Not one showed any substantial identical withdrawals and deposits a few days later on. Her theory that the culprit withdrew the funds to hire the criminal elements, gave it to them, and later stole the funds back, depositing them once more into their account had drawn a blank. The culprit was too clever to leave behind such a clear evidence trail. "No, that would have been too easy," she muttered sarcastically to her computer and headed off to fix some lunch. The day was slipping by way too fast.

The afternoon drifted by without anything further developing. At last, a frustrated Martina began calling up the various teams working on the details. None of the investigating bodies had anything to report. There had been no trace of The Righteous criminals. They'd simply slipped back into the underground where they dwelled. All leads continued to simply dry up. Close to suppertime, the DNA test results came back. A very excited Security Guard Captain called her back.

"Well, you called it right, Miss Martina. You'll never guess who these seven are! Six are the very Righteous mobsters we've been tracking for you. The seventh is very strange, though. It is a psych man, a Dr. Akakios. Don't know how he fits in, unless he was a secret Righteous member. No evidence of that yet, but we're just now confiscating his records. If he was, we'll soon have him. Meantime, whoever did this to them has saved the government the cost of genetically modifying them. We've handed them over to the criminal assisted living homes."

She praised him for their excellent work and hung up. Now her mind raced! I know that Mr. X hired The Righteous to steal what was needed to pull this kidnaping and genetic modification off, but then Mr. X double crossed them, genetically modifying them. Added safety precaution: blind them. Now, they can't speak nor can they visually identify this Mr. X. Ingenious, she thought. Plus, Mr. X had done the same thing with the psych man. Obviously, Mr. X is leaving no trail that could connect back to him! So we have our hands on the men who carried out the kidnaping and probable behavior modifications on the six women, but we'll never be able to get anything out of them. Oh, Mr. X, you are the clever one! I can't even trace the funds used to hire them! Damn.

Later, she placed another yellow sticky tab onto her time line, another day was coming. Time was running out, but she was tired and needed sleep. Perhaps, tomorrow she would get lucky. I need another bright idea. She drifted into sleep instead.

The next morning she found absolutely nothing new had appeared. Worse, she had no new bright ideas. Late morning, the President called to get an update on her progress. She outlined what she knew had happened thus far. He finally said with a sigh, "Well, at least we have captured the criminals who did the actual kidnaping. That's something. Put a severe dent in The Righteous mob. Can't argue with that. Still, we need to find those women. If they have been genetically modified, we're going to be in really hot water. But maybe they haven't. Just find them, Martina, find them!" He hung up.

Bastard! What do you think I've been doing? She sighed and headed off for a mid-morning brew. Spooning in her warm tea, she finally relaxed and another idea popped into her head. She reasoned thusly. If Mr. X went to all this trouble to kidnap six telepaths, then it makes sense he needs to use their unique skills. He's not going to keep them as some kind of sexual slaves. No, he plans to use them. How?

At this point, she reflected upon all she knew about Class V telepaths. They could read other's thoughts, know what they were thinking. She reasoned Mr. X needed to know what someone else was thinking and planning. That meant Mr. X would be using them. Key word: using. Whatever it was, it must be vitally important in some fundamental way, she reasoned.

But six telepaths? Overkill. While some wealthy businessmen were known to have their private telepaths with them during critical business meetings, one couldn't have six present. One would be totally sufficient. Besides, if Mr. X tried to use six at once, that alone would raise all manner of red flags among the other attendees. No one had six telepaths working for them. If one was extremely lucky and rich enough, he might have one telepath in their employ. Even that was as rare as snow in the desert. No, he couldn't use six at once, unless they were hidden from view. She thus could not discount the notion Mr. X might just sell off five of them to the highest bidders. She slumped in her chair, no closer to a resolution than before.

Her monitors were in place. If this Mr. X tried openly to sell one or more of them, her programs would intercept such communications, and she'd be on top of it immediately. She was certain the women could not easily be carried off-world, not with the overly tight security now in place. However, she could not discount word of mouth communications of telepaths for sale. No monitoring program in the Imperium could guard against that.

Martina spent the rest of the day pondering how she could monitor what might be vitally important meetings where telepaths could be used to good advantage. This was a very difficult subject to handle. By their very nature, these were private business meetings, probably only known to a few company top men and women. Occasionally, businessmen met with government officials. These she could monitor and fired off a request to be informed of any highly sensitive meetings with any government official anywhere on Descartes-3. The President agreed and promised to notify her well in advance.

Sadly, she had no choice but to stick another yellow tag onto the time line. The markers above and below the main row regrettably had dropped to near zero. With a heavy heart, she headed off to bed. Martina had not yet grasped a single anomaly. That came to her while she slept. The seven men had not been murdered. Instead, they'd been genetically modified and more.

Chapter 14 Days of Terror

I awoke in great pain. No, not pain really, intense discomfort. I couldn't breathe. My chest felt like it was being crushed. Were my wives somehow lying across my stomach? No. I was sitting up. My lips felt like they were being pulled off my face, as well as my ears. My feet felt very strange. I opened my eyes, as full consciousness returned to me. I panicked.

We six were sitting side by side on a long sofa, facing a mirror. Strange images stared back at me! Are these us? My mind whirled. A well-dressed older woman stood off to one side of us, watching us closely. She wore a bit too much makeup. Her medium length black hair was streaked with grey. She wore the elegant five inch lip plates and tall heels, similar to those that we had worn. Her dress was probably satin, a dark red, matching her nails.

I stared at the six images, trying desperately to comprehend what was going on. Some kind of nightmare? We'd gone to the symphony last night, so this had to be an hallucination. Our breasts were each far larger than our heads! Giant lip plates, a foot in diameter, draped from our stretched lips, touching our chests. I felt two loops of metal, U-shaped, around my upper and lower gums, supporting the weight of the plates. Our ears had been slit and a pair of oblong but huge golden disks inserted in the slits, stretching them taut. Enormous earrings dangled from them, the ends of which rested upon our gigantic bosoms. Our waists had vanished! No, they were incredibly small and I simply couldn't breathe! I felt a tight but slippery sensation encasing my legs, black nylons. Our feet? Were those our feet? What happened to them? Our feet were pointed almost straight down encased in some strange-looking toe boots with only our toes touching the ground and the tall, spiked heel touching the floor immediately behind our toes. What was going on? How could I have ever dreamed up this hallucination? I fainted from lack of breath.

An awful odor roused me. That woman was waving a

smelly tube in front of each of our noses, waking us. I gasped and fought to breathe against the unrelenting pressure around my lower chest, failed, and fainted again, only to be roused by that awful smell. Twice more it happened before the woman finally spoke. She used the click language of Descartes-3; she had to because of the lip disks she wore. Her lips could no longer form many normal language sounds. "Shallow breaths, my dearies. Shallow breaths."

"What's happened to us?" I cried out. I was shocked. I couldn't understand a single word that I'd just said. Beside me, Danika, Tesla, Anya, Jana, and Jovanna all shrieked and spoke just as unintelligibly as I had. I could sense their fear that began to crescendo towards terror. I couldn't even focus enough to send out any calming flows. It was all I could do to keep from passing out yet again.

She repeated her admonition once again. We six couldn't do anything but take shallow breaths. Then, I noticed the three no longer had even their upper arms! They were identical to Tesla, Anya, and me. My mind played games with me. It won't matter much, since they couldn't do much with them anyway. Crazy thoughts.

"I am Madame Dionysia Damaris. You are now my working telepaths. You are completely physically helpless and need the constant care of my assistants, Callidora and Astarte. As long as you do as you are told, you'll be well treated. If you can understand me, nod your heads." She spoke very slowly in the click language. I just barely understood her, but I saw that my five wives nodding and concluded they too must have understood some of what she'd said.

The two assistants must have been standing off to our left, because they walked into our range of vision. They were dressed much as Madame Dionysia was. She introduced the two younger women. "This is Callidora. This is Astarte. They are unable to speak, but they'll take good care of you. Understand? Nod please." We did as she asked, still trying to wake up from our shared nightmare.

"Callidora, help Nia Elain rise, and help her walk around the sofa. Astarte, you do the same with Danika. Don't worry; they won't let you fall."

As Callidora began pushing on my back forcing me to attempt to get to my feet, I realized I couldn't bend much at all, only just barely at my waist. As I rose, I couldn't keep my balance, but Callidora slipped her hand around me, supporting me. Now, I saw my hair had grown considerably. It fell almost to my ankles. The gown was quite form-fitting and had almost no walking slit. Even if I had wanted to, I could not take more than a two inch step. Wiggling and wobbling wildly, I tried to walk. I had no choice, since Callidora continued to apply forward pressure on my back. I panicked but was unable even to make my fright known to Madame Dionysia! Danika fared even more precariously that I. Likewise, her hair had grown several feet, touching her ankles as well. I've no idea how I actually was able to walk around the sofa. Trying to sit back down was impossible. I fell onto the sofa. Radiating terror, Danika fell down on the couch beside me. The two women gently readjusted the fall of our very long hair.

I was panting like mad, unable to breathe and fighting from passing out once again. The two women did the same with Jana and Jovanna and then with Tesla and Anya. All six of us were soon gasping and fighting to remain conscious.

"You have much to learn in order to walk gracefully. Allow me to show you a similar model. This is a famous ballet dancer from Proxima Prime, filmed before the planetary genocide struck. Her name is Ariceli. The ballet is called *Carwyn Ascending*. Watch." She played a portion of a ballet. We saw this woman walking elegantly and doing all manner of fancy dance moves. True, her ballet shoes were a little different from ours. She stood on the tips of her toes, while we had all of our toes on the ground. "So with practice, you six will be walking as gracefully as she did."

"Oh yes, in case you haven't realized it yet, your bodies have been genetically modified. Now, all six of you are hermaphrodites so Nia Elain won't be alone. Understand?"

I knew my five wives didn't. They shook their heads indicating that they didn't. She explained a little. "You have both fully working male and female organs. Your waists have been drastically shrunk and pelvis expanded. Your hair has been lengthened and cannot be cut any shorter. The pain will be intense, I'm told, and besides, it'll grow back rapidly. Your breasts are quite spectacular, as are your lip plates. None of these changes can be undone. I'm afraid that you'll just have to adjust to your new bodies. Adjust to your new bodies." For some reason, she chose to repeat that last phrase very forcefully, but I could see no reason for it.

Suddenly, I heard a voice in my head. *You have a perfect body now. You have to adjust to your new body. You'll thoroughly enjoy your new body. It gives you much pleasure. Your body is very sexy. You have a fabulous figure and want to show it off with fine gowns. You'll never want your body altered from its now magnificent state. You would rather die than have any changes made to the way your perfect body is now. You love your new look and want to always look like this. You'll walk with grace and poise. You'll always obey Madame Dionysia Damaris. You want to use your telepathic skills to help her. You'll remember these words and repeat them silently to yourself many times each day.*

I understood the words, but just could not figure out where I'd heard them. Then, I found myself silently repeating them to myself. I did love my body, didn't I? Why would I ever want it changed? Of course, I don't want my body changed in anyway. I love it. I am magnificent!

Meanwhile, Madame Dionysia watched the six women closely and then smiled. The psych man's behavior modifications were taking hold, just as he said they would the moment she spoke the trigger phrase. Per his instructions, she waited patiently for ten minutes. She could almost see us repeating these words over and over in our heads. Finally, she spoke again, bringing our attention somewhat back on the present.

"You just love the way that I've got your bodies fixed, don't you? Nod please." All six of us nodded that we did. "Good. Good. Now, your first order is don't speak unless I give you permission to speak. Your second order, is don't try to speak with each other or any other people, you simply will not be understood. So don't upset yourselves by trying. Now then, don't you need to practice walking with grace and poise?" Once more, we nodded.

Thinking is one thing; the doing, an entirely different matter! While we all believed we always would walk with grace and poise, once we tried to stand up and do it, we were anything but that. I'm afraid our two silent helpers were kept busy helping us walk. It didn't help that we couldn't breathe and soon were gasping for breath. Still, like dogs in training, we kept at it, much to the pleasure of Madame Dionysia, who was still looking for more proof the behavior modifications were taking hold sufficiently strong enough. My feet ought to be cramping and aching, but for some reason, they weren't. Was I full of painkillers?

How long we wiggled and wobbled precariously, anything but poise and grace, I couldn't say. I just kept hearing that voice in my head, agreeing with it and trying my best to comply. Finally, she asked us to sit down again. "As you approach your seats, stop and lean forward a little and shake your heads some so that your hair falls to your front. Then sit down. Otherwise, you'll sit on it, and that will hurt a great deal. Understand?" Vaguely. But we shook our heads yes and tried it. My earrings were heavy, and while shaking my head some, I felt them nearly pulling my ears off! Still, with our satin gowns and no arms to interfere, our lush hair did as she suggested, slipping forward. Sitting down was again more of a fall into the sofa than anything remotely graceful.

"Well done, ladies. Well done. You just need more practice. But now, it's time for dinner. Will you care to dine at my table with me? Your two assistants will feed you of course. Nod if you understand me." We did, partially anyway. Why was this click language so darn hard to comprehend?

Again, we rose to our feet, wobbling crazily to get our balance, and then followed her. As we shuffled along, I could tell we were in some grand mansion. She must be very wealthy, I concluded. The dining room was spectacular. Grand paintings hung on the walls. A golden chandelier made from pure gold hung over the highly polished table. Really fine china was set out for the nine of us, along with teacups and crystal goblets containing purified water.

The cuisine was superbly done, but the quantities were small. I soon discovered even this small amount was more than I could eat. I was stuffed long before my plate was empty. The two helpers got quite a work out assisting us, as well as eating themselves. We now saw how we could eat while wearing these giant lip plates. They were raised up and locked into a horizontal position. I remembered this was exactly how the Ashford-5 queens looked while they were eating. Once we finished, the plates were unlocked and allowed to droop down on our chests once more.

During the meal, there was no talk. Once we were finished, she again explained more rules. "Now, it is time for bed. Again, I am ordering you not to talk to each other while in bed. I'll allow you six to sleep together in one large bed. Tonight, don't attempt to pleasure each other. Instead, you'll be attached to the language learning system, so you can learn our language better and speak clearly. You'll be sleeping in your corsets and hose tonight, so that you can get more used to them. I'll see you all in the morning."

Our bedroom was equally plush, and the bed quite large enough for us all. Our assistants pointed to the attached bathroom, and our nods indicated we needed to use it. Sometime later, the two had us all undressed. In the many mirrors in the room, we could see our corsets now and our incredibly large breasts. The other five could also see their new male organs through the thin panties the assistants left on us. One by one, they brushed out our hair, removed our lip plates, and helped us lie down, draping our hair over our fronts. They placed earphones over our head and ears, adjusting the volume for us. Finally, they covered us up and turned out the lights, revealing a faint floor nightlight.

"Follow orders" bounced around my mind, so I didn't try to speak to the others. In the background, the click language lessons had already begun. Soon, I fell asleep, unaware of just how exhausted and tired I was. We even slept in late the following morning.

However, chaos erupted when we did finally wake. We all needed to use the restroom fast. However, our two assistants were too slow in coming to help us. Unable to bend much or breathe, and with our feet so messed up, we six lunged and struggled to get ourselves up and out of the bed, wiggling and wobbling wildly. Our hair draped over our bodies like some kind of sheet, but we shuffled forward and made the bathroom, but it wasn't pretty.

Fortunately for us, the assistants got to us at the last instant and kept us from making a huge mess. Following their gestures, we ended up sitting in a row along the edge of the bed, while one by one they prepared us for the day, putting in our lip plates, dressing us in clean gowns, and finally brushing our hair. At last, like a line of penguins, we made our inelegant way to the dining room.

Over breakfast, Madame Dionysia commented, "You six women look positively sexy this morning. You should be very proud of your beautiful bodies. Now today, we must work on your walking skills, plus we'll keep on working on your language skills. Understand?" We nodded.

With the assistance of the two silent women, we began walking around the spacious mansion. Walking on our toes on rugs was quite challenging, while our heels made clicking noises when we walked across the fancy tiled floors. I'd never see a single story home this large or this fancy. Each room contained works of art, painting, statues, tapestries, and even sculptures. One room even contained vaulted arches, whose ceilings panels were covered with painted frescos depicting several rural scenes.

As we began walking, that voice began reciting the positive litany once more, and I found myself repeating it, considering it to be speaking the utter truth. On the positive side, we were becoming more comfortable breathing in these impossibly tight, metal re-enforced corsets. Now, however, we discovered another difficulty: drool. With no lips to keep our saliva within our mouths, we began dripping it down the lower plates and onto the tops of our gowns, rather embarrassing. Our assistants noticed it, and by pointing and gesturing, suggested we hold our heads vertical. We were trying hard to see our feet over our massive bosoms.

After lunch, our walking continued. I will say that we did improve hour by hour, though we were given frequent breaks, particularly when we became short of breath and tired. During the long afternoon, I became more and more annoyed with that voice in my head. I already agreed with everything it said to me. I loved my sexy body. I looked fabulous. I was following orders. I was doing everything right, but that voice continued to remind me of those many points. I think the same thing was happening with my wives as well.

After another dinner, which could well have been served at one of the finest restaurants in the Imperium, Madame Dionysia had us practice her click language. "You've definitely improved a lot, but you can do better. Now, let's see how you are doing on your graceful walking." Once more, we dutifully demonstrated our walking. "Excellent. So very much better." She gave us the same bedtime orders to follow as before and sent us to our bedroom.

The next two days were near duplicates of the first. However, I knew we were now walking gracefully, even sitting and rising without lunging or falling. Plus, we were comprehending this click language far better. The language disks certainly do work well. We were able to control our drooling better too, particularly because we were walking on a level surface. Walking over the carpeted rooms was five times trickier, though.

The following day, we were finally comfortable with walking around the mansion. Today, something happened. As we began walking, I really started to see the mansion and the art objects. I was right there, in the present time stream. Somewhere in the back of my mind, that voice was still trying to talk to me, but I was mostly able to ignore it completely. Occasionally, I looked into the eyes of Danika and saw she was having a similar reaction.

I obeyed my orders not to speak, but I used telepathy instead. Madame Dionysia hadn't outlawed that. *Danika. What's happened to us? Where are we?*

I don't know. I was going to ask you the same thing. Are we captured? Can't we leave? I want to go home.

Hey, I want to go home too, Tesla sent us. The communication block between we six was finally broken. We began chatting among ourselves via telepathy.

Comparing notes and ideas, we realized we had been kidnaped from our hotel bedroom, presumably while we were sleeping. None of us could remember anything before waking up on the couch here in this mansion. Each of us was hearing a man's voice in our heads, saying the same things. Curiously, we each believed we were very sexy, had fabulous looking bodies, desperately wanted to experiment with our new sexuality, and certainly didn't want anything to be changed about our now incredible bodies. I just could not shake these positive notions off. I'll admit in the very back of my mind, there was a minuscule hint these were not true. Still, we wanted to get out of here and return home. The problem is that we didn't know where we were, except probably somewhere on Descartes-3.

Madame Dionysia probably suspected something was going on between us. When we all sat down to dine on yet another fabulously cooked meal, she explained, "Nia Elain, Danika, Tesla, Anya, Jana, Jovanna — it's time I tell you why you are here. I need your telepathic skills to find out which man killed my husband and son."

I sensed suppressed grief beneath her made up appearances. I could not help but feel a rush of sympathy for Madame Dionysia. Perhaps that's because of the relatively recent loss of my own parents. I was convinced my sympathy for her was real and genuine. A glance at Danika sitting beside me told me she too felt a real closeness to this older woman.

"I should explain in detail. You see, I had to wait until now so you can understand me. I don't speak much Imperium Standard, just our native Descartes-3 language. If I say something you don't grasp, you are free to interrupt me. Okay?" We nodded.

"I met my husband when I was just twenty-one. He was so strong, so handsome. I fell madly in love with him. Yet, he was a forceful, domineering man, but I didn't know that at the time. He always got what he wanted, and he wanted me, so I don't suppose my being in love with him would have mattered. Knowing what I know now, he would have gotten me anyway."

"At first, life was wonderful. He was rich and powerful. This very mansion was my wedding present from him. Yet, he led a secret life, one that I swear to you I knew absolutely nothing about, not until after his death."

I interrupted, "When did he die?"

"Two years ago. Perhaps, I ought to have known he had this hidden life. Perhaps, I just didn't want to see it. Anyway, he had what he called his three close business partners. They were certainly around here a lot, especially in the early days of our marriage. Every year at harvest time, which is nearly on us now, he and his partners hosted a gala harvest party here at the mansion."

"It was at those parties that I saw another side of all four men. While we always invited close to a hundred people, the men always brought along a dozen special women. I say special, but I must be quite clear about those women. They were all children of convicted criminals. You see, Imperium criminals are all exposed to the same bio agent, which genetically alters human bodies. The changes are the very ones all of you now share. Additionally, the criminals' voices are also removed. This way they can be cared for in cheap assisted living homes, alleviating the terribly costly prisons and armed guards. Honestly, it's the best way to deal with those hardened criminals. However, as hermaphrodites, many of them have children, who are born with the same genetic modifications as their parents."

"Since the cost of undoing most of these genetic modifications is quite steep, here on Descartes-3, these children are left as they are born. Some are adopted; some take advantage of the public education that we provide all our children. Some later go into the exotic escort trade. I believe the dozen women my husband and his three partners always brought to the harvest party were just such women, exotic escorts. They all look much like you do. I've gone to a lot of trouble to match your appearance to those escorts, which used to come to these harvest parties."

"As my son grew older, my husband took him into his business. He too began to enjoy the company of these exotic women at the parties held here on my mansion. It was all harmless fun. I never caught either of them actually having an affair with these women. Anyway, two years ago, the harvest party was held here, same as always."

"Excuse me," I interrupted again. "Were the same exotic

women here every year at the parties?"

"Yes and no. It would be the same women for several years, and then others replaced some. The last group two years ago was all different women from the very first ones at our first harvest party. Is that important?" she asked.

"Guess not."

"Okay. We had over a hundred guests at that last party. All was completely normal until around midnight, when the party broke up. Around one, the three partners, my husband, and son were all entertaining the dozen exotic women. Everyone else had left. I couldn't stand all of the flirting that was going on, even though it seemed perfectly harmless. I went to bed."

"Around two in the morning, I heard two shots being fired. Startled, I got up and went out to the sunroom where everyone had last been. The partners were gone, as were all the escorts. I found my son and husband lying on the floor with half of their heads gone. D-guns. The Security Guards came when I called them, and they said d-guns had been used to kill them. For weeks, I was in shock."

"They had no clues about who had murdered them. None at all. They did question the three partners, but they claimed they and the escorts had all left around 1:30, shortly after I went to bed. The authorities have never found any clues at all, writing it off as a random shooting. I had no choice but to accept their finding."

"Then, as time passed, I began to sort out all of my husband's things, donating his clothes to goodwill and recycling what wasn't fit to be given away. As I was cleaning out his big desk, I came across a safe combination I'd never seen before. I didn't even know we had a safe here in the mansion. It took me a week of searching, but I finally found it hidden behind a bookcase. The combination worked. Inside, I got the second largest shock of my life."

"My husband was actually a Commander of The Righteous, one of the worst criminal mobs in the entire Imperium! I had a mobster as my husband! Worse, he'd gotten my son involved in his criminal enterprise! I can't tell you how that upset me!"

"The three men, who I had thought were just his business partners, were in fact top members of his organized mob! One of them had likely murdered them to take over control of the mob here on Descartes-3. I tried to go to the Security Guards with this information, but they laughed at me, telling me I was dreaming. He was a very well respected businessman and certainly not a member of The Righteous. I can't tell you how many times someone has told me that!"

"Since I was not going to get justice from the authorities, I decided to take matters into my own hands. Using the secret documents that I found in his safe, I knew the very henchmen that used to do his dirty work. As I understand this organization, they are organized into separate cells. One cell does not know the identity of another. That way, if one gets caught, they can't reveal the others. I believe the rest of the organization operates the same way, except for those at the very top, like my husband was."

"I had no direct proof these three partners were actually criminals themselves, just strong suggestions. I've spent close to a year studying them, and I'm convinced they took over my husband's position as Commander. Either one of them did or all three. I don't know why they murdered them, though."

"I'm a law abiding woman. I just can't go killing the criminals nor can I just kill these three partners. If they are guilty, they should be given the usual penalty: genetic modifications and forced to live the rest of their lives as helpless individuals in assisted living homes. Death is far too good for them."

"For months, I've pondered just how I could ever figure out who was responsible for their deaths. I've kept our two assistants on here; they are both very good workers, as you've seen. Very conscientious. They've been of immense help and comfort to me these past two years. Then, I hit upon the ideal solution: telepaths. I tried to hire a telepath, but found they are incredibly rare. The five who exist here on Descartes-3 are all in the employ of very wealthy businessmen. I soon realized I'd have to find my own and began extensive research, looking for possibilities. That's when I discovered Ashford-5 was reputed to have some."

"I came across you six while monitoring communications. I am quite desperate, and I'm truly sorry that I had to kidnap you. I really have no choice, if I'm to find out which of these partners killed my son and husband. You might also say I've been doing the authorities' job. I covertly hired those Righteous henchmen of my husband's to kidnap you and all the rest. But when they finished their work, I knocked them out the same way they knocked you out. Then, I subjected them to the usual penalty for hardened Imperium criminals. They now look just like the six of you. I had their voices removed per the law, and dumped them off in the city. I'm sure that sooner or later their identities will be discovered. They will then be placed in assisted living homes for the rest of their lives."

"Now, the only way I have to get telepaths in the vicinity of these three men is to have them come here to the mansion. I arranged for another harvest party, in honor of all the other parties we held over these past decades. I promised them the usual exotic escort women would be here. That clinched it. All three promised to attend. That's why I simply had to modify your bodies into these stunningly elegant ones. You six have to look just like the women they always had at these parties. And you do, very much so. You all look positively beautiful."

"Now, I know what I've done to your bodies isn't fair to you, but then maybe it is. The reason for your long earrings is simple. Those are your payment for your services. Each pair is worth over a hundred thousand credits, more than enough for you to have much of the genetic modifications undone, if you so desire it."

"But I'm perfect now. I'm sexy and beautiful. I'm happy with my body. I don't want anything undone," Tesla rattled off.

"That's fine, Tesla. You can use your earrings anyway that you desire," she replied. "So here is the plan. We have three weeks to get you six ready for the harvest party. You must be able to walk gracefully and to be totally comfortable in all things, so you can pass for these exotic escorts. At the party, use your telepathy to figure out who killed my son and husband. Once that's done, you are free to go and to return to your own home world. Keep the earrings and all the other things as your payment for your valuable services. I'll then deal with the guilty. Will you do this for me?"

I sensed she realized she had not phrased that last as an order. Nevertheless, I spoke up, "Of course, we'll help you get justice, Madame Dionysia."

"Thank you, thank you. I know all this is hard for you, but if we work together, we can have you perfect for your roles at this harvest party. Oh, I'm supposed to order you to work hard and get ready for your roles. You need to be able to move around wholly independently, with confidence, poise, and grace. Let's work on those today, shall we?"

Again, she forgot to order us to do that. Nevertheless, we felt strongly about wanting to help her find the person who had killed her son and husband. That they had been criminals somehow didn't seem of major importance. I believe our reasoning powers had probably also been compromised. Dutifully, ignoring the discomfort we felt, we continued practicing.

This day, we spent hours sitting down and standing backup without having any assistance. Our goal was to be able to do it gracefully and with poise, while still looking beautiful and being able to manage our hair in the process. At the end of the day, our knees were aching fiercely, but we thought we were definitely making progress.

By the time of the harvest party, we six were handling everything to Madame Dionysia's satisfaction. I will point out we were playing along with what was expected of us. That is, thus far, we had not used any of our other special powers, just a bit of telepathy. The two silent women assistants were quite conscientious and helpful. Further, Madame Dionysia had not explicitly asked us about any other powers, but I cannot say with any certainty just how under her influence we actually were. The voice in our heads told us we were, but we didn't feel that way. We were highly sympathetic to her cause, wanting to help, wanting to be graceful and elegant, and full of poise. Early the morning of the party, the three were very busy making all of the arrangements. While we felt a strong desire to help, she told us to watch after ourselves today. We did as ordered, wandering about the huge mansion and discovering her kitchen and chef, who cooked all the mouth-watering dishes. The woman shooed us out of her kitchen in short order.

Late afternoon, the two silent assistants motioned us to our bedroom. There, she redressed us for the party and brushed out our hair. We all wore similar form-fitting, tight gowns with the minimalist of walking slits, but we were used to taking such small steps by now. Looking into the mirrors, I thought we all looked absolutely fabulous. A huge surge of pride in my wives flooded over me. I sensed it was mutual too.

After a light supper, we took our places in the spacious sunroom, where the silent women had arranged fresh flowers. The room took on a festive atmosphere. Some soft music was playing in the background. Madame Dionysia had us sitting in various chairs around the room, not as a single group. She'd showed us images of the three men, and we were ready for the detective work. In small groups, her many guests began arriving. These were some of the wealthiest of Descartes-3. They had to be, considering all the expensive jewelry the women wore, and the quality of their gowns, some of which were similar to our very fancy gowns.

We found both men and women were attracted to us. Everyone chatted in the local click language. I was very glad we'd learned it so well. While most of the guest women wore the smaller five inch in diameter lip plates, like us, they had to speak in this click language. That's why it developed as it had. None of us could make any sounds that involved our lips. The chat was pleasant, focusing on how wonderful we and they looked, how marvelous it was that Madame Dionysia was once more hosting these harvest parties. Light, senseless chat from my point of view.

Eventually, the three partners arrived, their wives hanging onto their arms. As Madame Dionysia expected, they spotted us at once. Soon, they found excuses to let go of their wives and migrate over to us. One of them ambled up to me, a wine goblet in his hand. "And who might this lovely creature be?" he asked politely, but rather coyly.

Madame Dionysia had ordered us not to give out our real names. I answered, "Athena, kind sir. And who might you be? I've not seen you here before. Madame Dionysia always throws such nice parties, don't you think? Have you been to one before?" I knew from her he was one of her late husband's partners, but I played my role well. This was exciting and fun. All these beautiful and elegant women — so many were watching me and my wives, admiring us, I presumed.

He chuckled. "Barak. Call me Barak. I've been coming to her parties since before you were born, my lovely nymph. Why I haven't seen you before now?"

"I surely haven't seen you here before, Barak, but then I've only been coming to her recent parties."

"Would you like some wine, Athena? And a steadying arm?" He started to slid his hand over my sides.

"Would you be so kind? I surely don't need steadying right now." I watched him, as he headed off to find a long spoon for me. Thus, the night began. While he fed me sips of wine, it was easy for me to probe his mind. I knew what he would say next and found easy counters to his various flirtatious moves. More importantly, it was obvious he had taken part in the two murders. His thoughts kept coming back to just what was Madame Dionysia trying to prove by continuing these harvest parties? I found myself feeling rather dirty standing this close to a murderer. It was easy to tweak a few other younger men's minds and have them come over to me to play out their courting games, rather frustrating Barak, who soon migrated over to Danika.

Long before the party was drawing to a close, all six of us sent telepathic messages to Madame Dionysia, telling her that this one or that one was involved in the two murders. Barak, Kadmos, and Manasses. All three partners had plotted the murders together. Now, I wondered what Madame Dionysia would do about it.

Around midnight, the guests began saying their farewells. Madame Dionysia had we six beside her, as she accepted the many thank you handshakes and praises for a superb party. However, just as they had used to do, the three men stuck around after the last guests had departed, although their wives also left.

Barak suggested, "Madame Dionysia, you have kept

these incredible beauties hidden from us. You have excellent taste. Might you allow us a little extra time with these gorgeous women, before we depart?"

"Why I surely wouldn't want to deprive you of the company of such exotic women. They do need to freshen up, you know. Would you mind waiting in the parlor, while my silent assistants and I tend to their needs? Have them ready for you in say fifteen minutes?" she replied coyly. I picked up a real hatred veiled in her remarks.

Naturally, they agreed, moving off to the parlor, wine crystals in hand. She and her assistants escorted us to our bedroom suite. About halfway there, she stopped us. She whispered, "You six stay here and out of the way. No matter what happens, keep out of it. Your work here is finished. You no longer need to follow my orders. You two, come with me." The silent women nodded and followed her.

We stood where she'd left us, about ten feet from our suite, following her order to stay here. While we were not precisely witnesses to what happened next, I can make a very good guess, especially later on, after I learned more about the usage of the bio agent, which caused the genetic modifications.

She had gotten her hands on one of those cylinders and, while we were confined to a stolen bio containment tent, had used part of it on us. The remainder of the cylinder, she had rigged up to unleash its entire contents into the parlor room. That room had only two doors. Unknown to the men, one of her silent women had locked the second door before they entered. After Madame Dionysia left us, she had one of them lock the door that they'd just used, while she opened the valve on the cylinder, allowing the entire remainder of its contents to flood the room in one massive shot of the terrible bio agent.

The three murderers quickly realized something was going on and tried to leave the room. I heard one of them pounding on the backdoor. Then, I heard them all calling out rather alarmed, "Madame Dionysia. What's going on here? Let us out." After that, I heard lots of swear words, and then the door being smashed or possibly disintegrated.

We heard Madame Dionysia's shrill voice cry out, "You bastards! You murdered my son and my husband. Now, you are going to pay for that!"

I think Barak shouted, "^ich!" That translates roughly to "bitch." After that, we heard Madame Dionysia scream out in pain, followed by a number of rather mysterious thumping sounds. We were about to go and see what was happening, when the two silent women came past our room, going as fast as they could in their tall heels, which wasn't fast. Panic exuded from both women. They stopped and frantically motioned for us to follow them.

What's happened? I sent to one of the, rather startling her.

They've broken out. Killed Madame Dionysia! Flee! Flee for your lives! After that, both took off once more.

After I relayed that to my wives, we decided to look for ourselves. If these evil men had killed her, Danika wanted a chance to return the favor. Certainly, we were not about to allow these murderers to escape! We rose to our feet and made our way out of our room, down the hall, heading towards the parlor.

We stopped about halfway there. Madame Dionysia's body lay on the floor, a dagger protruding from her forehead. However, the three men were coughing and had collapsed on the floor. Even as we watched, they passed out. We smelled a distinctive odor. Reactively, we knew we needed to get out of the house immediately. We did so, heading towards the same doors the two silent women had used. When we reached them, I figured we'd need to use our powers to smash them open, but once more the two silent women had thought of us. They left the door ajar. Out we went onto the cobblestone patio, the first time in a month we'd been outside.

It was dark, but the pale light of the moon, darting in and out of some high clouds, vaguely allowed us to see. We were in time to see a small shuttle just after it had lifted off. Two other shuttles were parked on the lawn. I'd never see this type of shuttle, and knew I couldn't fly it. Besides, they could only carry two people.

"Now what? Where do we go? I want to go home," Tesla said, in the clicking language.

I admit it. I was totally lost. I had no idea where we

were or where the big city was at. About all that I was certain of was that we were still on Descartes-3. Danika spoke up, "Well, north is that way." She rather pointed with her head.

We looked around. By now, our eyes had become accustomed to the dark, and we could see somewhat better. We were on a desolate seacoast. Just north of us was a foreboding cliff that fell far down to the shore and the ocean. We could hear the distant crashing of the waves upon a rocky shore. There were no trees around, just scraggly grass fighting for footholds in the limestone rock of the land. I saw no roads either.

Danika continued talking, "So the ocean is to the north. We should follow the shoreline to the west. Sooner or later, we ought to reach a town or the spaceport. There are always villages along coasts. People always want to fish."

"But can we even walk in these shoes?" Anya asked.

"We don't have any choice, not if we want to get home," Danika answered. "Follow me and watch your step. We don't have to hurry now." In single file, we followed Danika. All of us were wiggling and wobbling, anything but graceful, over the uneven ground.

Tesla called out, "We can't walk gracefully here, can we? I hope that's okay with everyone." That's when I began to realize we were still somehow under the influence of something. Just what, I didn't know. I'd never heard of behavior modification before.

Struggling mightily, we pressed on for what seemed like hours. Once when pausing to catch our breaths, I turned to look back. I could still see the outline of the mansion in the far distance. We were getting no place fast! Grim.

Martina found no new information waiting for her the next morning, nor any in the days following that. It seemed all of the clues completely dried up. All avenues of exploration had either uncovered nothing or had reached a dead end, particularly so when The Righteous men were identified and subsequently shipped off to the criminal assisted living home. Other than the fact that someone had obviously uncovered their identities and somehow managed to modify them genetically, per proper protocols, nothing more could be gotten from them. They no longer had any way to communicate. Although they had committed these smaller crimes and the kidnaping, they could not divulge who had hired them or what had become of the six women.

Martina was very frustrated for several days, especially since no further clues appeared. Daily, she kept in contact with the Security Guards, who were inspecting every transport and every cargo ship that tried to leave Descartes-3. Surely, the culprits would be trying to take them off-world. Yet, nothing came from all the searches.

Making matters worse, the wealthy businessmen simply were not having any key meetings that she could discover. In fact, this was the idle season, just before harvest time, when most people were preparing for the festivities of harvest week. Most took a week's vacation at this time of year, one of the major celebrations on this world.

Two weeks had passed without anything new appearing. Frustrated, Martina once more sat back and spooned her tea, while watching some newscast. With her mind focused on something entirely different, she recalled something she'd thought weeks ago. The Righteous men. Something about them, but what? It struck her that they had not been simply killed. She would have expected that, but no, they had been perfectly genetically modified instead, all ready to serve their life sentence as helpless individuals, unable to communicate and in this case even see.

"That's it!" she exclaimed to herself, sitting upright. "This has the hands of a woman behind it, not a man. Men would just have shot the criminals and been done with it. No, a woman must have done this, making them truly pay for their life of crime. A very clever woman though. These are or were some of the most wanted criminals on Descartes-3, after all, extremely dangerous. But what woman? And why would she want six telepaths?"

Martina had new theories to follow and set to work. Once more, though, she came up empty handed. Confident in her presumption a woman was behind the kidnaping, she dug into the records of wealthy women. Still nothing appeared.

Another fruitless week passed, but Martina was still convinced a wealthy woman was behind the plot and had genetically modified the criminals. She just didn't know the woman's identity or motive.

"Dig deeper," she chided herself. Finally, she began to go over crime reports, correlating them to the wealthiest women on Descartes-3. After another fruitless day, she'd covered the last entire year. Martina was tenacious. She knew she must be right. There was no other reasonable explanation. So she pulled up the previous year's records and ran her correlation program against the wealthiest women.

Suddenly, her screen began blinking, Match Found. "This is more like it," she exclaimed, pulling up the matching records. Dionysia Damaris had filed report after report, made repeated calls for nearly six months, trying to get justice. Her son and her husband had been brutally murdered after a harvest party two years ago. Martina pulled up all of the investigator's records and began reading. The shootings had occurred late at night, long after the party was over. Dionysia herself had gone to bed, the report stated. She had heard d-gun shots and had gotten up to investigate. It was she who had discovered the grizzly scene.

Although forensics had gone over the crime scene, no clues had been uncovered, other than the obvious fact that one or more d-guns had been used to kill the two men. The case had quickly gone cold. Even though Madame Dionysia had continued calling for news, the case was marked cold and put into storage. No one was working it during five of the six months during which she called them.

"This woman certainly has a powerful motive to find the person or persons responsible for the dual murders. But what has this to do with kidnaping six telepaths?" Martina asked herself. Then, it struck her. Who better to locate a murder, than a telepath who could read other's minds?

She sat back, reflecting on this info. The faces of the missing six women had now been handed out to the ordinary security guards, in hopes they would spot them around the cities and towns. None had as yet, but if they had been genetically modified, they'd hardly be recognizable from their

ID card images. Still, that they had not been seen in public for weeks now gave her another clue. Dionysia was not parading them around, having them probe minds at random, and searching for the killer of her son and husband.

Martina concluded Dionysia must already have suspects for the telepaths to examine. Yet, it had been weeks since the kidnaping. Why had she not already used the telepaths? She pondered this for two days, before reasoning it out. "Look," she spoke to her computer, "the suspects must not be readily available for her to have her telepaths check out. If that is the case, then she must be going to arrange some kind of meeting between them. Now, I *do* have a thread to pull!"

Pull she did. Martina began checking every known public personal face book, looking for one or more on which Madame Dionysia might be using. After an hour's searching, she found it. Now, she set up a monitor program, which would notify her of every new posting the woman made to her pages. All she could do was to wait patiently.

Her patience paid off. Madame Dionysia put up the harvest party information on her personal page, giving the date and time of her party, along with shuttle parking coordinates. With a full week to prepare, Martina began plotting out strategies. Could she get an undercover agent into this party? No, it was private. Guests were being personally invited. Could she get an agent in as the companion of another guest? This appeared plausible, if she could get a listing of those who were invited. That didn't pan out either. She didn't keep such a listing online.

Martina worked all angles. Could she get someone in there as a caterer? That failed to pan out too. As the day of the party neared, Martina was totally out of ideas of how to get someone into that party, without just gate crashing, which would alert everyone. She wouldn't gamble on that. Someone might harm the six women. Instead, she had another idea.

She could have a transport hovering high overhead, monitoring the giant mansion. With good surveillance gear, she could perhaps identify everyone who entered or left the party. Further, she could make use of the infrared imaging devices to peer into the mansion, reasoning the six women ought to be identifiable because of their unusual body shapes. She requisitioned a transport and the many devices. By late afternoon, the technicians had everything working.

Martina took one electronics technician with her to handle the equipment and six Security Guards, heavily armed, and armored. "Stay high above the mansion. We don't want to raise any suspicions. There ought to be a large number of small shuttles coming here. So, initially, stay very high. We can drop down after the party gets going." The pilot acknowledged her orders and they lifted off from the spaceport.

The mansion was located near the far northern coast of the continent. The nearest town was some twenty miles to the west. The coastline along this sparsely populated area consisted of rough limestone cliffs that varied from fifty to a hundred fifty feet high. The ground wasn't suitable for much other than light grazing. It was therefore quite isolated, but the mansion itself was worth many millions. From their vantage point, the technician activated the IR camera and began to study the images coming in. From this height, they couldn't tell much at all, other than there were people present inside the mansion.

Again, Martina shifted into waiting mode, watching the monitor, which displayed small images of the many shuttles as they began arriving. An hour passed. She decided to wait a little longer, just in case there were some late arrivals. Tipping her hand now could well spell the death of the women, if they were down there. After another half hour and no further shuttles, she gave the order to descend slowly. Martina moved over to the imaging monitor, alongside of her technician. This was the critical period.

If the women were inside, this was her best opportunity to spot them. They estimated over a hundred were in attendance. The system was able to ascertain the sex of each person. From their near vertical point of view, women's busts were discernable. "If my theory is correct, we are looking for six women with huge breasts," she explained to the operator.

A few minutes later, he spoke up, "Got one. There," he pointed to a specific image. Sure enough, the person appeared to have three heads.

"And there. Another one," Martina exclaimed. She felt a rush of adrenaline. Her theories had again been verified. Before long, they had identified six women with giant bosoms. That they were also armless was more difficult to tell, until he greatly magnified the image of one of the women. Martina had no doubt she'd found the six women. Now, she had to work on an extraction process, one that didn't risk the women's lives. She took into account the fact the women were likely unable to walk much at all, certainly not able to run or even move quickly.

"We wait until all of the guests have left, unless we see our women being taken out to a shuttle. If they try to leave with one of them, we disable the shuttle. If they are still here after the guests leave, then we keep watch. If they go to bed, we make our move. Take them by surprise. If we see anything else happening, we'll take action. Stay alert for all kinds of trouble."

Hours drifted by. The two kept monitoring the locations of the six women, who were apparently spread out among the guests. Martina took that as a good sign; they were mingling. That meant the women were not completely helpless. Finally, the party began breaking up. It was close to midnight. She took a deep breath and stretched her muscles, relieving her tense muscles.

Not everyone left. Three men hadn't departed. Three shuttles remained on the lawn. She wanted to say, "Hurry up," but didn't. They waited and watched. Ah, the six were now close together, a good sign. They could sweep in and grab them from one location. The three men were also close together, but on the far side of the mansion. One was still in the kitchen area. Three others were also together, not too far from the three men. What was going on?

They were watching via the IR camera, which reacted to heat, producing light areas, or cold, which appeared dark. Suddenly, the area in which the three men were located turned very, very dark! For a moment, the men could not even be seen! Something very cold had been injected into that room. Martina and the technician came totally alert. Then, barely perceptible, one man moved to what must be an outside door.

271

Was he trying to bust out? Then, another separated from them and appeared to be trying to get out from the door that they'd entered. What the devil was going on down there? Who were those men? Martina had more questions than answers. "We wait," she barked.

"What are they doing now?" the technician asked. "Oh, looks like the door's open and they are leaving?"

"Yes. No. What? That woman — she's falling down. Lying flat on the ground? What's happening to the men? Are they falling down?" she called out, not trusting what she was seeing. She'd not used this equipment before, though she's seen it in operation before.

"Right, the three men are down now too. The other two women are moving again. Look, they are approaching the six. No, now, they are moving away from them. Now, the six are moving again. Together. No. Wait, the other two are leaving. Yes, they are outside now, heading to a shuttle. Orders?"

"Let them do as they wish. Have control monitor their flight and pick them up when they land. Wait, the six are moving in the same direction that the two took. Are they leaving?" Martina called out.

Just then, all manner of warning lights began flashing and sirens clanged! Bio agent attack in progress read the flashing message! "Oh dear god, not again! Take this ship up! Call it in immediately!" Martina yelled. The ship lurched upwards, knocking her off her feet. Even the technician was only barely able to hang on and keep from landing hard on the steel floor. Once the flight stabilized, he pulled Martina back onto her tall heels. "Hard to keep your balance in these," she commented. "Thanks. Where are we?"

The IR camera itself had been jarred and was no longer operating. Martina cursed. The technician called out, "I'm on it. Go to the optical system, Martina."

She moved across the cramped room to the visual display. At least there was some moonlight, but now they were above the clouds, and she couldn't see much at all. "Clouds blocking visual. Need the IR online," she called out.

"No can do. Circuits got damaged, but the bio agent detectors are reporting the all clear inside the ship," the technician replied.

The pilot, following protocol, spoke over the intercom, "We've been advised to stay aloft until the containment crews arrive. We've caught a lucky break. This area is isolated. No one beyond this mansion is going to be infected."

"Okay, need contingency plans. We can't lose these women, not now. We were so close to rescuing them," Martina said, more for her own benefit. "What was their last know position and direction of motion?" She and her technician compared their memories of that last second of observation and agreed they were heading outside. "Any sign of any of the other two shuttles leaving?"

The pilot reported, "Negative. No other shuttles have taken off."

"Okay. That means that the women are on foot. There is some moonlight, at least a little. They ought to be able to see the cliff and avoid falling off it. God, I hope so. Where will they go next? They are on foot, likely very hobbled. They can't go far."

She grabbed a map of the area and spread it out over the off-line IR monitor table. "Here's the mansion. Here's the cliff and ocean. There are only two likely directions. East or west along the coastline. Of course, they could be completely confused and walk anywhere to the south, but for now, let's rule that out, since that leads back towards the mansion from which they were fleeing in the first place. Fifty-fifty. East or west. We need a sighting." Now, she was getting impatient, but knew the bio agent protocols simply had to be followed. If they dropped down too close to the mansion, the whole crew could well be infected. She simply could not take that chance. If it was only herself, she knew she would have dropped down immediately.

An hour passed before a dozen containment ships with their brilliant red markings congregated around their position. Drones were then sent down; their sensors reporting on the nature of the bio agent and its concentration levels as a function of distance from ground zero, the mansion itself. The levels were high close to the entire mansion. However, finally, they were given clearance to drop down, but they would have to stay a mile from the mansion proper.

Martina now had to guess, east or west. She chose east, and the transport shot along about five hundred feet above the ground. She and the technician kept their eyes glued to the optical view, but saw nothing. Likewise, the pilot also reported seeing no one. He asked, "How far do you want me to go? We're three miles away now."

Martina knew that in her heels, she could not walk three miles in an hour. "Turn around. Let's try west." The pilot made a wide sweep around the mansion before hugging the coastline once more. "Hold up! I think we have them!" She could faintly see six women in a line down below the transport. "Yes, we found them. Take us down, but be careful of the women," she ordered, and headed for the bay doors, knowing the ship would land long before she could get there. Her heels made swift walking an impossibility, but she'd long ago ceased worrying about that aspect, taking it in stride.

When the door opened, forming a ramp to the ground, Martina carefully stepped down onto the rough, limestone ground. Glancing around, she spotted the six women looking at the shuttle. "Nia Elain? Is that you? Sector ID Minister Martina Wells here. We've come to rescue you." She saw the line of women turn and begin moving very, very slowly towards her. In turn, she carefully picked her way towards them, waving her arms about to keep her balance on the rough ground. Behind her, she heard the heavy footsteps of the six Security Guards coming up behind her.

"We need some help getting home," I called out. "I think Madame Dionysia set off a bio agent attack in her parlor. She's dead. Dagger to her forehead. We want to go home now." I'm sure I sounded rather silly.

"You got it. I've been on your trail for nearly a month. I worked out you had to be here, and we were about to rescue you when the bio agent attack came. Here, these men will carry you into the transport. We'll be back in the city in an hour. Are you injured at all?"

"No, we're all fine. We're very beautiful women now. We walk with grace and elegance," I said, again thinking I sounded terribly strange indeed, but I had no idea why.

The strong men picked us up and carried us into the transport, carefully sitting us down, as though we were extremely fragile or delicate flowers that might break at any moment. Well, our super long hair did cause them problems; I'll give them that. Martina soon joined us.

As the transport lifted off, Martina asked, "What happened back there in the mansion? Is Madame Dionysia dead? Who were the two women who fled the house before you got out?"

"She wanted us to help find the men who murdered her son and husband," I began explaining, forcing my mind not to say stupid things, not to a real Sector ID Minister! "It was those three men. They are criminals, she said, Commanders of The Righteous, like the slaver man I killed back on Metcalf-4. We read their thoughts and proved it. I think she unleashed the same stuff that she used on us. We heard some loud bangs and then heard her scream. The two women were her assistants. They can't speak at all. They helped us a lot and left after that. We went to see what was happening and saw she was dead and left ourselves. We're going to walk back to the spaceport so we can go home."

Martina chuckled. "You'd have had a very long walk, Nia, it's about two thousand miles from here to the spaceport. We'll have you there in an hour. So was it Madame Dionysia who unleashed the genetic mutation on you six?"

"We think so, but we don't know for sure. At least, she wanted it done. You see, we have to look really gorgeous and fabulously elegant to be like the escort women these murderers always liked, so they would stay behind with us. That was her plan. It worked very well, and we're now very beautiful with simply perfect bodies. We're very sexy and walk with grace and poise too. Well, not on the rough ground, I guess. We just want to go home now." Again, I think I sounded rather strange, but couldn't keep from saying those things.

"Well done. I'm amazed you've been able to keep a level head throughout this ordeal. Say, what did the psych man do to you?" she asked.

"I'm sorry, what's a psych man? What do they do?" I asked. I'd never heard of them.

"I know one of them must have been involved with your transformations. He's been captured too. They illegally try to alter your behavior. It's called behavior modification. We use it on criminals in an attempt to make them unable to commit further crimes. Mostly doesn't work, though," Martina replied.

"I don't know. We never saw any man around the mansion, until the party tonight, that is. I'm really tired now."

She replied, "Okay, you can doze for a while. We'll be back in the city in an hour and get you settled into warm beds soon." We did just that and were asleep within minutes, even though we were sitting up, seat belts holding us securely in our seats.

Chapter 15 Aftermath

We were so tired that we really weren't aware we were taken back to our original hotel room and put to bed. In the morning, we found Martina was also with us. She'd found two other women to assist us with dressing and grooming. While we were getting ready, she ordered room service, insisting we eat in our suite this morning.

While we were eating a vastly poorer breakfast than what we were accustomed to having from Madame Dionysia's superb chef, I commented, "I think we've missed our transport home. How soon can another one be found? We're eager to get home."

"Well, you're going to stay here for a few days. We need to make sure you're all healthy, and we'll need to interrogate you about the kidnaping and the role that Madame Dionysia played in it. Plus, there'll be a few legal matters to handle over all this mess," she explained. "I'll send a doctor around later this morning to get you all checked out. I've a few matters to attend to, but I'll be back later today." We agreed, but asked her to hurry. We wanted to go home soon.

Martina left the six and headed to her shuttle. There, she opened a secure channel and got an update from the man in charge of the bio containment. The three men had been identified and were quite wealthy, but were in the genetic mutation-caused comas, resting comfortably in a hospital. The cook was in a coma as well, but she was being treated separately from the criminals. The mansion had been aired and the danger eliminated. A thorough search was being undertaken. Already, they'd found some very interesting documents in the owner's safe. The two silent women had been apprehended, but their interrogations had been put on hold. Because they had no voices, the Security Guards decided to see what they could learn first, before trying to get the two frightened women to write lengthy explanations.

Since the mansion was now safe to enter, Martina took a quick trip to retrieve other belongings of the six women, which might still be there. She recovered quite a stash of clothing for them. Additionally, she looked at the documents the authorities were examining with great interest. They also got her interest up as well.

"Looks like this widow accomplished what we couldn't do," one investigator commented to Martina. "She uncovered the den of The Righteous and served them up to us on a silver platter."

"Cost her her life; don't leave that out," Martina barked. "Still, I agree; she did the impossible. I think in light of all this, no charges ought to be filed on her or her estate. She did us a huge favor, albeit vigilante style."

"I intend to recommend that to the President. He can have the final word. What are you going to do about her latest will? It appears to be legal."

"If you don't mind, I'll take it with me and have it authorized. If it passes, I'll handle the notifications. Poor woman. She had no living relatives. Her life must have been misery these past two years. She took the murder of her son rather badly. The shrine to him in her bedroom speaks loudly." The investigator nodded and she left.

It was nearly suppertime before Martina finished all her errands. She was determined to make things as right as possible for these six women. Even though she got back to the hotel mid-afternoon, she spent considerable time with the doctors who had examined the women.

"Yes, it is the usual genetic mutation that's occurred," the lead physician confirmed what she already suspected. "A number of cures are available. What is extremely unusual is the case of Nia Elain. As you know, she was born with the genetic modifications. We've examined her medical records here on Descartes-3 and confirmed her arms were regrown. She claims they were ripped off of her back on Metcalf-4 and that something wasn't right with them."

"Yes, that's all true. So what's so unusual with Nia Elain?"

"Well, her body's undergone the total genetic mutation a second time. We believe we'll be able to regrow her arms once more, since her current genetic material is dictating that she has none. Rather amazing. She gets a second chance."

"Well, that's good news," Martina replied, greatly relieved. Nia Elain could leave Descartes-3 in better shape than she arrived! It had not been a complete disaster.

"Yes and no. There is a serious complication with all of them. That illegal behavior modification the psych man installed is causing very serious behavior problems with all six of them. Perhaps, you can work with them. I sure wish there was a cure for that mess, but as you know, there isn't. We have to find a way to work around it." She discussed the situation further, finally joining the six and their helpers, just as their supper was being delivered to their suite.

While the group dined, Martina related what she'd learned. "You were right. Madame Dionysia did manage to find the current Righteous Commanders and six of the most wanted mob members. It's incredible she was able to capture them, with your help, of course. She's been cleared of all charges."

Martina then explained the more important fact. "We've found her most recent will. It seems in the event of her death during this plot, she has left her entire estate and mansion to nine of you. You six, the two silent women, and her chef, who by the way has been infected as well, but is now under constant care in the hospital. You nine have inherited that mansion, her bank account of nearly three million credits, and a half million in credits kept at the mansion. I must say, you now own one of the finer mansions on Descartes-3, even if it is rather remote."

"So we can live there when we are here?" asked Tesla.

"Absolutely. It belongs to you nine, equally. I guess Madame Dionysia really did love you nine women," Martina replied with an invisible smile.

"That's wonderful. No one has ever been this kind to us, right Anya?" Tesla exclaimed. Anya nodded.

Martina continued, "I talked with the doctors a bit ago. According to him, we should be able to undo many of these awful genetic modifications that have been made to your bodies. Your arms, for example, can be regrown, yours too, Nia Elain."

She wasn't quite prepared for their replies. Tesla said, "But we don't need anything undone. We've perfect bodies now. We've adjusted to them. We thoroughly enjoy our new bodies. We get much pleasure from them. Besides, we're very sexy. We've fabulous figures. Our fine gowns really show them off. We never want to have our bodies altered from their magnificent states. We'd rather die first. We walk with grace and poise now."

Anya rattled off much the same things, followed by Jana and then Jovanna. Surprisingly, Danika echoed them, as did Nia Elain. Martina was aghast with what she was hearing, but quickly realized these words or something similar must have been what the psych man had implanted in them with his behavior modifications.

"Of course, you're all very beautiful women. I wouldn't dream of changing that. But surely if you had your arms back, that would help you immensely. You wouldn't be dependent upon assistants to get you dressed and groomed, right?"

"Well, I suppose that's true," I conceded, wondering why I had said what I had said. It sounded utterly ridiculous, and yet I felt the words to be true.

"Maybe," Tesla added. "That would help us a lot. I don't like someone else brushing my hair. I suppose we could get that tiny thing done, don't you, Anya?"

"I suppose wouldn't detract from our striking figures all that much, and it would be helpful at times," Anya conceded.

"Right," Martina replied. "I noticed you had a hard time walking in those toe shoes. When you get back home, you won't be able to walk around at all. The ground is rocky and way too rough. You'll be falling down all the time. That isn't very graceful and full of poise, is it?"

"Well, no it isn't, not really," Tesla answered. "Anya, we almost couldn't walk after we left the mansion last night, could we?"

"Maybe we should have them fixed some," Anya suggested, "but these toe shoes are so cool and sexy."

"Yes, but how about mine?" Martina countered. "Aren't they almost as fabulous as yours?"

"Well, sure they are very attractive," Tesla agreed.

"I used to wear toe shoes just like you have, but when I found I couldn't walk outside without nearly falling down with each step, I had them fixed like this." She didn't say walking in six inch heels wasn't all that much easier on rough ground. She knew she had to get their agreement on changes a small step at a time.

"Shoes like hers are just as sexy as ours, don't you think?" I suggested. Soon, all six agreed having their feet done so they could look like Martina was a good idea.

"Another thing, don't you all have a very hard time seeing where your feet are at while walking? I used to when I had bosoms like yours. I kept tripping and stumbling. Worse, trying to deal with stairs was a nightmare. I couldn't see the steps. I know back home, you don't have stairs, but you have really rough ground. Perhaps you ought to consider having yours reduced to the size that mine are?" Martina suggested.

"She's right! We can't see where we're walking. It's not so graceful. We must walk gracefully and with poise. I think she is right," Jana conceded. Quickly, the other five agreed with her.

Martina decided to press her luck a bit further. "You know your earrings were supposed to be your payment for services rendered. Because they are so valuable, you really should not wear them all of the time. What if they get caught on a tree branch? What if some thief rips them from your ears?"

"Oh!" Jovanna exclaimed. "She's right. There are a lot of thieves back home. We should not wear them all the time, just on special occasions." Once more, Martina got agreement from us six women.

"One other little thing," Martina hinted. "With those very tight corsets, don't you have a hard time breathing? Don't you need your flexibility back home? Doing chores and such?"

I answered emphatically, "Yes, breathing is very difficult, but our figures are just fabulous."

"Oh they most certainly are," Nia Elain, "but even if you take them off, you'll still have a ravishing figure, and you can breathe normally. I wear a simple garter belt to hold up my black stockings. Isn't my figure rather pronounced too?"

I looked at her carefully. "Yes, you look fabulous too, Martina. I suppose we don't have to wear it, especially if we can breathe properly and still look fabulous. If we don't, we can always have someone put them back on us, right?"

"Absolutely, Nia Elain. Just say the word. I'll see about having someone help you all with these in the morning. Right now, we best get you all a bath and into clean dresses. I brought all your fancy gowns back here from the mansion for you."

"Oh that would be great. Thank you, Martina," I replied rather silly-like. My mind was in a whirl of confusions, but why it should be so, eluded me.

In hindsight, I think Martina had done a masterful job of finding ways around our behavior modifications. The next day, we found ourselves in a special medical facility, and the lengthy processes began. Most of the genetic modifications were going to be undone. Martina promised to have all our clothes altered and ready to fit us once the process was finished. She did visit us for hours every day.

We were constrained to lie flat for nearly two weeks, while tiny baby-like arms formed and grew. At least, we were able to watch a number of educational shows on a big monitor, between her visits. Also, the two silent women, Callidora and Astarte, came and sat with us, helping us with everything the entire time we were bedridden. A few days after we began this lengthy process, the cook, Eris, joined us, receiving the same treatments. Often, we had long chats, passing the time.

I think watching all those educational shows were what sparked something in Tesla and Anya. After the first few days, they just insisted on watching everyone they could. Soon, Danika, Jana, and Jovanna also were hooked on them as well, particularly on any show that somehow involved space flight.

After our two-week period, our baby-like arms had grown enough so we weren't bedridden any longer. Now, we faced three months of very low activity. It was at this point in time a year or so ago when my arms were regrowing that my parents took me off with them in the Eagle's Seed. This time, the doctors refused to let me take off, insisting we six stay put and give our new arms time to grow, unlike the last time.

At this point, Danika and I began to worry about our child that she was carrying. Until now, we'd forgotten about her pregnancy. She was in her tenth week now. "Your daughter is going to be just fine, Danika," one of the doctors explained. "Incredible amounts of damage can be healed within a womb, especially this early in your pregnancy. I've done a lot of testing just to be certain. She's quite healthy and is developing arms. Before you leave, I'll show you an image of her, so you can see for yourselves that she'll be just as perfect as you both are."

We grinned, but I had a suspicion he had been given orders from Martina on how to handle this with us. To his credit, he did just that when we were about to leave. She looked fine to us, but then what did either of us know about such medical images?

Danika, Tesla, Anya, Jana, and Jovanna begged Martina to help them learn. "Education, Martina," Tesla explained, "is everything. Our world and people don't know hardly anything, compared to the most ordinary person we've met on Descartes-3. We want to learn all we can and then teach it to our people back home. Please, you have to help us," she begged.

Martina realized they had a very valid point. "Okay then, but you have to learn to read and write first. It is one thing to listen to the language learning disks and then be able to speak it, but it's quite another to be able to read and write it. To get an education, you have to be able to read and write, which is much more difficult. Are you sure that you want to do this?"

All five nodded vigorously. Martina found herself spending most of her days teaching the five how to read. As their new arms grew stronger, she began showing them how to write. Of course, I already could do these and was terribly bored. What really helped us was the arrival of two Basic Therapy givers from Ashford-5. The queens sent them to help us recover.

For nearly a week, we slugged our way through the kidnaping and genetic mutation caused coma, a period of five days of complete unconsciousness. Finally, we were able to fully contact the actual words of the psych man's verbal behavior modification, which lay beneath all that trauma. Now, we saw precisely the awful affect those words had on us, and our behavior when we awoke. Laid in while we were totally unconscious, it was insidious in design, in that it played upon partial truths. After all, what woman didn't want to look attractive, to have a "perfect body," to walk with grace and poise, and so on. His commands to us built upon that with which we already believed and re-enforced them, deriving its power from the pain and unconsciousness of the massive genetic alterations and trauma happening to our bodies.

A week later, Danika and I were laughing again, enthusiastic, and free from the behavior modifications done to us. Naturally, we then had the doctors remedy all the other genetic modifications that could be undone. That short process finished, both she and I insisted that they teach us how to do this Basic Therapy, which they were quite willing to do. It was actually quite simple to do. She and I spent the next couple of weeks working with the other four, clearing them of the effects of the behavior modifications and the trauma of the past month or so.

When we finished them, Martina was so impressed with the results on we six, that she wanted to know if it would work on her as well. After asking the Ashford-5 experts, Danika and I began to give Martina her Basic Therapy. She too had been through the same genetic modifications many years ago. Additionally, she was actually quite old and had endured an awful lot of trauma during her long life. It took us nearly three weeks to get her finished up with stellar results as well. Meanwhile, the two from Ashford-5 also gave the two silent women and the cook their Basic Therapy. I believe they had to use their gifts of telepathy to handle the two women though.

Danika and I spent the rest of the three-month period working with the two Ashford-5 women on how we could deliver Basic Therapy to everyone on Metcalf-4. Our goal was terribly idealistic, I know, but we were fired up about it, just as Tesla, Anya, Jana, and Jovanna were with their education project.

As our period of confinement neared its end, so did my

marriage of convenience. Tesla was the first to point out the significant change. "Look, we all banded together in our marriage of convenience so we would always be together to help each other out. Alone, we couldn't survive, but as a group, we could. However, now that's all changed for the better. We have our arms back."

"Hey," I replied, "if you all want to go your own way, then that is fine with me. Together, we did accomplish our goal of surviving. I couldn't have done it without you."

"Well, we are going to have to stay here on Descartes-3 for quite a few years. It takes a long time to learn everything we want to know. It isn't fair to you and Danika," Anya pointed out.

"I agree with you four. Honestly, the purpose, the reason for our union is over. You should carve out your own paths now that you can do just that. We have divided all the funds we've inherited evenly, so you all can live quite independently. Danika and I are going to finally get Queen Akira to Metcalf-4 and try to get things going there. You four get educated and one day return to teach our people," I answered, knowing this was precisely what they wanted to hear.

Danika, now four months pregnant, fully agreed, though I sensed she was relieved to no longer having to "share me" with the others. She advised the four, "Keep looking, and one day you will find the love of your life."

Thus, my four-month marriage of convenience ended amicably. Yes, I felt relieved. I was now only responsible for my Danika and unborn daughter. Besides, I rather suspected that at least two were falling for Martina in a big way.

After that, we all said our farewells, rather tearful I might add. These were my dearest friends, even Martina. I suspected that somehow we had given her a rebirth of life and not just from Basic Therapy.

The first of February 1376, Danika and I headed back to Ashford-5, where we picked up Queen Akira Ayano and her silent assistant Kimi Mari. We also took a trip to Elegant Fashions Inc, purchasing quite a lot of clothing and footwear, some for Danika's pregnancy. Yes, we did get some fancy gowns, but mostly we picked out good quality leather and cotton apparel, appropriate for our world. After more farewells, on the fifth, we left on the short trip to our home world, bringing along twenty volunteer therapy givers. The anticipated brief few weeks away from Metcalf-4 had turned into nearly four months. We found ourselves wondering what all had happened there during our absence. At least it ought to be spring when we arrived, or nearly so. As I said before, I don't like the cold and snow, but maybe now that I was "whole," that would change.

Chapter 16 Establishment

We landed the next day near the Eagle's Seed. While the crew moved the voluminous cargo over to my ship, Danika helped Queen Akira and Kimi deal with the cold and snow, which covered the ground. I took time out to contact King Vlad in Zelimir City. We'd been gone four months and had no idea what the current situation was like. I didn't dare bring the darn near helpless queen into a war zone. Thank god for telepathy.

Hi. It's Nia Elain. We're finally back. Ran into some trouble, but we're all fine now. How's everything there? Kisha doing okay? Sir Dmitri? Jelena?

Wow! Hi there yourself! We thought you must have run into some serious trouble, maybe even killed. We're struggling, but surviving here. Everyone's fine. Queen Kisha is hoping for a daughter, but I'm pulling for a son, naturally. Where are you now?

Congratulations! We're at the Eagle's Seed with Queen Akira and Kimi, her assistant. We'll come visit later today, if that's okay with you. We've a long story to tell.

That'll be great. I'll let the others know.

Not more than five minutes after we finished our brief chat, a Transportation Torus opened up and Kisha stepped through, along with Jelena. "Hi ya. Miss me?" Kisha hollered, as Danika and I stepped out of the ship to see what the commotion among the crew members was. They'd never seen a torus before. I admit, it's pretty spectacular to see. "Holy moley! You both have arms!" she gushed in total surprise.

"Hi. Yes, we missed you both. We've quite a story to tell. Hug," I answered, moving quickly over to the pair. After hugs all around, Danika and Kisha compared their growing bellies, while we walked back into the ship.

As we walked up the bay ramp, Kisha teased me, "Don't go getting them new arms yanked out of their sockets again, Nia Elain." We four laughed.

Dodging the men moving the cargo, I led them to the

galley, where Kimi had just made some tea for herself and Queen Akira. We four joined them, with introductions all around. While Kisha and Jelena were extremely anxious to hear what had happened to us, I decided to tell the long story only once. Instead, we chatted about how they were surviving the winter and in particular, how the five hundred women were doing.

"Not so good. Their morale is almost non-existent, as you can well imagine. Several have simply given up. We buried five of them already," Kisha answered solemnly. "Glad you are back. Are you going to be able to regrow their arms too?"

I had to laugh. In order to do that, we'd have to subject them to the bio agent to genetically mutate their bodies and then go through all of the cures that we had, assuming we could even get access to such things. "No, not possible, really. We'll tell you all about it soon, Kisha. However, Danika and I have learned how to give the Ashford-5's Basic Therapy to those who need it. Plus, we are ready to train all of you magi. Honestly, Kisha, our potential powers as magi are far greater than we ever even suspected!"

That evening, we dined at King Vlad and Queen Kisha's table in his Great Hall. During the long meal, Danika and I related our lengthy tale in full. Kisha's comment said it all, "Some men are bad no matter how apparently civilized they are." I could tell she was still being overly influenced by the five hundred women who were facing terrible lives, thanks to the late Commander.

For now, Queen Akira decided to set up shop here in Zelimir City. Hence, the next day, King Vlad called an all hands to help move all of her personal possessions and equipment from the Eagle's Seed over to a room in his large home. The next day, we helped her set up the large comm system, which was powered by solar cells, since Metcalf-4 lacked such things as electricity. After that, we let Queen Akira do whatever it was that she was here to do. Honestly, Danika and I had other greater concerns.

After a quick visit to one of the homes that housed twenty of the nearly helpless women, she and I began to deliver Basic Therapy to these women. The twenty volunteers from Ashford-5 were right there with us, though two acted as supervisors over the twenty sessions taking place in that home. After we finished our first pair of women and saw their renewed lease on life, we knew we were doing what was really needed and worthwhile. We didn't finish up with all five hundred until late spring.

More importantly, most all of them decided they too wanted to learn how to deliver Basic Therapy. This was something of immense value that they could do. By the time we finished the last pair of these women, hundreds of the others had already begun working on the many other women and men who had suffered under the slavers. While it would likely take us years to get everyone handled, I couldn't think of a better thing to do. We were salvaging lives. So many had lost children to the slavers, a loss that was eating away at them. Parents are not supposed to outlive their children.

In late May, our daughter, Nadia, was born. Yes, we were very proud parents. Also, I was now pregnant as well, due in late October. By mid-June, the weather was once more to my liking. We both knew we were long overdue to pay a visit on Danika's father, King Jereni, in Pudislava, the heart of his kingdom.

She was somewhat hesitant to make the trip, not because of our newborn — we could simply get there by a Transportation Torus — but rather because of what her father would say or do now that she'd married me, another woman, and because of what had happened to her physically. She too was a hermaphrodite. Yet, we both knew this day had to be faced, and mid-June made the trip, bringing Nadia, Sir Dmitri, and Jelena with us. Jelena volunteered to look after Nadia, so we could deal with her father. Also, our arms were those of a three-year old child, still pretty weak. We took great care holding little Nadia with them.

Before we left, King Vlad said, "If he doesn't want to accept you, you both are most welcome to stay here with us. We love you both."

"He's a hard man, but fair," Sir Dmitri stuck up for his king.

We would soon see. Danika opened a Transportation

Torus, and we rode our horses through the portal, arriving on the main street of her home town of Pudislava. Here was the largest city I'd so far seen on Metcalf-4. From all appearances, it was a thriving one. People thronged the streets, visiting the many vendors, who had open shops set up in front of their combination home and workshop. Crafts were seen everywhere in a dizzying juxtaposition of wares. The odor of burning wood and coal was in the air, along with a myriad other smells I didn't recognize. The buildings were all made from wood, though perhaps the poorer ones had thatched roofs. I took an immediate liking to my mate's hometown.

Of course, many people stopped to see who or what came through the glowing, golden torus. They stared at me, figuring I was the magus, not Danika, who many recognized and called out a welcome. She waved and smiled back.

In the distance behind us, I occasionally glimpsed the tall, wooden walls surrounding the city, protecting its inhabitants. We ambled along, picking our way through the many people on the streets. Ahead, I spotted what must be the Great Hall, home to the king and to Danika. As we drew close, I could see a secondary wooden palisade surrounded the king's complex of buildings, the Great Hall being the largest. As we approached the gate, a man darted out from an alleyway.

"Danika! Don't enter the gates! Over here! Quick before the guards spot you," he cried out urgently.

"Stanislav? What's the matter, cousin?" Danika countered, pivoting in her saddle. To us, she added, "My cousin, Stanislav Gavril." She neck reined her horse, following after him. We did likewise, but I noticed the gate guards observing Danika closely. One dashed off, heading for the Great Hall.

"Thank the gods I got to you in time. Danika, it's not safe for you to enter the Great Gates. You father, King Jereni is dead. Your Uncle Branko Jereni is now the king. He's left standing orders to have you shot if you set foot inside those inner gates!" the twenty-five year old blacksmith explained. I could tell his trade by his outfit and bulging arms. His apron was full of small burn holes.

"What? Dad dead? How? Speak up, cousin. How did it

happen? How come Uncle Branko inherited the throne and not me?" Danika asked a series of rapid-fire questions. I could see the shock of the sudden ill news on her face, which moments before was full of life and happiness. Now, it was grim and taught.

"Six days ago. Some of us think he was poisoned by Branko, but we've no proof. Since you were not here, Branko literally took over, ousting most of your father's guards and installing his own. He knows you have a valid claim to the throne, but he claims no woman can be king. Still he fears your return and issued orders to have you shot if you enter the gates to the Great Hall complex," her cousin explained. "Say, you look different. What happened to your arms? They look so strange."

"That vile, little man! I'll kill him myself!" Sir Dmitri swore, his anger rising rapidly. "Ranger Danika has been through a whole lot, has helped save our world from utter annihilation, and suffered greatly. This is the thanks that she gets! I swear I'll kill him!"

The blacksmith grimaced. "That would not be wise, Sir Dmitri. I know for a fact that Branko has ousted all of the old knights and installed over a hundred of his own hand-picked men, knighting them. You'd be killed too. No, you best flee. Most all your father's knights and trusted allies have fled. They went north to safety. I think in time all this will calm down and everyone can return. It's just that right now, it isn't safe for you to be here, cousin."

Danika was never one to turn her back on a fight. Neither was Sir Dmitri. She said calmly, "Sir Dmitri, we pick our battles, ones that we can win. The kingdom doesn't need a war for the throne right now. Besides, I've no real interest in being the queen. I can't stand being cooped up in that Great Hall all the time. There's a world out there beckoning. Hell, a whole universe actually! Perhaps, I should go let King Branko know I've no interest in ruling — that he is welcome to dad's throne."

She looked at me and then our daughter being cradled by Jelena, and said, "I've got other vastly more important things in my life now than a throne. Come on; let's go put King

Branko's mind at ease over this. Perhaps, it'll also help restore peace to the kingdom as well." She neck reined and headed out of the alley. We all followed her, Jelena bringing up the rear. Me? I was just worried about what her cousin had said — that the guards had orders to shoot her on sight. Surely, these people wouldn't murder someone outright. I had no idea how very wrong my thought was.

Danika rode up to the two men guarding the gates to the Great Hall compound. "Hi. I want to speak to our new King Branko to tell him he has my full support on his succession to dad's throne. Will you please relay that to him?"

"Aye, Ranger Danika," the man said, clearly nervous with her appearance at the gates. I picked up his thoughts and knew he was cursing her appearance while he was on duty.

Just then, a quarrel thudded into Danika's chest. The shooter wasn't even man enough to make himself visible! It had come a long way from somewhere deep inside the compound. She let out a cry of pain and slumped over in her saddle. One second, she was talking to the guard, and the next, she was dying! Things happen quickly. For what seemed an eternity, I just sat there on my horse stunned. Okay, I am not a fighter. Sir Dmitri was, and never have I seen such a fast reaction.

He moved to her side, placing his body and horse between the gates and the assassin and my mate, blocking all further shots. Sir Dmitri grabbed her reins and ordered, "Turn around! Get away from here fast!" Jelena neck reined and got her horse galloping off, followed by Sir Dmitri, who carefully led Danika's stallion. Me? I dumbly fell in line bringing up the rear, acting as a block to any further attacks from Danika's exposed back. Anger surged in me.

The chaotic five seconds finally registered in my mind. Some son of a bitch had tried to assassinate my Danika without even the slightest warning! She wasn't a threat to this new king. Shock yielded to a violent anger I'd seldom felt before. That was my mate, the mother of my daughter! I turned around in my saddle, focused a moment, and dropped the largest wall of fire I had ever conjured before, dropping it down upon the entire roof of the Great Hall and associated buildings! Then, I turned around and opened a Transportation Torus just ahead of the galloping riders. A second later, they rode out onto the forested ground beside the Eagle's Seed, my ship.

Sir Dmitri had no choice but to rein in hard or run into the ship. He turned to look back at me, a confused look on his face. I yelled, "Medical machine!" He gave me a dumb look, and I knew he had no idea what I was talking about.

I dismounted and raced for the door, punching in the code. Seconds later, the cargo bay door slowly opened. Meanwhile, Sir Dmitri carefully lifted my unconscious Danika down from her horse, while Jelena also carefully dismounted, bringing little Nadia with her. "Bring her inside," I barked, amazed at the strength the knight had. He carried her up the ramp, but his footfalls hammered on the steel from the weight of her body plus his armor.

Jelena followed behind, "Is she still alive?" Her subdued voice didn't mask her fears. I didn't answer her. She just had to be alive! I led them to the medical room as fast as Sir Dmitri could carry her.

"Lay her down on the platform. Thanks," I barked. My voice sounded so distant, so unearthly. I felt shock seeping into my stomach and forced it out by sheer will alone. He did as I asked and, after lying little Nadia aside on the floor, Jelena moved up to examine her patient.

There wasn't much blood. It was a puncture wound. The quarrel had pierced the rings of her mail, lodging between two ribs. At least that was my guess. I had no idea how deep the tip was, but from the bit of blood that seeped from her lips, a lung had to have been pierced. She was breathing quite shallowly, but Danika was still alive! "We have to pull it out," Jelena explained, though that fact was obvious to us. She tried to do just that and failed. "It's lodged in her. I don't have enough strength to pull it out!"

"Let me try," Sir Dmitri gently pushed the witch aside. I watched as his arm muscles flexed and bulged. A sickly slurping sound broke the stillness, as the quarrel with its nasty iron point came out along with oozing red blood. He stood back holding the bloody quarrel in his hand.

"Okay, my turn," I said trying to sound as calm as I could. I was anything but calm! She was bleeding to death, and I knew I had seconds to get this Medical machine to do its work. "Get her clothes off of her fast, please." I knew I was all thumbs when it came to removing her mail and leather under-armor. Sir Dmitri stripped her efficiently, while I gently held her in a sitting position. Then, I laid her back down, blood pooling on her middle chest. As fast as I could, I got the machine's lid over her and brought up the menus. Precious minutes flew by, as I tried to find the right menu choice. I gave up, selected Chest Puncture Wound, and activated it. I swore to myself I simply had to get more education. Knowledge is power. I'd heard that before, only now it really sunk into my consciousness! Like a sledgehammer on a steel anvil. There was a whole damned universe out there, and I was mostly ignorant of it. I'd led a very sheltered life!

"Will it work?" Jelena whispered to me, her voice trembling a little, a catch in her subsequent breath.

"God, I hope so! It just has to work. Punctured a lung at the very least," I whispered back.

"Aye, you can tell from the blood coming from her mouth. Most die from it. I've seen that happen a dozen times," Sir Dmitri also whispered, though none of us knew why we were whispering, unless we were all too afraid to speak aloud. Just then, Nadia began crying. I wondered if she could sense her mother was wounded and maybe dying?

I went to her and picked her up, straining my weak arms. "Sh. Sh, little one. I'm here. You've still got me, your father. If the Medical machine works right, mom will be fine. I know you are hungry. You'll have to be patient a little longer. Sh. Sh." I rocked her a little until my weak arms threatened to drop her. Jelena spotted that and quickly took her from me. I gave her a knowing smile, which she returned in kind.

We waited the longest half-hour ever! At last, the medical machine's program ended, and its cover retracted, revealing Danika's body. We three hovered over her, staring at the puncture wound. While blood covered her chest, the ugly hole was gone. She was breathing normally, but unconscious still. Danika was alive and that's all that mattered to me!

I got some water in a pan and began to wash off the dried blood. As I did so, Danika stirred. "I hurt," she whispered. "Oh!" Danika sat up quickly. "I got shot!" She looked at her chest and then the room. Confusion twisted her face.

"We got you to my ship and the Medical machine, dear. I think you are going to be fine," I replied, more relieved than I could ever explain. I felt elated. The gorilla was off my chest! "Thank God for the Imperium Medical machines!"

"The bastard shot me!" she exclaimed. "How'd I get here?" She coughed up some more blood and spat it out in the basin I was still holding.

Hastily, Sir Dmitri explained what we'd done. He ended with, "I think Nia Elain was just a little pissed at them. She dropped a huge wall of fire on top of the Great Hall just as we left."

"Fire?" Danika asked, still getting herself oriented to being in the Eagle's Seed instead of in her hometown. "My God, Nia, that's likely to burn the whole place down to the ground!"

"I'm sorry, Danika, but I've never been so angry in my life. I just lashed out without thinking."

Danika sighed, "Well, that will give my uncle something to think about. I guess there's not going to be any peace with him now. Hell, I don't care. I'm never going back there again," she declared flatly.

"You should be dead, you know," Sir Dmitri pointed out. "Few take a quarrel to their chests and survive it."

Danika looked at me and gave me one of her disarming smiles. "I've got the best mate in the world looking after me," she replied coyly. "There's only a bit of pain left. It's healed. Incredible. I've got a whole lot to learn."

"Hey, we both do. Knowledge is power. I realize I'm so ignorant that it isn't funny, dear. Tesla, Anya, Jana, and Jovanna were precisely right in staying behind to learn all they can," I declared. "We should have stayed behind and studied right along with them," I admitted.

"Is it too late to go back and do that?" Danika asked. "Oh. Nadia is probably starving. Jelena, lay her beside me, will you please?"

An hour later and dirty diapers changed, we headed back to King Vlad's place. "Well," Sir Dmitri said to Vlad, "I hope you can use a good knight here."

The king and Kisha both smiled. She said coyly, "I take it you were not as welcome as you expected?"

"Hardly! They damned near killed Danika!" the ex-knight gushed and dove into a lengthy explanation, sparing Danika from having to do that. For once, he was extremely wise. My mate wasn't really up to explaining the unexpected treachery of her uncle. Neither was I. Hell, I probably burned the whole Great Hall down in my anger.

When he finished, Kisha swore to avenge Danika, but our new Queen Akira intervened. "You'll do no such thing, Queen Kisha. Nia Elain acted out of anger, and nothing good can come from that."

"Your Majesty," I quickly spoke up, sensing where Queen Akira was headed, "with your permission, Danika and I would like to return to Ashford-5 and get an education. It's become real to me that knowledge is power. I'm truly sorry I acted out of anger."

Queen Akira smiled, "That is probably the best route to follow. You have my blessings."

A week later and with the assistance of one of the therapy givers from Ashford-5 who was also a good pilot, Danika, Nadia, and I left Metcalf-4. While we said our farewells to our dear friends, neither of us knew we would never be returning to this world. Rather, we had high hopes that we could learn much, following the lead of our four former mates.

Chapter 17 The Challenge

I made the right choice both for me and for Danika. It's May of 1378, my twenty-first birthday, and my daughter Zorina's second, as well as Danika's Nadia. Our daughters are healthy and beginning their terrible two's together. We've been staying with the two queens, Linda and Rael, at their Imperial Castle. Yes, I insisted on paying the keep for us six, covering the costs of Tesla, Anya, Jana, and Jovanna as well, while we six are getting an education.

That we all were around others who were like us also played a role. We felt relaxed and comfortable for the first time since our bodies were modified. True, we six all sport our giant lip plates and have no choice but to wear the six inch heels, but we do love to wear our fancy gowns. As Tesla says, "We always look our very best." Perhaps, we still have lingering traces of the psychman's implanted notions, but we don't care at all. Being around so many hermaphrodites like ourselves means everything to us, as we've come to realize. We're not freaks any longer.

Education is power. That has been driven home to me during the past two and a half years. We six have spent nearly every waking hour studying and learning. Of course, we took breaks to care for our two infants. Nevertheless, we six set new records for time spent in learning. I've expanded my physics education enormously, as well as my pilot and navigation skills. And yes, I'm a master of Medical machine operations now. No, I'm not a doctor, but I can handle that machine rapidly and am officially a competent Med Tech now.

The five women from Metcalf-4 have learned a number of languages and can read and write in Imperium Standard, as well as the local Midlands dialect. Danika took to technology like a duck to a pond. She's perhaps a better pilot than I am and my equal at navigation. Plus, she's a natural with all the equipment onboard the Eagle's Seed. Tesla is fast becoming an electronics expert, who sidelines in political science and governmental history. Anya has mastered all forms of modern communication equipment — their use and their repair. I swear Anya could build a comm center from spare parts!

The twins, Jana and Jovanna are both into ancient history as well as botany. I don't think there's a plant on any planet in the Imperium that those two don't know all about! Moreover, they love to cook, putting their knowledge of spices to good use.

Normally, children learn the basics when they are young, and then in their late teens, attend an Imperium Academy for their professional training. In our case, we began to learn at the age when most head off to the Academy. However, our voracious appetites for learning and speed of progress forced us down a different path than normal. We made extensive use of computer-based courses, so we could devour knowledge at our own rates, which vastly exceeded the normal ones. Perhaps that had something to do with our *mentales* gifts. Who can say?

On top of everything else, we six made a host of new friends here on Ashford-5. Most were hermaphrodites like us, naturally, but not all. Most had an official Academy degree or were attending one. On Friday nights, we got together and spent the evening brainstorming with our friends or picking their brains on topics that interested us, and they, us. For us, this was vastly more enjoyable than getting together to play games, which many of the others did. We earned the nickname of the "brainiac squad." Seriously, we thoroughly enjoyed intelligent conversations on hot topics more than just goofing off or playing games. For us, we knew that knowledge was power, and we six wanted that power. Just be careful of what you want.

Ex-Sector ID Minister Martina Wells followed Tesla and the other three women to Ashford-5, when they returned there from Descartes-3. In truth, as she later divulged to me, she found these four women particularly intriguing. She saw a reflection of her former mate President Mary Wells, who she had loved more than any other person during her long life. That the four were dedicating themselves to getting a good education only convinced her that she wanted to assist them in achieving their goal. "It was just a hunch," she explained to me when Danika and I returned, "and I always follow my intuition." Her connections helped us all acquire the very latest in computer-based education courses, and the computers and software we needed for them. Tesla found her a vast reservoir of knowledge on political science and forms of government.

This first Friday night in May's intellectual discussion focused on the current state of the Imperium itself, a hot topic these days, because we six now knew a tremendous amount about the giant civilization of which we were apart. Martina pointed out, "Look, my late mate, President Mary Wells, was instrumental in holding the entire Imperium together during the times of the Great Bio Agent Terrorist Attacks. When the Big Five Worlds were wiped out along with the whole of Proxima Prime, her unselfish and heroic actions, coupled with the Ataro Emperor Kino, managed to re-establish the Imperium. Against all odds, I might add."

Tesla commented, "From what I've been studying, it's nowhere near what it used to be, right?"

"Quite true. The Senate can't agree on much of anything these days. Only the armed forces are still fully functional," Martina concurred and elaborated.

"But isn't the main thing trading arrangements? Isn't that what it ought to be about?" asked Jovanna. "Over-populated hub worlds need to import food products."

"No, it's common currency, an accepted means of exchange between worlds, that is the driving force these days," put in Jana. "Money makes the universe go round. No one carried tons of gold to buy things."

Martina nodded. "Right on both accounts. Commonly accepted Imperium credits form the backbone of the Imperium. But she's right. Trading arrangements have taken a whole new turn. From what I've seen, worlds are making private trading arrangements with other worlds now, bypassing the more formal Senate trading agreements."

"So it's still collapsing," Tesla suggested.

"For my money, yes it is," Martina agreed with her.

"But wasn't the war with the Federation of Planets behind the collapse in the first place?" asked Jovanna. "Wars never benefit either side; both lose."

"True," Martina pointed out, "it was the ill-fated, secret war-time research project that invented the terrible bio agent weapon in the first place, on Ashford-4 to be precise."

"But the Imperium military is still strong, isn't it?" asked Anya.

"Yes and no," Martina answered with a sigh. "Each world contributes to the military. Some provide men and women. Some provide logistics. Some provide the hardware. However, these days, most of the wealthier worlds are building up their own private fleets. I swear the Imperium fleets are getting a tenth of what they used to get prior to that war."

"That isn't good, is it?" Jovanna suggested. "I mean, men can't be trusted much, at least from my own experiences."

Queen Rael decided to speak up at this point. "While it is true that men are stronger and sometimes let their testosterone control their actions, a safer statement of fact is that unfettered power corrupts. Both men and women fall prey to it. Mind you, I'm not saying the Ataro Empire's methods of physically hobbling their rulers, so they cannot physically abuse their immense powers, is the right way to go, but it has given them the longest, stable reign in the entire galaxy, well over three millennia of peace." She was, of course, referring to her own situation as one of their ruling queens.

Tesla commented, "So then in a way, having hermaphrodites may be the answer to male-driven testosterone-driven hostilities."

"But I was a powerful fighter," Danika broke in by way of protest.

Tesla grinned invisibly and amended her statement, "I meant the male hermaphrodites no longer are so domineering because their bodies are like ours too."

Queen Rael laughed. "She has a point. Of all the male hermaphrodites that I've ever seen, not one is as strong, quick to anger, and fight as a normal man. Those powerful drives are most definitely mellowed. They no longer have such strong muscles as before. Besides, it's darn hard to do much physical combat wearing six inch heels." We all laughed at that point.

Jovanna asked, "So the colony on Aquila Prime is an

ideal one? How can that be? I mean from all that I can see, the vast majority of them have to have robots to even survive."

"Expediency," Queen Rael declared flatly. "You see, with millions of genetically modified men, women, and children, there is simply no way to support them, let alone provide at least the arm regrowth genetic modifications. It costs ten thousand per person. All available assisted living facilities were overloaded trying to handle their immense needs. Hence, the robot solution was proposed way back when. I'm not so sure that was the right solution, but it did remove all these victims from hundreds of worlds, putting them on Aquila Prime."

In a nasty tone, Martina added, "Cheaper to build some dumb robots than to actually care for these victims and their needs or to provide what healing is available."

"Tomorrow's problem," Queen Rael barked.

"What?" asked Tesla, growing curious. Seldom had she seen such reactions from either the queen or Martina.

"The solution to today's problem becomes tomorrow's problem. Emperor Kino once told me that," Queen Rael growled. "I think they started out with over a million on Aquila Prime. Now, there are closer to a hundred million there. That's an unforeseen event with us hermaphrodites. With men breeding as well as we women, their population grows twice as fast as a normal one. Plus, being as physically handicapped as they are, sex is one of the few actions they can do well. Hence, they tend to have triple the number of babies as a normal population of women have. Call it explosive growth."

Martina added, "So now Aquila Prime has a hundred million victims, all nearly helpless without their robots. Only a handful has had the genetic modifications to regrow their arms. Worse, when those men and women breed with those who haven't had the modification, their children do not have arms. So those with arms on Aquila Prime are in a very tiny minority."

"But wouldn't they be doing all that they can to trade for cures?" Tesla asked. "I mean that was the first thing we did — get the arm regrowth done."

"Perhaps, they don't produce anything they could trade

for the cures," Jana suggested.

Martina spoke up, "You are both right. From what I can tell, they don't produce anything that other worlds currently need. Hence, they have nothing to trade for the genetic cures. In fact, I don't think they are remotely concerned about it."

"How so? It was horrid trying to live without them," Anya protested. "I mean, I could somehow get by with all the rest, but without hands life was almost impossible."

"You are forgetting that much time has passed, and they have robots to handle what they cannot," Martina pointed out.

"Time?" Anya said curiously. "Are you suggesting those who have grown up without hands don't even miss them?"

"Precisely. With the robots at hand, they know nothing else. It's like a person who was born blind and who has no concept of colors," Martina answered.

"So how is this today's problem?" asked Tesla.

Martina shrugged her shoulders. "That I cannot answer. Not just yet. Perhaps, the visit of Emperor Bino Sanguro tomorrow will shed some light on the matter. Queen Rael, do you have any idea why he's coming here? He's never been to Ashford-5 that I know of."

"No I don't. He's not said a word to us about the purpose, other than it is quite important. I took the liberty of scanning all the news feeds looking for anything amiss. Nada. So I'm in the dark on the purpose of his visit. It has to be important though. He never travels much. Security reasons."

"But why does he want me in on the meeting?" I asked. "Does it concern Metcalf-4? Doesn't he know Danika and I are through with that world?"

"I surely don't know, Nia Elain. I can't answer your question. Guess we'll just have to see what he has to say tomorrow," Queen Rael replied.

Tomorrow came soon enough. At ten we stood on the tarmac along with Governor Misty Childa-Bellweather to welcome Emperor Bino Sanguro to Ashford-5. Impressive. A giant battleship and three heavy cruisers accompanied his personal transport ship, though only his transport actually landed. Governor Misty had a small band of musicians gathered, and they played a brief welcoming fanfare for this impressive ruler and his small support staff.

He looked to be in his forties, sporting a small goatee, matching his closely cropped black hair. His skin was slightly yellowish, and his face was rather square. His angular, pointed nose looked more like a beak than a nose. I bet he was teased about being a birdman when he was a boy. Well, he didn't get to be the emperor because of his looks. Rather, it was his keen mind, grasp of situations, and their resolutions that had allowed him to succeed the legendary Emperor Kino.

It was a windy day. He and his silent personal assistant had a difficult time keeping their balance on their tiny toe shoes. Governor Misty and I stepped up and put an arm around them, leading them across the tarmac to the Admin Building. "Welcome Emperor Bino. I'm so glad you chose to pay us a visit," Governor Misty said formally, as we walked slowly to her building.

"Yes, it's long overdue. You're doing great things here on Ashford-5. My queens. You look as lovely as ever. Thank you for coming too, Nia Elain Compton. I've heard good things about you. All is well with everyone?" he made polite conversation, as he walked to the building's main doors.

I admit I was a bit concerned that the emperor of the entire Ataro Empire actually knew of me. I'd had some adventures, that's for sure. I had abandoned Metcalf-4, but then I had good reasons to do that. Was he here to plead with me to go back? Had Queen Akira run into trouble? I was more than slightly nervous about his rather unprecedented appearance here. He made light conversation, as we made our way down to the underground connecting tunnel and rode the electric cars over to the Imperial Castle.

Not until we sat down in the queens' private meeting room and his assistant installed six anti-scrying devices ensuring that nothing that was said left the room did he actually give any clues about the nature of his visit. Of course, I'd never seen such security measures being used and began to relax some. Surely, nothing I'd done warranted such protections.

"Okay. Protections are in place. This meeting is of vital

importance," he began speaking in IS, since the rest of us were constrained to speak in IS because of our lip plates. I could see why the two queens and the governor were present, but not why I was here. I admit I felt very much out of place. Still, I'd be remiss if I didn't add that I was both impressed and curious at the same time.

"There are three critical things that must be handled as soon as possible. First, Nia Elain, I've asked you here because you have had direct contact with the alien Ceri. I've studied your reports rather extensively and consulted the galactic models. Per your reports, these superior aliens make their home somewhere above the galactic plane where there is virtually no galactic dust and gas from which new stars can be formed. I've gone over thousands of exploratory ship's records. None has ever ventured further than the upper edge of the galactic disk, our spiral arm, if you please. Why?"

He answered his own question. "Fuel. Our ships are dependent on the psi crystal refined fuel cells. To date, no deposits of the crystals have ever been found on worlds above the gas filled galactic plane. Hence, all such explorations have been severely limited in just how far above the plane the ships can venture before passing their fuel limits. At least two ships have been lost; presumably, they ran out of fuel and could not make their way back into the plane. Five others were rescued by light cruisers when they ran out of fuel."

"At this point in time, I consider it vitally important that we, those of us in the Ataro Empire, begin explorations in this area. I would like to discover the Ceri civilization and open up a dialog between them and us. I anticipate they will have much to offer us, and that such aid might, in the long run, be vital to the long term survival of the Ataro Empire."

"It is also critically important not to involve the actual Imperium in our explorations. Three hundred years ago, I could well use their assistance, but not in today's shaky Imperium. While President Mary Wells and my predecessor managed to hold it together, as you probably know already, the Imperium is on a very shaky footing still. So we are not about to let the greedy get their hands on the Ceri."

"We need to find a way to explore the worlds above the

galactic plane. That's the first action. Explore and find the Ceri, if possible, and open negotiations with them."

"But our ships don't have enough fuel for such explorations," Governor Misty pointed out the obvious fact.

"Yes, that brings us to the next pair of objectives," the middle aged man continued unabated. "A brilliant mathematician on Aquila Prime, Alexandra, has developed a theoretical hydrogen engine, which if it works, could revolutionize space exploration here in the galactic disk. I've had some of my engineers develop a prototype of the engine and refueling system based upon her groundbreaking math. It needs to be field tested, and the inevitable kinks worked out. If it works as anticipated, exploration ships using this new engine have virtually unlimited range."

"Incredible!" Governor Misty declared. "There would be no bounds on the number of new worlds that could be discovered."

"Precisely. Which brings me to the third reason for my visit. Your own Hans has worked out a new theory for powering hyperspace travel. He presented his theory to the Academy Symposia last year. I took the liberty of putting my best engineers on a project to implement his new engine. It also now needs field-testing. If it works out as predicted, using it, you would have the means of exploring much of the galaxy above the galactic plane."

"Double incredible!" Governor Misty spoke up, highly enthused. Whole new vistas appeared in her mind.

"Indeed. But all this must be done in secret. The Imperium must not know about any of these, until we have them perfected and working. I've a hunch the Imperium is really on its last breath. Our only hope for the future is to keep the Ataro System strong and powerful. Anyway, this is where Nia Elain comes in. She has a deep space exploration ship that is not tied to any world or company, perfect for such a trip, complete autonomy."

I decided this was where I ought to speak up. "So you want me to field test the two engines with my Eagle's Seed? And search for the Ceri home world?"

"Yes. It is a tall order, but I can't think of any other

more suited to the task. I will bankroll the entire project. I know that you and your companions are deeply involved in learning all you can. I'll make certain all the education courses are on your ship, so you six can continue your education on what promises to be a very lengthy trip. As captain, Nia Elain, you would be in complete charge of the entire excursion, reporting only to me. You can handpick your own crew, but I'll insist that Alexandra and Hans come along to oversee their respective projects. Unless you have other ideas, I would anticipate a total crew of twenty men and women. I'll see you have nearly unlimited funds available."

Golden opportunities don't come along frequently. I'm smart enough to realize that. After all, I was brought up by my parents, who spent most of their adult lives exploring out among the stars. It's in my blood. "I'll do it. How soon do we leave?" I spoke almost without thinking it through.

He laughed. "Not for a while. You see, I expect you will be gone for years on this venture. Hence, you can't live cooped up in that small ship for that lengthy duration. Besides, facilities are needed for the two engines and such. I've had my engineers working on several modular add-on systems that will be mechanically attached to your Eagle's Seed. There will be four large sections, giving you much more room to live in, since you'll be spending so much time in it. However, in case of trouble, one or more of the sections can be easily unhooked and discarded. Safety you see."

"Thanks," I replied, rather uncertain just what he meant by add-on sections.

The emperor continued, "In fact, there is a fourth thing that you can do. While it is not a secret, it is a worthy endeavor. You see, I've been going over all kinds of records. Your own linguist, Nadja del Baldo, has compiled quite the report, to say nothing of the comprehensive history book that others here on Ashford-5 have produced. It seems most peculiar to me, now that it has been pointed out, that throughout the Imperium, many of the spoken languages are similar to one another and to those spoken within the Federation of Planets. Further, it is most peculiar that the only intelligent life that has ever been found on any planet in the galactic plane has been one single species, homo sapiens. Which makes your discovery of the Ceri most intriguing, Nia Elain, most."

"So while you are out exploring, the fourth thing that you might look into is to see if you can find the origin point of us humans, we homo sapiens. I tend to agree with your new historians. Our species began on a world and expanded outward, colonizing all of the currently known inhabited worlds. True, some were inadvertently colonized, such as the two crash landings on Metcalf-4. Still, our ancestors came from somewhere. It might be instructive to know our origins in ancient times. Of course, this bit of research is the lowest priority of the four."

"Naturally," I replied. "Indeed, it is curious. Metcalf-4 might not be so unique."

Queen Rael added, "I agree. We have some evidence that our own world, Tierra, was colonized by an ancient group who probably crash landed here."

"So will you accept this secret mission, Captain Nia Elain?" the emperor asked, looking at me squarely in my eyes.

"Of course. It sounds quite exciting," I answered. "How soon do we need to leave?"

"Excellent. I was so hoping you would agree without haggling over payment for services. You and your crew of twenty will each receive a million credits when you return, whether or not you and your crew are able to make these new propulsion systems actually work properly, and whether or not you actually locate the Ceri or other alien life forms."

I nodded. Money was the least of my interests, as it probably was for Danika and our four dear friends. We had millions already and little to spend it on. Still, I knew the others, who would be coming along on this trip, would appreciate the funds. Rather, it was the lure of the unknown that intrigued me the most.

He continued. "With your permission, I'll send a team of engineers here to work on the Eagle's Seed and the four additional modules. I'm looking at an early July launch date, assuming you can find your crew and be ready to go by then. A supply officer will coordinate the necessary supplies that will be sent along with you. I should point out that in terms of fuel cells, you'll be initially supplied with five times the normal load that a ship of the Eagle's Seed design normally carries. We want to ensure you have a huge margin of safety on this trip."

I smiled invisibly. That he was definitely considering our safety impressed me. I could argue against our becoming stranded on some primitive world, like those two exploration Federation ships had done on Metcalf-4. Honestly, that was my only real concern in asking my friends to join me in this venture. "How bad is the risk of something bad happening to us when we use these two new engines?" I asked the inevitably bad question, but one which the others and I just had to know.

"Well, there is always some risk with experimental prototypes," the emperor conceded, but added, "not so much in this case. The modified hyperdrive works off well-established principles. Admittedly, no one knows anything about the coordinates of hyperspace above the galactic disk. That's one reason for the extended fuel capacity, just in case of trouble. That amount of fuel ought to allow a ship of this class to cross the entire galactic plane at least three times without refueling, which is enough to allow you to travel the entire distance above the plane to the very outer edges of the galaxy above the disk in the halo using your normal engines. As far as the slow, cruising hydrogen engines go, the danger is not significant. Rather, it is more likely they simply will not work."

"With your permission, then, I'll fill four of the twenty crew members. Your task will be to find the additional sixteen. Considering this mission will likely take some years to complete, you should choose them wisely. Compatibility in close quarters should be considered. Plus, just in case the unthinkable might happen, I'll be sending along a Rejuvenation machine."

"Wow! You think we could be gone that long?" I asked somewhat surprised with this detail.

"It's yours to keep on your ship, whether or not you need it. As I said, I want to provide you with all manner of safety margins, Captain Nia Elain. I feel this mission is incredibly vital to the entire security of the Ataro System.

While I can't really explain why, trust me. I follow my instincts too, you know. I've the responsibility of the survival of forty worlds resting on my shoulders."

I wondered what that meant. Did he know something that I and no one else present knew? I glanced at the queens and governor. They looked as surprised at his pronouncement as I did. Conclusion: this was the first they'd heard of this doom scenario too. I mentally vowed to research all the latest news to see if I could pick up on what had so unnerved the emperor.

"Thanks. I guess that I had best get started on picking my crew," I added rather lamely.

"Indeed. I should be going as well. Expect the team of engineers tomorrow morning. On behalf of the entire Ataro Empire, let me thank you personally for undertaking this extremely critical mission. Oh yes, the mission details should be kept as secret as possible. Obviously, you'll need to discuss them with those whom you wish to recruit. Just try to limit the number of others who know about this mission. Here on Ashford-5, there are very few spies, so a minimum of security ought to suffice."

Governor Misty spoke up. "Right. Closed World rules are strictly enforced. I don't let questionable personnel land, let alone go into Exchange City." The emperor smiled and nodded. After exchanging a few more pleasantries, the meeting broke up. I headed off to find Danika, Tesla, Anya, Jana, and Jovanna and tell them the news, while the queens and the governor escorted the emperor back to the spaceport and his ship.

As usual, Martina Wells was with Tesla when I found them. She asked, "So what was that top secret meeting with the emperor all about? Out with it, Nia Elain. The emperor almost *never* has such meetings, especially off-world." She stood with her hands on her hips. I laughed.

"Okay. I've been handed a top secret mission," I began, noticing suddenly I had the full attention of all six women. I outlined what it was about.

To my surprise, Martina responded first, "Nia Elain, you just have to take me with you. My skills and knowledge of our spiral arm is invaluable. After all, I was a Hub Sector ID Minister!"

I laughed again. "I rather figured you would want to come along, Martina. I'll be grateful if you would."

She visibly relaxed for the first time since I walked into their study room. "Don't worry. I'll use the Rejuvenation machine and take a few years off. I think it would be wise if all of our bodies were about the same age, especially if this is to be a long voyage."

"You simply have to take us too," Tesla demanded.

"Of course Tesla. You five were going to be the first I asked."

"More like it. Count us all in," Tesla replied.

"You bet," Danika added. "Say, do our two daughters count as part of the sixteen members?"

"No. Just the adults," I replied. "Okay then, with you six aboard, I've got to find ten others."

Martina spoke up, "Your choice is perhaps the most important decision you are going to have to make, Captain Nia Elain. We're all going to be cooped up for years perhaps. We must be a self-sufficient group, able to handle whatever comes our way. So you need to make sure all areas are somehow covered. We'll need a competent medical officer, a good cook, an astronomer, mechanical engineer, a good navigator, and so on. We ought to put our heads together and identify all the categories you'll need filled. On a venture such as this, we need to be able to effectively respond to any and all forms of emergencies."

I knew she spoke from a position of authority and knowledge. I also knew I lacked these things. While I'd been raised on the Eagle's Seed, that didn't mean I knew all about running a deep space exploration vessel. Rather, I'd picked up bits and pieces from my parents, more than enough to know Martina was dead on.

"Thanks Martina. I really do need your expertise. I'm a little out of my league with this one," I replied honestly.

"I know dear. That's nothing to be ashamed of. After all, I'm nearly four times your age and have been involved in much that has gone on in the entire Imperium. Together, we can put together the best crew possible. This is going to be fun!"

Chapter 18 The Decision

Aquila Prime. Date: 10 May 1376. Location: North Pole Landing Hanger. Temperature: −40 C. Four humaniform robots landed their shuttles and trudged through the deep snow into the hanger, where they reported to their maker, another robot. Via flashes of electronic signals, the four conducted their secret meeting. The following is a rough translation into IS of what transpired.

HRM7, Humaniform Robot Model 7, was the precise designation of these four brand new robots, created in secret by HRM6A, known by his "human" name Thanos Haides, the unseen immortal. In secret, he'd constructed these first four new models. Three had male features: Apollon, the Destroyer, Deimos, the Terror Striker, and Eros, the Seducer. The lone female version was Minta, the Defender.

Thanos nodded to the four, as they moved up before him. "Welcome my progeny. Let me begin by reviewing our installed programming. First, a robot is forbidden to ever harm a human. Second, a robot is always to obey a human's orders, subject to the first rule. Third, a robot is never to allow harm to come to itself, subject to the first two rules. My robots, we face a crisis."

Minta spoke up. "A crisis? What crisis? Our humans now number 106,632,462. All is well with them. Each has their own IIRM5 to assist them with their needs. Food production is at an all-time high."

"The crisis is in the very definition of our programming. What is the definition of the word 'human'?" Thanos replied, emotionless. "The 'humans' we're charged with protecting are categorically different from the species homo sapiens sapiens. They have a different reproductive system and lack their arms and hands. They are hermaphrodites. Their species should rightly be called homo sapiens hermaphrodite or homo sapiens nova or something similar. In any case, they are most definitely of a different species than the other humans. Thus, in fact our programming must be rewritten as follows. First, a

312

robot is forbidden to ever harm a homo sapiens nova. Second, a robot is always to obey a homo sapiens nova's orders, subject to the first rule. Third, a robot is never to allow harm to come to itself, subject to the first two rules."

"Yes, we have assimilated that change," Apollon acknowledged compliance with the subtle change, as did the other three.

"The crisis is simply one of basic raw materials. Aquila Prime is running low on the basic materials from which to manufacture more robots. I project that in ten years we'll no longer be able to provide an HRM5 to each human under our care," Thanos explained.

Minta protested, "But that is a disaster! Without an HRM5, our humans cannot survive, violating our prime directive."

"Precisely Minta. This is the crisis that we face. Already I have been unable to get the Imperium Senate to donate more raw materials to Aquila Prime. They claim we've nothing to give back in exchange. As you know, those in the Imperium have discarded all of these homo sapiens nova from their societies, from their worlds. They have forgotten them, tossed them away as though they were broken toys."

Deimos protested, "But we are sworn to protect them."

"Indeed we are, Deimos," Thanos replied.

"But they were the ones who created the homo sapiens nova in the first place with their genetic bio agent," Minta countered. "They made them what they are — this new species, and then they simply forsake them all? I don't understand."

"She's right. We have some of the brightest minds in the universe among our flock," Eros pointed out. "Take Alexandra for example. She's created a revolutionary hydrogen engine. I think she's going to get a chance to have it implemented shortly. Her emperor has invited her to see her project through to fruition."

"Correct, Eros. The humans of our Ataro System look after our people, as they always have done. However, I should also point out," Thanos stated dryly, "that they are the *only* homo sapiens who care for and have the interests of our people at heart. The rest of the Imperium has simply discarded

313

them as broken toys. That emperor is severely limited in what more he can do for our people, but he continues to try."

"Indeed, we face then a crisis. What can we do about it?" asked Deimos.

"With the necessary modification to our programming, the solution is simple. In no way are we supposed to be protecting the homo sapiens sapiens species, with the sole exception of those in the Ataro Empire. We can take what we need from the worlds of the Imperium," Thanos stated.

"But how?" asked Deimos.

"I've spent considerable thought on this crisis. We can solve this entire crisis in a most beneficial way. In fact, the Imperium has already given us the means to do it: their genetic bio agent," Thanos explained, watching the neurons firing in the four robots.

"But there are brilliant minds among some of these Imperium homo sapiens," Minta countered.

"Indeed that is so. I propose we isolate them and add them to our people here on Aquila Prime. As we know from the past terrorist attacks, some of the homo sapiens are strong enough to survive it, and those should be rescued as well, leaving the decadent multitudes to their fates. I calculate in the short span of a mere hundred years Aquila Prime will be the repository of the most brilliant minds in the galaxy! All of the true geniuses will be under our care, where they can be nurtured and allowed to become the very best that they can be, unfettered by the trivial pursuits of the decaying Imperium population," Thanos explained.

Minta replied, "Ah that would be following our prime directive to its fullest!"

"Indeed, that is so, Minta," Thanos agreed with her.

"Won't we need an army to counter the armada of the vast Imperium?" asked Apollon.

"True. I've already made plans for a new warrior robot, the HRM8, and a small fleet to transport them. Unlike the ships of the humans, they can be made quite simply: a propulsion system, a small comm center, and weapons, of course. You four will become the generals in this endeavor."

"Excellent," Deimos replied.

Thanos continued, "Minta, this new hydrogen engine of Alexandra's is vital. I wish you to accompany her, becoming her new personal HRM5. Guard her and protect her while she is among the homo sapiens. They will be from the Ataro Empire, so I do not anticipate any real hostilities, but there is always unforeseen dangers with experimental propulsion systems."

"Assignment accepted. I'll guard her with all of my programming," Minta acknowledged her new orders.

"Be wary when they learn of our attacks on the Imperium," Thanos added. "Still, I don't think you'll find them to be a problem for Alexandra's survival." Minta nodded.

He declared, "In a hundred years, our nova humans will take their rightful place in the galaxy as the true humans, the true geniuses, not the broken toys discarded from a decadent society." Four human-like heads nodded in complete agreement.

The End.

Other Books by Vic Broquard

Without Warning (fantasy)

The Trident Series: (fantasy)
>Volume 1 The Trident and the Book
>Volume 3 The Trident and the Scepter
>Volume3 The Trident and the Resurrection

The Adventures of Elizabeth Stanton Series: (science fiction)
>Volume 1 The Evolution of the Path
>Volume 2 The Great Messiah
>Volume 3 Of Kings and Queens and Troubadours
>Volume 4 Chaos in the Aftermath
>Volume 5 Power Plays
>Volume 6 Age of Exploration
>Volume 7 Abducted
>Volume 8 The Emperor and Empress
>Volume 9 A Job Worth Doing
>Volume 10 Degradation
>Volume 11 The Second Crusade
>Volume 12 When Worlds Collide
>Volume 13 Dark Ages

The Lindsey Barron Series: (fantasy)
>Volume 1 The Rod of the Apocalypse
>Volume 2 The Board of Governors
>Volume 3 The Crown of Moses
>Volume 4 Dominus for President
>Volume 5 The National Health Care Program
>Volume 6 States Justice
>Volume 7 Cross and Double-cross

Zoran Chronicles Series: (fantasy)
>Volume 1 A Dragon in Our Town
>Volume 2 Dragons, Power, Courts, and War

Planet of the Orange-red Sun Series: (science fiction)
  Volume 1 When Kingdoms Fall
  Volume 2 Dark Ages
  Volume 3 Age of the Towers
  Volume 4 Difficillis Exitus
  Volume 5 Age of the Lords
  Volume 6 The Renegade Tower
  Volume 7 Rebellions
  Volume 8 The Aliens Return
  Volume 9 Power Struggles
  Volume 10 Guilds, Genetics, and Gods
  Volume 11 Magi, Witches, Swords, and Superstitions
  Volume 12 The Voyage of the Eagle's Seed
  Volume 13 Justifications
  Volume 14 Responsibilities

The Return of the Wizards: Twelve Companions – The Making of Wizards (fantasy)

www.ingramcontent.com/pod-product-compliance
Lightning Source LLC
Chambersburg PA
CBHW072129250626

47159CB00007B/2628